Dedicat
Genova,
With warmest wishes,
Your Sailor of Heart,
Naomi C. ...

HELL AT SEA

HELL AT SEA

NAOMI C. DESIDERIO

Tate Publishing & Enterprises

 TATE PUBLISHING
& Enterprises

Tate Publishing is committed to excellence in the publishing industry. Our staff of highly trained professionals, including editors, graphic designers, and marketing personnel, work together to produce the very finest books available. The company reflects the philosophy established by the founders, based on Psalms 68:11,

"THE LORD GAVE THE WORD AND GREAT WAS THE COMPANY OF THOSE WHO PUBLISHED IT."

If you would like further information, please contact us:
1.888.361.9473 | www.tatepublishing.com
TATE PUBLISHING & Enterprises, LLC | 127 E. Trade Center Terrace
Mustang, Oklahoma 73064 USA

Published in the United States of America

ISBN: 978-1-5988679-9-2

07.01.15

To my shipmates worldwide.

I was called to a mission, and it was this - to love.

ACKNOWLEDGMENTS

With all my sailor heart, I thank my veterans of the war at sea and their wonderful wives for their gifts of friendship, historic memories, and invaluable moral support, while I plied my course of writing *Hell At Sea*. There are good, decent people on both sides of the battlefield. Sadly, the majority of the veterans I name here are now on "Eternal Patrol." "Sailor, rest your oar." I apologize, as well, if I have overlooked any special name of a person who helped me.

Horst Bredow, director and founder of the German U-boat Archive, Cuxhaven, Germany, and his wife, Annemarie; Horst Boettcher, U-618; Captain Louis Cafiero, U.S. Merchant Marines; Richard Calabro, USS Charles H. Roan, and his wife, Mary Jane; Ken Conover, USS Collett, and his wife, Betty; Harry Cooper, founder/director, "Sharkhunters, Inc."; Peter 'Ali' Cremer-Thursby, CO, U-333, author, *U-BOAT Commander*; Mike DelRusso, USS Card; Hans Eichner, U-504, U-642, and his wife, Friedl; James Ewell, Lehigh Valley Pennsylvania Chapter U.S. Submarine Veterans World War II; Heinz Falk, U-616, and his wife, Christel; James Galbreth, USS Ellyson, and his wife, Betty; Bill Geary, USS Borie, USS Darter; Herbert Georgious, former director USS Ling Memorial, Hackensack, New Jersey; Otto Giese, U-405, U-181; Ernst Goethling, U-26; Jochen Gruetzmann, editor, "Schaltung Kueste," and his wife, Anni; Peter C. Hansen, U-124, naval intelligence, author, *Execution for Duty,* and his wife, Monika; Reinhard Hardegen, CO, U-123, and his wife, Barbara; Gerhard Held, L.I., U-618, and Marianne; Heinz Heuckeroth, U-168, and Friedi; Stan Hicks, USS Taussig; Wolfgang Hirschfeld, author, *Feindfahrten,* U-109, U-234, and Irmgard; Georg Hoegel, U-30, U-110, author, *Embleme Wappen Malings,* and Dora; Ben Hugo, USS Borie, and Connie; Siegfried Koitschka, CO, U-616, and Waltraud; Konrad Lewitz, U-60, U-178, and Ilse; Bob Maher, USS Borie, and Sandy; Jak P. Mallmann-Showell, author, *U-BOATS Under the Swastica,* historian; Karl-Heinz Marbach, CO, U-953; Edward Miller, USS Spence, and Claire; Victor Nemeth, USS Hale; Jesse Parker, Navy, Korea, Vietnam; Thomas Quinn, USS Ordronaux; Pat Repoli, USS Taussig; Captain Bill Ruhe, USS Sturgeon, author; Edward Rumpf, author, historian, U.S. Army, Korea, and Jackie; John Ryder, USS Perch; Martin Schaffer, USS Redfin, former president of Lehigh Valley Submarine Veterans, and daughter, Joan; Walter Scull, USS Aulich, and Jean; Erik Skurbe, U-552, U-96, U-1007, and Meta; Robert Straub, USS Guavina, USS Amberjack; Erich Topp, author, *Odyssey of a U-BOAT Commander,* retired Rear Admiral, Federal Navy, West Germany, CO, U-552; Steven Truax, historian; Herbert A. Werner, author, *Iron Coffins,* CO, U-415, U-953; Ken Williams, president, New Jersey "Tin Can Sailors," and Ann; all the veterans and crews of USS Borie, USS Ellyson, USS Taussig, U-616, U-618/Z27, the Lehigh Valley Chapter, U.S. Submarine Veterans, World War II, the Gudgeon Chapter, New Jersey Veterans of World War II; the New Jersey "Tin Can Sailors," U.S. Submarine Veterans, Inc, and the American Merchant Marine Veterans of the Dennis Roland Chapter, who so kindly welcomed me to their reunions and meetings.

Very special thanks to Peter C. Hansen, Robert E. Straub, and Erich Topp for their kindness in reading my old raw drafts for nautical details and battle scene direction, and to Sister Colette Tolder, my former English Literature professor for her enthusiasm after reading a more recent draft and suggesting I cut it 100 more pages. To the kind people at Tate Publishing, who were very patient and helpful: Jessica Lay, Janae Glass, Dave Dolphin, and Brandon Rahbar. Thank you for this honor of being published!

Of great help to me, as well, were the photo record, *U-BOAT War*, and the video, *The Boat*, by photojournalist, Lothar-Guenther Buchheim, and the book, *Operation Drumbeat*, by Professor Michael Gannon. Any errors in my novel are strictly my own, and I take full responsibility for them. Any resemblances to personages, still living or on Heavenly patrol, are unintentional.

Finally, with deep gratitude to my wonderful family, cousins, neighbors, and friends who prayed me through my recent serious illness, enabling me to bring my "little boat of dreams into port," and to my precious family here at home in Cranford, who well experienced my ups and downs through twenty-three years in this ongoing project, loving me, in spite of it all: my beloved husband, Jim, and my dearest children, Philip, Laura, and Vincent, and now my sweet granddaughter, Maya Michele, and especially to my beloved Mother, who believed in me from the beginning, but could not be with me at the end.

Besatzungsliste U-115

(Crew List - U-115)

Kapitaenleutnant Herbert Ketter

Kapitaenleutnant (ING) Alois Geissler, L.I.

Oberleutnant zur See Paul-Karl Ullmann, IWO

Leutnant zur See Dietrich Heubeck, IIWO

Marine Assistenz Arzt Gerhard Moeglich

Obersteuermann Heinz Weber

Obermaschinist Diesel Hans-Joachim Holleder

Obermaschinist E-motor Herbert Lange

Oberboots Maat Wilhelm Scholz #1

Obermechanikers Maat (T) Werner Brunnig

Oberfunk Maat Konrad Lieb

Oberbootsmanns Maat Gottfried Becker

Obermaschinen Maat Gerd Schwabl

Obermaschinen Maat Walter Jung

Bootsmanns Maat Franz Wirth

Funkmaat Georg Schatz

Maschinen Maat Wolfgang Bommer

Maschinen Maat Karl-Heinz Hochstaetter

Maschinen Maat Horst Thomas

Maschinen Maat Adolf Kuhnl

Maschinen Maat Hans-Guenther Greise

Maschinen Maat Dieter Graef

Matrosen Hauptgefreiter Leo Kuhlmey

Matrosen Obergefreiter Kurt Mohan

Funk Obergefreiter Helmut Lange

Funk Obergefreiter Georg Kolbig

Mechaniker Obergefreiter Franz,Josef Mueller

Mechaniker Obergefreiter Christoph Schaub

Mechaniker Gefreiter Bernhard Uphoffner

Matrosen Obergefreiter Horst Struckmeier

Matrosen Obergefreiter Heinrich Oesterweise

Matrosen Obergefreiter Maximilian Senghas

Matrosen Obergefreiter Otto Randtel

Matrosen Obergefreiter Franz Wachsmuth

Desiderio   Page iv

Hell at Sea

Matrosen Obergefreiter Hans-Juergen Luther

Matrosen Obergefreiter Wilhelm Feiler
Matrosen Obergefreiter Hans-Dieter Meyer (Koch)
Maschinen Obergefreiter Klaus Winkelhofer
Maschinen Obergefreiter Adolf Bieber
Maschinen Obergefreiter Christian Zech
Maschinen Obergefreiter Reinhard Schade
Maschinen Obergefreiter Paul Honnscheidt
Maschinen Gefreiter Theo Brinkmann
Maschinen Gefreiter Siegfried Krueger
Matrose I Fritz Baier
Matrose II Josef Kutzop
Heitzer I Herbert Giske
Heitzer II Karl Braumann

- 1 3 -

PROLOGUE
BdU Headquarters, Paris - April 14, 1942

Admiral Karl Doenitz, chief of Nazi Germany's U-boat Force, regarded the young lieutenant commander at rigid attention before his desk.

"Your first watch officer, Paul Ullmann, accuses you of dereliction of duty on this patrol, *Kapitaenleutnant* Ketter. What do you say to this charge?"

An angry shadow crossed the young lieutenant commander's broad clean-shaven face. He refused to give in. "Nothing, *Herr Admiral.*"

The admiral rose stiffly, as if he'd become an old man before his time, and walked to the tall window overlooking Avenue Marechal Manoury. For a long while he surveyed the ragged Paris skyline, then came around, his lean flat face ghostly pale in the late afternoon light.

"I like you, Ketter. A Knights Cross winner and risk taker, like your good friend, Hardegen of U-123!" The Admiral bestowed a paternal grin on his young lieutenant commander. "You know well I admire such bravado in my captains. Therefore, I will not ask you what went on aboard your boat during the return from America. It was a most unusual circumstance you dealt with, one that has no precedent in our Navy to my knowledge. And one, by the way,

I might have found most intriguing in my days at sea in the First War."

The young lieutenant commander did his best to suppress his shock. A brief smile played on his thin lips. So, there would be no court-marshal after all?

The admiral whisked his hand over the mound of folders scattered on his desk. "Your record is impeccable, Ketter. You have sunk many ships! That is what I expect of my captains! Yet, there is one last thing I want you to do before you leave this room."

"But, of course, sir." The young lieutenant commander snapped his heels in ready obedience, his mind warring between doubt and relief.

"I want you to eliminate one or two details from your war log." The admiral regarded his young lieutenant commander with a knowing expression.

"Sir?"

"We want nothing of the 'little incident' to remain for prying eyes. Do you follow me, Ketter? It must be as if the whole thing never happened."

Never happened? Never happened! The young lieutenant commander would never forget! And his mind drifted to his beloved fiancée who waited for him at the base hospital in Lorient. They must get married as soon as possible on his return.

However, the admiral had other plans. "Now, *Kapitaenleutnant,* one final thing, we need bold experienced commanders, like you, to pass on the torch to our eager, young trainees. Therefore!" The admiral bent to the desk and began scribbling. "I am assigning you as instructor to report to the training school at Pillau on the Baltic day after tomorrow, where you will drill new commanders in our latest attack methods."

The young lieutenant commander answered bluntly, "Yes, sir!" He understood, and he must obey. The dream for any personal happiness ended abruptly.

CHAPTER 1
Whiting, New Jersey - May 6, 1986

The telephone jangled on the wall next to the refrigerator. Sixty-two-year-old Mary Ann Carlino glanced up from her solitary evening meal of fish sticks, green beans, and macaroni and cheese. *It's got to be Doris Kendall,* she thought with a weary sigh. *Probably wants a ride to the meeting tonight, and oh, that poor woman can talk, talk, talk til the cows come home.*

Mary Ann got up to answer the phone on the third ring. "Hello?"

"Ah, hello, Mrs. Carlino?" A man's hesitant voice greeted her on the other end of the line.

Mary Ann gripped the receiver. Tony's doctor! Something had happened! "Yes, this is Mrs. Anthony Carlino," she answered, her heart racing.

The man continued, "Mrs. Carlino, my name is Steve Anderson, and I'm a historian writing a book on the submarine operations of World War II -"

Oh, good Lord, what now? Mary Ann grumbled to herself. *Hadn't there been enough of these calls through the years? History buffs crawled out of the woodwork, wanting to interview Tony about his service on USS Starfish and his two brutal years in Japanese captivity. For Pete's sake, let the poor man alone!* She often wanted to scream at these intruders.

Yet, Mary Ann interrupted her caller as cordially as possible. "Mr. Anderson, please. My husband isn't here. He suffered a stroke a few months ago and is presently in the Home for Disabled Soldiers up at Menlo Park. He doesn't want to talk about his war days anymore. He's had enough, as you can well understand, I'm sure."

Enough, yes. It would be four months May 18th since the devastating stroke, which left Tony paralyzed on his entire right side and unable to speak coherently. Mary Ann had hoped to care for Tony at home, but the children, especially Mary Beth, had insisted it would be too much for her to handle. "After all, Daddy wasn't the easiest man to deal with when he was well," they concurred. And so, Mary Ann had given in and was making the lonely, 60-mile drive, up and back, on the Garden State Parkway to Menlo Park every other day to visit her husband, who sat in a slump of anger and defeat, while life went on without him.

"I'm sorry to hear about your husband," the historian's voice broke into Mary Ann's brooding thoughts. "I remember my grandmother had a stroke when I was eight, and Mom had to place her in a nursing home. Ma always felt guilty for sending Grandma away, so I can understand how it must be for you."

"That's kind of you to say so, Mr. Anderson." Mary Ann felt somewhat amenable toward her caller but wanted to end the conversation. She must finish eating and get ready for the altar/rosary meeting at 7. "Mr. Anderson, thank you for calling. I'm sorry Tony can't be here to talk to you. He had some heart-rending stories to tell about his POW time in Ofuna."

"I'm certain he did, Mrs. Carlino . . ." Anderson seemed to be stalling. "Ah, with all due respect to your husband and his fine service in the war, I was really hoping to, ah, talk to you, about your own experiences in March 1942?"

Mary Ann's knees buckled and she nearly dropped the receiver to the floor. "What are you talking about?" She gasped, pretending ignorance.

The historian wasted no time in explaining his reasons for phoning. His calm voice sounded far away, as if he stood on the other side of the ocean. "Please bear with me, Mrs. Carlino. I think I mentioned before, my interest in World War II submarines centers on the War in the Atlantic. I've been concentrating on a campaign called *Paukenschlag* , when a handful of German U-boats was operating off the east coast of the United States in early 1942."

Mary Ann couldn't reply. She felt as if she was plummeting through the floors of a tall building, while Anderson blithely related on and on about his research. "As part of my work on *Paukenschlag*, I obtained several declassified documents from the National Archives in Washington, D.C. . One of the documents concerns a German submarine, the U-115. The commander's name was Herbert Ketter." Anderson paused. "Ah, Mrs. Carlino, are you with me?" His voice called down the shaft of time.

"Yes, I'm here," Mary Ann said softly. She'd been "here" for years, waiting, waiting.

"Mrs. Carlino?"

"I said, I'm here!"

"I thought maybe you'd hung up on me?"

"No, no, I wouldn't do that." Mary Ann struggled to her chair at the table and bowed her head into the palm of her hand. She'd been found! At last, she'd been found!

Anderson stepped carefully through the unknown minefield of her past. "You recognized the commander's name, didn't you?"

"Yes!" She felt like crying.

"Mrs. Carlino, I'm sorry, I don't mean to cause you trouble or bring back any unpleasant memories from the war. " Anderson sounded genuinely concerned on the other end of the line. "With your husband at the Soldiers Home, maybe this isn't the best time for getting into this thing. Perhaps it would be best if I called some other time?"

"Mr. Anderson, wait!" She had to know. The memories were too close. "May I ask, how did you find me?" She felt exhausted, like a helpless rabbit struggling in the hunter's snare.

"Well, I'll tell you, Mrs. Carlino, it took some hard digging to find you. Tracing old newspaper stories of the time and other records, which, by the way, I'd be glad to share with you. That is, if you'd like to see them?" Anderson hurried along. "What I was hoping for is that we can meet sometime in the near future? Say, this coming Saturday, if this would be all right with you?"

Saturday? This Anderson fellow was certainly in a rush! "I guess. I don't know," she acquiesced. "I don't think anything is going on this Saturday." Her mind tumbled from one thing to the next. Were Kate and the children driving down for the weekend? She'd have to disappoint them and tell her grandchildren, "No, Na Na can't have you come down this week because someone else is coming to see her. Na Na has a long-hidden story of her own to tell from the Second World War. Something you'll never believe. Something I've always wanted you to know, but could never say."

"Mrs. Carlino," Anderson hesitated, "I feel it only right to tell you that I would never publish or say anything about your private memories without your permission." He became most insistent. "You have my word on that!"

Mary Ann was shocked by the historian's discretion in telling her this. She had never considered that her experience might be printed up in a magazine or book. It seemed too far fetched. Too controversial. "Thanks for letting me know, Mr. Anderson."

"By the way, there's something else you should know." Anderson's enthusiasm had become irrepressible. "I have greetings for you from a mutual acquaintance."

"Greetings?" Mary Ann frowned. "From whom?" She asked warily.

"Well, you see, Mrs. Carlino," Anderson replied with a bit of intrigue, "I was over in West Germany back in March. While there,

I met again with retired NATO Rear Admiral Herbert Ketter at his home in Bremen to discuss his war patrol of 1942. And before I left his place to return to the States, he told me if ever I managed to find you, I must, quote: 'please give to you his heartiest greetings.'"

Mary Ann slowly hung up the phone. For a long while she stood before the refrigerator door and stared at the magnet photos of her six precious grandchildren, who lived in Virginia and northern New Jersey. Then her eyes drifted to a bevy of notices from St. Elizabeth Ann Seton Church and the Village Four clubhouse, and the med-alert cards listing Tony's doctors and their phone numbers and the various prescription drugs he'd taken prior to his stroke.

It came to her. Quietly at first, like a gentle breeze blowing through the scrub pines in the backyard. Then it grew and grew, a great anvil chorus of wind and rain and thunderous ocean waves. He's alive. He's alive? *DEAR GOD, HE'S ALIVE!*

Mary Ann whirled about and glanced at the phone on the wall. Who could she tell? Who would possibly understand how she felt?

Kate, yes. She must call her daughter right away. Mary Ann lifted the receiver and began to dial the familiar number.

No, wait! Calm down! Think! Think what to say first!

Mary Ann set the receiver back on the hook and leaned against the kitchen doorway to calm herself. In the end she decided to inform no one about the historian's phone call, but took a long walk down Molly Pitcher Drive to the clubhouse lake, where she sat in the warm stiff grass beside softly lapping water.

CHAPTER 2

A green plaid cotton shirt strained over his portly stomach. He wore wrinkled brown corduroy pants, black Dunlop sneakers from Bradlees, and silver-rim bifocals. Historian Steve Anderson fumbled with his bulging leather briefcase and extended his right hand in greeting. "Hello, Mrs. Carlino, it's a pleasure to meet you."

Mary Ann shook Anderson's hand then stepped back from the open front door into the paneled sunroom. "Won't you please come in, Mr. Anderson?"

Did he detect the hint of a Brooklyn accent? Anderson mused. That's where she was from originally. He entered the pleasant little sun room, furtively appraising the older woman. So, this was the lady with the fantastic history, he thought. Barely coming to his shoulders in height, Mrs. Carlino wore a pink and beige floral blouse and beige polyester slacks. Shallow pockmarks from a youthful spate of acne marred her ruddy cheeks and a faint white scar was just visible on her forehead beneath her short bangs. Her chin length silver blonde hair gave her a rather girlish appearance, but her blue eyes, friendly, open, honest, and maybe just a tad anxious, caught Anderson's attention immediately.

"You had no problem finding your way here?" Mary Ann asked.

"Oh, no, your directions were perfect." Anderson smiled and

shrugged his shoulders. "Although when I turned onto Hudson Parkway, all the houses looked alike."

Mary Ann laughed. "Oh, I know what you mean. When they built these retirement communities they forgot we old folks might get lost in the maze and not find our way home!"

Anderson laughed in turn, as he glanced around the little sunroom. Before the four oblong windows, a large Bradford flowering pear tree spread its leafy branches over the front yard and gently curving street. Newly-planted pink and white impatiens grew at the base of the tree and overflowed green plastic planters along the paneled window sill behind a large wicker sofa in the sunroom. On the opposite wall near an antique oak desk, a wood framed clock ticked quietly, its small gold pendulum swinging back and forth, back and forth, above a grouping of photographs. Anderson planned to check out those photos later for any historical interest.

"You have a pretty cozy place here," Anderson said. "Heck, I'd retire in a second to a place like this. My wife would give anything to get out of the Philly area."

"How about we sit in this room to talk, Mr. Anderson?" Mary Ann suggested. "The lighting here is better, and it's more cheerful."

Wow, Anderson thought, *this historic lady certainly seems eager to get this interview started,* and he had a pretty good idea why. "Sure, it's fine with me, Mrs. Carlino." He set his briefcase on the sand-colored carpet near the coffee table. "Listen though, please call me Steve."

"Alright, Steve. And you can call me Mary Ann, okay?" Mary Ann directed with a wave of her hand. "Now you just make yourself at home. The rocker over there is very comfortable, or would you prefer the sofa for better lighting? Fine. That's fine, and set your briefcase up on the coffee table, if you wish. Ah, good, that's it."

"Thanks!" Anderson lowered his bulk to the sofa. He noticed how Mary Ann's blue eyes followed his briefcase, as he heaved it onto the coffee table. She seemed quite edgy, not knowing what to expect to have come popping out of the bag.

As he opened his briefcase and carefully removed several manila file folders, Mary Ann casually seated herself in a gold plaid wing-back rocking chair opposite. Suddenly she bounced to her feet. "Steve, would you like something to drink before we get started? Maybe a soda? Or how about a cup of coffee? I made a fresh pot before you came."

"Ah, no thanks, that's okay." Anderson shook his head. "I had lunch not too long ago. Right now, though, I want to thank you for agreeing to see me. I know my phone call last Monday evening came like a bolt out of the blue."

Mary Ann slowly seated herself, touching nervously at her short gray-blonde hair. "It did, yet I'm glad you could come, Steve." Her eyes met his with bright intensity. "You have to know that, after all these years, I was quite shocked to find out that Captain Ketter is still alive."

Anderson nodded. "He's going to be very happy when I tell him I found you. As a matter of fact, I've been trying to call his home in Bremen these past few days, but he must be away somewhere. Always on the go, that guy!"

Mary Ann glanced out the window. "You alright, Mary Ann?" Anderson asked carefully. "You sure you want to do this?"

Mary Ann smiled over at Anderson before settling back in her rocking chair. "Yes, yes, don't mind me. Just a little overwhelmed, I guess," she replied.

Feeling somewhat sheepish, Anderson leaned forward and drew his GE cassette tape recorder from the briefcase. "Ah, Mary Ann, would you mind if I recorded our conversation?"

"No, no, not at all, Steve. At last my memories can be put down for my children and grandchildren to keep."

Her enthusiasm reassured Anderson and holding up the plug to the recorder, he looked around quickly to locate an electrical outlet.

"There's an outlet right by the end table over there." Mary Ann pointed behind the sofa.

"Great! Thanks." Anderson arose awkwardly, plugged in the recorder and sat back down with a hearty sigh. "Remember, Mary Ann, if you get tired or don't want to go on, let me know. We can always continue this interview another time."

"I'm sure I'll be fine." Mary Ann replied.

Anderson cleared his throat and slowly pressed the record button on his machine. *Here goes!* he thought, most eager about interviewing his historic subject.

"Today, May 11, 1986, I will be conducting an interview with Mrs. Mary Ann Carlino at her home in Crestwood Village, Whiting, New Jersey. Forty-four years ago, only three months after the United States entered World War II, Mrs. Carlino experienced a most unusual journey."

"Yes." Mary Ann's voice came softly in the background like a final "Amen."

"Mary Ann," Anderson turned to her with a serious expression, "do you mind if we start your account on the night of Friday, March 13, 1942? At the time, you were only, what, eighteen-years-old?" Anderson's voice drifted. He felt on the brink of history, like staring into a vast golden treasure that had laid unclaimed for years.

Mary Ann smiled faintly. "Yes, that's right."

Anderson folded his hands and leaned toward his historic subject. "Mary Ann, I read the account by the U.S. Coast Guard about what happened that night at Sandy Point, Long Island. You had actually been walking on a restricted beach, is that correct?"

"I was, Steve, though at the time, I didn't think about what I was doing. I'd been warned by my girlfriend's parents not to wander too far around the area." Mary Ann pressed her lips together. "But like the silly gal I was, I wanted to go down to the beach."

Anderson listened closely, mindful of past accusations against her.

"Steve, you have to believe I was not a Nazi sympathizer or contact!" Mary Ann struggled to reveal herself. "A lot of folks back then wouldn't listen to me or try to understand what I had been through. Now, maybe with you, I'll finally have the chance to talk about what really happened, and how it affected me." She pressed her hand to her heart. "For too long I've carried the burden. Kept everything quiet, so as not to offend sensibilities, especially my husband's."

Anderson eased back on the sofa, duly satisfied. This is what he'd hoped to hear. He knew by Rear Admiral Ketter's account that this experience had a much different twist.

Mary Ann continued her recall without hesitation. "I was only going down to that beach for a minute or two, and like any self-assured young person I felt nothing would happen to me. If I just hurried down to the beach, enjoyed a quick stroll in the fresh open air, and got back to my girlfriend's beach house, no one would know.

"And, oh, I was in love, Steve!" Mary Ann blushed. "Puppy love it was. I had fallen for this fellow who was in training up at our submarine base in Groton, talk about coincidence, right? His parents ran a deli on Nassau Boulevard in our old neighborhood, and I had just received a letter from him that day. Oh, Steve, I'm going on and on here, not making any sense."

Anderson shook his head. "You're doing fine, Mary Ann. Just tell your story the way you remember it. Things'll straighten out as we go along."

Mary Ann clenched her hands together. A tiny round diamond glittered on the gold band on her left ring finger. "I told all this to Captain Ketter that night, but I knew he thought I was crazy." She grew subdued, her eyes searching out the sun porch window to that long-ago scene Anderson could only imagine. "Ketter spoke good English then?" he asked.

Mary Ann looked up, startled. "Oh, he spoke it quite well, as did his first watch officer." She hunched her shoulders instinctively, as if enduring some private pain. "Yet now I look back and realize my open confession might have softened the captain's feelings toward me and possibly saved my life."

Anderson was momentarily unsettled. Certainly, Ketter could have killed her in the circumstances, but thank God, he hadn't!

Mary Ann assumed a far away look. "I remember it all, Steve. How I felt when I ran into those German seamen on the beach. I thought, at first, they were sailors from a merchant ship, which a U-boat had sunk out at sea. The newspapers were filled, at the time, with reports of ships being torpedoed and survivors coming ashore all covered in oil, or badly burned and suffering from exposure. It was a terrible time, as you know!

"Anyway, even though I was scared at being alone on the beach with those men surrounding me like hungry wolves, I wanted to get help for them. That's all I could think to do, I was in such a panic."

Anderson was flabbergasted: "Then you actually conversed with the German saboteurs! What did they say to you?"

"One of them told me they were fishermen from Southampton," Mary Ann replied. "Their vessel had run aground in the bay," he said. And, of course, that made sense, since there were crates and other supplies scattered over the beach. Then the next thing I knew, I was fighting for my life! One fellow jumped me from behind. I was sure I was going to be killed! I expected to hear gunfire or feel the sharp point of a knife plunge into me." Mary Ann trembled involuntarily, tears sparkling in her eyes. "I heard a lot of arguing. I knew they were fighting about what to do with me."

"Did they rape you, Mary Ann?" Anderson asked gently.

"No, no, thank God!" Mary Ann shook her head. "They roughed me up a bit, for they were in a big hurry, you see. They gagged me and bound me with rope - I had no chance, at all - and next thing I knew I was headed out to sea in a rubber boat." Mary Ann closed her eyes. "It was dark and cold, everything moving fast. I was certain I was headed for my death. Perhaps to be dumped overboard to drown.

"I remember being dragged onto the iron deck of this monstrous black ship. Men were everywhere, flying around like ghosts, but

I couldn't make out who they were. I could hear them mumbling among themselves. Several hands undid my ropes, and I was hauled to my feet in a flash. My shoes kept slipping and getting caught in those long wooden deck slats. . . .

The tape recorder rolled. For many hours it would roll, except for occasional stops to add a new blank cassette, or to refill a glass of soda, or to use the bathroom. Forty-three-year-old Steve Anderson, amateur World War II naval historian and hopeful book author, junior high school Social Studies teacher on the side, married to Patricia Strayer Anderson, father of two teenaged daughters, Laura and Jennifer, settled back on the sofa overwhelmed to know he would, at last, possess both sides of this amazing wartime account.

- 2 8 -

CHAPTER 3

Wind and waves roared in the chaotic black night like hungry lions squabbling over mangled prey. The freezing air was cold enough to slice flesh from bones. Eighteen-year-old Mary Ann Connor, newly released from the ropes that bound her, gazed up through stinging tears to a squat platform, which rose ominously from the center of the narrow ship. Along the curved summit several dark heads waited against a hazy background of shredded cloud and faint stars. Suddenly a rude shove sent Mary Ann tripping and skidding along the slippery deck toward a dark cavern below the platform. With a cry of shock she slammed into an invisible iron ladder. "What? What?"

"'Plees' to go up fastly!" A man mumbled in poor English.

Mary Ann refused to climb the skinny ladder, hanging onto those icy side bars for dear life. However, her rowdy captors easily pried her hands loose and hoisted her, kicking and screaming, onto the second rung of the ladder. Her foot slipped suddenly and down she went, striking her forehead on an iron crossbar. "Ooowww!"

But the jostling men wasted no time in getting her where she had to go. Strong arms forced her higher, higher toward those dark heads at the summit. Then a sly hand made its way slowly up her bare thigh toward her private area. "Stop that, you moron!" Mary Ann landed the culprit such a kick in the stomach that he nearly tumbled overboard. An explosion of laughter ripped the air. Vile pirates at a midnight raid, these men had in the bag a real one, and they weren't about to let go the prize!

Frenzy ruled the night. Everything whirled in black confusion. Mary Ann hung suspended between the black deck below and the open sky above. More hands reached down from overhead and seized her by the shoulders of her coat. They hauled her, like a sack of grain, over the blunt metal edge of the high platform and yanked her to her feet on the upper deck. Immediately a flurry of hands reached out to steady her on the careening deck, but Mary Ann slapped them away with a vengeance, producing more raucous outbursts from the faceless phantoms that surrounded her.

Shadows floated toward her, bumped her, touched her. Someone slipped in from behind and boldly gripped her breasts beneath her coat. Mary Ann let out a howl that echoed for miles.

"*Sei ruhig! Allen sei ruhig!*" An angry scowl jolted the unruly mob.

Silence reigned at once. Only a strained coughing fit revealed any fragments of the high tension that dominated the scene. Mary Ann stood alone, weeping, choking, shivering violently, on guard against further aggression.

"*Bitte?*" A soft voice inquired at her side. The man attempted to take her arm, but she threw him off. "Don't touch me!"

Phantoms stirred restlessly. Men murmured among themselves. Directives were given. How to handle their lively catch!

Again Mary Ann heard the word, "Bitte," spoken in an apologetic tone. The man's hand gently tested her, sought to tame his frightened charge.

And so, Mary Ann allowed herself to be taken. Better this than the mayhem she had endured to this point! Wanting desperately to get inside somewhere, anywhere where it was warm and light and protected, Mary Ann submitted.

Her faceless guide led her among closely-milling shadows near the upper railing. Far below in darkness she glimpsed faint white-caps churning and frothing against the ship's bulging flank. Dare she consider a jump to escape this horror? She actually veered toward the railing to judge the height of her jump, but her ghostly companion tugged her into a narrow, pitch-black space at the forward end of the high tower.

Near the center of the enclosed area two stumpy fat poles poked skyward. *The ship's exhaust pipes?* Mary Ann wondered briefly. Then her gaze swung to the vast expanse of broad, heaving ocean and starry sky stretching beyond the iron wall of the tower enclosure. Even in the grip of this horror her soul could be stirred at the sight of the heavens!

Suddenly Mary Ann's guide brought her to a standstill in the tight walkway. *What was there?* A red circle glowed in the deck like a cauldron of molten iron. *My God!* Mary Ann made out the vague image of a man squatted beside the open pit. His comely, bearded face reflected the eerie firelight. Buried to his hatband in the protective nest of his padded coat collar, the man gazed up at Mary Ann and smiled pleasantly, as if to assure her of his honorable intention. Then he lunged for her, caught her by the coat sleeve and began to pull her toward the fire.

"Let go of me! You let go!" Mary Ann yanked her arm from the man's grip and toppled back into a solid wall of male bodies. The men howled with delight and promptly sent her careening toward that smiling, bearded lunatic and the flaming hole he guarded.

Now, for the first time, Mary Ann gazed into the depths of Hell. The entrance of the open hatch led down a treacherously narrow ladder, which plunged from the rim of the iron hole through swirling vapor clouds to a glinting metal floor far below. On a nearer level a man looked up. He frowned momentarily upon glimpsing Mary Ann, definitely trying to be certain of what he was seeing in the open hatch above, then swung away fast, his excitable voice relaying the news of her astonishing appearance.

"Please don't make me go down there! I'll never make it! I'll fall! I'll get killed!" Mary Ann was pleading with the bearded man.

But it didn't matter. Nothing mattered! The men jammed her into the open pit, with loud grunts spiced liberally by heady curses, and planted her feet securely onto the top rung of the steep ladder. Down, down, steadily down, down, they pounded her, until Mary Ann was neck deep in the fiery hole of Hell.

CHAPTER 4

"Steve, all the while I was screaming like a banshee, 'No, no, no, no, no!'" Mary Ann cried out. "It's a wonder they didn't bash me on the head!"

"What a welcome aboard!" Anderson laughed.

"I tell you, Steve, I nearly lost my mind. I had no idea what kind of ship this was that I should be entering it down a small hole on a skinny ladder. But there I was, up to my neck in the open deck hatch." Mary Ann laughed lightly. "More like a monkey hanging from the sides of its cage in a zoo! But those fellows had to get me down that hatch quickly—"

"That's true," the historian cut in. "Their boat was sitting wide open in the bay off Long Island, and all that noise and yelling could have attracted unwanted attention from shore."

"Indeed, we were already under weigh," Mary Ann smiled ruefully. "But now the best is yet to come, if you care to call it that?

"So, there I was, making my way down the ladder very, very slowly, that good-looking fellow topside in the hatchway watching me go down. I was hanging on white-knuckled and praying the Litany to all the Saints in Heaven when it hit me full force."

The stench! It enveloped Mary Ann like noxious sewer odors rising from street vents in the New York City subway system. Odors of sweating human bodies and sewage mingled with the sharp sweet smell of diesel fuel and the grease-laden wafts of a meal cooking somewhere below. Mary Ann clung to the ladder. "Dear Lord, it stinks in here!"

She felt on the verge of passing out when a pair of strong hands grabbed her by the waist and brought her to stand on a small platform midway down the tower ladder. Blinking about in the lurid haze Mary Ann encountered a white toothy grin in an apple round face. The young man - the one who had gaped up at her when she looked down the hatch - regarded Mary Ann with the sweetest expression she'd ever seen. His mop-topped straight black hair under a small pointed gray cap, which tilted rather dangerously toward his right eye, hadn't seen a barber's scissors in weeks. With a pencil-thin mustache scouring his upper lip the fellow resembled, for all the world, a younger version of Clark Gable in the movie, "Gone With The Wind."

Mary Ann lunged for the man. Just the look on his face! A kid really. Mary Ann nearly wrenched the fellow's head off his shoulders. "Help me, please! Get me outta here!"

Clark Gable tottered off-balance, a sheepish grin splitting his round face, as he careened into a row of little trumpet-shaped tubes and black electrical circuits. All the while he waved frantically to ward her off. *"Bitte, Fraeulein, bitte, bitte!"* But Mary Ann continued to hammer at him, beside herself with desperation, tears spilling down her cheeks. "What's wrong with you, you nuts or something? I said, I need help! Help me! Pleeeze!"

The wide-eyed young man pointed urgently above their heads. Large black boots were coming through the round hatch hole onto the second rung of the ladder. "Oh, God, no!"

"Bitte." Clark Gable sprang to his feet and pushed Mary Ann toward a connecting ladder at the edge of the small tower platform. In a tirade of terror, she hooked onto his foul jacket with fierce cat's claws. "For Heaven's sake, what's this dumb 'bitter' you guys keep saying? Can't you speak English? I said I need help!"

Those black boots were practically on top of her. The descending man's leathery presence filled the small tower space where she struggled with the apple-faced Clark Gable. In a daze of defeat and cowed by the presence of this new arrival, Mary Ann clambered down through a shiny metal tunnel toward the grated floor at the bottom of the ladder. For a second she dared to look up. That lovesick Clark Gable was peering at her over the edge of the platform. Then he backed away and looked no more.

The big boots were coming fast, threatening to crush her fleeing fingers. Mary Ann scurried as fast as she could down the last few rungs of the tower ladder, until her feet finally touched the solid iron floor at the base. There she shrunk aside, trembling violently, against a bulging yellow wall and stared into a small crowded space. The room was a profusion of switches, meters and other strange equipment. One wall glowed with tiny green and red lights, reminding Mary Ann of Christmas tree bulbs. Dials and wheels of various sizes sprouted from the walls and floor, and beneath the low ceiling above her head thick bundles of wires and pipes snaked about like twisted jungle vines. To her right, two large steering wheels jutted over a low bench. *It must be the way they drive the boat,* she thought. Yet no one sat there at the moment.

And then she saw them. Several men stood stock still among the wheels and pipes and gadgets. They stared at Mary Ann as at a vision from Heaven. Their pale sweating faces glowed with unearthly radiance in the dim red lighting which bathed the cramped spaces. Devils in the fires of Hell, those men watched her with keen interest, calmly measuring her, waiting to see what she might do.

One tough-looking fellow in a faded work shirt, his sleeves rolled to his elbows, leaned against a table, calmly chewing on something. *A cow chewing its cud!* Suddenly he heaved a loud 'skawwt!' and spit on the gleaming metal deck at Mary Ann's feet. She inched back instinctively. A fearful-looking devil elbowed the bold spitter in the ribs, then leered at Mary Ann with a gap-toothed grin. *See what we think of ya, lady!* His wild man's eyes seemed to say.

Those big black boots came clumping down the ladder, and Mary Ann found herself face-to-face with the bearded man from the hatch above. His sparkling eyes flashed at her through the ladder rungs. *Such a handsome man!* She nearly gasped aloud. Then he turned his back to her and ambled away into the room to join the gloating on-lookers.

More men poured down the ladder. A steady stream of boots, pale whiskered faces and squeaky overcoats, they came down, accompanied by the brisk aromas of sweaty animal leather and damp, cold night air. Mary Ann choked in the tight press of male bodies, shuddered before the inevitable grins and stares, trembled under every blast of coarse laughter that exploded from one or another of them.

Another pair of boots smashed onto the metal deck plate at the base of the ladder. A slightly-built man wearing a crumpled white cap with a circular, mildewed emblem above the black hat band quickly pushed near Mary Ann. At once, she felt the raw power of this man, noted the way the other men had stiffened in deference to him, and concluded he had to be the captain of this horrible vessel.

Indeed, that small statured, sharp nosed fellow with the white cap shouted and gestured like a madman at his loitering men. Several fellows, including the handsome, bearded one with the dark peaked hat, slid past Mary Ann, though not without quick, curious glances in her direction. Others ducked into a low, round hole in the wall forward. Mary Ann watched them disappear, one by one, like rats into a sewer.

CHAPTER 5

The captain swung to Mary Ann, his eyes flaring in shadow beneath his low cap. "Miss," he announced, "I am the *Kommandant* of this 'Ooo-boot'! We go at once to my Quarters!"

"Oh, thank God, you speak English!" Mary Ann lunged for the man. "Help me! Please help me!"

But the man wasted no time with her. He grabbed her arm, practically lifting her off her feet, and flung her toward that low, round hatchway where the other men had vanished. She felt herself going. No will of her own. No chance to fight or plead for understanding. Her legs buckled like sticks, as the irate captain forced her down into the metal tube, and she ducked forward, a timid turtle poking its head from its shell, to peer into the circular hatch. Only a stained green linoleum floor could be seen on the other side.

How to get through this crazy hole gracefully? Mary Ann lifted her right foot slowly onto the curved hatch floor, as if testing the chill water of a swimming pool. Immediately her coat fell open and her A-line skirt rode up her knees, exposing her tattered slip and pale soiled thigh. Embarrassed before the captain, she struggled valiantly to hold her skirt hem down with one hand, while clinging to the curved hatch frame with her other hand.

"Go, go, go, go, go!" The captain shouted at her back.

"I am! I am! Give me a chance to figure it out!" *Oh, this was awful! Absolutely awful! No way to treat a girl!*

Suddenly Mary Ann lost her balance and tumbled against the side of the tube. "Help!" She slid to the curved floor, her legs splayed fore and aft like a high school cheerleader going to the ground in a split. She was stuck! And each time she tried to pull up and right herself she slid back into the silver hatch cradle. With a final wince of effort she strained forward, leg muscles burning, and caught the rim of the hatch with both hands and pulled herself through the hatch to the other side. It didn't matter about maintaining modesty anymore. *So what if that captain got a gander of her bare legs!*

Mary Ann crawled out of the hatchway into a narrow corridor on her hands and knees. *Now, why hadn't she just done this in the first place?* Then rising to her feet, all wobbly and breathless, she squeezed against a paneled bulkhead, as the captain swung through the hatch opening, boots first, and landed with a solid thud in front of her. For a second he glanced at her with his dark, angry eyes - as if to gauge her sanity, or lack thereof - then brushed ahead of her in the narrow walkway beneath overhead light bulbs with flat metal hoods.

A forlorn little shadow, Mary Ann followed after him to see where he would go, for she didn't want to get lost or left behind. But it was only a few steps down the corridor before the captain halted and spun to face her. His finger pointed to a green curtain to the left of the narrow passage.

"In here!" He barked.

Mary Ann moved trance-like along the corridor, touching every here and there at the bulkheads to maintain her balance in the swaying boat. At one point she drifted near an open doorway to the right of the passage and glanced in at a frail-looking youth with the soft, wispy face of an angel. He sat in a tiny closet with black earphones hooked over his straight dark-blonde hair, and when he looked up and saw Mary Ann, his jaw dropped in amazement and his blue eyes blinked like the neon signs in Times Square.

"*Herr Kaleu!*" He gasped, looking from his captain to the girl.

But the captain ignored the lively fellow in the closet. There was no need for an explanation. Only for concentrating on one's duty.

Sensing this keenly, Mary Ann crept to where the captain waited by the green curtain. She dare not delay!

When she passed the green curtain, sight of the tiny compartment space surprised her. The room contained a low narrow bed which hung only a foot or so above the floor. It had side rails, like a young child's bed, and a thin pillow propped at the head. Beside the neatly made-up bunk stood a small desk with an overhead cabinet and several shelves lined with books and folders, reminding Mary Ann of Aunt Louise Cassidy's oak secretary in the hall back home. A small lamp bolted beneath the bookshelves dangled a rusted pull chain and beamed a bright halo of light onto the scored desktop. More wooden cabinets with round, rusted-gold handles filled the space above the bunk beneath the boat's exposed iron ribs.

"Sit!" The captain ordered, as he threw down the metal rail at the side of the bunk.

Mary Ann stepped past the captain, not wanting to brush against him in the tight space, and sat on the olive-green wool blanket, which covered the bunk. Then she looked up in alarm. The captain had reached around with a jerk and yanked the green curtain across the doorway, blocking off the admiring gaze of the angel-faced man in the closet across the way and closing her in with him.

CHAPTER 6

The man leaned into the small wooden desk and crossed his arms in a comfortable way across his frayed, gray-leather jacket with a sliver of yellow wool lining sticking from the collar. His closely-set brown eyes beneath black arched brows stared down at her past a prominent nose that hooked slightly at the bridge. Along his broad jaw line a black ragged beard crept, then shot up into an arrow shape beneath his lower lip. Oily strands of black, tangled hair poked out around the shiny band of his soiled white peaked hat, adding to the man's unkempt appearance.

A pirate! Mary Ann shivered. The name, "Black Beard," popped into her mind. This horrible captain was surely a pirate, what with the way he stared at her with that smug grin playing about his thin purple lips. All he needed was an eye patch to complete the picture.

"*Und sooo,*" the captain murmured, mindlessly toying with his black whiskers.

Mary Ann would have none of it. Her eyes watering with the effort to speak, she demanded to know: "What's going on around here? Who are you anyway? I want some answers right now, you hear me?"

Yet she knew! The horrible reality seared her soul. She didn't want to believe it. Or else, she reasoned desperately, she had accidentally stumbled onto a secret wartime exercise the Navy was conducting? *Oh, dear God, let it be that and not something else!*

The captain's hand dropped to his side, and he came forward with a start. Mary Ann fell back against the bulkhead, fearing a burst of anger from the man, or worse! Instead, she saw him smile, though his smile certainly didn't indicate amusement. He seemed greatly perturbed beneath that pleasant smile. He cleared his throat abruptly, and then began to address her in his shattered English:

"I say it to you again, I am the *Kommandant*, or as you say it, the 'Cap-ee-tan.'" The nasal pitch of the captain's voice scoured Mary Ann's nerves. She could hardly understand him, or was she just too frightened to hear him clearly in the creaking boat?

"Mi-ne nah-me ist Herbert Ketter, of the rank of *Kapitaenleutnant*, or in your Navy, Lieutenant Commander." With a sudden flourish the captain extended his hand to Mary Ann. "*Und* now, Miss, you must tell it to me, what is your name please?"

Mary Ann stared at the captain's wide dirty palm. She had no intention of taking his hand. *She knew! She knew!* She could not deny the evidence!

"So, you wish not to say your name to me?" The captain coaxed humorously.

Mary Ann glared up at him - Lord help her! - and jammed her hand under her coat. "You're German!" She spat at him, her head whirling like a toy top with the force of her deadly pronouncement.

The captain grinned in a benign way then slowly withdrew his hand. "It is as you say it, sweet girl."

Mary Ann wasn't sure what possessed her just then. Perhaps her 'Irish' rose up to take control, just like when Daddy was cornered by someone in an argument or faced a critical moment. She came out fighting mad, ready to put that Nazi captain in his place.

"How dare you!" She shouted, her teeth clattering like marbles in her head. "Y-you bring me here and knock me around like I was a bag of someone's dirty laundry!" *Wow, was she frantic!* "Now you look here, you-you captain, I don't know what's going on around here, but I won't have anymore of it, you understand? You take me back where I belong, or else!"

She didn't know what else. She couldn't believe her gall in addressing that Nazi pirate in this manner. Why, he could murder her on the spot! *Dear Jesus in Heaven, just look at him!*

The captain regarded her with black brows arched in surprise. "I see," he nodded, as if agreeing to her demands. "*Und* now you must know, my sweet girl, I am not in the habit of taking pretty young ladies from the enemy shore!" With that, his head flew back and short bursts of laughter shot from his open mouth. Small yellowish square teeth showed between his thin lips. Then his eyes swung down to her, where she sat trembling, yet defiant, on his bunk. "Besides, a woman on board of a 'soop-marrrine' means bad luck for the crew, yes!"

Mary Ann heard the word, 'soop-marrrine.' Tried to make sense of it. 'Soop-marine'? Submarine? *A German U-boat was a submarine!* That explained the crazy round doors, the ladder coming down from the top, the small compact rooms –

"Oh, my God!" Her anguished cry rang in the tight quarters.

The captain's grizzled face loomed closer in swirling fog. "You are here on a German 'Ooo-boot,' and I am the Capee-tain!" He pronounced with great authority, though it was apparent he, too, was frazzled by the situation.

Madness surged up in Mary Ann like a volcano about to explode. Everything spun into crazy elongated shapes: the captain, the soiled green curtain across the doorway, the desk with the little halo of light, the wall with two hanging photographs and a chipped, rusted mirror. She saw them in the far haze. Mother, Daddy, the boys, her little wee Maggie. drifting away on a cold, dark sea, their hands raised in final farewell.

"Nooo!" Mary Ann's wail of agony resounded down the submarine corridor into the Officers Room and the galley. The captain's legs uncrossed fast, as he bent to Mary Ann. She saw his bearded face coming at her like a death mask.

"Calm yourself at once, Miss!" He ordered. "You do what I say, nothing goes wrong for you!" His large dead-fish pale hand was reaching for her.

"Don't you dare touch me, y-you Nazi!" Mary Ann scrambled to the head of the bunk by the desk, her arms and legs flailing wildly.

The captain staggered against the desk. Mary Ann watched him going, an exaggerated move, as if her harsh words had formed a fist and slugged him in the stomach. For a long while the man remained immobile, his fingers pressed to his eyeballs.

Mary Ann stared at him in alarm. Had she upset him that much? She saw this clearly, then wilted into fearful silence and waited to see what he might do.

"Miss." The captain dropped his hands to his mouth and pulled down on it until it elongated into a large red 'o.' His weary blood-shot eyes scanned the linoleum deck as he continued speaking quietly, but firmly:

"You have come to be on board my boat by my men who do not know what to do with you. They find you walking on the beach, what can they do?" His eyes darted to Mary Ann, where she sat visibly shivering and weeping.

"My men say to me they are not murderers. They think only to save your life. Now!" The captain's nasal voice went up ever so softly in a sing-song tone at the end, putting a final cap to the discussion. "You are here with us, yes?"

CHAPTER 7

A bit of hope pacified Mary Ann at the captain's quiet tone. "Then you'll be taking me back to shore soon?" She heard the man's sigh of resignation as he stretched his head forward to consider her demand.

"I think for now, sweet girl, you must understand, this is—"

"*Herr Kaleu?*" A voice interrupted from the passage on the other side of the green curtain. The captain straightened up fast, scowling. "*Ja, kommst Du her, Leutnant!*"

The green curtain parted. A man peered in. Why, it was the handsome, bearded fellow from the ladder! Mary Ann jerked up in shock. His crystal-blue eyes pierced her like diamond arrows, then jumped to his Commander, who motioned impatiently for him to enter. Looking somewhat embarrassed yet impishly delighted by this summons, the handsome "Leutnant" put his fist to his mouth and squeezed his bulk into the tight compartment space next to his captain. His full lips dared to form a smile for Mary Ann, which he carefully screened from his commander.

"Young lady," the captain pronounced in his accented English, "this is my Second Watch 'Off-ee-ser,' Dietrich Heubeck."

The officer named Heubeck stiffened appreciably at the introduction and bowed to Mary Ann with exaggerated formality. *A real show-off,* Mary Ann marveled grudgingly, momentarily forgetting her terror. Then Heubeck turned to his commander, and both men spoke together in German for several moments, obviously discussing her and her predicament.

Mary Ann felt quite confident they were planning how to get her off the boat and back to shore. This was such a silly mistake, after all! So, she must just stay calm, maybe say something to the captain in due time, make him understand how this whole mess was something that got out of hand and could easily be rectified.

Suddenly the captain swung to her, taking her off guard. "My watch officer says to me this is a very nice surprise to see a pretty young lady sitting on my bunk!" And the men laughed as if this situation was greatly amusing.

Her insides curling with rage at the subtle implication Mary Ann wanted in the worst way to hurl a retort at the Captain. *Just get me out of here, you lousy Nazi!* If only she had a baseball bat, she'd conk these fellows on the head and make a run for it.

But the captain proceeded smoothly: "Naturally, my dear, we cannot be too careful with this thing. There is every reason to believe that something has gone very wrong with our little shore operation. Perhaps you are a spy, yes?"

The blood drained from Mary Ann's face. *A spy? Surely these Nazis couldn't be thinking such a thing of her, an innocent victim?* "Sir, I'm not a spy!" Panic rumbled in her bowels.

The captain's eyes narrowed to slits, boring into her, studying her every twitch. *Dear Jesus in Heaven, he didn't believe her?* "I'm no spy! How could I be a spy?" She whimpered.

The captain signaled his second watch officer to another conference. Again, the two men huddled together, talking on and on in their swift, guttural German, while Mary Ann shrank further and further into the corner of the bunk, her frazzled mind jumping from one horrible possibility to another. *What if these Nazi seamen tried to get information out of her? Things she didn't know, and they wouldn't believe her! What if they searched her, or worse – Oh, God, no! – made her undress? Tortured her? Physically attacked her?*

Now, the captain was gazing down at her with his dark eyes. "My officer cannot speak English so good, therefore I must translate for him what you say to me, yes?"

With a polite nod, the man named Heubeck acknowledged this fact, then calmly pulled a pen and small writing pad from inside his rumpled jacket pocket. The interrogation was about to begin! Blood rushed in Mary Ann's ears like the flood waters of doom. Or was it the sea lashing at the U-boat's outer hull? Mary Ann felt her head split apart with loud, cracking sounds. Or was it the creaking of the submarine's whale-size metal body as the boat turned on the sea and roared along, its powerful diesel engines hammering in the vast distance?

The captain glanced at his second watch officer, then scratched absently at his whiskers and murmured in English, just loud enough for Mary Ann to overhear. "How can we properly explain this thing, Dietrich? That a sweet surprise comes to us here from America?" The captain shrugged, grinned knowingly at his second watch officer, then sighed and looked up at the ribbed overhead, as if pondering a puzzle.

Mary Ann warily watched the men. Was it her imagination, or had they become less threatening? It seemed the deathly atmosphere in the compartment had changed to one of complaisance. She sensed that these men would not harm her, after all, but seemed to be just as stunned and confused as she was about her sorry plight.

"Sir?" Mary Ann's voice sounded like a mouse squeak in the crowded compartment that was meant to hold only one person. She felt as if she was standing outside of herself looking in through a tiny round window at the two German officers standing a mere half-arm's length from her. "How soon will you be taking me back to shore?"

The captain's brow lowered. He looked askance at her, and Mary

Ann trembled anew to see those clouds of anger rising in his belea-guered face. Yet she went on, cautiously, insistently. *Lord knows where she was finding the courage!*

"It's getting so late, sir. My girlfriend and her parents will be wondering where I am." Maybe Helen Marie, and Mr. And Mrs. Flynn were aware she was missing, or maybe they weren't? Prob-ably they were asleep, not suspecting in a million years that some-thing like this could be happening. After all, she had sneaked out of the house in the dark around 10:30PM. "I'm sure they're already out looking for me right at this moment!" She insisted. *Such grand hopes!* Then an ominous realization popped into her mind: Helen Marie and her parents wouldn't be up for hours. They would have no idea she was gone, since her bedroom door was closed. They'd think she was sleeping late and not want to disturb her!

"So please, sir," she choked, "what if you take your submarine in closer to the beach. I could swim the rest of the way!"

The captain's face reddened. Mary Ann pleaded desperately. "I won't tell a soul I was here on your boat, or even that your boat was out here off the coast! I'll just tell my girlfriend and her parents that I got lost and fell in the surf while I was out walking." Mary Ann gestured down at her soiled wet clothes. "See? They'll believe me!"

An ear-splitting roar filled the small compartment as the cap-tain broke into loud bellows of laughter. "Heubeck!" He elbowed the startled officer at his side and translated what Mary Ann had said. The second watch officer laughed in turn, though a trace of sympathy filled his blue eyes. Then the captain came back to her, his face an emotionless mask. "My officer says you are very brave to want swim back to the shore."

Mary Ann felt the sting of the captain's sarcasm, but pressed her case willfully. "Well, sir, I'll show you, I can and will do it! And I promise I won't say anything to anyone when I get back either!"

The captain grinned amiably, his thin lips stretching back to reveal his small even teeth. "It is very nice for you to be concerned for my boat and crew." He rumbled.

"Yes, sir." She couldn't help that part of the plan. *Anything to placate him! Get him on her side, so she could get out of here!*

Then coughing off to the side, the captain wiped his mouth on his fist and gazed at her, his dark eyes probing, "How far can you swim in the Atlantic Ocean in March?" He inquired.

"Well, I'm sure I can do it, sir." She replied with enthusiasm. *He appeared convinced?*

"Can you swim two or three kilometers in the cold water? In the darkness? In that coat and skirt you wear?" His eyes fell over her too boldly to relay the message.

Mary Ann nodded resolutely at each question. "Yes, sir, I'll do it, believe me!"

The captain sniffed, remained silent momentarily, pondering the magnitude of her determination.

Mary Ann considered something else. *Now, why hadn't it occured to her before?* "Sir, if you think I can't make it by swimming, then how about the Coast Guard or Navy? If you radio in to them about me, they can come under a flag of truce and get me." The image of Indians and cavalry meeting on a vast plain with peace pipes and banners waving filled her mind.

The blast came like cannon fire. "Enough senseless talk!" The captain raved. "I don't have time for this baloney!"

Mary Ann recoiled in shock. The second watch officer jumped to attention, his blue eyes searing into Mary Ann with the bitter truth.

"I think, sweet girl, you will be much better off to remain right where you are!" The captain drew out the last words in his nasty nasal voice. His eyes did not leave her face. "*Und* now I have some questions for you, Miss America, who tries my patience greatly! You will answer them, yes? Then perhaps in time I must answer any questions for you. Is this agreeable? Or must I strangle you into submission!"

CHAPTER 8

Cowed to tears, Mary Ann felt her mind collapsing slowly, one section at a time, like a building crumbling beneath the battering of a wrecking ball.

The captain rumbled. "My reliable second watch officer you see here will write down what you answer to me. I translate for him. Do you understand what I say to you?"

"Yes." Mary Ann swiped at her runny nose with the palm of her hand. The captain had assumed his authoritative stance and stood glaring down at her past his curved nose. "Now, you will tell us first, what is your name please?"

Her name? Why did it matter? She was nothing but a dead person!

"Your name please?" He repeated, his face softening slightly to encourage her. "It would be very nice to know the name of the pretty girl who comes on my boat late at night."

What, pretty? Mary Ann thought. *Surely he's lying! She wasn't pretty at all, at least not to a lot of the fellows back in high school!*

"Mary Ann," she conceded quietly.

"*Bitte,* louder!" The captain cocked his ear.

Mary Ann jerked forward. "Mary Ann!" she hollared.

"Aaah," the captain sang out, "'Mari-an-ne,' what a lovely name, Marianne." He caressed her name with his lilting accented voice, seemed very happy, indeed, to at last know her name.

How she loathed the man! Though she had never truly hated anyone in her life, Mary Ann despised this black-bearded Nazi U-boat captain, what with the way he looked down on her, all high-and-mighty and so sure of himself and his power over her.

"*Und* now," he crooned, "what is your family name, Marianne?"

"What? Family name? Oh, yeah, my full name is Mary Ann Theresa Connor!" She burst out. "So now you know it, okay?"

The captain's boots scraped the deck as he changed his stance in the tight compartment. "Connor." he mused. "You are Irish then, yes?" He studied her face.

Mary Ann gripped the bunk mattress, glanced warily at the second watch officer. The Nazis disdained anyone who was not of German descent. But she answered with conviction: "Yes, I am! One-hundred percent Irish, and proud of it!" *Let the captain put that in his pipe and smoke it!*

"Ah, yes, the German people like the Irish people very much, Marianne Connor." The captain's reply relieved her growing concern, though it added to yet another worry. *Might he become too familiar with her?* "We have no quarrel with the good people of Ireland." He said.

Yeah, well, you have a quarrel with me! Mary Ann wanted to blast the man to Kingdom Come, but remained silent instead, searching desperately in her mind for a way to win him over into letting her go, now that he seemed a bit more amenable toward her.

"*Und* now, I must ask you, where is your home, Marianne Terese' Connor?" The captain sidled closer to his second watch officer, though he kept a critical eye on her.

Mary Ann answered promptly: "I'm from Brooklyn, New York. Greenpoint section. Humbolt Street." For a fleeting moment, she saw her home. A piece of Heaven on Earth, it was. Aunt Susie and Mama on the front stoop, little wee Maggie and the Rossi twins cutting out paper dolls on the parlor floor, Daddy and the boys huddled around the kitchen table playing penny poker.

"Brooklyn!" The captain's gasp of surprise rattled her. "What are you doing so far from your home?"

Mary Ann nearly laughed aloud to see the stunned expression on that Nazi captain's face. "I told you before, I'm visiting my friend, Helen Marie, and her family in Sandy Point this week."

The captain no longer paid attention to her. He was busy talking to his second watch officer, who frowned in concentration as he listened. Mary Ann wondered at their apparent discomposure, then the captain turned back to her with a forced smile.

"Now, Marianne Connor, you must answer correctly. What were you doing so late on the beach by the home of your friend?"

Mary Ann answered truthfully. "I was going for a walk, sir."

"*Und* do you always spend your holiday walking alone on the beach at such a late hour?"

"Well, no, sir. Just tonight. It was the first time I was ever away anywhere in the dark like that."

"*Ja, und* tell me, why were you out on the beach in the dark tonight?"

"Sir, it had nothing to do with you, if that's what you're driving at!" Mary Ann waved her hand. "I'm not a spy! Helen Marie's father had warned me not to walk the beach, that it was off-limits because of the war, but I went anyway, thinking I won't go far or stay long. Just a quick walk down and back. Nothing more!"

"So you failed to obey the warning of your friend's father?" The captain sounded like Monsignor Walsh in the confessional at St. Catherine's, and Mary Ann answered the captain, as if he was the Monsignor, though she felt very childish and stupid. "I wanted to see the ocean, sir, with the stars shining over it, and then I got to praying as well."

The captain's head jerked back and his mouth curved down. This certainly wasn't the answer he had expected from her, but Mary Ann went on chattering, determined to convince him of her innocence: "I never got to see a clear night sky in all my life, sir. Oh, I can see the lights of Manhattan from the roof of our apartment build-ing- and that's spectacular, believe me, with the searchlight on the Empire State Building and everything! But I never saw a really dark night sky with the stars shining over the ocean. It was like looking at Heaven!"

Mary Ann stumbled on, trembling with the effort to confess her revelation. "I felt the urge to pray, as I said, sir." Yes, she readily admitted this to the Captain, though he was a Nazi with no decent human feelings or faith in Almighty God. "The feeling comes to me sometimes, and I have to go somewhere quiet and alone."

"Ah, *ja, ja,*" the Captain eyed his second watch officer as if to confirm her insanity, "this is most interesting that you go to the for-bidden beach to see the stars and to pray."

"Yes, well, I pray all the time, sir, not just on the beach tonight. And you know why?" She rocked forward, mindlessly daring him, "it's because I care!" *Oh, Good Lord, why was she babbling on like this? Was it her nerves, or that desperate need to explain to people what she did, so they wouldn't misunderstand her or her intentions?* "I stop to think about what is really important in life, not like what's going on with this war, with all the killing and dying and people hating each other!" She wanted to add, "Like you Germans, thinking you're the master race, and wanting to take over the world," but she wisely refrained from doing so.

The captain straightened up, his thin lips pressed together in a grim line. She had shocked him, that's for sure, and it rattled her to think she had gotten so presumptuous, but didn't the man need to know the truth of where things stood?

"What is important?" The captain mumbled to himself, while the second watch officer waited to the side, his blue eyes leaping back and forth between Mary Ann and his commander. "So, you think about what is important, Marianne Connor. This is most interesting that you KNOW what is important!"

Mary Ann sensed the storm brewing and braced herself to

receive its punishing winds. "Tell it to me, Marianne Connor!" The captain practically seized her by the shoulders. "I want to know what is so important that you know!" He pointed to his wide-eyed second watch officer. "I am certain my officer here wants to know also! All of my men want to know what you know! You say it to us, what is important! Apparently you are the only one who knows!"

She blinked up at him. She wanted to say, "God," but remained silent, wary.

The captain waited for her answer that did not come, then turned away in disgust, ignored her as she deserved. He was speaking in German to his second watch officer, who hurriedly scribbled in his little notepad. *Was he actually recording what she said?* The captain spoke on, pointing with his thick forefinger at something the second watch officer had written. Then the captain laughed out at some private joke and swung back to Mary Ann on the bunk.

"This entire thing intrigues me, Marianne Connor." *So he wasn't going to give up the argument after all?* Mary Ann shivered with wonder and apprehension. "You are all alone on the beach. It is very late. Almost midnight. You are there to see the stars. And to pray." Mary Ann lowered her eyes, her cheeks burning, as the captain harangued in his caustic tone. "You are thinking about what is important. You are seeking solutions for yourself and the entire world! Most commendable!"

"Yes," she murmured beneath his verbal lashing.

"*Und* then, there you are! You meet my men on the beach! Incredible! You just happen to be there, lost in your prayers and looking at the stars when and where my men are there, too!"

"Yes, that seems to be what happened." Mary Ann felt closer to death than life.

With an exaggerated move, the captain lifted one large booted foot onto the edge of the bunk near her thigh and leaned down to her. For a long, terrible moment he remained silent, observing her, seeking any cracks in her story. She feared he might touch her. That he definitely want to touch her to see that she was real!

"I must know something further, Marianne Connor." His breath, stinking of stale cigarette smoke and digested food, was in her nostrils. Mary Ann didn't want to breathe in that man's foul air and turned her head down and away. "What else were you thinking on the beach?" He reached over and tapped the little notepad his second watch officer held. "What you say to me will not be written here. You say it only to me." The captain came back to Mary Ann. "For me it will be most interesting to know the mind of a pretty young lady from the United States, since she wishes to talk freely with me, yes?"

Mary Ann stared down at her icy hands lying clasped in her lap. She had brought all this on herself. The captain was baiting her, she knew. He'd tear into anything she'd say, and she fiercely regretted blathering so openly.

"I was thinking of the war and how tragic it is." She began her confession hoarsely. "I was asking God to protect—"

"Who? Who do you ask God to protect?" The captain's shout deafened Mary Ann and rattled his second watch officer, who stood by shyly looking on this surrealistic scene of his commander bickering with an American woman.

Mary Ann glanced up at the two men, her face twisted with the start of fresh tears. That Nazi captain waited. *Such a harsh, triumphant German face!* Her breath caught in ragged gasps. "I was praying for everyone, sir," she murmured.

The captain stared at her, then grinned, those thin purple lips stretching back over his small teeth. "A very nice gesture that you pray for 'everyone!' Perhaps, then, you have prayed for me?"

Mary Ann didn't answer, though it troubled her that Jesus Himself said a person should pray for his enemies. Now the enemy stood before her. His face loomed clearly, and his dark angry eyes sought something. Assurance? Could it be possible that he, too, hoped for her prayers for his battered Nazified soul? But she determined not to give him the satisfaction: "I was thinking of my family, especially my brothers who might have to go into the service, if the war goes on for a long time." She avoided the captain's sharp gaze. "I was also thinking about some fellows I knew in high school who are already in training." Her mind drifted to Bobby Lawson.

"Of course, of course." The captain leaned back on the desk and slid his hands into his jacket pockets. "We all pray for our own, do we not, Marianne Connor?"

She nodded. *Was he mocking her? Him, pray?*

"Do you find that so hard to believe of me, Marianne Connor? What does your American propaganda say of us? That we Germans, the so-called 'Hun,' the National Socialist hordes, seek to destroy the present world civilization?" A chill shot up Mary Ann's spine at his words. "I am a Catholic, the same as you, Marianne Connor. I think very much to my large family, to my grandparents and many aunts and uncles and cousins in my old birthplace in the south of Bavaria. I think always to my parents in Frankfurt, and to my friends and classmates who are at sea, and to my younger brother, Hans, who fights in the desert of North Africa.

"Do you find this so difficult to believe that I pray, Marianne Connor? I pray for my homeland! I pray for this war soon to be over! I never wanted for this damned war in the first place!"

Shocked by his tirade Mary Ann whispered, "I'm sorry, sir."

The man glared at her. "You are sorry for me, Marianne Connor. Why?" His smile was cold and distant. "So then, it seems we think the same after all, yes? We know what we know. That there are things we must do, even if we do not like it. There are things we cannot control, but must do them."

She nodded, unsure to what extent she had committed herself in agreeing with the man. He thundered on at her:

"Ja, be sorry for me, Marianne Connor, and pray for me, also. Many of my friends are already dead in this war! Some lie on the bottom of the sea in their fresh graves. Bombs come each day on our cities. Our people die! Yet we are willing to sacrifice to claim victory for our homeland!"

With that, the captain put his back to her and motioned the second watch officer into the passage outside the green curtain, leaving Mary Ann alone in the tiny stale Captain's Quarters to come to terms with what he had said.

"Steve," Mary Ann Connor Carlino regarded the historian on the sofa across from her, "I sat there on that bunk in complete shock after those men went out of the compartment. I was shaken up, feeling sad and guilty and so many other emotions I can't begin to say. Yet I wasn't as afraid of the captain anymore, for I think by then, I was already admiring him somehow. Also, I suppose I knew I wouldn't be going home that night, or any night after that. I was very sure I wasn't going to survive. Not that the men would kill me, no, Steve. But that I was going to die with them in their submarine somewhere along the way. I was going to be one of the many millions who were dying all over the world in that terrible war."

Anderson had been listening intently. *What was there to say?* He recalled the memories, which *Konteradmiral* Ketter had shared with him during his interview at his home in Bremen-Oberneuland, of the first night Mrs. Carlino had come aboard his boat, who she was and what went on. This entire thing seemed incredible! Plus the fact that this extraordinary human interest story had remained under wraps all these years. Well, it was understandable, in light of postwar revelations, especially with the Holocaust and other Nazi atrocities making the headlines. But he, Anderson, would make sure that this magnificent tale of an American girl taken prisoner on a German U-boat didn't stay buried any longer. Enough years had passed for people to come to know and accept that there were many decent young German soldiers and sailors who fought and died in that war. Too many good men and women of all nations had sacrificed their lives for various causes, right or wrong, that they had served!

CHAPTER 9

"Heubeck," Kapitaenleutnant Ketter murmured to his '*Zweite-VO*' beyond the captive girl's hearing, "you know that the young woman said she visits in Sandy Point with friends." Ketter's mind still tumbled from their verbal exchange. He had not expected such a challenge from the bedraggled little American lady. She had definitely touched a raw nerve with him, reminding him further of a truth he could not escape. "So," he rasped irritably, "the navigator has brought us too far to the west after all. What in thunder went wrong?"

"That blasted coastal fog, *Herr Kaleu*. We couldn't make out the shore so well." Heubeck replied.

"And so, our charts weren't the best either," Ketter growled. "Now we have this little mess to deal with. I will treat the matter as I see fit. The young lady is no security threat to our assignment, you and I both know this. Our boat was off course by several miles. As for the *Abwehr* fellows, they are on their own back there. If anyone searches for her and finds them, it's out of our hands. Let Berlin deal with it."

"Quite so, *Herr Kaleu*. But what is to happen now?"

Ketter scratched his jaw, an easy, satisfied gesture. "While the young lady is our 'guest,' I will let her have use of my Quarters. This will afford her some privacy."

"Jawohl, Herr Kaleu," Heubeck nodded thoughtfully.

Ketter coughed into his fist and glanced in at the terrified young woman on his bunk. *Such a feisty little lady!* He must be careful with her. Her sweet freckled face with the sad purple bruise above the right eye intrigued him. His men had roughed her up good! "Heubeck," he condescended to his *Zweite-VO,* "until further orders come, I think my good, reliable officers can include the young lady in their schedules. For the moment, she can enjoy a cup of hot coffee from the galley and some dry clothes. See that she gets these."

"Jawohl! Certainly, *Herr Kaleu!"* Leutnant Heubeck agreed enthusiastically. "But then it can be possible she is to remain on board with us for the duration of our patrol?" He sounded quite too thrilled at the prospect.

"Nothing is certain at this point!" Ketter scowled, his head aching at the very thought that, indeed, the young woman must be kept on board. He'd love to do as she demanded, take her back and dump her on shore. "But I can't order the young lady to be thrown overboard, can I?" He smiled ruefully.

"Aaah, then she must stay with us!" Heubeck gushed, then checked himself appropriately. "Yet I do feel sorry for her, *Herr Kaleu.* She is so frightened. And she has been taken from her home and family. How will she survive with us?"

"It will not be pleasant for her, or for us," Ketter grumbled. "She must survive as we do, *Herr Zeite-VO,* one day, one moment at a time, yes?" Ketter was irritated with Heubeck's concern for the girl. He wanted no competition. *Ah, let it be! Such a thought!* "And we must consider, if there is difficulty with the *Abwehr* agents in America and it can be traced to her -" Ketter shook his head, a sardonic grin crossing his face. "Well, it must be too bad. We would never get word of this anyway. Our *Herr Admiral* Doenitz, the 'Big Lion,' at U-boat Headquarters in Kerneval, would certainly be informed, and so our little American lady will disappear without a trace the moment this boat reaches port. It would be a sad thing, if this must be, Heubeck."

Ketter stole another glance at his unexpected passenger. "Ah, well," he sighed wearily and examined his watch, "I will be alone with her for a moment, *Leutnant.* I wish to explain some things to her about our wonderful 'cruise ship.' Then, in a few minutes time I will make out the radio report to send along to '*BdU*' , informing them of our completed mission and that this sweet civilian comes on board with us. What a row that will cause!"

"Jawohl, Herr Kaleu." Heubeck followed demurely behind his commander and poked his head into the tiny Quarters where the girl sat. "But *Herr Kaleu,* maybe you must not be so harsh with her after all?"

Ketter shot him a look of towering annoyance. "You do not mind about this, *Leutnant!* Carry on with your duties!"

"Yes, sir!" Heubeck promptly departed.

With his officer out of the way, Ketter shoved near the girl and began to gather up his books, the war log, and other supplies from the desk and shelves in his personal compartment. Occasionally his eyes swept the young woman on his bunk. *So unbelievable to see her there!*

"Marianne Connor," he cracked in English. *Must sound harsh! Keep her in line!* "I will leave you here for a short time, because I am a very busy man." He noted the expression of panic on her face. "I will give you a stern warning. Under no circumstances are you to leave these Quarters and wander about unescorted on your own. Do you understand what I say to you?"

The young woman nodded, shivering and weeping quietly.

"I normally do not contain a prisoner on board my U-boat unless he begins to fiddle with the knobs and wheels and taps, ha, ha. However, in your case, my men may forget their purpose in this boat, if you move about freely. For your sake I must keep you here where it is, at least, somewhat private for you, yes?"

He went on: "My officers will attend your needs as best they can. You need something, you ask them. My second watch officer will bring coffee to you very soon. Now I take my things from here to make room for you. We must all play a little waiting game." He pushed on the green curtain to exit the compartment.

"Captain, please!"

That sweet voice! Ketter swung to the young woman, delighted with the prospect of another verbal confrontation with her. He'd never known such a spirited, out-spoken woman like this. *Was she typically American?* He wondered. "You have something you wish to say to me, Marianne Connor?"

Her frightened eyes dropped to her lap. *What, nothing now?*

"I am waiting!" Ketter kept his hand on the edge of the curtain, as he studied her, the tangled, dark auburn curls that fell over her shoulders, the gentle curve of her cheek. "You wish to use the WC?" He grunted.

"What?" Her teary blue eyes came up.

"The WC!" He scowled. "How you say it in America?"

"I don't know what you mean." She shrunk back from him.

"You must make water! Pee pee, yes!"

Her eyes grew large with awareness. She shook her head vigorously in the negative.

"I see." He brushed his nose with his fist and cleared his throat. "Then, one final warning, Marianne Connor. I will remind you most forcefully that my crew is composed of excellent, trained sailors and mechanics, as well as good officers over them. During long periods at sea, their tempers and desires become sharp as the razor. Therefore, you should not tempt them!" He winked at the young woman to drive the message home. *Yes, those innocent blue eyes widened with fear. His words were having the desired effect.* "You can believe that life on a German U-boat can become very routine and boring. Days and days on the sea,"

Ketter rambled on, relishing her increasing discomfort. "It is a long way from port and the arms of a generous woman. You remain in here, you will be safe. And remember, Marianne Connor, a U-

- 6 0 -

boat man's duty is to the boat and crew. Your duty is to stay out of the way!"

That said, Ketter stepped into the passageway and yanked the curtain closed on her. *Heck with it, there was nothing more to be done anyway.*

CHAPTER 10
Chorus - The Radiomen

"You hear that, Konni? If I were in there, I would not treat that poor girl so harshly as Ketter does!"

"The Old Man knows what he must do, Schatzi. Don't be so concerned."

"When I looked up before and saw her in the passage, I nearly went through the overhead! I think to myself, can this be? A girl here? And all alone? Where has she come from? I mean, my God, what else can happen on board this boat on Friday the 13th?"

"News of her capture has surely spread among our comrades. The Old Man must have a firm hand for sure!"

"Ah, Konni, listen, she cries again! I will jump right over there and take her in my arms!"

"Ha, ha, no, Schatzi, you must stay here at your post like a good boy."

"There, Ketter stands in the passage. Look at him! He is in the foulest of moods. I feel sorry for all of us, now that this thing has happened. What have he and *Leutnant* Heubeck decided about the girl, that I'd like to know?"

"Shh, keep it down, Schatzi. The Old Man will hear us and then there'll be trouble for us. Now give me that folder. There's work to be done."

"Of course." Schatzi secured his headphone set over his right ear, his angel-blue eyes sparkling.

CHAPTER 11
Chorus - The Crew

The news had, indeed, traveled fast throughout the German U-boat. From the bow compartment to the aft torpedo room, it was known: an American woman was on board and being interrogated by the *Kommandant* in his Quarters at this very moment!

"Any of you pigheads in the *Zentralle* get to see her? Come on, tell us, what does she look like? Sexy, yes!"

"You should've heard her scream when Feiler made her go up the ladder to the *Wintergarten*! Got her on the bare leg and received quite a reward - a kick in the gut, ha, ha!"

"There's no more room in this sewer pipe for another stinkin' body!"

"Yeah, but it's a woman's body, Theo! Think of it, we have no need to return to port, boys! The comforts of port are now available at sea! All we have to do is go off duty and line up!"

"No more saltpeter in tonight's meal for me, ha, ha!"

"It's nasty bad luck with that female on board."

"Ah, Senghas, you keep saying that! Cut it out, will you! It's giving me a bad feeling."

"Put that comb away, you blockhead. Why bother looking pretty, when she'll never see any of us back here in the e-motor room?"

"Yeah, well, maybe I plan a little visit to her, Erich!"

"For my part, fellows, I want nothing to do with that 'Ami' dog. Lisette waits for me back at the Dancing Bar!"

"Ah, so, listen to this! I'm sure Lisette is doing just that, waiting for her 'babyface' sailor to return from sea! Yes, yes, we all know she does just that! She screws with no one else, ha, ha!"

"I overheard the Old Man telling the *EVO* on the bridge that she could be part of some counter intelligence plot."

"It's too coincidental, Willi. Even if enemy intelligence knew we were coming, they'd have endless miles of American coastline to patrol. Besides, aren't you boys excited it's a girl? A real, live girl! Here! On our boat! If this boat runs into any trouble, I'll gladly die with her in my arms!"

CHAPTER 12

Mary Ann huddled against the paneled bulkhead in Captain's Quarters, her legs drawn up beneath her damp coat and skirt. She had formed a protective barrier against the putrid bone-chilling atmosphere in the German submarine, and like a caged animal, sat staring with dry, saucer eyes at the soiled green curtain. Only her ears functioned. Tuned to the alien environment she distinguished the crew's laughter and foreign shouts above the distant steady clattering roar of the boat's diesel engines and the muffled rush of water against steel.

"*Fraeulein* Connor?" A man's voice called suddenly from the other side of the drawn curtain.

Startled from her torpor, Mary Ann sat up, on alert for another encounter with the Germans.

"Ah, *Fraeulein* Connor, *bitte*, you are there?"

"Yes! What do you want?"

The curtain slid aside. Crystal-blue eyes peered in. Second Watch Officer Dietrich Heubeck entered the compartment with a slight nod to her. In his hands he balanced a flat baking tray, which he politely extended to her with a pleasant greeting, "*Bitte schoen.*"

Somewhat relieved to see this man and not another, mainly the captain, Mary Ann dared to sneak a peek at Heubeck's offering, which turned out to be a cup of steaming black coffee with the consistency of motor oil and an unappealing, lop-sided sandwich with gray, greasy-looking meat oozing from the bread onto the white porcelain plate.

"Bitte?" The officer indicated that Mary Ann should take the tray from him.

Not wanting to appear ungrateful, she dutifully complied, lowering the tray to her knees with trembling hands.

Then she saw them. Tiny gold swastica emblems ringed the edges of the plate and saucer and glinted menacingly at her in the lamplight, as if to taunt her that, yes, yes, you are here on this death ship, a doomed prisoner with no escape. It was like viewing the skull and crossbones run up the mast of a pirate vessel! Her breath caught in ragged gasps. *She would hurl the tray across the room! Toss it in that German officer's face!*

Heubeck either failed to note her agitation, or else it had no affect on him. Instead, his calm voice came above the pounding of the submarine engines and the awkward staccato 'tap-tap-tap' of someone working away on a typewriter nearby. "In mine poor English, I say to you, welcome on board of our boat, *Fraeulein.*"

He welcomed her? Was he out of his mind! Mary Ann couldn't meet his blue eyes. "Thanks," she murmured, her lips pressed thin and cold with tension. Yet, she had to admit, she felt no animosity toward the man. Perhaps, only a glimmer of interest? For he was quite a good-looking fellow and seemed to be trying very hard to please her and make her feel comfortable, if one could be made comfortable in a situation like this.

Heubeck stood by the partially-open curtain watching her, clearing his throat, from time to time, and nervously tugging at his dark blonde whiskers. *What was he waiting for?* Mary Ann wondered. *Wasn't he going to leave the compartment? Let her to herself?*

But he had no intention of leaving. "Eat, please." He directed with a friendly smile, when he caught her looking.

"I'm not hungry." She mumbled, avoiding his gaze. The meat in the sandwich, whatever it was, smelled rotten. Or was it everything on this lousy Nazi U-boat?

Yet, Mary Ann felt compelled to cooperate with the second watch officer. Besides what would be the harm in taking a little sip of the coffee? It might help warm her up a bit.

So she lifted the cup in her shaky hands and swallowed a gulp of the black brew. "Oooh, aagg!" Mary Ann coughed. For sure it tasted like the fuel oil odor that permeated the boat. Then she carefully lowered the cup to the saucer with the gold swastikas and glanced up at the second watch officer.

"Goot?" He inquired cheerfully.

"It's okay, I guess," she mumbled.

"Okay? Okay? What is that, okay?" The man suddenly came alive, boldly mimicking her response. He pointed to the sandwich. "You must eat, okay, okay?"

Mary Ann was flabbergasted by the officer's behavior. *How dare he poke fun at her!* Then like a gushing fire hydrant, the second watch officer launched into bright conversation, in German, of course, talking on and on, and laughing and gesturing as if, for all the world, this was a normal, friendly get-together at Sammy's Hot Dog Store on Manhatten Avenue. *What had gotten into the man?*

"Ah, now, now, don't look at me that way, sweet girl! That you could only know what I feel for you in my heart, yes!" Heubeck wanted so much to bring some cheer to that helpless, frightened little lady. She was certainly in a very sorry situation, and it would be so good for her to know they all suffered these deprivations together, as he later explained to the Old Man about his attempt to serve the young woman her first meal on board the boat.

"That is canned liverwurst you eat, see? Unfortunately we have no more fresh meat on board of our U-boat. When the men pass through the control room our first days out from port, they sneak slivers from the fresh hams and smoked sausages that hang from the pipes. But still, the *Obersteuermann* can't catch them doing this!"

Ah, if only the young lady would smile for him, Heubeck thought. He was very sure he could coax a smile from those pretty lips. *Come, come, sweet girl, smile for me. Make me happy. Maybe I can feel better, too?*

"I got the Cook to fix that sandwich especially for you," Heubeck explained enthusiastically. "Naturally, *unser Smutje* complained about having to do this extra work, as he always does when he feels put upon by one of us men. The bridge watch topside happened to be hollering for coffee, so *unser Smutje* was really sour, ha! He'll be even more upset if you don't eat, sweet girl. So, come, I don't want a pretty girl like you to starve on board of our U-boat."

Mary Ann had grown increasingly frustrated throughout his monologue. *What, in Heaven's name, was the man going on about? Was he crazy or something?* "Just go away! Leave me alone!" She cried. "I don't want anything from you or anyone else around here! Nothing, you understand? Just take me home! All I want to do is *GO HOME,* do you understand me?"

Mein Gott, this isn't going right, Heubeck winced under the young woman's angry barrage. "Dear girl, you must be calm, or the *Kommandant* might remove me from your care, and that we wouldn't want at all, believe me. The stone hearted 'Pauli' would be sent to replace me, and he is not so pleasant."

Just look at the girl! What could he say? That he, too, wished to go home? They all wished to go home! God, look at the girl. She was crying like Lotte did back in the Tiergarten that dreary November day before his departure for France. This little one reminded him of Lotte. That vulnerable look. Yes, this was his downfall in love. He had found it so attractive in Lotte. And now he wished to comfort this little one, take her in his arms, kiss her, love her—

Calm yourself, Dietrich! You can't be thinking this stuff. It's all behind you now. Don't let this sweet one mess with your brain. Heubeck bent to the young American woman on the Old Man's bunk and attempted to speak to her in his poor halting English. *If only he hadn't done so poorly in his language skills at the Gymnasium!* "Miss Connor, do not cry. Please make to relax," he said.

Mary Ann realized the man was trying to be kind to her, but this didn't help her feel better. It only seemed to make things worse, for she didn't want to like him so much. *Those blue eyes. That nice smile. The way he spoke.* She wiped at her tears with the sleeve of her coat, then lifted the baking tray with the coffee cup and uneaten sandwich on the swastika plate and held it out to the second watch officer. "Here, maybe you better take this stuff back. I don't want it." *No, she didn't want anything anymore, except to lay down and die.*

The second watch officer reached for the tray. The boat took a sudden roll to port, turning away fast and changing direction. The tray slipped from Mary Ann's grasp. In horror, she watched as the cup and saucer and plate with the dreaded swastikas shattered on the green linoleum deck. As if to drive in the insult further, the sandwich landed with a plop on the officer's thick soled sea boots and spread its sickly gray contents on his pants cuff, and the baking tray went banging and clattering, like the cymbal from a drum set, into the center passage where it disappeared from sight.

"Oh, no, it was an accident, I'm sorry!" Mary Ann clasped the sides of her head in panic.

For a long moment, the second watch officer stood stunned and

- 7 0 -

silent, then reached up and pulled back the green privacy curtain to peer into the passage. Across the way, the angel face radio man sat in his tiny closet, looking from the second watch officer, to her, to the mess on the deck as if to say, *Now what's going on?* Then he reached over for the baking tray, which had wedged itself in a corner beneath his radio equipment, and handed it to the second watch officer, who quickly seized it from him with an authoritative growl.

Mary Ann warily watched those men. Was it her imagination, or did the second watch officer seem to be straining not to laugh out? Yet laughter rumbled up his throat, causing him to cough in crazy fitful bursts. The angel face man eyed the second watch officer with a cat-like grin before pulling his head into his tiny work compartment and whistling softly, biding his time until the big blow arrived.

The second watch officer stooped down and began to peel the slabs of purple-gray meat and squished bread from his boot. Mary Ann leaned near the edge of the bunk and observed his every move. With a casual air of indifference the officer flipped the soiled sandwich onto the tray, then reached around, here and there on the linoleum deck, picking up pieces of the broken crockery and depositing them on top of the battered sandwich.

"I'm sorry, I didn't mean to drop the tray." Mary Ann repeated in a deathly-still whisper, certain she would be chastised for her carelessness. The officer's blue eyes leapt up to her. She jerked back, heart pounding. *That man! He was so - oh, he was so fine!*

"Ah, my little captive bird, I will not harm you. You must not be so afraid of me." Heubeck arose and glanced at Schatz over in the radio room. *That Funker was getting a real show here, that's for sure! Well, let Schatzi say all he saw to the other men. After all, they were envying their Zweite VO this special duty!*

"So, sweet lady," Heubeck leisurely stirred the contents of the tray with his forefinger, "you must not lose your temper and throw the food about, if you do not like what we serve on board our U-boat. I know that, most of the time, I myself am tempted to throw the meals - overboard to the fish, ha, ha!"

Schatzi exploded in the radio room. "It takes a cast iron stomach to digest *unser Smutje's* galley fare, *Leutnant!*" His laughter came like ringing bells, merry and fetching.

Heubeck bellowed at Schatzi, while his eyes locked in on the startled girl, "See, Miss Connor, none of us likes the meals either! So, we understand why you did this thing. You should not apologize for throwing the meal away!" He winked at the young woman. "Who cares about broken dishes on a German U-boat, yes? This sort of thing happens all the time." He grabbed the bulkhead in the rolling boat, the baking tray wobbling in his hand, and pretended he was falling. "You see, it is not unusual for a meal to be lost in a bucking submarine! It is a matter of gaining one's sea legs! So, for now, I will tell *unser Smutje* that this was an 'act of God.' You enjoyed his wonderful canned liverwurst sandwich with green mold garnish, but unfortunately it got away from you!"

Schatzi was howling over in the radio room. "Good excuse, very good, indeed, *Leutnant!* 'Act of God.' *Unser Smutje* will accept that explanation just fine!"

Suddenly Heubeck noted the slight upward turn at the corners of the young woman's lips. Was it his imagination, or had his sweet little American charge smiled at him? Ah, yes, the hoped-for result had been achieved! Then just as quickly her smile vanished, as if she had second thoughts about her reaction and regretted it.

Heubeck lay his hand on the green privacy curtain. *One last look at her, ahh. If only you knew what I feel as this moment, sweet girl,* he mused. In his poor English he spoke to her a last comforting assurance. "Good night, Miss Connor, good night. Please not to worry anymore."

The young woman's soft reply came unexpectedly, "Yes, good night, sir."

Heubeck watched her ease down on the bunk, her back against the paneled bulkhead, as she curled into a tight ball. *How small she looked!* Her wide eyes no longer saw him, but stared past him, seeing something far away. Heart moved with tenderness Heubeck stepped into the passage and drew the curtain on the girl. Then he caught Schatzi's eye in the *Funkraum.*

"Ah, well, what else is there to do, *Funker?*" He shrugged his shoulders and started for the Wardroom.

"We can keep doing what we do best, *Leutnant,*" Schatzi called after him, "and that is to be good *U-bootfahrer.* Fight and win our battles as they come to us!"

CHAPTER 13

Mary Ann stared at the swaying green curtain, with the thin outline of the bright lights from the corridor along the ragged edges. She must not think of that man and the way he had fussed over her. She - the plain-Jane who never went out with a fellow - except for ole slow-poke Paul Wittles, who took her to the Junior/Senior Prom last year. How could she even consider this good-looking German officer might be attracted to her? *What was she thinking anyway? Such thoughts were traitorous, weren't they?* She pressed her hand to her eyes. *One does not moon over the enemy, no matter how nice looking he is.*

Burrowing into the narrow bunk she determined to focus on getting off this stinking boat. *A girl on a German U-boat, with all these sailors? Well, they'd be nuts if they thought they could get away with this. No way! And that captain - he'd better do something! Some kind of plan to get her back to shore and home to her family!*

"*Fraeulein?*" The second watch officer was back again? Mary Ann propped up on her elbow, waited with anticipation, little chills of delight chasing through her.

Again: "*Fraeulein, sind Sie da?*" No, the voice sounded different. More high pitched.

But Mary Ann replied readily, "Yes, come in."

The curtain parted, and a boyish face popped through the opening.

Billy? Billy Baker! Mary Ann gawked in astonishment at the youth. "Gee whiz, I don't believe it," she whispered. "Where'd you come from?"

The sailor nodded to her, *"Tag,"* as his thin freckled face, topped by carrot-colored hair beneath his small pointed cap, flushed to deep scarlet. *Oh, yes, he looked exactly like Billy Baker in Algebra II class junior year. Imagine! Him, here! On this enemy vessel!*

"Well, don't just stand there, come in!" Mary Ann gestured to the timid sailor.

Into the compartment he shuffled, all gangly and laden down with a pile of folded gray clothing - a button-down work shirt on top - and a brown canvas bag, which swung from his right shoulder. A broom was wedged beneath his left armpit, and as he stumbled toward Mary Ann and tossed the supplies onto the bunk; the broom came flying as well, narrowly missing her head.

"Whoa, easy, Billy!" Mary Ann ducked, eyed the broom with distrust, then blinked up at the German sailor. "You almost got me on the head." *He didn't mean it,* she knew. By the look on his face he certainly needed more reassurance than she did. This shy red-headed fellow seemed unsure, oh, not about her, but about who and where he was. She sensed they were both victims of a horrible nightmare. Yet he had no choice but to serve and obey, while she could fight for her freedom and escape this wretched boat.

Then her attention went to the gray clothes and faded-brown canvas bag he had dumped on the bunk. "What's all this stuff for? Surely, it can't be for me?"

"Ja, ja." The sailor mumbled.

Mary Ann dared touch the sailor's arm. "Listen, Billy, whoever you are, please inform your captain I won't be needing all this stuff." *Good Heavens, the sailor jumped a mile. One would have thought she was poison or something!*

"Ja, ja!" He grabbed the broom and began to sweep up the bits of broken crockery shards on the deck with the diligence of a determined underling.

"You know, I'm not staying here, Billy. There's no way that's going to happen. But I do feel sorry for you, being stuck in here. Wish I could take you with me, when I go back to Greenpoint. Get you out of this mess."

Of course, the poor red-headed sailor didn't understand a word she said. He merely mumbled, *"Ja, ja,"* his eyes downcast in submission. Then he produced a dirty rag from his wrinkled trousers pocket and stooped to wipe up the spilled coffee on the linoleum deck. The rag swished back and forth, back and forth, missing half the spill, because poor Billy was in such a rush. *Typical fellow,* Mary Ann thought. *Just like Eddie and Jack. Mama always has to make those two brothers of mine do their chores over again since they don't do them right the first time. . . .* Mary Ann's eyes filled with tears. *Her brothers! Would she ever see them again?*

The red-headed sailor's startled gaze met hers. Then like a shot, he was out of the tiny compartment as if his very life was on the line. *"Gute Nacht, Fraeulein, gute Nacht!"*

"Goodnight!" Mary Ann called after him.

CHAPTER 14
Chorus - In the bowroom

"So, Oesterweise, tell us, what happened back there on the beach?" Bernhard Uphoffner leaned on Max Senghas' shoulder as they sat crunched together on the floor boards.

"You know something out of the ordinary like this happens, it don't set right with me." Senghas mumbled, shaking his large semi-balding head.

"Shut up with that crap, will you!" Otto Randtel shouted from the lower bunk. "Just let Heini and Kurt get on with the story."

"Yeah, Senghas, what in blazes would you have done? That girl came flying out of nowhere, like a ghost risen from the grave!" Heinrich Oesterweise scowled.

"Let Max be, fellas. You know how superstitious he is." Christoph Schaub scooted closer to his mates. "Go on, Hein, tell the story. We're waiting."

Heinrich lovingly stroked a starboard torpedo, which gleamed chillingly in its rack in the glare of the electric overhead bulbs. "Kurt and I were unloading the dinghy, yes? Braun, the leader of that cussed group of know-it-alls, had gone up into the dunes for a look around. I was near Winkler, the fat pig who complained most of the voyage. What a tough guy! He didn't like the lower bunk we gave him, ha, ha!"

The gathered sailors swatted at one another:

"I am a special agent of the *Fuehrer!* I deserve better accommodations than this sewer pit!"

"I demand my own private stateroom with a bath, a desk, a chair, a bed—"

"My own yacht to sail to America!"

"Good riddance to the jerk! Who the heck did he think he was?"

Heinrich waved, "Listen up, you wise guys! This Winkler fellow was ordering those other two nitwits around. He wanted them to get a crate of explosives away from the surf. They were going to bury a lot of that stuff and come back for it, once they got established inland.

"Well, here comes that female, flying along, I tell you. Winkler saw her and right away blocked her way. The bonehead was in control, very smooth and calm. His spy training must have done him some good, after all, ha, ha! Anyway, Winkler started talking to the girl real nice in English. They spoke for a short while, and I guess she started asking too many questions."

"Ja, ja." Kurt Mohan spoke out for the first time. "Winkler waved to Hein and me to get back to the dinghy and get the heck out of there. She wanted to go for help. Something about phoning the Coast Guard about us being shipwrecked."

Oesterweise piped in. "So, I start walking past her to see if another person might be coming along the beach. Maybe she had a companion, a nice boy, you see, and they were out carousing on the beach, you know, ha, ha!"

"Ooooo!" The sailors clapped each other on the back.

"Then I see Braun coming around in the dark," Oesterweise continued. "He knew there was trouble. So, I right away jumped the girl!"

"Aah, *ja, ja!*" Shouted the enthusiastic chorus of male voices.

"Soon Kurt followed, and we had that little female down in the sand, holding on like this—" Oesterweise demonstrated his hold on a nearby shipmate, who pummeled him playfully in the stomach. "We didn't know what to do next with her!"

"I'd know what to do!" Otto Randtel jerked his fist in the fetid air. "Rape her!"

"Ah, *ja, ja!*" Rejoined the chorus.

Kurt Mohan bellowed, "That pig, Braun, wanted us to strangle her and take her body off-shore and dump it over the gunwale, but I couldn't do this thing. No way. Maybe our high and mighty agents from Berlin have the stomach to murder a woman, but not me."

"Killing her wouldn't have solved anything. What if her body washed ashore?" Oesterweise gazed around at the men. "Then that would be 'it' for our illustrious Winkler and his associates, so I told Kurt we must bring her back to the boat. Let the Old Man decide what to do with her."

"Ah, *ja, ja,* the Old Man, he is a tough guy!" Rang the rowdy chorus.

Oesterweise scrambled forward, the better to present the story with just the right emphasis. "So, here I come, up to the *Wintergarten.* Of course, Ketter expects a prompt report, but he did not expect our little 'surprise package' from America! But before I can explain about the situation, he hears that girl screaming down on the main deck. Ah, I tell you, the Old Man let out with such curses that it made even me blush!"

"Worse than a pirate over spilled rum!" The chorus roared its approval.

Mohan rubbed his hands together with delight. "The woman put up a heck of a fight on that beach! Knocked me flat several times!"

"Oh, ho!" Someone shouted.

"And she's kind of a small thing, too. Not much taller than you, Ottochen!" Mohan pointed to his mate in the lower bunk.

"Get outta my hair!" Otto Randtel swung up angrily. "You block-heads are always on me about my height. Yet whose eyes does Ketter rely on up on Third Bridge Watch? Mine!"

Popping static suddenly broke into the rollicking laughter in the bow room. The *Kommandant's* voice snapped over the boat's intercom system: "*Achtung,* attention men—"

"Now what?" Senghas growled.

"Someone should have timed us on that beach exercise." Heinrich Oesterweise whispered to Christoph Schaub. "I never moved so fast in my whole life." Then Heinrich threw himself over the rail of his top bunk and landed on his side. Otto Randtel reached up and stabbed him in the ribs. "Ouch! Cut it out, will you!" He shouted.

"Quiet!" The gravelly voice of the section officer, Willy, warned from aft near the open hatchway. "The *Kommandant* is explaining about our new 'crew member.'"

"You mean, our 'extra ballast'!" A mate snorted.

CHAPTER 15

Imprisoned in the commanding officer's small quarters, Mary Ann also recognized the captain's voice booming over the U-boat's intercom system. His abrupt German words assaulted her as surely as if the man was physically beating her on the head. Unable to endure his thundering voice Mary Ann clamped her hands over her ears and buried herself in the corner of the bunk, defiantly kicking at his soiled-linen pillow. How she loathed touching anything that was his! The battered sea blanket, the stained, stinking, twisted sheets beneath her, the mildewed paneling on the bulkhead, the cabinets, the scratched-up writing desk, the very air in the boat reeked of that vile Nazi pirate.

"There's no way I'm staying here!" Mary Ann croaked aloud, and envisioned herself scrambling up the control room ladder, the men snapping at her ankles, like wild dogs, to drag her down, while that horrible Nazi captain shouted and cursed orders. But she would climb fast and free into the night and leap over the side of the U-boat, far, far down into the dark, lashing sea and be swept beyond reach.

Mary Ann sat forward. *Could she do it? Oh, yes! Oh, yes!* The round hatch was but a few steps away. *She must go for it, now, now NOW!* She jumped off the bunk and seized the green curtain, but a man's scowl erupted in the passage. Many feet trampled by suddenly. *What was going on? Why were men running around just when she tried to make a break for it?*

Sickening, bowel-wrenching fear paralyzed Mary Ann, as she considered what she'd nearly done. She slunk back onto the bunk in a daze. How could she have dared to try? *It was out-right suicide, Lord help her!*

"Dear Jesus, save me, rescue me from this horrible place!" Her whispered screams were lost in the chaos that surrounded the Captain's Quarters. For a long while she lay sobbing, then—

"No!" She slammed her fist into the captain's pillow and sat up. "I'll wait, bide my time. I won't give in. I swear I won't! I'll find a way out of here, one way or another, believe me!"

- 8 2 -

CHAPTER 16

"How 'bout we take a break, Mary Ann?" Historian Steve Anderson suggested, as he clicked off the recorder.

Mary Ann gaped around, shocked to find herself grounded in the pleasant sunroom of her retirement home in Whiting. "Alright," she said wearily.

"Besides," Anderson held up his hand, "I have something I think you might like to see." He rummaged through several manila files in his briefcase, and then lay a folder on the coffee table. "This, Mary Ann, is the British copy of the radio transmission sent to U-boat Headquarters in France the night you were captured."

"My goodness!" Mary Ann rocked forward in her chair to see the thin, yellowed sheet of paper Anderson had pulled from the file.

"Okay," he murmured, then pointed a finger along the faded details. "The radio report of your capture went out from U-115 about 3:38 on the morning of March 14, Eastern Standard Time, or 9:38 Central European Time, to a transmission station at Kalbe on the Elbe River near Magdeburg, Germany."

Mary Ann carefully took the document, fearing it might disintegrate in her hands. "I don't believe it," she murmured. "The British knew about me?"

"Well, not quite that you were the prisoner, only that the Germans had captured a person." Anderson said. "You have to remember, in the war everyone was reading everyone else's radio traffic, trying to figure where the enemy was located and how to attack him. The message about you probably raised an eyebrow or two at Bletchley, but no one could have done anything about you. Sadly, there were more important things to worry about, Mary Ann."

"I know. I gradually figured that out." She nodded.

"By the way, for your interest, you might like to know that the U-115 was a Type IXC submarine built for long-distance operations. About the size of your husband's sub, USS Starfish. Now, you'll see here," Anderson indicated some numbers on the paper Mary Ann held, "when Ketter sent the message to Headquarters, U-115 was already located approximately thirty nautical miles southeast of New York. The boat had traveled pretty far from the drop zone where you were captured, so you wouldn't have made it to shore had you jumped overboard that night."

"Steve, I was crazy enough to try!" Mary Ann perused the yellowed sheet in her hands. She read the words silently to herself:

"Operation Ambrosius Successfully Completed. American Civilian Apprehended. Interrogation Revealed No Connection With Present Operation. Await Further Orders. U-ketter."

"It's so brief. So without emotion." Mary Ann glanced up.

"Typical military," Anderson grinned. "They're not out to write novels."

"I know," Mary Ann replied, "but who would guess at the myriad life's dramas being played out behind these stilted words?" Her gaze drifted off, as memories swirled about her like river eddies. "Who could know what would happen from one moment to the next?"

CHAPTER 17

The green curtain snapped aside. *Kapitaenleutnant* Ketter entered the compartment with a determined stride. Mary Ann scrambled up on the bunk, raking at her disheveled hair. *How dare that Nazi captain walk in on her unannounced! Just who did he think he was?* She prepared to fight the man, but he only regarded her with amusement as he slid the curtain across the doorway.

"So, Miss Connor, just please relax." He then pointed to the brown canvas bag at the foot of the bunk. "Have you yet looked to see what we give to you?" He asked.

"No," Mary Ann huddled in defiance.

The captain pursued. "I think perhaps you must already wear your new clothings?" His eyes slid to her to relay the veiled order. "I suggest you change out of that coat and skirt you wear and put on these fatigues at once." Then he began sorting through the other supplies which "Billy Baker" had tossed on the bunk in his mad rush to get out of there.

"Ah, I see all the necessary things are here. This is good!" Ketter held up a long-sleeved gray shirt with two breast pockets and a row of silver buttons down the front. "These are not so fashionable, Miss Connor, but they are the standard apparel among the members of our U-boat Force."

Mary Ann attempted to fire a retort, but the captain cut her off. "Ah, and here! A small towel and cloth and a bar of saltwater soap. Wonderful!" He lifted the soap cake to his nose. "The soap does not smell so good as the perfumed soap women like, but it will get you clean. My men have performed quite a search to find these things for you, my dear! They do anything for you. Unfortunately, there is no toothpaste or brush for your teeth. Such personal items belong to each man in his sea gear. I have toothpaste. You will use this. Use your fingers—"

"I don't need that stuff, captain!" Mary Ann blasted. "Get it all out of here and then listen to me, cause I have a plan. One that will work, if you'll please cooperate with me. No more waiting around, or wondering what to do, when the answer is right in front of you!"

The captain cocked his head. *So the game continues?*

"That little boat I came here in tonight, remember? Let me have that!" A hiss escaped the captain's mouth and his eyes rolled to the overhead. "I can row to shore!" Mary Ann begged, "Then you can go your way and I can go mine, and we'll forget I was ever here."

In a tirade, the captain flung the gray shirt onto the bunk. "Enough of this nonsense! Who gives the orders in this U-boat!"

"I don't care!" Mary Ann slammed her fists on the bunk and leapt to the deck. *Just like that! Time to go! Good God, the look on the man's face!* Mary Ann bumped past him rudely. *So what? He deserved it!* She was through the curtain and into the passage. The open hatch beckoned. A hawk-eyed man in the closet observed her abrupt appearance. *Where had the angel face fellow gone?*

It was over in a second. The captain seized her and hurled her back into the compartment. "Where are you going, Miss Conner?" He sounded truly mystified that she should dare to run out on him. "Must I shoot you to settle you down?"

A threat? He would never shoot her, she knew and swung at the man with all her might. But her fist merely grazed the captain's whiskered chin. She felt the stiff, jaggy bristles of his beard on her knuckles and looked up in shock to see the man's angry eyes. His broad face, marred by weathered creases and strands of jet black beard jutting from scattered pores in his sallow skin, loomed closer. He was her height, perhaps only slightly taller in his boots. *She could take him on!* And again Mary Ann swung at that loathsome Nazi face.

The captain ducked fast, caught her wrists and forced her down onto the bunk. "Enough!" He slapped her cheek hard. Once.

The blow rippled in waves along her jawbone. The captain's arm was rising again. "Noo!" She scrunched her face and turned away from the expected strike. *What, nothing?*

Suddenly a woman's high-pitched opera voice blared over the U-boat's intercom system. Scowls of protest erupted deep in the boat, and Mary Ann realized the crew had overheard her struggle with their captain and wanted to hear more!

Mary Ann lay sobbing beneath the captain's weight. In whirling haze she saw his brown eyes flecked with strange gold dots. His twitching body indicated a latent male desire that both stunned and terrified her. "I am very sorry, Marianne Connor," he murmured through the singing voice. "If I could, I would let you go from here and not suffer this fate with us any more."

Mary Ann tried to absorb the reality of this man who lay heavily on top of her. She felt things she didn't understand or want to understand. "Get off me, I can't breathe!" she gasped.

The captain rose slightly, yet continued to press her down with his iron legs. "Miss Connor, you must understand this situation. We are at war with your country. So!" His mouth formed the terrible words. "For now, you must remain our prisoner." That mouth, thin, straight, commanding, pronounced the deathly fate. "There is nothing I can do for you any more. Do you understand what I say to you, Marianne Connor?"

She nodded her head in his soiled pillow, as tears of defeat seeped from her eyes.

The captain rose slowly, a check against any further attempt on her part toward hysterics. Mary Ann watched his broad, bearded face recede against the steel, ribbed overhead, and then dragged herself into the corner by the desk, her only refuge in this oppressive enemy world. The woman's singing voice had dropped in volume and, in the distance, the boat's diesel engines pounded on and on like primitive jungle drums signaling war.

"I must wait for further orders," the captain was addressing her in a gentle, more intimate tone. "When these come, then I must do in this situation what I am told by my superiors. My officers try to make you as comfortable as possible in the meantime. But we also intend to carry out any orders. I do not like it that you should be on this U-boat, but-" he sighed long and satisfied - "like all of us here, you must not fight against your fate, but accept it."

Mary Ann watched how the captain's lips curled around each word and found herself wondering what it might be like to be kissed by those thin lips. *Oh. Good Lord, that such a thought should even enter her mind!* And she felt disgusted with herself.

"You have entered into a new world, Marianne Connor. If you wish to survive, then you do as you are told. The safety of this U-boat and the men of my crew are my first concern. For now, you are with us, yes?" His voice trailed up in a sing-song lilt, so subtly final.

Mary Ann felt like a naughty child who has been soundly chastised. Through a haze of confusion and cold stabs of reality - *I am here! I am really here!* - she saw that the captain held the brown canvas bag in his hands. Opening the zipper with a quick stroke, he produced a shiny steel canister.

"You need to know these things," he began the lesson in submarine survival. "This cylinder contains oxygen. I will not turn this nozzle, but in emergency, you have only to put on the mask and do this" - he pretended to turn the nozzle on the canister - "and then you have oxygen to breathe, yes?"

Tears of despair welled in Mary Ann's eyes, yet she remained silent and listened. She did not question. She did not argue. She did not dare interrupt him.

- 8 8 -

More things came out of that brown bag. The captain conducted the demonstration as if he was a teacher explaining ordinary, everyday facts to a group of bored students. "Another part of the safety gear, the potash cartridge." He held out a rectangular metal case for Mary Ann's inspection. "It will absorb carbon dioxide from the air during an extended diving procedure. This schnorkel connects from the cartridge and then, this mouthpiece you see, goes into your mouth. You place it between the teeth and bite down firmly. This rubber clamp goes on the nose so that you will not be tempted to breathe in any bad air from the boat. In such an event, off-duty personnel are instructed to go to their bunks and rest. You will receive this instruction also."

What kind of event? What instruction? When? From whom? Mary Ann's addled brain tumbled from one fearful thought to another, as the captain continued his tedious lecture.

"You wear this cartridge in front of you, like so -" he brought the metal case to his chest - "these straps go over the shoulders and then - "he crouched, a deliberate, bold demonstration to let the message sink in - "they come up between the legs to connect in front of you." His eyes slid to her. "Now you see why you must not wear a skirt on board of a 'soop-marine,' Miss Connor." He seemed much too delighted to explain that fact.

Such a crude, awful man, he was! Mary Ann looked away, repulsed, her face burning with indignation, as the captain busily removed the safety equipment from himself. His nasal voice droned on. "These things, you must not be afraid of them. I am certain you will not have to use them, but you must be familiar with them." Mary Ann dared glance at him. His eyes jumped to her as he replaced the cylinder and cartridge in the brown bag. *"Und so,* the first survival lesson is completed, yes?"

How she despised the man, the way he looked down at her over his curved nose! Yes, he seemed to be trying to be nice, but Mary Ann sensed that something more was going on, and she sure didn't want to be giving him the wrong impression.

Then he was reaching above her to an overhead cabinet. "I think there is enough room up here for your things." He opened the locker door and something started to slide out. *"Nein, nein,"* he quickly slammed the little door shut, then stretched above her, leaning heavily on the bunk with his shins, his tattered dark blue sweater riding up to reveal a grayish undershirt and a sliver of pale skin. The scent of the man, a sharp, unwashed odor and a kind of sour-lemonish smell, which she now associated with him, made Mary Ann nauseated.

"Ah, here, I do not have so many things." He held the canvas bag aloft. "Your gear can be placed in here also." Then he backed down with a satisfied grin. "Now, you see, Miss Connor, you will be most comfortable." He calmly adjusted his ragged sweater over his leather belt. *"Und* now, I insist that you change into those fatigues at once. I will leave you alone for some moments to do this, and then we will make a small, but necessary trip to the WC. You call to me when you are dressed." With that, the captain whirled about on his booted feet and exited the compartment, drawing the curtain across the open doorway.

CHAPTER 18

Mary Ann remained riveted in the corner of the bunk after the captain walked out. A dull headache thumped in her forehead from the strain of encountering him, and for a moment she touched along her cheek where he had struck her. Yet she could not forget how the man had looked as he lay on top of her. That triumphant German face, his narrow eyes calculating his advantage over her.

She heard his nasal voice on the other side of the curtain just now. He must be talking to the hawk-eyed man in the closet across the way. Deep-throated, *"Ja, ja's,"* cracked through their conversation. First, the hawk-eyed man said something. Then the captain's abrupt voice answered, and she trembled to think how the captain had behaved with her. How she felt about him at this moment! Then her eyes darted to the gray fatigues at the foot of the bunk. *She must wear those crummy clothes? Dress like on of his men?* "Not on your life!" She mumbled.

Suddenly the captain's voice came near the curtain, calling out in English, toying with her. "You are dressed yet, Miss Connor?"

"Not yet, sir!" She shot back.

"I shall wait only one moment longer," came the patient reply, though not without a teasing tinge. "Do not take so long to remove your clothes, or I must come in there and undress you myself?"

"Why!" *The nerve of that scoundrel!* "I'm hurrying as fast as I can, sir!" She snapped back at him.

Then with trembling hands Mary Ann slid off her damp overcoat and laid it aside on the bunk. She undid the buttons on her green cardigan sweater - a homemade Christmas gift from Mama and Daddy - and loosened the waist buttons of her blue and green plaid A-line skirt. *These clothes were all she had left of home, all that connected her to her dear ones! No!* She refused to undress. Only the overcoat remained on the bunk. The rest of her clothes would be worn under those hideous German fatigues. Mary Ann reworked the buttons on her skirt and sweater. *Have as little skin contact as possible with anything German! This way, when rescue came, she had only to grab her coat and run. Not worry about leaving anything behind on this Nazi vessel.*

With a thump she flopped back against the paneled bulkhead and struggled to shove her brown and white saddle shoes into the leathery fatigues pants legs. Then she stuffed her skirt and slip into the wide waistband and yanked the belt tight, only to discover there was no extra belt hole to accommodate her small waist. *Oh, well, she wouldn't be in these dumb pants for long anyway.*

Her eyes on the curtain for fear the captain come flying in and catch her off guard, she quickly pulled on the gray shirt with the offensive odors of grease and sweat emanating from the wrinkled folds. *Some German had worn these filthy fatigues before handing them over to her? That figured!* Mary Ann buttoned the five tarnished silver buttons down the front of the shirt, and then scrambled into her small refuge by the desk. "Alright, captain, I'm ready!" She called.

The curtain flew back. Mary Ann was sure the man had been hoping to catch her in a less than desirable condition. He ambled into the small compartment. "*Ah, so, gute!*" His eyes looked her over. His lips pressed together. *Might he laugh at her?* "Well, I see, and now you are feeling more comfortable, Miss Connor?" He inquired gently.

"I guess so," she mumbled.

"Let me say, you look very much prettier in those fatigues than any of my men look, ha, ha." Then the captain extended his hand to Mary Ann, his thick sausage fingers waving in quick jerks. "You will come with me now! There is no more time to waste!"

Mary Ann shrunk back. "Where are you taking me?"

"You will go to the WC!" The captain seized her wrist and pulled her to the edge of the bunk.

"Hey, wait, hold on! I don't have to go!" *Yet she did!* She didn't want him taking her like this! Her feet were getting tangled in the sea blanket, which slid with her to the deck.

"Do not force me to become angry with you yet again!" The captain roared.

Mary Ann found herself standing only inches from the man's glowering face. His eyes dropped to her mouth. His smile came slowly. "You are coming with me at once to tend to your private business, is this clearly understood, Marianne Connor?"

"Yes, sir," she whispered.

CHAPTER 19

The captain flung open the green privacy curtain and led Mary Ann into the brightly lit passage. Across the way, the lean, hawk-eyed man - the replacement for the angel-face fellow - sat in the tiny closet. Small, white, circular fuses framed his head, and a black headphone set hung over his dark, wavy hair, though one ear remained tuned to activity in the boat. In one corner on a small shelf the record disk with the woman's soft, sad singing voice spun around and around on a phonograph machine.

The man had been intent on a book, but now he glanced up at Mary Ann with round, luminous hawk's eyes beneath black brows, which met in a storm line above the bridge of his nose. His lips parted into a smile, which produced impish dimples in his cavernous cheeks.

"Our chief radio-sound man, *Obermaat* Konrad Lieb." The captain introduced Mary Ann to the man. "He is on duty. Later, another man comes to relieve him at the end of his watch. Someone must always be on duty in the radio station at all times!"

Mary Ann nodded shyly at radioman Konrad. "Hi," she said quietly.

Konrad bowed deeply in his chair, very pleased that she had spoken to him. "Hallo, *Fraeulein!*" His voice cracked like summer thunder.

The captain squeezed Mary Ann's arm. "Next here," he directed her view to another small compartment space filled with strange mechanisms, "the sound room, yes! When the boat travels underwater, the radioman becomes the sound man. He can hear very many noises. Schools of fish, whales talking together, the screws of a merchant ship, or the higher whistling sound of the destroyer in pursuit." He leaned into Mary Ann to relay a confidence. "The sound man is our boat's ears under the sea. He alone knows what happens beyond our steel drum."

Then the captain directed Mary Ann through a narrow, rectangular doorway at the end of the passage. "Officers Quarters!" He announced with bravado. "If you wonder where I now sleep since you presently have my bunk, I will be here with my officers. Normally, the *kommandant* of a U-boat does not give up his bunk to anyone, but only a badly injured seaman. For now, I think you must need more privacy than I do. Later, we find a bunk for you in the Petty Officers Room."

Mary Ann wasn't paying attention to the captain. Instead, her gaze had become riveted on two bunks along the right side of the officers' room. A narrow table, its leaves folded down to enable passage, stood bolted before the bunks, and sticking out into the cramped aisle from under the table a pair of heavy, thick-soled shoes lay crossed in repose. A slender man, his white-blonde hair slicked back in a stiff slab, sat propped in the opposite corner of the lower left bunk, as if he was sprawled on a sofa at home.

"Paul-Karl Ullmann, my *Erste Wach Offizier*, my first watch officer, Number One, or as you say in the United States Navy, Executive Officer." The captain brought Mary Ann to a standstill before the blonde god. "Well, *Herr EVO*, here is our unexpected guest!"

"Yes, Captain Lieutenant, I see her," the blonde god replied in perfect English.

He was definitely not impressed with her appearance. Indeed, Mary Ann sensed malevolence in the man, that he would rather kill her than look at her. His finely-chiseled face and blue, lashless eyes remained aloof, forbidding, like stone.

The captain attempted to humor his sullen officer. "Her clothes are a bit too big for her, don't you think so, Pauli? Our supply man must yet find her another set of fatigues from one of our shorter crew members."

Ullmann looked away with a slight, annoyed grin. However, a loud voice inquiring in German erupted at Mary Ann's back: *"Was ist, Herr Kaleu?"*

The captain whirled about, pulling Mary Ann with him. *"Ah, so,* Weber!" he greeted the interloper.

Mary Ann confronted the Devil himself, the nasty fellow who had leered at her when she came down the ladder into the control room. In an exaggerated show of respect, Weber removed his dark peaked hat to reveal thin oily hair sticking out around chapped, flappy ears flecked with dandruff. His grin widened appreciably, displaying widely spaced, broken teeth edged with brown tobacco stains. *But it was his eyes - devil's eyes!* They bored into Mary Ann like drills, tore her clothes from her body, lay bare her soul.

Mary Ann fell back in alarm, much to the amusement of the officers. "What is this? My navigator frightens you, Miss Connor?" The captain squeezed her arms playfully. "Weber says to me you tremble like a little puppy, and indeed, I can feel this!"

Mary Ann did not repulse the captain's touch, but felt, instead, the sudden need of his close physical protection. In no way did she want to meet these odious men of his crew, especially not this creepy-looking fellow.

The captain went on, jumping from English to German and back for the sake of introducing Mary Ann to the Devil. "This is Heinz Weber, our boat's navigator and third watch officer. Also, Miss Connor, Weber is the supply petty officer on board this boat." He tugged possessively on Mary Ann's arms for emphasis. "My man, Weber, orders the food provisions for several weeks of sailing on patrol. He

- 9 6 -

says to me that he has come just this moment from 'getting a fix' on our boat's position!"

Mary Ann wanted to get away from that short, repugnant devil of a man. *Put a brick wall between him and her.* He was practically in her face, as the captain rambled on and on: "Weber knows the sun and stars intimately. He says he is on intimate terms with the stars in the Heavens. Ah, ah, ah, he wishes to be on intimate terms with a pretty young woman, yes!"

Weber emitted a grunt of satisfaction at the English translation. His eyes did not leave her face, as he blustered on and on to Mary Ann in excitable German. Flecks of saliva flew from his foul mouth and dotted her face. Weber wanted Mary Ann to know something. He seemed most insistent that the captain relay the message to her.

"A real romantic here, after all!" The captain laughed. "He is not normally like this, Miss Connor, but he says to say to you, he sees stars in your eyes. My man wants to know the young woman with stars in her eyes. See what a nice effect you have on the men of my crew?"

Mary Ann nearly collapsed. *She had no intention of influencing these lousy Nazis, let alone that fearful naivgator.*

Clapping "his man" Weber soundly on the shoulder, the captain directed Mary Ann forward. "Come, come, Miss Connor. We must now proceed to our destination."

"You are escorting our little American lady to the 's–house,' Captain Lieutenant?" The first watch officer called out sweetly.

The captain swung around, "For her sake, *Herr EVO,* we will refer to it as the 'WC.' Now forty-nine men and one pretty young lady must share the same toilet space on this blasted barge. Unfortunately we have no place marked exclusively for *Damen.*"

Ullmann roared out, fully milking the situation. "I am sorry for her, Captain Lieutenant! What rotten luck! But then, too, she cannot have the nice luxury to water over the side of the boat like we do up on bridge watch!"

Mary Ann wanted to fade into the deck upon hearing this crude explanation. *These men were terrible! No fellows she knew back home ever talked like this in front of a girl!* The first watch officer thundered on, his loud voice laced with sarcasm. "Perhaps we must use the outdoor facilities and leave her the 'head' down here for the sake of 'privacy,' Captain Lieutenant!"

"This will not be necessary, *EVO.*" The captain guided Mary Ann toward another rectangular doorway ahead. "We shall keep arrangements as they are. And so, I see the *LI* is not yet returned?"

"No, Captain Lieutenant, he remains in the motor room. Some problems with a pump."

"I see," the captain leaned into Mary Ann to confide yet another revelation. "I must also mention to you about our own Alois Geissler, who is the *Litender Ingenieur,* the chief engineering officer who also bunks here with us. I am certain you will meet him in time, but he is the heart of our boat. He knows every machine and every bolt with his eyes closed. If something breaks or malfunctions he is right there to fix it. So, you see, Miss Connor, you will be safe on board this boat with all of us. We have a good boat, yes!" Ah, the captain was so pleased with his boat and crew. They were "all" that mattered to him!

Then in a bold move the captain seized Mary Ann's hand. *What, in Heaven's Name, was this? A pleasant stroll in the park?* Mary Ann tried tactfully to remove the man's strong grip, but he held tighter to her. "Also, Miss Connor," he continued pleasantly, "the *LI* has the added responsibility to keep his eyes on the fuel supply. During dives or submerged attacks he must keep the boat properly balanced, fore and aft, like the man on the tightrope. Otherwise, the boat will sink at one end and breach the surface of the sea at the other end and make the perfect target for an enemy airplane or destroyer."

Unable to focus on the captain's ominous words, Mary Ann glanced back at the navigator and first watch officer, concerned that they should notice how their captain held to her hand. *Might they get the wrong idea? Think the captain had a thing for her?* POW! Mary Ann slammed head-long into the Wardroom doorway in a blinding burst of stars.

The captain came around fast, "You are fine?"

"I think so," she rubbed her aching forehead. *How she wanted to cry!*

"You must always watch where you go in these small spaces, my dear," he chastised her playfully, and then stepped ahead of her into the next compartment.

Following hesitantly after him Mary Ann encountered a balding man in a gray T-shirt marked with a huge eagle clutching the terrible swastika emblem in its sharp talons. The man stood before a small counter, punching and slapping a mass of pale, oily bread dough in a huge steel bowl. Beads of sweat shone on the man's forehead in the bare overhead bulb, and Mary Ann rued the thought that some of those sweat drops from his hefty jowls might fall into the dough. Another man, stripped to the waist, sat on a wooden crate in the narrow passage forward, pealing a large heap of potatoes.

"*Guten Morgen, Smutje!*" The captain bellowed in German, as he entered the confined galley space.

"*Morgen, Herr Kaleu!*" Both men returned the captain's greeting with forced enthusiasm.

"Our boat's cook, or as we say it, *unser Smutje!*" The captain waved Mary Ann's attention to the low-browed man whose hairy fist pummeled the dough.

The cook's eyes carefully avoided Mary Ann, more from shyness than hostility, she realized. Then she peeked around the tiny kitchen space, instantly fascinated by the little black and white porcelain stove that was jammed into a corner beside a white metal cabinet. A steel nameplate on the stove read, "Vosswerke." On the farthest of three electric burners lining the stove top a kettle emitted a rushing cloud of steam, and on the nearest burner a huge steel pot awaited the potatoes. A protective rail, like those on the bunks, surrounded the stove top, undoubtedly to steady the cooking pots in heavy seas. Pots not in use hung from hooks in the overhead, along with huge spoons and ladles, which swung back and forth like pendulums beneath snaking pipes and bundles of electrical wires.

"*Und so,* what do you think of this galley?" The captain thumped Mary Ann's side with his elbow, and she backed away quickly, disconcerted at his sudden rough handling.

"It's kind of cozy, I guess." She answered quietly, and then observed a small ladder, which ascended into a dark cavern above the galley. *A possible escape route?* Mary Ann strained on tip toes to look up the ladder to a sealed hatch with a large wheel. *Could she manage to open it?*

"Cozy, yes?" The captain was laughing heartily. "A woman always likes to be in the kitchen. But now you see, our Hans-Dieter is a busy man in this galley. Three times each day, he must prepare meals for our crew, and very often these men eat at different times because of changing watches and other situations. Since we are on Central European Time, we eat breakfast in the evening, yes? Ha, ha! So, *unser Smutje* is a man who must always work hard, though he has help from the men up front in this U-boat."

The sweating cook frowned at his captain and Mary Ann, annoyed that they should be standing there so long discussing him when he had work to do. Mary Ann noted that the cook had a mind of his own. He wasn't going to be easily intimidated by anyone, let alone his captain. Naturally, the captain was egging him on, teasing him in a friendly, bantering manner, but the cook merely replied in blunt tones as he pounded at the oily mass in the bowl with his huge fist.

"*Ah, so, gute, gute, sehr gute.*" The captain switched to English. "You make a nice meal, yes? One to please our pretty guest here, *Smutje!* And so, Miss Connor," he let his hand slide along her back, and Mary Ann recoiled from his continued attempts to touch her. Still, the captain pursued, grasping her wrist tightly as if to remind her he had sole right to do as he wished with her.

"The cook says he will make a special dessert for you today, my dear! *Unser Smutje* is an excellent pastry maker and hopes you will like what he makes for you."

Mary Ann nodded politely at the cook, since his suspicious eyes seemed to await a response from her.

"You are pleased, Miss Connor?" The captain goaded Mary Ann. "You have won our cook's approval. Now, we will not disturb him any longer, but move on to our destination." The captain released Mary Ann's wrist and pushed ahead into the next compartment space. "Come, come, my dear," he called back to her, "the cook, as you see, is a very busy man, the busiest on this boat. He rarely rests, yet his meals are amazingly adequate."

Smiling weakly at the disgruntled cook, Mary Ann followed after the captain. He moved past the young man peeling potatoes and placed his hands on the man's slender, bare shoulders. The sailor looked up and smiled at his commanding officer

"Miss Connor!" The captain shouted back to Mary Ann suddenly. "Do you know our cook wants to open a restaurant on the fashionable Kurfurstendam in Berlin, when this gawdawful war is over? Our cook is a good man, yes? You be good to him, he is good to you!"

Mary Ann sidled past the potato man. She glanced at his naked, white shoulders and caved-in chest and thought, *she wouldn't want to date a scrawny fellow like that.* She felt the young man's gaze checking her out as well, and looking back to be certain that he was, found herself sprawled on the deck among several wooden crates. The captain hurried back to her and the potato man was instantly on his knee by her side.

"What happened?" she blinked at the two men.

The captain's grizzled face loomed above her against the glare of the electric lights. A soft wave of nausea skimmed her stomach. *Oh, please dont' let me throw up!* Mary Ann begged inwardly, as she struggled to her hands and knees.

"Here, here," the captain grasped one arm and the potato man held the other to assist her to her feet.

"I don't feel very good," she mumbled.

"But of course," the captain chided gently, "you must yet develop sea legs, Miss Connor. It must take time, yes." And he chuckled as if at some private joke, before starting off ahead of her in the weaving passage.

"We are now in the Chief's Quarters," the Captain slapped an empty bunk to the left of the passage, "and this runs into Petty Officers Quarters."

Her head spinning in slow motion Mary Ann stumbled along behind him. The captain's hearty voice sounded more and more far away in the submarine haze. "Altogether here, twelve bunks and fifteen men," he called back. "One goes off duty and sleeps in the other man's stink!"

Mary Ann reeled past even more bunks and glimpsed a man lying on his back reading a large manual beneath a small flare of light. Another man looked up at her from a lower bunk and followed her progress with wide-open eyes. Someone else slept on a top bunk, his arms folded comfortably beneath his head. It was the cute angel-face fellow from the radio closet! He lay, like a sleeping cupid, amidst an array of little charms on strings and dozens of photographs and pencil sketches taped to the bulkheads.

"Come, come, Miss Connor!" The captain's fierce growl from up ahead reminded her not to dally. He waited by yet another circular hatch, gesturing for Mary Ann to go through the opening at once.

There was no worrying about her skirt riding up this time. Like a champ, Mary Ann bent down and crawled through the hatch on her hands and knees in her baggy fatigues, then shimmied out into a dim, cluttered room that extended into a distant tunnel. *How far did this boat go?* she wondered. Many faces materialized in the dusky gloom. At least twenty men crowded into the narrow space. They were loafing on bunks, stretched out on wooden deck planks, or peering over bulging hammocks swinging from the overhead. What a mess! Clothes, books, shoes, dirty dishes, all sorts of personal items, filthy socks, underwear - *ooo, don't look at men's gotchies! And the smell, oooeeee! How could those poor fellows exist in this place?*

At once the captain emerged from the low hatchway and started toward an oval iron door to the right. *"Was ist los? Wie ist da?"* He pounded on the hatch in a terrible fury.

From behind the door came the muffled sound of shuffling feet. A sudden hollow 'whoosh' indicated a toilet flushing. Then the door-knob rattled and the oval hatch scraped inward, revealing a minuscule toilet compartment with a silver sink bowl bolted to the barren wall and a large porcelain toilet perched on slatted floor boards. As the red light above the washroom doorway winked off a tow-headed fellow, his face a distorted sea of red and white pimples, struggled with his belt and squeezed his bulk through the narrow doorway.

"Entschuldige, Herr Kaleu," he nodded to his commander, then spotted Mary Ann hiding behind the captain. At once his eyes danced with delight. *"Ah, Herr Kaleu, das Maedchen!"* He gaped at the miraculous presence of the girl.

But the captain's patience was strained to the breaking point. Mary Ann cowered, as he fired verbal volleys at the awkward seaman, who stiffened with ready obedience, *"Jawohl, Herr Kaleu! Jawohl, jawohl!"* His face and neck red with embarrassment, the poor sailor dove headfirst among his mates into the cave, where he was pounded mercilessly and wrestled onto a lower bunk near a gleaming cylinder.

Now the captain shoved Mary Ann toward that tiny toilet cubicle. "You will use the WC and get out at once!" He growled.

Mary Ann didn't want to go in that toilet! Not with those fellows gawking at her and laughing like maniacs! She glimpsed the large toilet and noticed yellowish brown streaks dribbling down the thick base onto the wet metal floor grating beneath the wood slats. *How disgusting!* Behind the toilet, pipes and wires coiled about in semi-darkness. Mops and brooms leaned in one corner near a bucket overflowing with dirty rags.

"Please, captain, I don't have to go!" And yet, she did! *Real bad!* Cold, fear, dampness, nausea were taking their toll. "I forgot my washcloth and soap! How can I wash?" She stalled for time.

Naturally none of this mattered to the captain. Into the foul cubicle Mary Ann went, prompted by his roaring impatience and the crude laughter of his men in the cave.

"There is no time to waste!" The captain's broad, bearded face peered at her through the open hatchway. His dark eyes flashed lightning bolts beneath the brim of his dirty white hat. "Fresh water is severely limited on board this boat! You will use the sink in my Quarters to wash, if you want for this. Do not attempt to touch any valves or pipes in here, do you understand? Do not flush the WC when you have finished, or you will get a face full of—!"

Howls of laughter rang in the background.

"But sir, what will I do?" she cried.

"Just do your business and get out!" The captain's scowl was cut off by the slamming of the metal hatch. He'd shut her in the WC. Left her to do what she must in an atmosphere reeking with the vile stench of forty-nine German U-boat crewmen.

CHAPTER 20

The return trip through the narrow passageway crowded with off-duty crewmen talking and laughing and staring at her proved a nightmare. Her head retracted between her shoulders like a timid turtle, Mary Ann hurried after *Kapitaenleutnant* Ketter, who tramped ahead of her in his huge sea boots, calling out to various men along the way in his loud, excitable voice.

Suddenly a man blocked Mary Ann's path, as she exited the galley into the Wardroom. She glimpsed the dark blue of a leather jacket and stepped aside to go around the man, but he simply swaggered in front of her. Mary Ann moved left, he moved left. Right, he moved right. *What was this?* Back and forth, back and forth, their sidesteps became a crazy little dance, accompanied by low snickers.

"Excuse me, please! Let me get by!" Mary Ann looked up perturbed and met the Devil's eyes. Navigator Weber grinned at her with his tobacco-stained teeth, and Mary Ann felt her insides twist with revulsion and alarm. Already the captain had exited the Wardroom far ahead in the haze, leaving her to face down this dreadful man by herself. Then seeing his advantage, Weber pinned Mary Ann to the bulkhead. At once his hands pressed into the many layers of clothing she wore, seeking his soft targets.

"Stop! Cut it out!" Mary Ann shoved frantically against the man, which only seemed to increase his determination to conquer her. Slamming her hard against the bulkhead again and again Weber sought to kiss her. Up, down, right, left, Mary Ann turned her head to avoid that slobbering mouth. *Would no one help her? Get this human python off her?*

Then with a grunt of disgust Weber thrust her aside, discarding her as so much trash. She felt the sharp rejection like a slap in the face and saw blazing anger in the Devil's eyes, that she had dared to humiliate him before his comrades. No, he would not soon forget this rebuff, but would have her again at a time and place of his choosing.

Tears stung her eyes as Mary Ann stumbled off through the Wardroom past the gloating first watch officer, who sat in his corner lounge before the folded-down mess table, his taunting mouth wide open, his white teeth gleaming with chilling mockery. Down the passage by the radio/sound compartments the captain stood by the green curtain. He observed her approach with blank eyes. *Wasn't he concerned about her struggle with Weber? Didn't he care?*

Furious inside to be left to the wiles of the wolf, Mary Ann vowed to tell off the captain about his lack of protection. And yet she knew by the look on the captain's face that he would not tolerate any complaints about his men. How she managed to survive was her problem, not his.

"*Und so*, the dutiful journey is over, my dear." The captain sounded most amused, as Mary Ann crawled onto the bunk and huddled in the corner near the desk. How she resented that man's condescending attitude. "Yeah, no thanks to you," she mumbled under her breath.

The captain was busy checking his watch. "Good! So now, I must warn you, we will dive in approximately one-half hour's time."

Mary Ann popped up fast, the incident with Weber immediately forgotten. "What?"

"The sun comes up, we go down," the captain pronounced airily.

"But I thought you only did that in battle!" Mary Ann didn't know how much more trauma she could endure in this appalling Hell.

"No, dear, we dive many times a day," the captain replied. "And so, you must be prepared for this event. It is training for the crew to keep them alert at all times. We must balance the boat, fore and aft, as supplies are used up and the weight shifts. Also, we look for any operating defects in the boat, for we do not want to find these during an emergency."

Chills raced up Mary Ann's spine. "I see." Then she glanced up, pleading, "then you'll be letting me know any time you plan to dive?"

"I will try to forewarn you of any future dives, Miss Connor." The captain seemed distracted, then with a sigh he came down to Mary Ann and regarded her directly, his dark eyes caressing her face. "You must understand that, if this boat is attacked, there is no way I can warn you, Miss Connor. You must remain here on the bunk, out of the way of my men, and stay calm."

"But!" Mary Ann groped, her mind dazed with shock, and then she grew sober. *So this was submarine life? This is what Bobby Lawson would know when he got out of training in Groton and sailed to the Pacific to fight the Japanese?* The thought brought Mary Ann a sudden sense of awareness and empathy, even as she confronted this German captain. He was reaching to an overhead locker, then backed down quickly and tossed a shredded rag and small cake of soap at Mary Ann, who grabbed for them as if diving for a ball hurled by the short stop to first base.

"You will wash now," the captain proceeded to lift back the lid of the nearby desktop, revealing a small white porcelain sink bowl with a single faucet. What a surprise!

"I'll be washing in there?" Mary Ann blurted.

The captain paid her no heed. Instead, he turned the faucet valve and a small jet of water gushed into the sink.

"So, Marianne Connor," he began yet another lecture, "a 'soop-marine' is built for diving and running silently beneath the sea. You will hear and feel many strange things, but these will be normal. You get used to them in time." He shut off the faucet and whirled to face her.

"Wash quickly! Again, touch no valves that you see in the boat. All of this will be done for you by me or by one of my officers. Soon, as well, a meal comes here to you. I advise you to eat." Finally his dark eyes, filled with a trace of regret, came to her in the corner of the bunk. "So, my dear," he rumbled, "you are fast learning, it is not a pleasant thing to be at war?"

"No, it isn't, sir," she murmured.

"This is a very unfortunate experience for you, Miss Connor. I do my best to arrange for your comfort and security, but now it is for you to cooperate and adjust. With this, I cannot help you. It must happen here." The captain tapped the side of his head and turned abruptly to walk out of the compartment. The green curtain snapped shut behind him.

CHAPTER 21

Of course there would be no hot water to wash in. Not here! Not in conditions like these, Mary Ann reasoned as she dipped her washrag into the numbingly cold water in the sink basin. Her stocking feet spread to keep her balance on the listing deck, she gawked, for a moment, at her image in a chipped mirror, which was bolted to the bulkhead near the curtain. *Ugh, what a sight!* Not that she much cared what those German sailors thought of her, but, as always, she looked a fright when fellows were around, what with her tangled hair and her face aglow with flaming-red pimples. *How she loathed her acne!* Recalled how fellows avoided her like the plague back in high school. Those memories stung! Naturally the pretty, fair-skinned gals got all the attention, while she, the ole "has been"—

A deafening shrill scattered Mary Ann's brooding thoughts like dry leaves before a wind storm. Instantly the deck dropped forward, pitching Mary Ann into the shelves above the sink. *Good God, they were diving! It was no half hour as the captain said it would be, that liar!*

Hard men's shouts exploded in the passage above the ear-splitting claxon, *"Gehe! Gehe! Schneller!,"* as off-duty personnel dashed downhill in the passage. The green curtain bucked and flapped with their mighty passing. In blind panic Mary Ann hauled herself onto the slanting bunk and gripped the side rail as if she could halt the U-boat's resolute plunge into the depths and drag it back to the surface.

"This is nuts! NUTS!" She wailed in the chaos. Her ears popped painfully with the increasing pressure. Her eyes frantically searched the ribbed overhead, expecting the sea to burst through the boat's iron sides any second.

The curtain dangled aside and part of the radio room became visible across the way. There, calm as could be, sat the hawk-eyed Konrad. He rode backwards in his swivel chair, seemingly unperturbed by events. Sensing her look, he leaned into the passage and regarded her. Then he smiled with his deep-dimpled cheeks and white teeth and nodded in a friendly way, but Mary Ann could only stare back at him, too frozen with fear to react.

Into the ocean depths she hurled with the enemy crew. Mary Ann felt the hurling down like a passenger train roaring off the edge of a cliff into an endless ravine. Then - silence. Silent drifting down, down, down. The claxon stopped its furious clanging. The bawling men had reached their diving stations. Only a slight creak protested somewhere beneath the linoleum deck. Soft hisses faded and died. *The boat was emitting a final sigh of relief?*

Mary Ann kept her eyes on Radioman Konrad. Her one stoic guide in the unfolding bedlam, she judged all things by him: his calm expression, his pale hand lying loosely on a piece of radio equipment, his long legs crossed in an X under his chair.

Suddenly a jarring bump followed by screeching, scraping sounds forward in the boat slammed Mary Ann into the paneled bulkhead at the head of the bunk. She grabbed the captain's pillow and keened a plea to Heaven: "Lordy! Lordy! Save me! Save me!"

The boat gradually leveled out, then settled with a slight list to port. The green curtain swung across the bunk compartment, and Radioman Konrad vanished from view.

The boat lay still. No sound. No movement. No endless swaying or bouncing or creaking or banging. Mary Ann felt her muscles collapse from the strain of hanging onto the rail. Her stomach lurched, her face screwed up, yet she managed to swallow the hysterical sobs which threatened to erupt from her. For now, she lay entombed in irrevocable silence on the ocean floor with the German enemy.

Beyond Mary Ann's curtained-off world, this was how things transpired that early morning before the sun rose over the eastern rim of the Atlantic: the shrieks of the diving claxon jolted the U-115 men to electric action, taking their over-active minds from those lazy, satisfied musings of a vulnerable young woman alone in the CO's Quarters. Off-duty diesel stokers, e-motor mates, torpedo mechanics, and ordinary seamen poured from bunks and nooks and crannies, and bounded for the bow torpedo room, as petty officers shouted and cursed at their stumbling heels: "Faster! Faster! Go, go, go!"

The men of the second bridge watch tumbled down the ladder, striking the iron control room deck with violent thuds, and scrambled to reach their emergency posts. *Kapitaenleutnant* Ketter, the last to leap down the hatch, slammed and dogged the lid cover against the tongues of seawater that swept into the horseshoe of the bridge.

The boat dropped away bow-first with a powerful hiss of escaping air and the turbulent roar of seawater entering the ballast tanks beyond the bulkheads. Already, Chief Engineer Alois Geissler stood in his customary place behind Seaman First Class Fritz Baier and Petty Officer Werner Brunnig, who, both breathing fast and shaking off the chill from topside, manned the hydroplanes. Teeth-gritting Franz Wirth, the control room mate, had spun closed the overhead air valve of the diesel engines, when the electric motors took over the drive.

"Chief!" *Kapitaenleutnant* Ketter hailed Alois Geissler. "We'll go to the bottom! The depth in this area is about one hundred meters, where we will lie in wait!"

"*Jawohl, Herr Kaleu,* very good!" The chief engineering officer bellowed in reply. "There is no sense tempting fate during daylight hours, in spite of reports that American defenses are flimsy!" And he smiled at Ketter with the knowledge of a shared secret.

Ketter sidled near Geisser and eyed the creeping depth gauge as it circled toward the black numeral 50. "We will rest up for the hunt tonight, Chief. While we are in the area, we, too, shall partake in the great 'American Turkey Shoot,' yes?"

Geissler grinned at the analogy, while Ketter blustered with enthusiasm. "The 'Amis' will not soon forget, this is the German version of Pearl Harbor!" Ketter sniffed proudly, rubbed his nose, and then tipped his head around to view the other men in the control room.

Geissler's eyes flashed with the knowing. "Ah, *Herr Kaleu,* this is excellent incentive for the men. They crave action. This is, indeed, the great opportunity for our German U-boats!"

Ketter nodded. He felt very pleased with his tip-top crew. They were ready. They would always be ready, and he would not cease in driving them to well-oiled perfection.

CHAPTER 22

The U-115 lay on the continental shelf several miles off the coast of Barnegat, New Jersey. The submarine dozed in a state of hibernation. Only the essential life-sustaining machinery and equipment remained in operation, with a skeleton force of men on duty. *Kapitaenleutnant* Ketter had ordered the rest of the crew to their bunks. Off-duty men could read, sleep, play games, or do other quiet activities, and not move around any more than necessary, in order to preserve oxygen for the twelve hours they were under.

As morning wore on, a spate of writing emerged from various compartments, including letters home, since the men must wile away their spare time. Naturally, many creative compositions, including a poem discovered in the brown, leather-covered notebook in the WC and later copied and posted on a bulkhead in Petty Officers Quarters, centered on one subject:

> "I saw her as they brought her down;
> Sweet blue eyes, hair, soft and brown.
> The fear she showed went straight to my heart.
> One glimpse of those legs, my pulse gave a start!
> They led her away to private seclusion,
> But not before I had made a conclusion:

When we reach port some weeks from now,
In this fine, old boat, our worthy 'sea cow,'
I will ask the young lady for a special date;
Let her know a U-boat sailor can really rate!
I will take her to a sidewalk café,'
To sip 'Apertif' in a romantic way.
We will stroll to the fishermen's wharf for our lunch.
In her arms will be flowers - a magnificent bunch!
I will buy her silk stockings and a pink and white gown,
The best of them all in the whole harbor town!
And as evening comes creeping, and shadows grow long,
I will hold her so close and sing her a song.
A sweet kiss on her lips, a soft word in her ear,
She will have nothing more to fear!"

Occasionally, the sound man on duty whispered a report of propellers passing in the vicinity of the submerged U-boat. Once even, a ship steered directly overhead, its huge pistons beating rhythmically throughout the hull of the silent submersible.

"How can we let targets like that get away?" Someone grumbled in the bow torpedo room. "I never heard so many ships!"

"Shut up, you wait. The Old Man promised we would share in the booty, and we will!" Another mate scowled. "The 'American Hunting Ground' is teeming with game! There will be plenty left for us to shoot!"

At mid-day, canned ham sandwiches and potato soup made the rounds. A steward, little "Billy Baker" himself, brought the meal to Officers Quarters and to the captive girl in the Captain's Quarters. A select crewman from the bow and stern compartments each carried the appropriate supply - never any "seconds" - of soup and sandwiches to his own hungry mates.

As the men ate their meals, *Kapitaenleutnant* Ketter wandered into each compartment in his felt-soled slippers and stopped to exchange small talk with his crew. He found the men in good spirits, anticipating the coming night of action. A few men produced photographs and other mementos of home to share with their "Old Man."

"See, *Herr Kaleu*, my little brother, Karlchen, he has joined the *Waffen-SS Leibstandarte*.

I also have an older brother, Albert, who is in the mountain troops -"

"This is my fiancée, Herta. I plan to marry her on my next leave home. She is beautiful, isn't she, *Herr Kaleu?*"

"Ah, yes she is, Wachsmuth. You are a very lucky man!"

Likewise, it could not fail that some of the men boldly inquired about the unexpected passenger and how she was faring. Ketter answered each query with the same reply, followed by a paternal grin, "she survives nicely."

Then Ketter stopped by the sound room. He nodded at Georg Schatz, manning the hydrophone, sweeping the dial around the sonar scope.

"Lots of activity upstairs, *Herr Kaleu!*" Schatz whispered excitedly. "American shipping goes on as if it were peacetime, ships traveling singly and on a regular route, with no escorts that I can detect. It's incredible!"

Ketter leaned on the sound room doorway and folded his arms comfortably. "And we lie in wait, just beyond the enemy's greatest port, Schatzi. The ships go in and out of New York harbor through a strait called the Verazanno Narrows. My good friend, *Kapitaenleutnant* Reinhard Hardegen, took his U-123 very close to the Narrows in January. He said he was overwhelmed by the lights of Manhattan and Brooklyn." Ketter took momentary pleasure at the thought of his little lady prisoner from Brooklyn lying mere footsteps away in his bunk. "Ah, my friend from the U-123 told me there were lights as far as the eye could see, Schatzi! No black-out in war time! The night was like day, and Hardegen said that he sat there in the midst of it all, not a soul in America sensing his war-like presence!"

"That's something, *Herr Kaleu!*" Schatz gasped. "Then you, too, are planning to go close to New York that we might view the bright lights of the city?"

"No, Schatzi, I am not so daring as that." Ketter replied with a grimace. "By now, the harbor is undoubtedly mined and closely guarded. I would not desire to sit so openly in the city lights." Then he uncrossed his arms and placed his right hand on the edge of the sound room doorway. "Yet, wouldn't it be a fantastic prospect to sail up around the island of Manhattan and go under the famous Brooklyn Bridge? Wouldn't that be some story for us to bring home to port, Schatzi?" Ketter's eyes flashed, and he laughed softly. "But I shall play a cautious game and operate only on the approaches to the great harbor of New York, so we have plenty of elbow room to dive in an emergency."

"I agree, *Herr Kaleu!*" Schatzi wondered at his usually grim commander's sudden talkativeness.

Ketter patted his young hydrophone operator on the shoulder and started toward the control room hatch, but he was stopped by the sound of a stifled sob from his Quarters. Ketter drifted near the drawn curtain, listened, waited. The young woman had been left alone long enough. He must go in to her.

"Miss Connor?" He inquired. "May I speak with you please?"

He heard soft shuffling, knew she was preparing to encounter him. Then her sweet female voice replied, "Yes, come in?"

His heart responded with a wild thump, as he pulled back the green privacy curtain and entered the compartment.

CHAPTER 23

She was sitting in the corner of his bunk by his desk, wrapped in HIS sea blanket, her back propped against HIS pillow, Ketter noted with smug satisfaction. Her pale cheeks were moist with tears, which she quickly wiped away when she saw him. Her blue eyes regarded him with alarm, as he stepped into the compartment beside the partially-open curtain. It dismayed him to see her reaction. The young woman should know, by now, he meant her no harm.

Ketter glimpsed her forlorn little brown and white shoes on the deck beneath the bunk. Her half-eaten sandwich lay on a plate near her covered feet. Should he even try to win her?

"I see you did well through the dive," he announced. "You are now a fully initiated *U-bootfahrer*, yes?" He intended to humor her, to lighten tensions between them, but saw only her glance of bewilderment.

"Did you open your mouth to relieve the pressure during the dive?" Ketter pursued in a gentler tone.

"I don't know, I think so," she shrugged.

"Did this help you?" he asked.

"A little, I guess."

"You were frightened." he soothed.

She nodded.

"I am sorry you were afraid." Ketter noted the nearly empty sink with her washrag deposited limply against the closed drain. He'd take care of that later, but for now he continued talking: "The first time is always a frightening experience for someone who is new to a submarine."

"You don't say," she mumbled.

Ketter propped himself on the edge of the sink. "I recall vividly my first time, only two years before, when first I came into the U-boat Force. Before that, I was an officer on a destroyer, but I requested a transfer to U-boats." *Ah, did he note a glimmer of interest in those uncertain blue eyes?* "Yes, the first dive I make in a U-boat, I am not so brave as you are, Miss Connor." Ketter smiled warmly at her.

The young woman looked away. *What, no response? He must try harder!*

"It is very quiet, Miss Connor. Perhaps you must sleep after the difficult night you had." *After all, she would not find sleep this coming night.*

"I'll try to, captain." She huddled lower beneath his sea blanket.

"Goot! Ah, Miss Connor, perhaps there is something I can get for you? Maybe you must need something to help you to pass the time while you are here with us. U-boat men always bring along books, playing cards, board games, even musical instruments to entertain themselves when off-duty." Ketter gestured toward the appropriate locker in the passage, watching how her blue eyes followed along. "See? There we have a small library. You do not read German? No? Do you read French then? Two of my officers brought along several books in French before we sailed."

"I took two years of French in school." Her reply burst suddenly in the stillness of the sunken submarine. *Such a sweet lilt to her voice!*

Ketter became enthused. "Well, then I must see that you receive a book in French to read!"

"But I don't think I know French well enough to read a book, sir." She seemed embarrassed to admit that fact, Ketter noted.

- 1 1 8 -

"I see." *What could he possibly suggest to her?* "Well, then, what about writing? Perhaps you must write about this unusual journey you make with us? You record it for the future, yes?"

A light came into her eyes. "Yeah, that might be nice, sir!"

Ketter bent to the young woman on his bunk. "Ah, Miss Connor, it is very nice that you want to do this." And he confessed, confided, all at once. "I have much concern for you, that you are, ah, somewhat comfortable on board my boat. That I can make you feel secure in the situation. I hope you will understand when I must be harsh. We are at war, Miss Connor, and I must make many difficult decisions for the welfare of all on board this U-boat."

"I understand, sir," she nodded, though her eyes remained downcast.

"Well then," Ketter straightened up, "I will see to it that writing paper and a pen can be found for you. I have a spare notebook in the Wardroom, which I am not using. But of course, writing when the boat is sailing is difficult, as you must know already. But I look for anything to help you against boredom, yes?"

She seemed to be considering his words, and then glanced up at him with a timid smile. "That'll be nice, thank you, captain. I appreciate what you are trying to do for me." Her smile faltered.

Ketter felt momentary giddiness. He had not expected gratitude from his sweet captive. "Ah, Miss Connor, you are most welcome, indeed!" He leaned down to her, fascinated by that sprig of little, brown freckles dusting her slender nose. "How wonderful to see your smile, Miss Connor." She was shrinking into the corner of his bunk. "It will help me, if I can depend on your cooperation in this thing."

Should he dare to ask her? Yes, he wanted to know! "Do you mind it, if I talk further with you, Miss Connor? I wish very much to make you feel comfortable." *A fine excuse!* "I would also like to know you better. Is this agreeable to you?"

A nod again, merely.

"Miss Connor, will you speak to me of your home and family? Will this be very difficult for you to say?"

"No, sir," she replied quietly.

Ketter crossed his arms casually across his chest. "You must first tell me, perhaps, about your parents?"

The young woman began to speak at once, obviously struggling to fight down any painful emotions. "Well, sir, my Dad runs a saloon on the corner of Humboldt and Nassau Streets. He gives out free lunches to men who work in the neighborhood and to folks down on their luck."

"A good man, your Dad, yes?" Ketter added.

"Yes, he is. And my Mother, she does cleaning for other people. She has always helped out anyone who is sick or in need, bringing us children along, when we were young. Mama also takes in laundry from the convent over at St. Cecilia's Parish." The young woman halted, appeared about to cry.

"Please, go on," Ketter prodded gently.

"Well, sir, I have two brothers, Jack and Eddie. Jack is sixteen and Eddie is thirteen, and my little sister, Maggie, will be eleven years old on April 4th." The young woman seemed to cheer up at the mention of her siblings. "My brothers are so mischievous though" - she rolled her eyes - "like when they tied a rag to the sewing machine wheel and got the cat to chasing after it, back and forth, back and forth, you know, it got crazy!"

"And you? How old are you, Marianne? May I call you by your name, 'Marianne'?" Ketter urged, well aware of the warning signals against fraternizing too much with his sweet female captive.

"Um, I guess so, captain," she consented with a shy, perplexed glance in his direction. "I am eighteen, though I'll be nineteen the end of June."

"Eighteen? Ah, I see," Ketter rasped. *Eighteen? She was only eighteen? Good God, he felt like an old man at twenty-six.* "And so, you are still in school?" He asked.

"I am in nurse's training now," she replied.

"Very good!" Ketter reacted with enthusiasm. "I wish you very much luck in your goal to become a nurse! You will make an excellent nurse!"

The pretty, young Marianne was blushing. "Thank you, captain. I hope so. I hope I'll make it. I get so nervous about my exams. About failing. You know what I mean?"

"Of course!" Ketter grinned. "But I think that, after this experience on board my boat, you will find your exams a little less of a challenge for you, yes?"

The young woman's sudden laughter caught Ketter by surprise, brought his heart to a stand-still. "Oh yeah, I guess that's true!" Her eyes rolled up again, and she shrugged in a comfortable way. "I suppose I best start looking at it that way, for when I get out of here."

Penetrating warmth crept through Ketter, and he waved his finger playfully at her in gentle admonition. "I think, my dear, you must think about the future at all times. I am saying this to you, keep your goal of being a good nurse in front of you, in spite of what happens in between."

"I'll certainly try, sir." Her wide-eyed expression, indicative of a certain naive hope and youthfulness, reminded Ketter of what he had once been long ago - Eighteen, yes. At the time, he was brimming with lofty faith and ideals, as if he had the world by the tail. Adolf Hitler had become chancellor the year before. Indeed, Germany, like himself, was poised for a positive future. The humiliation of previous years, the Fatherland suffering political and economic chaos after the Great War, and he himself suffering nagging illnesses brought on by the rheumatic fever and poor nutrition in his childhood - Father out of work, a bitter, frustrated war veteran, Mother, pregnant with Inge, gaunt, determined, scraping together what she could. Yes, everything had changed for the better when he turned eighteen. New purpose and energy had seized both him and the nation as one. He and Germany had shared a common resurgence of power and personal pride. When he en tered Flensburg-Murwik for naval officers training with his Class of '37, the entire future lay before him. There was nothing that could stand in the way of this—

And now, this blasted war had come too soon, much too soon. Any rational person could see beyond the propaganda clap-trap in Berlin to the reality of the situation. Anyone with half a brain knew the entrance of the United States into the hostilities had placed the final seal on Germany's fate. It was only a matter of time.

These gnawing doubts continually gouged at the pit of Ketter's stomach. Symptoms of an old illness had been plaguing him recently, and he was relying more and more on the anti-spasmodic injections given by Moeglich.

And now, there she sat, the sweet, young Marianne from Brooklyn in the United States. What quirk of fate had brought her here? An angel? A hellion? A reminder of ideals long vanished? A thorny herald of the future, whose blue eyes stared in revulsion at what he was - the enemy warrior who served a mad government?

Ah, yes, he was falling in love with this young woman. He needed her! But not in the usual way. He needed her innocence and defiant strength as they existed right at this moment. Pray God, she would not lose these attributes on the horrendous journey she faced with him and his men. This last thought pierced Ketter's heart like a sword. The young woman would not survive the journey. He was sure of that. Her innocent light and spirit would be destroyed, and he would be responsible for this additional wartime tragedy.

Yet, as he looked down at her huddling in the corner, as far from him as she could get without melting into the paneled bulkhead, Ketter realized that he resented the young American woman's presence. Her words, her very attitude toward him goaded. Need he be reminded further of the fate that awaited him and his comrades? That, in spite of their tremendous sacrifices, Germany would be defeated again? And by her nation, the United States!

"So," Ketter sighed, "you are then eighteen, and you will be a nurse. That is, indeed, very nice, yes."

No longer certain what to say to her, Ketter extended his hand to the young woman. *Just to feel the softness of that small hand.* "I am pleased we have this chance to become better acquainted, Marianne," he said.

The young woman willingly took his hand. He held tightly to her hand in an effort to relay reassurance between them, but now she looked up at him, shocked that he held to her hand so long.

"I must go, Marianne," he regarded her closely, "you will be fine?"

She managed to pull her hand free, "Yes, captain."

"Now you will not cry anymore?" He hovered closer.

"I'll try not to." She unconsciously rubbed her hand in the blanket, as if to remove remnants of his touch.

"Good." Ketter swallowed a trace of growing indignation. "But then, you must rest."

"I will, sir, thanks."

Ketter stepped out into the passage with a backward glance at his captive. Already she had rolled away from him toward the bulkhead. Then his eyes met those of Georg Schatz in the sound room. The sonar man scrutinized him with a puzzled expression, undoubtedly wondering what had been discussed between him and the American. Scowling to himself, Ketter snapped the green curtain across his quarters and headed for the Officers Wardroom.

CHAPTER 24

Kapitaenleutnant Ketter entered the Wardroom in a foul humor. First Watch Officer Paul-Karl Ullman glanced up from his place at the mess table with its dingy, stained linen cloth, which was littered with the remnants of the mid-day meal. Chief Engineer Alois Geissler leaned back from his empty soup bowl and folded his arms behind his head. Both men watched as Ketter flopped onto the lower port-side bunk beside the mess table. At that point *Obersteuermann* Heinz Weber happened to wander into the Wardroom from his berth in the Chief Petty Officers Room forward and stood looking on his compatriots with his usual mischievous expression. The wolves had gathered?

"And so, how does it go for our American lady, *Herr Kaleu?*" Ullmann asked casually.

Ketter mumbled, "Why do you ask, EVO? You have concern for her suddenly?"

Geissler stretched his arms up, lacing his fingers together, and yawned loudly. "She must be a very desperate young woman, *Herr Kaleu.*" His arms dropped to his sides. "Have you informed her of the radio message we received from Headquarters before we dived?"

"I believe she already knows the reality of her situation, Chief," Ketter rolled on his side to bring Geissler into sight. "So, what is there to say? She must accept her fate, that's all."

Weber's grin revealed his brown, gapped teeth. His eyes danced with hungry anticipation. "How fortunate she is to return to base with us! A civilian prisoner. Contraband of the German Navy, yes!" His laugh was nasty. "She should earn her passage, don't you think, *meine Herren?* Perform certain tasks for us, in the meantime."

"Excellent idea, Hein!" Ketter cut him off, saw where he was leading. "Perhaps she can do some sewing for us. Peel potatoes. Wash dishes. Whatever else needs to be done around here. I will see to this."

"Make bunks. Clean the WC. Not bad." Ullmann mumbled.

"Shall she administer back rubs and foot massages as well, *Herr Kaleu?*" Weber suggested innocently. "This, I could very much use myself, ha, ha!"

The officers laughed congenially among themselves.

"Aah, no, Hein," Ketter replied, "we are tough men. We don't need coddled."

"So, what have you discussed with her before, *Herr Kaleu?*" Ullmann probed. "Are there some secrets you wish to reveal?"

Ketter shot a look at his first watch officer on the opposite bunk. "What are you driving at, Pauli?" He snapped. The laughter in the small compartment died instantly.

Ullmann maneuvered undeterred into firing position. "Perhaps you can tell us what you have discovered about the girl, *Herr Kaleu?* You were talking with her for quite some time. I assume you found her to be a sweet and cooperative prisoner, who readily says all she knows?"

"She will give us no trouble, *EVO*, so you need not be concerned," Ketter glared at Ullmann

"Why should I care, *Herr Kaleu?*" Ullmann stated easily. "You have her in firm control."

Chief Engineer Geissler stared hard at Ullmann, as if to warn him off, let the matter drop. After all, it was the *Kommandant's* business to talk to the female prisoner as he felt necessary. *Surely, there was nothing more than that going on? Or was there?*

"Well, Pauli," Ketter leaned comfortably against the mess table. "Maybe you'd be interested to know the girl is eighteen-years-old and is pursuing a career in nursing—"

"Ah, she is young, *Herr Kaleu!*" Geissler cut in. "Isn't the chap who serves us our meals that young?"

"Three of the crew are seventeen." Ullmann replied stiffly. "Most range between eighteen and twenty."

"Awfully young fellows coming into the U-boat service." Geissler shook his head.

"Indeed," Weber grimaced, "just kids really. What can they know? And more and more, we are at the mercy of their inexperience and incompetence, these little fanatics."

"So, what else have you learned about the girl, *Herr Kaleu?*" Ullmann doggedly swung the conversation back to the American captive.

Ketter scowled, "Ah, surely, *EVO,* you are still not thinking she is a spy, or worse" - and here, he guffawed - "like the mythical sirens, out to destroy us?"

The other men laughed, but Ullmann remained unmoved.

"I will tell you further, *Herr EVO,*" Ketter said, "our Miss Connor has consented to keep a journal, while she is with us."

"I disagree with this decision, *Herr Kaleu!*" Ullmann burst out. "You know it is against regulations for any of us to keep personal diaries and journals while at sea! She will record events of this boat and take note of anything of interest to the Allies!"

"Having her keep at journal is a good thing, if I may say so." Geissler interrupted in a complaisant tone. "What else is the girl to do to pass the time? This claustrophobic existence would affect her and cause further trouble for us. So, we keep her mind busy. Isn't this what our *Kommandant* advocates we all do?"

Weber smirked. "Then, too, we can learn those little 'hidden secrets' she has. We can swipe her journal and find out what she thinks of us stinking dogs! Read between the lines, yes?"

"Precisely!" Ketter rumbled. "It is my intention to confiscate her journal when we reach port, gentlemen. Nothing will leave this boat in her hands. So, you see, Ullmann, you have nothing to worry about!"

The first watch officer folded up one long leg against his chest. In spite of his 6 foot 2 inch frame, he had the capability of bending like a pretzel in the cramped spaces of the U-boat. "I am more concerned with—"

The strain in the Wardroom atmosphere was broken by the approach of Dietrich Heubeck from forward by the galley. He carried a cup and saucer in one hand and a plate of pastry in the other. For a moment, he stopped behind Weber and looked uncertainly on his fellow officers, aware that he had interrupted something of import.

"May I get by, please?" He nudged the stubborn Weber, who grudgingly stepped aside.

"Come join us here, Dietrich!" Ullmann indicated a space on the bunk next to himself. "We are just having a little discussion that should interest you."

"Not right now, Paul," Heubeck lifted the plate of pastry he held in his hand. "I'm delivering this little snack to the American girl. Our *Smutje* feels sorry for her, so he asked me to bring this coffee and left-over apple tart to her, since he has no time to do it himself."

"Aaah," Weber leered about, "around here there is much manly concern for our sweet American guest, is there not?"

Ketter scowled, "That's it, there's nothing more to discuss on the subject, gentlemen. Let it drop now!" He slammed his fist on the mess table, "Where's the fellow on clean-up detail? I want this lunch crap cleared away at once!"

"Crap." Ullmann mumbled in the corner. "There's more bullpippi piled in this hellhole than we can shovel in a year."

CHAPTER 25
March 14, 1942

Thanks to the second German officer who brought this notebook to me a while ago, but why bother writing? Who cares?

Twenty minutes later

I'll write. What else can I do? Just lay here doing nothing? My mind's in a whirl as it is, so I might as well let it all out, record for the future, as the captain told me. What future? Dear Lord, here come my tears. . . .

I must have hope! Dear God, be with me! I must rely on You as never before to get me through this terrible ordeal. How many times in my life You have been there for me and my family, so I must trust in You now to help me survive!

It could be worse, I suppose, a lot worse. The Germans have been nice to me, so far, but I'm going to keep my distance from them til I'm off this boat. Not get too friendly or ask for anything more than I absolutely need. Dear knows what could happen?

Where am I? Where am I? I keep hearing this song playing over and over in my mind in a haunting minor key, then it fades out in a staccato beat, like a hammer hitting a radiator pipe. Where am I? Where am I? Da-da-da-dddd-da.

My hand is so cold I can barely grip this pen to write my stumbling words. It's damp and chilly, like being in a tomb! That's what this is, a tomb! I've wrapped my coat and the captain's blanket around me, but it doesn't help me feel any warmer.

And I keep thinking back to yesterday. It seems like a dream, as if it took place in another world. Almost twenty-four hours ago, I was making my usual morning rounds on the 3rd floor with Martha Turner and Gladys Smith. We were all looking forward to going out for the weekend on the LIRR with Helen Marie and her folks to their beach house in Sandy Point. It was the first time I wasn't going home to be with Mama and Daddy.

I must mention here, too, I received a letter from Bobby Lawson. I was so excited I jumped around and around the dorm floor like a crazy lady! I couldn't believe he actually wrote to me. Me, of all people! I guess I figured I'd never hear from him. When I ran into his mother back in January, she gave me his address at the base. "I'm sure he'd like to hear from you," she told me. "He doesn't hear from many of his friends."

Of course, Mrs. Lawson had no idea how in love I was with her son, nor that I was ever part of his crowd back in high school anyway. But I kept my promise to write to him, and now Bobby's letter is here with me in my coat pocket, along with the blue seed rosary I received from Sister Mary Michael. But the letter is pretty much ruined from how I was brought on board last night.

Yet, it gives me comfort to know I have Bobby's letter here with me. Thank goodness, the Germans didn't search me and find his letter, and maybe use it against me, because of his military service. But one day, God willing, I will share my experiences of being on this submarine with Bobby. Wouldn't that be something? That gives me even greater hope!

Dearest Mama and Daddy, my cute, silly brothers, Jack and Eddie, and my wee sister, Maggie, dear Bobby, Aunt Susie, Aunt Dottie and Uncle Will, my cousins Patrick, Sean, and Brian O'Keefe, everyone back home, I love all of you! Pray for me! Please don't give me up for dead! Send out anyone to search for me! I am here, HERE! God help me!

CHAPTER 26

"Chief, bring boat to periscope depth," *Kapitaenleutnant* Ketter ordered quietly. "I want to have a look around first."

"Aye, *Herr Kaleu.*" Chief Engineer Alois Geissler gestured to an eager mate to open the release valve.

A great hiss of compressed air thrust seawater from the ballast tanks. The boat swayed like a cradle, then listed and shuddered and started to rise slowly, freely, through the sea depths, a ponderous iron whale mounting to the surface.

Ketter clambered up the control room ladder to the conning tower and slid onto the leather saddle seat before the periscope. Pressing his right eye to the black eye cup, he prepared to encounter unknown conditions on the surface. A destroyer might be lurking nearby, or an airplane could swoop overhead and spot the U-115's narrow hull on the surface. Ketter's hands toyed nervously with the crossbar of the periscope. He was most anxious to commence the night's hunt!

Down in the control room, Chief Engineer Geissler watched the depth gauge on the bulkhead. In tune with his *Kommandant* in the tower, Geissler made the boat obey as it should. Soon Ketter's hollow voice called down the hole: "All clear! Surface, Chief!"

With a distinct shock the boat broke surface into evening twilight and wallowed in a choppy sea. The diesel engines coughed once, hesitated, as if refusing to cooperate, then roared throughout the submarine, kicking the boat forward. The men at their action stations smiled and jabbered at one another. The boat was very much alive again.

A chill breeze from the northwest brushed the men up on second bridge watch. Along the western horizon, the hazy halo of New Jersey's shore lights glowed peacefully, casting a ghostly aura about the watch. Suddenly a bridge guard strained forward. He lowered his binoculars slightly to be sure then rammed them to his eyes in earnest.

"Captain to the bridge! Shadow approaching off starboard bow!"

Ketter had just seated himself on the chart trunk in the control room to await events, when the cry came down. In seconds, he was up the ladder again, through the tower, onto the bridge. He tore off his goggles and jammed a large pair of night binoculars to his eyes.

"Aah, a fat prize, indeed, men! She's full of the much-needed 'blood' for the Allied war machine!" Ketter followed the oncoming image against the glow of light from the distant shore.

"She's at least ten thousand gross registered tons, *Herr Kaleu!*" Horst Struckmeier surmised near Ketter's elbow.

"A nice tanker all alone without an escort. Unbelievable!" First Watch Officer Paul-Karl Ullmann had arrived on the bridge.

Ketter spun around to the men, his white cap an indistinct blur in the darkness, "Let's find out if our 'eels' work at the western end of the Atlantic as well as they do at the eastern end!"

"You bet, *Herr Kaleu!*" The bridge guards rallied.

Paul-Karl Ullmann bent to the voice tube. "Sound, on battle stations!" He prepared to direct the surface attack under the watchful eye of his *Kommandant.* Any disparity between the two men had been totally forgotten.

The boat maneuvered into optimum firing range. A bevy of

orders and acknowledgments flew from the bridge to the control room to the forward torpedo room and back to the bridge:

"Rudder ten degrees to port! Come to course one-eight-five degrees. Open outer doors! Flood tubes one and two!"

"Rudder five degrees port! Maintain present speed. Come to new course one-eight-zero and hold steady!"

"Stand by tubes one and two. Target distance one-thousand-three-hundred meters. Speed twelve knots, course sixty degrees. Follow up!"

For a few tense moments, the men on the bridge waited in rigid anticipation. U-115 drove stealthily toward her intended quarry, her diesel engines rumbling low and threatening like a ravenous beast. Paul-Karl Ullmann moved the target bearing device, keeping it trained on the approaching ship. His voice was steady: "Target angle sixty. Increase speed to fourteen knots, range seven-hundred meters. Set torpedoes for five meters depth. Ready to fire a spread of two torpedoes."

Down in the tower, the final information was repeated for entry in the war log. One last time, the aiming calculator adjusted the indicated changes electrically in the torpedoes. The doomed tanker swung toward the hunter. The moment was perfect.

"Tube one, fire!" Screeched Ullmann, as he pressed the firing knob. Then, some seconds later: "Tube two, fire!"

In the bow torpedo room, the senior torpedo mechanics mate pressed the respective hand-firing buttons. *Obermaat* Werner Brunning yelled back to confirm: "Tube number one, fired! Tube number two, fired!"

Two consecutive thumps forward in the hull indicated the torpedoes had left the tubes and were on their way. On the bridge, *Kapitaenleutnant* Ketter checked the luminous dial of his watch. Counted one, two, three. . . . thirteen, fourteen, fifteen. . . . *Don't let them miss!* Seconds ticked interminably. BOOOM! A wall of flame ripped open the night, followed by deafening explosions. Something struck the forward deck a glancing blow, sending Ketter and the bridge guards to their knees behind the tower housing.

"What the blazes!"

"Check for damage to the hull!" Ketter bellowed.

"Yes, *Herr Kaleu*, at once!"

CHAPTER 27

The late afternoon sunlight faded to deep gray. In the distance a roll of thunder announced the approach of a Spring storm. For a moment Mary Ann stopped talking and reached over to switch on the lamp on the end table, then continued her monologue:

"Steve, there are no words to describe what I experienced that night. My God, that ship must have been close! When the concussion wave hit the U-boat, I thought I'd split in half, that's how strong the explosion was. Immediately my first reaction was, rescue had come. The Americans were firing on the U-boat to get Captain Ketter to surrender me over to them." Mary Ann gazed out at roiling storm clouds gathered above the treetops at the end of the yard.

"My American boys were out there waiting on the deck of their ship," she murmured trance-like. "Soon I would be among them and brought safely home." She regarded the historian with a bright, crooked smile. "So, as was my habit at the time, I bolted off the captain's bunk into the passage toward the hatch. . . ."

A blonde sailor, crouching near the curtain, leapt to his feet, when Mary Ann shot out of CQ. *"Fraeulein, nein!"* He grabbed for her, but she streaked past him like a ball carrier going for the goal line and wriggled head first into the low hatchway. The harried mate scrambled after her, cursing and fuming, and caught her fleeing heels, only to come up holding her empty shoes, for Mary Ann was already through the hole into the control room.

Another sailor leaning on the inner control room bulkhead with a silver stopwatch in his hand looked down in surprise, as Mary Ann burst from the hole. *What is this?* But Mary Ann only saw the control room ladder dead ahead. The gateway to light and life above, it beckoned but a few short steps away. And somewhere up there, beyond this horrible Nazi prison boat, her American boys were waiting. She would swim to them, if she had to, crawl up the side of their proud ship, jump into their welcoming arms. Mary Ann saw it all in her desperate flight: her United States Navy sailors, flashing clean, white, happy smiles, would wrap her in warm blankets and hang onto every word of her incredible tale of sailing with the enemy! Oh, and the newspapers were sure to be notified! Reporters with popping flashbulbs would flood around her, when her rescue ship pulled into New York! Mama and Daddy and all the family would be there to take her home! People would visit! My God, she would be a celebrity!

Mary Ann bounded for that narrow ladder, her stocking feet slipping on the grooved iron plates of the control room deck. WHUMP! Down she went on one knee, genuflecting before the altar of her salvation, slamming her kneecap against the metal deck. Then she staggered up, groaning with pain, determined to reach the goal. Her right hand actually brushed the third rung of that blessed ladder to freedom before several disgruntled control room mates tackled her to the deck.

Like lions on the prey, they rode her down. Breaths huffed and strained, bones bounced painfully. With a short scream Mary Ann strained upright, her hand grasping helplessly at the empty air, then she tumbled backward, dragging the mass of male bodies with her.

She stared up dazed and disoriented. Wild red whiskered faces gaped down at her. Suddenly, Mary Ann had the crazy urge to laugh out loud. Just the silly looks on their faces! She wanted to shout at those men, "Surprise! I'm sure giving you Nazis a run for your money, ain't I? Oh boy, oh boy, oh boy!" For it all seemed so incredibly ridiculous - her, there on her back on the deck, and the exasperated men looking down on her as if this was some kind of juked-up football game.

But the situation was deadly serious. The mates dragged Mary Ann across the metal deck toward the forward hatch. She hit and kicked and screamed for all she was worth against the powerful male tide. Heads parted briefly. The men hove her into position to go through the hatch. In that moment Mary Ann glimpsed a small photograph bolted above the hatchway frame. The distinguishable black-mark mustache stood out in the pasty white face of the stone-eyed Nazi leader.

"Nooo!" Mary Ann's wail deafened a vexed mate. She struggled to break free, though her extremities were nailed to the deck by rock-hard men. Suddenly someone seized hold of her and brought her up roughly. Mary Ann gazed into the extraordinarily handsome face of Second Watch Officer Dietrich Heubeck. His crystal-blue eyes blazed with fury. He was practically chewing her face with his gnashing white teeth.

"To ze bunk, at once!" His breath stirred loose hair wisps on her forehead.

Mary Ann sagged in shock, "Yes, sir."

"Und remain zer!" He pounded her again then blinked around at the other men, as if somehow seeking their approval, which mystified Mary Ann in the depths of her despair.

The other men watched her intently, some with that surly look of satisfaction, others with somber expressions. *Were they feeling sorry for her?* The storm had passed. The sails had gone limp against the cross bars in the dead calm that followed.

Mary Ann slowly hauled herself up onto her hands and knees and entered the gaping metal tube. Battered, bruised, blinded by tears, her nose dripping clear drops onto the iron cylinder of the hatchway, she crawled toward the forward passage. The blonde sailor was there to meet her as she emerged from the hatch. He yanked her unceremoniously to her feet and led her, tripping and stumbling, toward the dirty green curtain surrounding her prison cell. The captain's stinking bunk awaited. Like a beaten, stray dog, Mary Ann slunk onto the rumpled sea blanket and curled into a tight ball against the bulkhead.

The second watch officer had followed, checking to be sure she did as he directed. He stood by the bunk and waited. Mary Ann peered up at him through her tears and wondered: was his handsome, glowering face just a mask to hide his true feelings? Did he really care?

No, the look on his face told a different story. She was nothing to him. He had his own priorities to deal with.

With a wince of pain, Mary Ann rolled toward the bulkhead and put her back to him. Now she understood much too clearly what had happened. *The Germans had torpedoed a ship!* A horrible, horrible sound, not to be imagined by the most hardened human ear. Beyond the iron walls of her imprisonment her cherished Allied seamen were flailing and drowning in the cold, dark Atlantic. They were dying, even as she lay in this Nazi vessel, alone, helpless, trapped, unable to help them or do anything to stop this murderous U-boat in its deadly rampage.

The soft whisk of the green curtain closing apprised Mary Ann that the second watch officer had finally exited the compartment. *Good, let him go!* She scowled inwardly. *These terrible Nazi sailors were muderers of good men and ships and deserved to be shunned!* Overwhelmed with despondence Mary Ann keened long and hard and tearless into the captain's stained pillow. She was but a shadow of her former self, her last energy wasted for naught, her heart and soul bereft of any hope.

CHAPTER 28

Observers in the eerie reflection of their man-made Hell, the men on the bridge of U-115 watched the burning fuel tanker with shocked fascination. *Aaah, the heat!* It scorched their faces, yet they could not take their eyes from the torrid scene.

"Verdammt!" Horst Struckmeier murmured reverently.

"Can any man have lived through that?" Gerd Schwabl asked the question that pricked at each man's conscience.

"Yes, there's a lifeboat! Poor luckless rats better hurry, the entire sea is aflame around them!"

The radioman's report came up from below. *"Herr Kaleu,* no SOS went out from the tanker. Apparently they had no time to get one off. Nothing on the six-hundred meter wave length."

"Stupid Americans! So sure of themselves, are they?" Ketter spat with disgust. "Why don't they convoy like their British cousins? For mercy's sake, look at that! Their coastline is lit up like a Christmas tree! Don't they observe a blackout, now that they are at war? Or will they sacrifice good men and ships so that their shore resorts can stay open? Curse them, their ships are easily seen by us against the light!"

"Herr Kapitaenleutnant, we must take full advantage of this situation while it lasts," Paul-Karl Ullmann replied at his shoulder. "The

'Amis' will come to their senses soon enough. There should be no mercy shown toward this stumbling enemy."

"Get him while he's down, yes?" Ketter leaned on the tower coaming and stretched his neck toward the distant shoreline as if to analyze the real face of the menacing giant, America.

A dark head popped from the open hatch on the deck of the bridge. "Permission, one man on bridge?"

"Permission granted. What is it, Scholz?"

"Herr Kaleu, I beg to report, there was a bit of a problem with the American prisoner," Scholz confessed.

Ketter exploded, "What are you talking about, man?"

"It seems our little girl made a run for it. She managed to get as far as the control room, *Herr Kaleu."*

"What in thunder is going on down below?" Ketter roared. "Who's to be watching her?"

"Kutzop, *Herr Kaleu."* Scholz answered briskly.

"Well, you tell Kutzop it will be the can on moldy bread if he doesn't keep her in control! She will interfere with our torpedo launches! Must she be shackled to the bunk? This is all I need!" Ketter fumed, then turned to his first watch officer whose tall frame dwarfed him by a foot. "Number One, let's get out of here. Head southeast. That tanker is the perfect beacon for any U-boat hunter in the area. Keep your eyes sharp, men!" He berated the watch, then muttered out of Ullmann's hearing. "Cursed little 'Ami' girl, she's a spunky thing, and I intend to tame her." He felt a sudden thrust of power in his loins at the memory of her struggling beneath him on his bunk. His chest heaved with desire. Such craving he must fight, if he was to accomplish his mission!

U–115 slid away from the sinking tanker into the wall of night. The bridge guards strained their eyes, vigilant for swift Allied retribution, but none was to come. In the crowded forward torpedo room, sweating men labored to lift two greased "eels" along their tracks into the empty one and two tubes. Chains clanked and rattled, breaths gasped, muscles strained at their Herculean task.

Ketter descended the tower ladder and propped himself on the chart trunk in the control room where he proceeded to mark the latest entry into the *Kriegstagbuch,* or War Log:

Sonntag, den 15 Marz 1942   (Saturday, March 14, 1942)
01.24 Uhr CET   (1924 Hours EST)

Mar. - Quadrat CA 8265   Loaded tanker in sight.
NW 5, Seegang 2.   Groener lists it as Esso
   Pittsburgh.

Lage 80 Halb bedeckt Kurs 60.   Determined that tanker
1009 mbm sehr gute sicht.   has 10,000 GRT. Headed North
   for New York. Two torpedoes
   fired from tubes 1 and 2.
   Tanker goes down. No sos
   recorded. One known lifeboat
   away. No coastal blackout yet
   observed by the enemy,
   though this is fourth month
   of war for them. Partly cloudy,
   very good view.

Later that night, U-115 sighted two more ships running alone on separate courses. One, a suspicious looking little vessel, which Ketter thought might be a Coast Guard patrol boat out searching for them, was given a wide berth. The other ship, a large freighter, U-115 chased and finally caught, putting one torpedo into her exposed side. The "eel" slammed into the engine room. There, men of the freighter's "black gang" died instantly, most of them scalded to death when the boilers ruptured, steamed alive like lobsters, cherry red, screaming in agony, as their flesh cooked.

The crippled freighter shuddered under the torpedo's impact, then drifted and rolled on its side, taking on a huge stream of water through the damaged hull. In a matter of minutes, her great hulk slipped quietly below the roiling sea surface and disappeared forever, taking with her several trapped crewmen, both the living and the dead.

U-115 glided over the sea's black surface, "ahead slow." She crept in slowly toward a dark cluster of two lifeboats afloat among the wreckage. Ketter had ordered the submarine's guns trained on the human forms, which lurked in the drifting boats.

"In case they should fire on us," he cautioned his men of the watch. Ketter stepped up onto a metal ledge and leaned over the tower to scan the littered sea. *This was his handiwork, his proud mark,* the ironic thought skimmed his mind. Faint moans came over softly splashing waves to port. Ketter's heart beat faster, as a ghostly lifeboat floundered toward U-115. He, Ketter, had been the cause of this human suffering. The men out there were no longer the enemy, but fellow seamen in peril, and he must assist them as best he could.

"Schwabl, hand me the megaphone!" Ketter gestured impatiently.

A seaman of the watch promptly stepped forward and handed up the megaphone. Ketter seized it, spun back to the lifeboat and brought the megaphone to his lips. His voice husky with emotion, he called out in his near-perfect English:

"Good evening, gentlemen, may I ask, what is the name of your ship please?" The sound of his voice echoed across the scene of destruction, frightening him with the force of its cocky strength. It seemed an abomination to disturb the dead and dying.

At once, a vague figure clambered upward in the lifeboat, clinging to its gunwale in a passing swell. "We are from the Patagonia Queen!" came the equally strong reply.

Ketter was pleasantly surprised at the sound of this lusty voice, and his resolve for his purpose returned. "What cargo did you have aboard?" He pursued.

"We had general cargo. That is all I will tell you," the reply held a challenge.

"Well, then," Ketter rejoined with grim humor, "you must send the bill for your cargo to Franklin Roosevelt! He should cover the loss of your fine ship!"

Silence answered U-115's commander. Only the waves thrashing against the submarine's flank reminded him of the truth. As a final gesture of humanity, Ketter shouted: "Man, have you any injured with you? We also have some supplies we can pass on to you!"

"We want nothing from you! We can manage on our own!" The gutsy voice answered from the darkness.

Ketter ducked his head from the verbal blow. "Then I bid you, good luck!" he called back. "Hope you make it! Sorry we had to sink you, but this is war!"

The lifeboat faded astern into the wall of night. Ketter slowly lowered the megaphone, then turned and jumped down onto the bridge deck. "Let's get out of here!" he scowled, his mind troubled by the sense that he, too, was sinking fast in perilous waters.

CHAPTER 29
Chorus - the Petty Officers

"I tell you, Willi, the Old Man takes too many risks. He runs on the surface in broad daylight, even as we approach Chesapeake Bay and the American naval base at Norfolk."

"Well, men, I heard it from *Leutnant* Heubeck that Ketter wants to get to the coast of North Carolina, to Cape Hatteras along the Outer Banks. We should be there sometime tomorrow."

"Ah, yes, there the warm Gulf Stream comes from the south and hits into the cold North Atlantic, creating high wind and wave conditions. Plus, there is the added danger of underwater hazards like Diamond Shoal. The area has been a challenge to mariners during the centuries."

"And the Old Man takes us to this place, Georg?"

"Ships, Wolfgang, and plenty of them! It is the perfect hunting ground. Many tankers loaded with oil and gasoline from Texas, Aruba, and Venezuela must make the turn past the Outer Banks on their way North. There will be ships filled with sugar and fruit and cotton. And we can get them while they run this dangerous passage!"

"Ah, Schatzi, you know so much, yes? Where'd you learn all this stuff?"

"You know our *Kommandant* has a scratchy neck, Karl-Heinz. He wants that blasted Knights Cross and can probably sink enough tonnage on this patrol to earn it."

"I think our *Kommandant* wants more than that, men. Did you hear our little girl this morning?"

"Ah, the girl. No, what's happened to her?"

"She took another fit, that's what! I happened to be going by CQ and got a look in at all the commotion. It took two of the officers and our good *Doktor* Moeglich to get her under control. Should have heard *Oberleutnant* Pauli. Plenty pissed off. He doesn't seem to like our little American girl."

"The guy's a hard-nose, a real National Socialist *Dumkopf*! I understand his father is a high police official in their home district."

"Who cares! That girl's a pain in the neck, crying and puking all the time. She deserves a good thumping, now and then, to straighten her out."

"Whoa, Wolfgang, some gentleman you are! I feel sorry for our sweet captive. And don't I know how she feels with the seasickness. I have often to carry my bucket with me on duty in rough weather."

"The girl needs some tender, loving care, and I, the expert lover, will provide it!"

"This is already happening, Franz, in case you haven't noticed. The Old Man nearly went berserk when he saw the restraints on her. Claimed he never gave such an order, but I heard him, plain as day. And now he's mad as a cornered rat. He has a feeling for the girl, I know this!"

"Don't we all?"

"What do you think, Schatzi? You're there in the *Funkraum*. Is there something going on between the girl and our Old Man?"

"Nothing unusual that I can see. They've had conversations, but nothing more."

"Do you overhear anything interesting?"

"No, Franz, I don't. I figure it's the business of the Old Man to talk to her."

"Ah, yes, he can go into his private compartment any time he wants to, and there she is! He has only to close the curtain—"

"That's enough, men! It's the *Kommandant* you speak of! No more loose talk, especially within earshot of the 'Lords'!"

"Look, buddy, you don't have to get so testy!"

"Shut your mouth, Wirth! I won't put up with any more garbage talk from you or anyone else in here!"

CHAPTER 30

The red light above the narrow washroom doorway winked off as the oval hatch slowly opened. Mary Ann emerged, pale and miserable looking, her matted hair plastered to her forehead like strands of washed-up seaweed, her eyes sunk in dark hollows beneath eyelids as thin as cellophane. Stumbling over the lip of the washroom doorway, she grabbed for Gerhard Moeglich, the boat's medic, who quickly hooked his hand under her armpit. His gaze of tender concern for his frail charge turned to a stony glare, when he spied a smirking face on a nearby bunk in the bow room.

At Moeglich's clipped order, the youth slid off his bunk with a grimace of embarrassment and entered the washroom door. The sound of the toilet pump working seemed to satisfy Moeglich, and he turned aside, Mary Ann in tow, and shepherded her into the bow room hatch.

Mary Ann clung to the medic's red plaid shirt front, as he dragged her to her feet on the yawing deck on the other side of the hatch. Deep in her suffering, she had no will of her own, but hung drooped forward, her stomach caved in from the force of continuous dry heaving, her head rocking with dizzy pain. She had stopped begging God to save her long ago. Now she wished only to die.

The medic, a large, homely man with a bulbous, red-creased nose, a stubby dark beard, and friendly green eyes, had been with her periodically throughout the day, but there was nothing he could give her to ease her nausea. The aspirin he offered to relieve her headache didn't stay in her stomach long enough. Yet Mary Ann felt comforted by the medic's presence, when he showed up, now and then, to check on her.

Moeglich's face bent to hers, so that Mary Ann felt his warm smelly breath on her cheek. They progressed along the tumbling passage through the Petty Officers Room, lunging back and forth against tiers of bunks. Several pairs of sympathetic eyes peered over bunk rails and around short gray privacy curtains to view the couple as they passed. For a second, Mary Ann raised her head to judge the distance to the end of the room. She glimpsed the *Smutje* far ahead in the weaving passage by the galley bulkhead. He regarded her halting footsteps with the gruff pity typical of a weathered seaman who has witnessed such agony as hers.

The distant, raging cry, *"Alarrrmmm"* - the fourth within as many hours - tore into her consciousness. Mary Ann looked to Moeglich, confused, begging. She knew the cry, knew what it meant, felt helpless before its looming result.

Moeglich reacted at once. With the thrust of a maddened bull, he hurled Mary Ann onto an empty lower bunk at the right of the passage. Her head slammed the metal frame of the upper bunk, and she collapsed in a flash flood of pain onto the thin leather mattress. She was just clear of the passage when the thunderous herd of men galloped by at knee level, heading downhill to the bow room. Their boisterous shouts, *"Schnell, schnell, gehe, gehe!,"* and the strident clanging of the diving bell bored into the angry new wound on her head.

The submarine angled sharply downward. *These drills, these drills, was there never an end to them?* Mary Ann wretched into an unknown crewman's stinking sheets. Yet, she welcomed the depths of the sea, for they provided relief from the perpetual, sickening, rocking motion of the boat and the chronic nausea that plagued her.

BOOM! An explosion hammered the submarine. KA-BOOM!

Another ear-splitting blast followed close on. The boat plunged and reared and screeched throughout its large steel structure like a can being kicked along a rutted back alley. Glass shattered with sharp tinkles. Light bulbs popped and blew, pitching the bunk compartment into total darkness. Through flashes of blue fire down forward, wayward bodies thudded about in the surreal scene. Mary Ann wailed like a hoarse siren in the chaos.

Dim emergency lighting blinked on and off, then on again to reveal the gray Petty Officers Room devoid of life. *The men were gone! The boat was going down!*

Mary Ann struggled up from the bunk. *She would not be left alone to die!* Blinded by blood from the gash on her forehead, she floundered after the men, who had vanished into the hollow ahead. Her feet in their flat-bottom saddle shoes skidded downhill along the slanting deck, as if she was on roller skates. She smacked into rolling food cans and rotted potatoes, tripped over scattered boots, books, and a loose cooking pot from the galley. As she reached for the open bow room hatch to slow her swift descent, she caught her left ring finger in the spoked wheel mechanism. "Ooww!" She stopped to extricate herself, frowned in dull wonder at her finger twisted at an unnatural angle, then plummeted head-first through the round forward hatch.

She catapulted into the bow torpedo room, which was perpetually cluttered with rumpled bunks, discarded clothing, and boots. Swiping the stubborn flow of blood from her eyes with the sleeve of her fatigues, Mary Ann glanced around. *The men! Where were they?* She saw ropes and chains dangling in the empty gloom. Deflated gray hammocks swung from the steel ribbed overhead, and the narrow mess table had loosed most of its contents onto the deck.

Then, in a dim cavern far ahead, Mary Ann spotted a hand waving. She distinguished loud whispers: *"Fraeulein, komme!,"* and noticed a gaggle of human faces near four large round white doors. *The men were there!*

Exhaling fretful little puppy whimpers, Mary Ann squirmed and clawed her way through the debris toward the men. As she came, many welcoming arms reached up for her, and she readily went in among them, shivering, gasping, and snuggling closely against a taut-muscled chest. Excited men's whispers waved around her like blowing summer grasses, yet she felt no fear. Here, at last, was the human contact she sought, the sensation of warm bodies, and the reassuring strength in the gentle arms that supported her.

Mary Ann settled in for the duration of the attack. A man's surprised gaze met hers, but she merely blinked up at him as if to say, *Don't mind me, I just dropped in for a visit.* The sailor's soft, curly, sandy colored hair rolled straight up like a board from his high forehead, and Mary Ann wondered that his hair had not seen a comb for weeks. She had the urge to touch it, but refrained from doing so. *Yet, didn't he have the sweetest expression?* Eyes sparkling in the bare submarine light, he glanced about the tight space to garner his shipmates' reactions. *Isn't this something?* His eyes seemed to say. *The girl is right here with us! Can you beat that?*

The U-boat leveled out at safe depth. No more explosions jarred the hull. Recovering from the trauma of the bomb attack, Mary Ann realized where she was. Many hands clung possessively to her. Wherever they could find contact, arms, legs, back, shoulders, and comforting hands touched her. A sailor in a black and white striped t-shirt cradled her to his chest, and Mary Ann was shocked to discover her own arm encircling his slender waist. Yet, she kept her arm where it was, did not dare move a muscle. *Let it be,* she thought. The sailor's fingertips gently searched through her tangled hair. She winced with pain, but did not stop the fellow from probing her wound. The sailor whispered around to his shipmates. His soft, deep, guttural tone washed over Mary Ann with the power of warm healing waters. She relaxed and listened and drifted in the sailor's tender attention. Her fears and seasickness had vanished.

- 1 5 0 -

CHAPTER 31

<table>
<tr><td>Montag 16 Marz 1942</td><td>Monday, March 16, 1942</td></tr>
<tr><td>22.26 Uhr (CET)</td><td>16.26 hours, EST</td></tr>
<tr><td>Mar. Quadrat CA 7914.</td><td>Wind force 2. Seas 4.</td></tr>
<tr><td>Seegang 4.</td><td>Visibility 8 nautical miles.</td></tr>
<tr><td></td><td>Partly cloudy.</td></tr>
<tr><td></td><td>Crash dive before U.S. aircraft,</td></tr>
<tr><td></td><td>possible identity PBY</td></tr>
<tr><td></td><td>Catalina. Two bombs.</td></tr>
<tr><td></td><td>Torpedo tube 5 is out of</td></tr>
<tr><td></td><td>commission. No other permanent</td></tr>
<tr><td></td><td>damage.</td></tr>
</table>

In German:

"She was right there among the men, Captain Lieutenant! I couldn't believe what I was seeing! I laugh now to think of it, how she must have gotten there with them. Certainly her first experience with the waterbombs motivated her."

"I'm sure this is so, *Obermechanikers Maat* Brunnig. That is all for now, you may resume your duties."

"Aye, sir, of course."

"Captain Lieutenant, the cut on her head needed five stitches. Naturally I had to remove some of her hair to reach it. Also, she sustained a broken pinky finger on her left hand. I set it with a small splint. Flinched at bit, during all this, but didn't cry out. She's a mighty brave lady, sir! I left her nearly incapacitated on a bunk in the P.O.'s room!"

"Yes, Moeglich, our little American lady is something else."

In English:

"And so, Marianne, you are feeling better?"

"Yes, I am, thank you, sir."

"It seems that you and the boat received some minor injuries from the depth bombs?"

"Yeah."

"And it was one of your fine aircraft from the United States which bombed us."

"It was?"

"Of course! What did you think?"

"Well, I don't know, captain. I didn't realize, but now I guess I know."

"Just remember what you experience, my dear. Write it in your notebook we gave to you that the Germans suffer, too. No one is an exception from this!"

"I'm pretty much realizing that, sir, believe me."

In German:

"So, Moeglich, we are making good time. In the early morning hours, we will reach our new area of operations. You may carry on with what you are doing for the young woman. Get her face cleaned off and the wound bandaged up. Give her any more aspirin for pain."

"Certainly, Captain Lieutenant, I intend to do so. I should be done here shortly."

"Very well."

CHAPTER 32

The U-115 submerged to wait out daylight hours on the 60-meter line off Hatteras Light early the following morning. *Kapitaenleutnant* Ketter had been unpleasantly surprised to observe numerous small pickets patrolling the Outer Banks, as well as frequent flights by reconnaissance aircraft. However, he soon discovered they were no threat, when an attacking seaplane dropped one bomb far from the boat.

"The 'Amis' have the right machines, but don't yet know how to use them," Ketter scribbled blithely in his war log.

That night, with plenty of opportunities abounding, bad luck plagued U-115, as she slipped in along the shallower shipping lanes to hunt. Two G7e torpedoes failed to find their targets, missing a 7,000 gross-registered-ton freighter and, some time later, a fully loaded oil tanker, just ripe for picking. The firing calculations had been perfect. Yet Konrad Lieb reported from the sound room that the second torpedo had taken a 25-degree heading off course and ran aground near the shore. Thankfully, it had failed to explode and reveal their presence. So, both intended victims steamed away unmolested, not even realizing they had been under attack by a German U-boat.

Ketter ordered the guidance systems on the remaining eleven

"eels" checked. *What in thunder went wrong?* He wanted to know. *Was there some incompetence on the part of the torpedo "mixers"?* This accusation goaded! Grumbling and cursing, the torpedo mechanics fell to, laboring to slide each 2,000-pound torpedo out of its tube or up from storage beneath the floor boards in the bow room to examine them. The men minded not so much that their Old Man was "biting heads," but they were here to "kill" ships, and could not do so. *The torpedoes' manufacturer was surely the culprit! Or perhaps sabotage during delivery from Germany to the loading docks on the French coast?*

Toward daybreak, off Cape Lookout, U-115 sighted another tanker coming up from the south and prepared a submerged attack. This time, the periscope lens fouled. U-115 boldly dashed to the surface to begin the chase, but Chief Engineer Geissler reported a break in the major cooling water pipe of the starboard diesel engine. *"Verdammt!* Take her down! Take her down!" Ketter roared in exasperation. Power must be cut in order that the pipe could be disassembled and the problem area welded and refitted.

Now the entire crew felt the weight of the failed attacks. This could be seen in the sharp glances, the wrench thrown down in disgust, the lips curled by curses, a short-lived argument among some mates over a petty matter. Yet, one thought seemed to prevail over any others, and it was cautiously whispered back and forth among several superstitious sailors:

"See? I have told you this would be. That woman's presence on board this boat is a curse to us all!"

"Her sad, sweet look cannot fool me. Perhaps she does some kind of magic closed off in the *Kommandant's* Quarters that protects her own ships!"

Another fruitless day passed in repairs on the sea floor. Tension aboard remained tangible. Ketter maintained the tone of the atmosphere by brooding on his bunk and yelling out for prompt reports. It now seemed most imperative that he regain the privacy afforded by his former quarters. Only his out-spoken first watch officer had the nerve to suggest this, "Throw the enemy dog into PO. Chain her up!" Ketter angrily spurned the advice.

These many long hours, over the course of two days, Mary Ann endured alone and seemingly forgotten in the captain's rightful quarters, except for the Spartan care schedule that had been assigned for her bodily needs. The embarrassing, but necessary trips to the WC, in the company of the hefty medic, revealed men in subdued states. There might be the occasional glance of recognition from one or another of them, or a passing half-smile, but mainly eyes were cast down, brows folded in deep concentration.

Cold meals, consisting mainly of canned meat sandwiches, came to Mary Ann, delivered by the red-headed sailor whom she secretly dubbed "Billy." He entered her tiny, curtained-off world with an exaggerated bow, laid the plate of food and cup of tepid coffee on the captain's wooden desk, then quickly departed, hardly daring to look at her. *Naturally, for she was such a hag!* she thought. Yet, Mary Ann did greet "Billy" cheerfully each time he came; she was so starved for friendship and memories of loved ones from home.

Throughout those desperate hours, Mary Ann turned to praying on her blue-seed rosary beads and writing prolifically in the notebook the second watch officer had given her. If it hadn't been for these two outlets she would have lost her mind!

A few excerpts from her journal follow:

". . . . I'm not sure what day it is anymore. Can't keep track, since everything here is the same. The lights burn constantly, no sunlight. Am fairly sure it's daylight out, when the boat is under the sea, and night when it's on the surface. This is all a bad dream. . . ."

"Am feeling somewhat better. My stitches still burn and my broken finger aches constantly, but that's to be expected. The medic gave me more aspirin. It helps a bit. I'm just grateful it wasn't my right hand finger that got broken, or I wouldn't be able to write. . . ."

"No one comes in here, not even the captain. Sometimes I hear him passing on the other side of the curtain. Can tell by his voice. Think he'd come in and ask how I am? No! It doesn't matter. I'm not as afraid of the men as I was at first. I suppose I'm getting used to things. . . ."

". . . . When I think of Mama and Daddy and the boys and my wee Maggie, it's as if my heart has gone shut. I can't cry anymore. I feel strange and empty, but somehow there's always this sense of hope that comes to me. I feel it when I pray. . . ."

Journal Entry (hours later):

"I have to write. Constantly write. It's a great release! I still have a headache, but it's calmed down. Even though the boat is moving, the sea isn't as rough.

"I know this submarine is looking for more ships to attack. I'll never forget these terrible, tense hours as long as I live! I can actually feel and hear the thump of the torpedoes being fired! I hang onto my rosary the whole time and pray for the lives of the men on those sinking ships. When one of the Germans shows up, I hide my rosary for fear he will take it from me."

"The boat made more dives today. Each time we go down fast, I fear more bombs will explode on us! Dear God, this is the worst terror I've known in my life!

"I think of my dear Bobby Lawson and all our submarine, battleship, and destroyer sailors, especially those killed or injured at Pearl Harbor. Now I realize, too, Bobby never felt anything for me. I carried quite a bright torch for him, last year at school, and prayed he would ask me to the Senior Prom. But of course, I was the crazy fool, dreaming the impossible.

"But here, he wrote to me, after all! The world has changed since December 7. The situation has changed our country, and because Bobby faces a frightening, unknown future, maybe he's viewing me differently, too. I am not that silly, homely girl he used to see in the hallway back at school. Rather, I'm a much-needed friend in uncertain times. It seems to take shock or tragedy to make us grow up and treat other people nicer. I've seen this happen quite a lot in my life. Events come around full-circle to teach us how precious life is and to be good to others, for time is short. Things can end suddenly.

"I feel sorry for everyone. Yes, even for these German sailors. They're just guys really. I don't hate them or think of them as 'Nazis' anymore. Some of these fellows are kind of cute, too, from what I see. But I try to hold that part of me in check. . . ."

"How did I feel when this submarine was bombed by one of my own airplanes? It felt like my body was being smashed and shaken til my teeth and bones disintegrated to dust. The fear and shock is indescribable! I can only imagine what it must be like when a torpedo hits a ship! Or, what it must be like for people in an air raid with bombs dropping on buildings, while they cower in a shelter underground? I'm torn apart to think how we humans treat one another! I can only imagine what

- 1 5 8 -

must be going on around the world right at this very moment! Who is hurting out there? Who is dying?

"Sadly, back home, I didn't pay attention to the news on the radio. Too busy with my own worries and keeping up with my studying. I didn't even think how the patients in the hospital might be feeling. I mean, I cared, but I was more worried about Sister Pauline suddenly showing up on the ward and finding something wrong with my work. So, this is my true confession of my thoughtlessness from the bowels of Hell."

"I look in the mirror here on the wall and don't recognize myself anymore. The bandage covers the right side of my head, like a lopsided little hat. The medic stopped by to check on me before and was delighted to find me writing away in my journal. Though he can't speak English, he has a nice way of calming me down. He's a decent guy.

"My face and hair are awful! Two large pimples formed on my right cheek, and my personal smell is driving me crazy. I need a good bath! So do these sailors. They look just as bad or worse than I do. It's awful how we human beings have to exist in a war we cause ourselves. Now I know why girls aren't allowed in combat."

CHAPTER 33

Scarlet flames licked along the length of the doomed ship's deck like the slow, deliberate strokes of lounging lions washing. Angry black clouds of smoke punched high into the night sky, fanning out across winking stars. Small internal explosions wracked the ship's interior, as the fuel tanker settled on even keel at 2,000 meters distance from U-115. Suddenly, a blood- red geyser blasted upward, showering the ghastly scene with fiery debris and sending swaths of acrid, choking smoke toward the men on U-115's bridge.

Kapitaenleutnant Ketter scanned the burning ship through his binoculars. A British ship, the name "Abbey House" emblazoned on her hull, she had been running darkened and unescorted on an erratic zig-zag course in the attempt to save herself in these treacherous American coastal waters, where the United States defense seemed not to care.

Disgusted, Ketter lowered his binoculars. "Where do they find the men to take such ships to sea in wartime?" His face was a snarling red mask in the hell-fire of the torpedoed tanker. "You couldn't pay me enough to sail those floating funeral pyres!"

"But, *Herr Kaleu,* you see our luck has turned for the better, has it not?" An enthusiastic voice enjoined from the starboard side of the bridge.

"Ah, yes, of course, Seaman Baier," Ketter replied with a sour cackle, then raised his binoculars once more to the burning tanker. "This is our third ship tonight, men! No more fooling around with our broken U-boat, yes!"

"Herr Kaleu, the tanker is sending out an SOS/SSS, attacked by submarine." Schatzi's report came up from the radio room.

"Good God, who can remain alive on that barge?" Ketter gasped.

"We must put another eel into her, *Herr Kaleu!"* First Watch Officer Paul-Karl Ullmann pressed near the UZO. "Send that tanker to the bottom at once!"

Ketter whirled about, "No, Number One, let's give the 10.5 centimeter gun a workout! Gun crew to action stations!" His order rang out.

Men scrambled madly to obey. Bodies popped from the deck hatch like jacks-in-the-box. Shadow men hurried to the *Wintergarten* at the rear of the bridge, slid down the ladder to the main deck, and rushed forward around the bulging tower to the bow. Ketter listened to the many feet scraping and pounding along then turned to his lanky first watch officer.

"Every eel is precious, as you well know, Number One!" He rumbled. "We will take out the tanker's wireless room, and then finish her off with nice round holes along the waterline."

"Aye, *Herr Kaleu!"* Ullmann snapped in agreement.

The gun crew had assembled down on the main deck in front of the tower to await orders to commence firing. Hans-Juergen Luther, as "layer," took up his station on the left side of the deck gun, while the "loader," Horst Struckmeier, removed the water-tight muzzle plug to a storage hole on the gun pedestal. Passed by many hands from the magazine under the floor plates below deck, the heavy shells came bumping up the hatch into eager hands.

Commanding the big gun, Second Watch Officer Dietrich Heubeck ordered the first round loaded and the gun breech closed. Then assuming a rigid stance, he cried out: "Forward gun ready for firing, *Herr Kaleu!*"

Ketter leaned to the voice tube and directed the helmsman in the conning tower: "Port ten, both ahead slow. Distance to tanker 1,500 meters. Steady up on one-nine-five. Both ahead two thirds." Then he grabbed the proffered megaphone and ordered the gun crew to action. "Permission to fire five hundred meters, ten rounds!"

In the meantime, U-115 was slipping closer to the burning behemoth. Waves of heat from the fuel tanker seared the men's faces on U-115's open bridge and main deck.

"The Old Man's taking us straight to Hell!" A bridge guard murmured in awe.

Suddenly, a remote command was issued below, and the forward 10.5 centimeter gun roared to life, its blinding muzzle fire startling the men on bridge watch.

"Holy Moses, that's incredible!" screeched the excitable Seaman Baier on Ketter's left.

Again, the gun blasted into the night, followed by another roar, then another. The first shell hit squarely on the tanker's flying bridge with a white burst. *Good shot!* Ketter observed grimly through his binoculars. Rounds two and three fell short of their intended targets, however, a result of U-115's unsteady headway in the rolling sea. Ketter gripped the iron tower plating, counted out the fourth, fifth, and sixth shots. Three shells exploded in close succession on the midship house and hull. The seventh round reached her mark - the tanker's radio shack, silencing once and for all that desperate SOS/SSS. Ketter thumped his fist on the tower edge with an abrupt show of satisfaction. *Good men, good!* As if in answer, an unexpected flash erupted from the tanker's stern.

"Herr Kaleu, those wretched dogs are firing on us!" Ullmann's high wail held disbelief.

"Verdammt!" Ketter cursed himself for sailing too close to the tanker. A British ship would have a gun after all! But who could

possibly remain alive to man that gun? Someone was definitely alive in that inferno, someone very determined and very brave. *The last man alive? Or an evenging ghost bent on U-115's mutual destruction?*

"Emergency, full back!" Ketter screamed down the voice tube to the engine room. He must present the narrowest silhouette to the enemy tanker's fire. Slip out of range quickly! The acknowledging bell clanged deep throughout U-115 with an urgent shrill, as the boat trembled violently with the effort to pick up speed. Another fire flash burst from the tanker's stern. Ketter cursed like a madman over his reckless judgment. He had exposed U-115 to unnecessary danger, making his boat the perfect target in the reflection of that tanker's hell-fire. He had thought to give his men a thrill, make them think him a right, fine, daring *Kommandant* who took risks to win success, and now, for sure, they had the whole blasted ball of wax.

An incoming projectile screamed low over the heads of the bridge guards. It crashed into the sea close alongside U-115, sending up a geyser of white water that drenched the huddled men. Down below on the main deck, the plucky gun crew was getting off an eighth round. Ketter wondered at the chaos of gunfire he had created and felt that wicked pride he liked in himself. The Old Man was giving his men many thrilling adventures to boast about when they arrived back in port!

A blinding flash sent Ketter hurling to the deck like a rag doll. He heard the shell tearing through the double-plated steel cladding on the outside of the tower, heard the terrified cries of his men as they fell around him in engulfing darkness. Except for the boat's pounding diesel engines blindly driving U-115 backward into the wall of night, all had become ominously still, as Death arrived aboard the boat.

Ketter found himself pinned to the bridge deck beneath a tangled heap of bodies. He attempted to move his arms and legs to test for any injury. *Get up, fool!* He exhorted himself. *Resume command!*

Account for your men! His heart pounded. Had he alone survived the carnage, this horrible result of his pride run amuck?

"Herr Kaleu?" A shaken voice inquired at his feet.

"Number One?" Ketter rallied, overcome by relief - and a sudden violent headache - and extended his trembling hand toward the voice. "Ah, God, it is you, Pauli!"

"Yes, *Herr Kaleu,* I am fine. A bit shaken up, but fine." First Watch Officer Ullmann refused his commander's outstretched hand and got to his feet unaided.

Another man, Oesterweise, by the voice, called from the darkness on Ketter's left. "As am I, *Herr Kaleu."*

"Ah, so, good, Heini!" Ketter exulted.

Shadow heads came up slowly, one at a time. Ketter groped along the fairwater, grasping each man in turn, then quickly scanned the main deck below. The gun crew remained on their feet. A miracle!

The fire of the enemy tanker remained as a brief sputtering spark on the horizon. The British ship slipped ignominiously into her grave. Suddenly a cry from Ullmann alerted Ketter to another crisis: *"Herr Kaleu,* we have a man down on the *Wintergarten!* It is the young Fritz!"

CHAPTER 34

The boat's diesel engines hammered like kettle drums, vibrating the iron bulkheads and deck with the force of an earthquake. Then abruptly the engines died, and the boat drifted in reverse, angling slowly to starboard, exhausted after its rapid retreat.

Alone in her tiny cell Mary Ann inched resolutely along her blue-seed rosary beads, the third decade, fifth bead. "Hail Mary, full of grace—" *What's going on out there?* "Blessed art thou among women—" *Why had the boat stopped? Was it damaged? Out of fuel? Please be with me, Dear Lord! Be with us all—*"Holy Mary, mother of God, pray for us sinners—"

With a violent clatter, the engines thumped to life again, driving the boat forward and gathering speed. Mary Ann closed her eyes tightly, breathed in and out, in and out. *Please, PLEASE be with me, Lord!* That helpless resignation to unseen events, the terrible bracing of oneself for blind impact, the cold penetrating fear that preceded further explosions, the frightful possibility of sudden death enshrouded Mary Ann in a thick, gray haze, as she burrowed shivering into the corner—"now and at the hour of our death. Amen."

The sudden commotion of men moving about in the passage did not attract her attention, at first. She'd grown inured to the chaos of men rushing back and forth along the corridor to their various duties.

But something was happening out there. Her curiosity roused, Mary Ann rolled over to the edge of the bunk and peered down, as always, at the space under the green curtain. *Good God, a man lay on the linoleum deck in the corridor!* His limp right arm was sprawled, in full view, beneath the hem of the curtain surrounding her prison, and his smudged fingers clawed weakly at the floor.

Mary Ann sat up fast. *Someone was hurt!* Without wavering, she slid to the deck in her stocking feet, taking care not to step on the grasping hand. Her own hand was on the curtain, but she quickly backed against the bunk and waited, as a crewman stepped alongside the fallen man.

What motivated Mary Ann to act, at this moment, was multi-faceted. Most definitely, it was the aftershock of battle and the accumulation of stress over many nerve-wracking hours and days. She was no longer in her right mind? No, quite simply, it was her heart. That this was an enemy sailor lying injured on the deck didn't matter. As a student nurse she had the obligation to aid, instead of sitting paralyzed with indecision on the bunk. If she was experiencing war, then she must force herself to view its results first-hand!

Slipping her blue-seed rosary into her fatigues pocket, she pulled back the edge of the green curtain, but a man's broad back blocked her view. She opened the curtain further. There, the captain, his dingy-white commander's cap smashed low on his brow, stepped gingerly along the opposite bulkhead near the radio room doorway. For now, thankfully, he didn't notice her standing by the open curtain, or surely he would have ordered her back on the bunk!

To the captain's right, Radioman Konrad stood pressed in the sound room cubicle, his sharp hawk's eyes cast down on a scene Mary Ann could not yet view. Konrad talked to the gathered men in a subdued tone, his sallow, heart-shaped face pinched with concern.

Then Mary Ann recognized the medic's voice down near the hatchway, though it did not hold its usual calm tone, but sounded harsh, even panicked. She strained on tip-toes to see what he was doing and accidentally bumped the broad-shouldered man in front of her. He instantly moved aside, not even realizing it was she, the prying American prisoner, who had bumped him. A sight way was opened up, and Mary Ann witnessed, for the first time, the horrifying results of combat.

Bathed to his elbows in blood, the medic worked with trembling hands to secure a cloth tourniquet around a mangled leg stump. The lower half of the leg was hanging by thin spaghetti strands of flesh, and Mary Ann saw jagged bone protruding from the raw, gaping wound. Her insides rolled sickly. *Oh, God!* The linoleum deck resembled the butcher's block at Sam's meat market!

"What happened?" Her cry burst like a gunshot in a silent canyon.

No man replied. Mary Ann slipped in closer to glimpse the injured man's head back in supporting hands. His wide-open eyes stared at the overhead in shock, yet he uttered no cry. His auburn hair fell in loose slabs from his pale forehead.

"Billy!"

Mary Ann's cry startled the men. She scrambled to reach the fallen sailor, but the man with the broad back swung his arm to ward her off. Yet, she could not be dissuaded. This was the sailor who served her meals! Her little red-headed "Billy Baker" from Algebra II class!

Don't let him die! Don't let him die! No, not like Tommy! The memory seared her brain. She was five-years-old. Blood splattered the trolley tracks and ran in the cobbled street outside her family's flat. Tommy's sweet face grimaced with pain. Mama's screams charged the sultry morning air. Neighbors and passers-by looked on in helpless, stunned silence. . . .

Do something! Do something now! Mary Ann spun to the bunk with her coat and the gray sea blanket lying askew near the bulkhead.

"Please, sir," she gestured to the disgruntled captain, who stooped by the radio room door, "put your injured sailor in here on my bunk. Don't let him lie on that cold, hard floor!"

Every man in the passage turned to look at her. *Who was she to give orders?* The captain glared at her, and yet she noted that his sharp gaze had softened. *Was it her imagination, or did she glimpse love in those dark, narrow eyes?*

The captain was on his feet at once, directing his men in urgent tones. The medic nodded his great shaggy head, and all together the men labored and huffed to lift the gravely injured sailor and carry him into the tiny quarters. Mary Ann retreated down the passage and watched as the men gently lowered "Billy" to her bunk. She dare not look to see how the medic maneuvered "Billy's" torn leg, nor did she note the pools of blood shimmering on the deck. She focused solely on the young sailor's gray face. *How strange it was to see him there on her bunk in the lamplight.*

The medic shoved another hypodermic needle of morphine through the torn gray trousers on "Billy's" thigh. Mary Ann felt the sharp stab in her knotted stomach, yet she remained firmly in place by the open green curtain among the helpless, milling men.

Someone bumped her. A stout sailor with a somber flat face was pushing a gray mop along the deck. The captain stood with his back to her, talking quietly to the medic. The hawk-eyed Konrad waited at the foot of the bunk, his lean shoulders sagged with defeat. The sailor on clean-up duty went about his grim business without a word.

Mary Ann reached out. She dared touch the captain's coat sleeve. Felt the give of soft flesh beneath the tough leather exterior. "Sir?" she inquired carefully.

The captain wheeled around with a jerk. *She had touched him?* His angry gaze cut her.

"Please, sir," her throat was dry as sandpaper, "may I help care for your sailor? Maybe even just to sit with him a while?"

CHAPTER 35

The captain frowned, uncomprehending. Mary Ann knew her request had taken him off guard. He seemed unable to focus. His lips puffed out. "But, of course." He conceded, then gripped her elbow and steered her resolutely toward the bunk.

"I feel so badly, captain!" She sought to explain her feelings in the rush. "My brother, Tommy, was run over by a streetcar, when I was a little girl, and I wanted so much to stay by him, but no one would let me, and I never got to say 'good-bye' to him!"

"You will remain by my sailor." The captain forced her down onto the bunk by "Billy." The wooden desktop gouged her back, but Mary Ann remained stoically "on duty," in spite of the discomfort. She had requested this assignment, now she must carry through.

The medic was watching her, but his gentle-ox face seemed to show approval of her presence by his badly-injured patient. Mary Ann nodded to the medic, then gazed down at "Billy," where he lay mainly in shadow, his young-kid face appearing ghost-like, smooth, and waxy. His eyebrows were little golden triangles in the lamplight, giving him the appearance of a plucky leprechaun. His ski-jump nose, peppered with light brown freckles, surprised Mary Ann. She hadn't noticed this feature about her little "Billy" before, and her heart swelled with tenderness and pity for the sailor. *Why? Why you, sweet Billy? Must you, so young and vulnerable, suffer pain and loss, because your crazy, far-off leader craves to dominate the world?*

Mary Ann glimpsed "Billy's" bloody leg stump at the foot of the bunk, oozing dark-red blood onto her coat. Bobby Lawson's letter was hidden in the pocket of her coat, but there was nothing she could do about it now. *Just let it go. Let it go. . . .* Then a thought struck her with such terrible clarity it took her breath away: *Bobby Lawson would not survive the war.* She felt this like ice to her soul. Knew, in that clairvoyant flash, he would perish at sea. . . .

Someone placed a hand on Mary Ann's shoulder and squeezed, startling her from her fearsome vision. "I trust you to remain by Seaman Baier."

Mary Ann squinted up into the captain's lined, bearded face. *He was close enough to kiss!* His familiar sour-lemon odor floated in her nostrils, bringing her an odd measure of comfort. "What's his name, sir?" she asked quietly.

The captain's eyes met hers. Their noses were mere inches apart. "His name is Fritz Baier."

"Fritz? I see." Mary Ann looked down at "Billy." "That's a nice name." *A funny sounding little name. Fizz! Pop! It suited "Billiy's" sprightly little kid face.*

On impulse, she placed her bound left hand on the sailor's arm. "Fritz?" She spoke softly. "It's me, Mary Ann, the American girl."

The sailor's eyes fluttered in response. *Had he recognized her voice?* "Shh, don't be afraid," she assured him. "I'm here beside you. Just relax. Relax. That's it, okay?" She rubbed his arm and noted the slow, shallow rise and fall of his slender chest. *He's dying!* She whispered to him, "Take it easy, dear Billy. God is with you."

Suddenly Fritz rose up on the bunk, scaring her half to death. His eyes flew open, and he stared hard at her, as if trying to relay a final message.

"You're getting ready to go?" She shivered in the intense blue light of his eyes. "It's okay. It's okay. You go when you're ready. God loves you!" Tears streamed down her face.

Then, relieved he'd been understood, little Fritz eased back on the captain's thin, gray pillow. His blue eyes remained locked on Mary Ann then slowly turned glassy, as he exhaled a long, relaxed sigh that trailed out, out, out.

God, take care of him! Take care of us all! Mary Ann begged in the wake of Fritz's quiet passing. Yet, she was not troubled by the sailor's death. Rather, she felt a deep, penetrating sense of knowledge and mystery to be a witness to this poignant moment when the soul departs the body. She truly believed that the ultimate goal of living was this final moment, when a soul passes beyond the pain and sadness and confines of human existence.

Through a haze of tears, Mary Ann observed the lifeless face of her little "Billy Baker" Fritz with the trace of blonde fuzz on the upper lip. What marvels he must be seeing as he steps into God's eternal Presence! Now, all questions would be answered for him, all mysteries revealed, all the suffering of earthly life be but a fast-fading memory. Mary Ann wondered that they all must envy Fritz his new freedom. He was out of the misery of war for all time, and like the knights of old, had entered the sacred halls of Valhalla, something she had learned - but did not quite understand until now - in her senior English literature class.

No, she was not afraid to be sitting on the edge of the bunk, on the sharp division between life and death, beside a dead German sailor, whose blank eyes stared at her from another realm. Instead, she felt humbled, privileged to be present at the side of a warrior who died in battle. That she could be present to comfort all warriors who fell, or would ever fall, on the world's battlefields! That they might find her there beside them, to comfort them and see them off on their eternal journeys. Yes, this was her call from God! This was what she wanted to do!

A hand brushed her shoulder. Mary Ann looked up to see the medic, who pressed close to view Fritz. "He just died," she murmured.

"Mmm," the medic draped his large hand over Fritz's forehead and drew it down gently, closing the sailor's lifeless, staring eyes. Then he backed into the passage at a respectful distance among a crowd of on-lookers. Mary Ann was surprised to see so many men in the passage looking in at her as she held vigilance over their fellow crewman. *Where had they come from?*

Then, from forward by the Wardroom, the tall, grim-faced first watch officer thrust his way through the crowd. His stony eyes jumped to Mary Ann and his face reddened with a fury she had never seen. He pushed toward her, bumping a smaller man out of the way.

"Come out of there at once!" He bellowed.

CHAPTER 36

Mary Ann couldn't move fast enough for the first watch officer, who swooped in on her like a bird of prey. Helpless, in shock from Fritz's passing and wedged tight by the desk, she struggled to extricate herself from the trap.

"I said, move, you stupid American female!" He yanked her up by the shoulder of her fatigues and flung her into the crowd of gawking crewmen, who scattered like beaten dogs. No one attempted to interfere, as the officer pursued her again and again through the corridor, "You understand me, you move when I say! You move when I say!" shoving at her and driving her into the corner by the control room hatch.

Then, satisfied, the officer strode away and confronted the medic, their German voices rising in angry exchanges. Several men drifted toward the Wardroom doorway, their heads lowered, not wanting to further witness the wretched scene. Only radioman Konrad remained, his brilliant hawk's eyes staring down at nothing under black thundercloud brows.

Huddled in humiliation and defeat Mary Ann glimpsed her little "Billy" stretched in death on the bunk in her prison compartment. He looked pitifully forlorn, a victim, too, even in death, of that insufferable officer. At once, a great, raging tide of despair overwhelmed

Mary Ann, driving out the last thread of hope she had clung to in this nightmare journey. *A sailor, dead. Loved ones, gone. Herself, a twig in the wreckage on treacherous seas. Mama, Daddy, Jack, Ed, Tommy, wee Maggie, Aunt Susie, Uncle Frank, Grandma Cassidy – gone, gone, gone forever!* She doubled over from the force of many well-placed emotional punches to the stomach and wept until it seemed her tears would flood the narrow passage and sweep unhindered into every compartment, dashing everything and everyone into a mangled pulp.

Then through the storm of her tears, Mary Ann saw the captain's white cap emerge from the round hatch. *Where'd he been? Why hadn't he been here before when she needed him?* The captain looked up at her, surprised to see her crying in the corner. "Ah, so, the young Fritz Baier is dead?" He inquired, as he glanced into his former quarters.

Mary Ann shook her head in the affirmative, but determined not to say a word about what had transpired between his first watch officer and her. "Yes, sir," she said quietly.

The captain stood close to her side. Mary Ann felt his nearness like a protective wall. He was a good man, a decent enough man. She saw exhaustion and sorrow sketched on his raw, lined face. Dampness from the open bridge, and chill and battle smoke clung to his leather presence. Again, Mary Ann's heart opened in pity for this vulnerable man, who shouldered the responsibility of a war ship and the men under his command. *That he must fight in this war and see men fall!*

In a timid show of sympathy, Mary Ann lay her hand lightly on the captain's leather arm. "I'm sorry about your sailor, sir," she said.

At once, the captain laid his rough hand over hers. For an awkward moment he patted her hand sporadically, as if testing her reaction, and then gripped her hand tighter, holding to the only secure anchor in his tragic world. The bond was sealed.

"What is this, Captain Lieutenant?" A voice exploded in English. "You accept the false sympathy of the enemy prisoner and let her by our comrade, Captain Lieutenant!"

The captain calmly stepped in front of Mary Ann and confronted his first watch officer. "So, yet you question what I do in this situation, *Herr IWO?* Do you not see what happens here?"

"I see only what I detest! It was, after all, her blasted Allied guns which killed this man!" The first watch officer pointed an accusing finger at Mary Ann. "You and the 'Ami' dog show much feeling for yourselves! I resent this!"

Mary Ann pulled back from the captain. *It was not this way at all! Surely she had not acted wrongly in sharing mutual grief? Yet, oh, God, it couldn't be denied that she felt growing attraction for the captain and his way of thinking and acting. And now, this was apparent to the other men? It was making the captain look bad! And it was all her fault!*

Like a cobra about to strike, the first watch officer glared down on the shorter captain. *Did he intend to harm the captain?* It horrified Mary Ann to see the captain swallowing that officer's verbal abuse, and she wondered, in a spasm of doubt, if the captain actually feared his towering first watch officer. Yet, a man, no matter his rank, should never humiliate his captain or question his actions. Or was this permissible under certain circumstances?

But, no, the captain was speaking, and he spoke in English, for her sake, Mary Ann knew, definitely reasserting his command: "I intend, *Herr IWO,* that the young lady be part of this with all of us!" He seized Mary Ann's arm and swung her before the first watch officer. "Let her know it all, *Herr EWO!* Let her know that we, too, are good men, who do our duty with honor!" The captain's thin lips curled back over his small, square, clenched teeth. "Let her see that we fight and bleed and die the same as her own people! Let her show this sorrow for us!" He gripped her arm. "Let her remember us in a good way to say to her people in the United States that we are NOT godless 'Nazi' hordes, but men fighting for our lives and our people. I think now she knows this, yes?" The captain laid his hand firmly on her shoulder. Mary Ann shrunk back in fear. The glowering f irst watch officer's cold stare registered his lack of faith in his captain's purpose. Unbounded hatred coiled like poison gas through the passage.

"Tonight, Marianne, you do right here! We are most grateful for this!" The captain's dark eyes locked on her. "And later, you will be with us for the burial of our young comrade!"

With a final, scathing look at his first watch officer the captain entered the round control room hatch. Mary Ann watched him step through the hole, his left leg leading, his shoulders hunched forward, then faced the first watch officer. But he had already turned away and was assisting the medic in opening out a length of white cloth. *The burial shroud.*

CHAPTER 37

Mary Ann looked on in sorrow as the medic and Radioman Konrad carried the shrouded body of Fritz "Billy" Baier from CQ into the passage. Already, blood was soaking through the shroud. There was no stopping it, or any reason to try. Squeezing against the bulkhead, Mary Ann let the men pass with their sad burden. She watched Konrad step slowly backward into the control room hatch and lead Fritz's body through the hole, while the medic gave support. It was a pitiful transfer, for the men bumped Fritz several times against the sides of the metal tube.

Two sailors promptly arrived from forward in the boat and solemnly entered the captain's nook, where they proceeded to strip the leather mattress of the bloody sheet and blanket, before hurrying away. With a jolt, Mary Ann realized that her coat with Bobby Lawson's letter had been swept into the bundle. *So, that was it. The end of another connection.*

Then she noticed a silver glint beneath the head of the bare mattress. *Her notebook? Thank goodness, no one had taken it!* Mary Ann crept into her prison compartment and pulled the notebook from under the thin mattress. Hugging the notebook to her breast, she sat cautiously on the edge of the bunk where her poor "Billy" had died, and pondered the disturbing events of the past hour. *What feeble words could she draw upon to describe the tragic drama? To think that, at this moment, such wartime tragedies were playing out in a million places around the world, on land, in the air, and on the vast sea beyond the boat's hull. She must write that! Get it down, while she could,* and she opened her notebook to begin.

Someone stood beside her bunk. She saw gray pants legs and large thick-soled shoes from the corner of her eye. *The first watch officer!* She jerked up fast, alarmed, and met the luminous hawks' eyes of Radioman Konrad. "Oh, hello!" She blurted in relief.

"Please, to come at once, *Fraeulein* Connor!" Konrad ordered in his thunderclap voice and extended a long, slender hand to her.

Mary Ann retreated. "Why? Where are we going?"

"You see. Come, please." Konrad's blue eyes encouraged. Then he pointed to her filthy stocking feet dangling on the deck. "Shoe!" He demanded.

"What? Oh, yeah," Mary Ann peered over the side of the bunk, "they're under there somewhere, I think." And she promptly slid to her hands and knees on the deck by Konrad's big shoes. He stepped back with a soft laugh, as she squinted into the dark, dusty space under the bunk for her shoes. There they were, back in the far corner. She had to shimmy part way on her stomach to grab them. "It's a tight squeeze under here," she called up to Konrad, then backed out of the space and got to her feet.

"Well, here they are." She held out her brown and white saddle shoes for Konrad to see. He was watching her with a quizzical expression. *Was she nuts?* Then he smiled at her with his beautiful white teeth and deep dimples that contrasted sharply with his short, black goatee and stormy brows. "Ah, *ja, ja. Schue!*" He boomed like a drum.

Feeling warm and lighthearted by his friendly presence, Mary Ann sat on the bunk and slipped on her shoes. Of course, she sensed Konrad's brilliant hawk's eyes following her every move. He seemed most amused by her bandaged left pinky finger, as she struggled to tie her gray laces. "Okay, I'm ready," she looked up with a smile.

Once again, Konrad offered his slender hand. "Come, *Fraeulein!*" And this time Mary Ann accepted his hand, then just as quickly pulled her hand away. "Ooops, wait, I forgot something." She snatched up her note book from the desktop and shoved it under the mattress. "There, now I'm ready." She turned to Konrad and willingly took his hand.

He directed her out of CQ toward the round control room hatch, where she bent into the tube, pressing her hands against the metal sides for balance in the swaying boat. Right foot leading, Mary Ann pulled herself from the yawning hatch into the red-dimmed control room before a gaggle of men on duty. They stared at her from the maze of controls and machinery. Slow smiles widened with recognition. *There she was, the American girl!*

A short, stocky crewman came huffing around a large metal box, like a Lionel electric train racing beneath a Christmas tree. His barrel chest puffed with authority, he delivered a heap of rubber garments at Mary Ann's feet. Just flung them there amidst snickers of amusement from the control room gang. But Mary Ann determined to remain unruffled, not let those fellows get her goat. Employ a bit of humor herself, if she must.

"I guess these are for me?" She sighed, then calmly stooped to retrieve the ample, wool lined rubber coat and a heavy duty pair of foul weather pants with yellow elastic suspenders. "Wow, this stuff weighs a ton!" She gasped, as she attempted to lift them into her arms.

The short stocky fellow waited a few steps away, his mouth turned down in a gruff up-side-down U. He was pointing to the long low bench before those two large steering wheels at the left side of the room, so Mary Ann dutifully hauled her burden over the iron floor plates to the designated spot. Naturally, no man there offered to help her with her load. That short fellow merely followed after her - she glimpsed him, jumping up and down like a monkey, making eyes at her back, much to the entertainment of his buddies - and directed her to be seated.

"Alright, alright, enough poking fun at me," Mary Ann grumbled to herself, as she sat on the narrow bench and began to separate the rubber pants from the bulky coat. Setting the coat aside, she ruffed out the pants, surprised at how long the legs were. *Surely, she would trip over the cuffs, like a fool, and kill herself!* She shoved her right foot into the right leg opening, but her flat-soled saddle shoe got caught in the fleecy yellow lining. Leaning back slightly to pull her foot out of the woolly lining - WA-UMP! - down she went, slamming her head on an iron steering wheel. The control room jerked up in a flash of white stars, and Mary Ann found herself wedged under the wheel, folded nearly in half between the bench and a wall panel.

"Help!" She squeaked.

Men jumped from the maze of controls, like racers coming off the starting block. They flew to Mary Ann, grabbed her arms roughly and lifted her onto the bench. "Ooww, ooo, my back!" She grimaced with pain and sat gasping for breath, her head whirling in confusion. *Why, that short stocky fellow over there seemed on the verge of a heart attack!* Mary Ann wondered that she had scared him half to death with her fall. Suddenly, she saw Daddy's face in her mind. How he always looked when something out of the ordinary happened, like the day Aunt Susie found a dead mouse in the water pan under the icebox. Daddy's mischievous blue eyes opened wide with surprise and his mouth pursed in with that long, low whistle of his.

"Woooeee!" Mary Ann let out a whistle just now. Pictured herself looking like Daddy. Saw the German sailors regarding her with cautious looks ranging between shock and delight. Mary Ann waved her hand to assure them. "I'm alright, fellas. I'm alright."

Yet, the looks on those sailors' faces: *Is this American girl coming apart at the seams?* Mary Ann burst out laughing. The laughter came from deep in her belly, shaking her frame in convulsive waves, as tears coursed down her cheeks. *What a release! It was grand!* And if she dared look up at those silly German sailors, the cycle started all over again.

"Garlic's bloomin'!" She cried with glee, using a phrase Mama used when family hijinks got out of hand. Jack and Eddie might be rolling on the parlor floor, snorting and weeping with merriment, over some monkey business they had pulled, especially on the poor cat. It went round and round like this at home. Jokes and pranks. *Never a serious moment. Not even at funerals—*

"Come, come, Marianne, there is no more time to waste!" The captain's stern voice snapped Mary Ann to her senses. She looked around. Where was the captain?

CHAPTER 38

Mary Ann spotted the captain's white hat in the red dimness behind the control room ladder, but did not recognize the man. His eyes were encased in large, black goggles. "Dear Jesus!" Mary Ann whispered in horror. The captain resembled the Japanese pilots she had seen in news reels about Pearl Harbor at the Nassau Movie House! *Their maniacal slanted eyes behind black goggles, those fearsome pilots had flown right at her on the screen!*

"Sir?" she choked.

The captain was staring at her with his big bug eyes. "It is very cold topside, Marianne," he bellowed. "You will be glad you wear those heavy clothings."

"Yes, sir."

Someone gripped her shoulder. She looked up, shaken, into the stone face of the first watch officer. "Get dressed at once," he ordered. Wonder of wonders, a brief smile cracked his face. *So, he, too, had found her amusing?*

"Yes, sir," Mary Ann replied quietly and bent to retrieve the oily rubber pants which lay askew on the iron deck. The first watch officer assisted her to dress in his own austere way, rushing her with grumbled German expletives to get her shoes into those pants legs, at once! and bringing her to her feet, while she struggled to adjust the yellow suspenders over her shoulders.

The short, barrel-chested fellow promptly handed up the coat to the first watch officer, who held the coat open for Mary Ann to put on. "Thanks," she mumbled, carefully sliding her left hand with the bandaged pinky finger into the left sleeve, while shoving her right arm into the right sleeve. She staggered a few steps under the weight of the heavy gear, her arms out for balance. "Ooo, boy!" Laughter rippled through the control room.

"Come, Marianne, there is no time to waste!" The captain called impatiently.

"Yes, sir." Mary Ann stumbled drunkenly toward the base of the control room ladder, where the captain waited in those menacing goggles. Suddenly the room went dark! She reached up blindly to discover someone had pulled a wool hat over her head. And she just knew who that someone was! Peeling back the edge of the hat, she turned to see the short stocky imp beaming at her. "Thanks a lot," she said, then reasoned that she'd asked for it. What with her clowning around, she was fair game for these men.

"Come, come! You are ready to climb up, Marianne?" The captain's goggled eyes flashed in the dim lighting. "First, my watch officer goes up, then you, and finally, I come after."

"Okay, " Mary Ann agreed. She would go up as requested. She didn't know why she was going up, and she didn't dare ask. Certainly, not a rescue? She knew better than to expect that. Yet, anything to get out of this rotten hell-hole!

With practiced ease, the stone-faced first watch officer nimbly mounted the narrow steel rungs of the control room ladder. Mary Ann watched his thick-soled shoes recede into the hooded tunnel extension, then she stepped to the base of the ladder and placed her hands on the vertical steel bars. *Dear Lord, how would she do this with a broken finger?* Looking far up the ladder, she observed the first watch officer climbing higher, higher. She thought he might wait to help her climb, but, no, he was gone far overhead into the night.

Mary Ann squinted. *What were those little lights shining in the black circle above?* She couldn't imagine what they might be. *Lights from a submarine control panel? No, wait - stars? Yes, they were stars!* She placed her left foot on the bottom rung of the ladder, determined to reach those stars, but the captain pulled her aside rudely.

"You can hold on good with this?" He held her bandaged left hand in her face.

"Well, yes, I'll hang on as best I can, sir." She was stunned by the captain's rough handling. *Was he out to prove how tough he was on her in front of his men?* Then he released her hand and nudged her to begin the climb. "I believe this of you," he mumbled.

Again, Mary Ann stepped onto the bottom rung. *She would not be afraid of the height,* she told herself. *No, not like that first night she came down into the boat.* Yet, her heavy rubber-clad body kept swinging right, as she toiled through the metal tunnel extension. Because of her useless pinky finger - what a surprise to discover how important a pinky finger is for gripping things! - she quickly found it helpful to wrap her left arm through each rung of the ladder as she hauled herself upward, a slow step at a time.

The captain came closely behind her, squeezing against the backs of her legs. *What was he doing?* His arms encircled her trembling legs. "You are fine, Marianne?" he bellowed up the tunnel.

"So far, I'm okay," she called back, very glad the captain was under her for support, *for Heaven knows, this was quite a risky thing she was doing!*

A big, lumbering rubber ball, Mary Ann planted both feet solidly on each rung, then hooked her left arm over each successive rung before moving onto the next step. Half-way to the star-lit goal, she emerged into the cavernous conning tower. A man squatted before a wall of white dials, his hand resting loosely on a control. He glanced up at Mary Ann, as she entered the tower. *Why, if it wasn't the apple faced "Clark Gable," that love-sick sailor she had encountered the first night she'd come down into the boat! Only he looked more pale and exhausted than when she first saw him.*

"Hi, how are you?" Mary Ann readily greeted the sailor. "See? I'm doing pretty good this time, aren't I? No more hollering!"

"Clark Gable" started to say something, but Mary Ann was already on her way up the tower ladder, with the captain's prodding, of course - no time to stop and gab!

She smelled the first wafts of cold, fresh, sea air. These drew her like a starving waif to a table of home-made bread. Mary Ann struggled up the last three rungs, leaving the captain down below. Her head popped from the open deck hatch into pitch darkness and biting cold air, which caught her like a slap in the face. *Oh, God, oh, God, oh, God!* she fumbled along the thick metal lip of the hatch for a place to climb out. Faint nausea skimmed her stomach. *Don't get sick! Please, not now! Not with the captain climbing under me!* Mary Ann slumped over the bumpy metal hatch lid and collapsed on the deck.

"Pull her up, *EVO!*" She heard the captain's blunt call above the roar of wind and waves.

The stout reply seemed to come from a great distance: "She's fainted, *Herr Kaleu!*"

Deep in fading consciousness, Mary Ann had to smile. *Just listen to those Germans,* she mused. As always, she was causing them trouble. And yet, she knew that they liked it somehow. They never knew what to expect from her.

Hands slipped under her armpits, and Mary Ann was hauled to her feet. She was certain she was laughing aloud in the cold wind. *This was great, great, great!* Her nausea had subsided, and she made out the captain's white cap rising in the darkness near her elbow.

"The fresh air has - keh, keh, keh! - stunned her, *EVO.*" He was coughing. "She breathes U-boat fumes for too long!"

"Ha, yes!" Came a jovial bark from the First Watch Officer.

The captain held her arm, "You are fine, Marianne?"

"Yes, much better," she looked airily off to sea.

Then she was led to the right near the shoulder-high wall to the rear of the tower walkway and accidentally bumped a shadow sailor on duty. He quickly squeezed aside to let her pass, then raised binoculars to his featureless face.

Immediately Mary Ann was struck by this ages-old image of a sailor's stoic vigilance of sea and sky. The image spoke to her, thrilling her with wonder and delight, and bringing tears to her eyes. *To think, she was actually witnessing this sea-going drama! She was actually living it!* She felt the wondrous stirrings of a miracle in progress that she herself belonged at sea sailing off to marvelous new lands.

CHAPTER 39

"Now, Marianne," the captain shoved near Mary Ann and pointed to the sky, "there are the stars you wished to see!"

Turning her head around and back Mary Ann beheld a glittering white band arched from one end of the horizon to the other. The illustrious Milky Way! Millions of stars hung in relief against the black velvet night, appearing like the twinkling lights of Manhattan along the East River. Her mouth fell open, tears started. "Dear God!" she whispered.

The captain pressed closer, claiming her. "You are seeing a night which every sailor loves, yes?"

"Oh my, yes!" Mary Ann held with bare hands to the icy metal edge of the tower wall. The sea wind whipped her left cheek, blowing loose hair wisps into her eyes and mouth, which she quickly wiped away. But she viewed everything quite well. The broad, heaving, black ocean stretched to the ends of the world, where stars dipped down to kiss the sea surface. And she, Mary Ann Connor, stood in the midst of this vastness, as if standing below the great vaulted ceiling of St. Patrick's Cathedral!

The sudden urge to sing out overwhelmed Mary Ann. She would join the grand Heavenly choir, shout triumphant "Alleluias" to the Lord. Indeed, she wanted to fly up to those sparkling light-gems and tumble down the brilliant aisles of Heaven into Almighty God's lap!

That she could leap up and gather whole armloads of those glowing orbs, cup them lovingly in her hands and bring them down, like strings of electric Christmas lights, to decorate the dark world!

The captain's voice sounded a deep organ note in the vast night. "You are here with all of us, Marianne. You are most special to my men and to me." He spoke in a windy, wooing tone near her left ear. His white cap, perched low on his forehead, moved against the starry background. She sensed his intentions all too well, felt the soft rush of butterflies in her stomach. *Was the captain attempting to court her? It was the perfect spot! The perfect opportunity!*

Mary Ann looked off quickly to the stern of the boat to avoid any sudden kiss, should it come, and glimpsed two narrow poles angled skyward above an assembly of large wheels. *The U-boat's guns!* she surmised, numb-struck by the reality of their menacing apparition. It seemed an abomination that such a beautiful, star-studded night must be marred by man's war-like presence. Could no one sail anywhere in peace on their tiny life's courses? Must there always be contention, that terrible sense of doom, and people scurrying about, like ants on a sidewalk, going nowhere fast in the larger scheme of events? Then - squish! The end! Snuffed out. Sunk in the depths of anger, greed, and hatred.

Mary Ann's heart ached with a strange, new longing. *If only people looked Heavenward!* She swung her eyes across the bright firmament overhead. *There it is - our true destiny! Our home port! Can't we put aside all squabbling and self-righteousness, and follow the Right Course by those stars?*

It struck her - she must write this down. Such momentous thoughts must be entered in her little notebook as soon as she got down in the boat. She must never forget how she felt standing here on the tower of this enemy submarine as it sailed under Heaven!

Looking off beyond the silent guns, Mary Ann glimpsed the faint white wake veil, like a bride's wedding train, trailing behind the U-boat. In the gloom the outline of a thick cable and a round, flat connector materialized near the edge of the tower below her chin. Then she noticed the shadows of several crewmen gathering on the rear platform. *How did they get there?* She wondered. Clipped conversation came above the brisk sweep of waves along the U-boat's flank.

Indeed, this was a wondrous journey! Her own personal moving classroom to learn the living experiences of men at war and—

A sharp tug on her arm brought her around to face the captain. *The kiss must come now!* "Marianne," he pronounced solemnly, "in some moments from now, we commend our Seaman Frederick Baier to the deep. I bring you here that you must share in this final tribute to him."

Oh, dear Lord, so this was why she was here! And she felt ashamed for thinking otherwise. "Sir," she replied in a quivering voice, "I'm honored to be here for Fritz, thank you for allowing me to be here."

More guilt stabbed her heart. How dare she admit to being "honored to be here" when her own Allied servicemen were dying out there, the tragic victims of vessels such as this one on which she sailed. *Good God, what was she thinking?* Mary Ann struggled to right herself in this ever-careening balance of emotions. Yes, she mourned for this dead German sailor named Fritz "Billy," but her heart cried for her own, too. Yes, for the entire world! There should be no "this" side or "that" side, she concluded stubbornly. Not after what she was learning on this journey.

The captain gently squeezed her arm - a lover's gentleness? - through the layers of her heavy coat and gray fatigues. "Good, Marianne, now I must go on to the lower deck to begin the sea burial for Seaman Baier. You will remain up here with Dietrich Heubeck, my second watch officer, who has charge of the watch. If things change up here, then you must be prepared to go quickly into the boat."

"Yes, sir." Mary Ann couldn't imagine that anything could disturb such a beautiful night, let alone a funeral service. Certainly she knew full well the horror of a sudden attack, but could something like that happen now? No, not with God so close to her under His bright Heaven! Yet, thankfully, blessedly, it never occurred to Mary Ann how she might possibly get down into the boat fast enough, with her broken finger and inexperience, should an attack come. She could not imagine that she would be left topside to drown or explode in a million pieces under the impact of an Allied bomb should the boat go into an emergency dive. She could not possibly imagine that the captain had, in spite of his growing fondness for her, already decided to sacrifice her to save his boat and men, and that this was the risk he was running to bring her topside for Fritz's burial service.

Mary Ann felt the captain pressing behind her in the narrow bridge walkway. Suddenly he gripped both her shoulders with his hands and his mouth came close to her ear. His right arm stretched over her right shoulder, he pointed a shadow finger to the dark horizon.

"Over there, Marianne, forty kilometer to the west is the coast of North Carolina in the United States."

Mary Ann nearly collapsed. "It is?" The stars blurred to smeary streaks with her tears. *Had this U-boat sailed so far from New York? Over there, over the edge of the world, far beyond reach and fading fast, was her country, her home, her family. . . .*

The captain was talking. "Our Seamn Baier will be buried in the United States coastal waters far from his home in Tuetsing. Maybe, one day, Marianne, you return to your home in Greenpoint, Brooklyn, you think of Fritz Baier and the many young sailors who die at sea in this war, yes?"

Mary Ann shivered. "I will, sir. I already am thinking of them." It stunned her to think the captain believed she might ever make it home!

He clutched her shoulders, murmured against her cheek. "After the burial ceremony I return here to you." Mary Ann felt his cold lips on her skin. *A kiss! Oh, please, no!* Then the captain was gone, a dark spirit slipping to the rear platform, his white commander's cap a faint indicator of his passage through his shadow-men.

CHAPTER 40

Another man pushed into the spot vacated by the captain. Mary Ann made out the vague outline of a bearded face, knew by the profile it was the second watch officer who stood at her left side. She sensed that he, too, was finding this the perfect opportunity to have a measure of close physical contact with her. *Should these men be showing her such overt attention? Should she even allow it?* She decided to remain calm, not say anything.

The movement of ghostly men down on the main deck caught her attention. "Billy's" burial service was about to begin. Mary Ann got up on tip-toes to get a better view, when someone pushed her from behind, nearly knocking her to the deck. The second watch officer grabbed her arm and propelled her from the narrow confine of the bridge to the open rear platform, where icy wind and spray caught her in a fresh fury, whipping her about like a flag on a pole. Her feet slid about on the wet deck, and she feared being blown off the platform. "Help!"

But the second watch officer had Mary Ann well in tow. His arms boldly encircled her waist, his chin pressed into her right shoulder, and his whiskers brushed her cheek. *Dear God, what was this? A lover's embrace?* The man held her like Ashley Wilkes held to Scarlett O'Hara in the barn scene in "Gone with the Wind"! A haze of emotions clouded Mary Ann's thoughts, and she strained not to cry out with ecstasy to be held so strongly by this handsome German officer. *Yet, how could this possibly be happening to her, the ole wallflower who could never get a date back home? It must be a dream!* Droplets of sea spray kissed her cheeks and trickled down her chin into her collar. She treasured this time beneath the stars, knew she would remember it for the rest of her life. And this, she recorded candidly, ardently for Steve Anderson, the naval historian, at her retirement home in Crestwood, for the moment, forgetting the main focus of her account. "Oh, she was in love, so in love, that long-ago night!" she sighed and went on with her sea tale.

Deep male voices carried on the wind. The voices rolled in a monotone chant above the continual lashing of the sea and the puttering of the U-boat's diesel engines under the tower housing. Mary Ann distinguished the captain's nasal voice intoning a verse on the main deck below. At intervals, his men, who clustered around her in the night, answered their captain. The second watch officer's fervent, melodic German played in her ear.

Chills of wonder raced through Mary Ann. She rode the waves of the present, relishing the fact that she was treated so tenderly by these enemy warriors. That they thought well of her, protected her, and treated her like a precious gem. Indeed, for the first time in her life, Mary Ann felt truly beautiful, attractive, desired!

From the protective embrace of Second Watch Officer Dietrich Heubeck, Mary Ann watched the drama of a live sea burial unfold. Shadow men on the rear deck lifted a dim-white shroud toward the edge of the deck. *Fritz's body!* Mary Ann heard the distinct splash, as his body slipped into the frothy wake at the side of the boat. For a second, she thought she saw the long white shroud flip away in the boat's turbulent wake. Or was it the flash of churning water kicked up by the U-boat's propellers?

The horrible awareness of Fritz sinking alone into the dark, cold sea depths, while this crowded boat of life sailed on without him, came like a jolt to Mary Ann. She imagined Fritz's eyes opening wide in terror to realize where he was.

Then, out of the rush of seawater closing over Fritz's grave rose the voices of many men singing in crude harmony. The melancholy chorus progressed like ocean swells, rolling up from the main deck to the platform, where Mary Ann stood in Dietrich Heubeck's protective arms. As the wave swirled past the couple and cascaded into the narrow horse-shoe bridge behind them, Heubeck took up the mournful melody, heaving with emotion and rolling his "r's" emphatically:

"Ich hatt einen Kameraden. . . ."

Mesmerized, Mary Ann listened to the impassioned hymn. She understood the word: *Kameraden.* "Comrade." This was the loss of a comrade, a friend, a brother. A shipmate! How many friends and brothers and shipmates were dying this night?

Mary Ann grieved in the midst of that star-lit funeral chorus, in the arms of the second watch officer, tears streaming down her icy cheeks. Then gazing up at the silent night sky, she imagined each star to be the little lantern of a fallen warrior going home to God. Those myriad stars, yes, each one a living soul of ones who had per- ished from the ravages of wars, human cruelty, disease, poverty. How she wanted for this to be so!

The second watch officer had mumbled something in her ear? She inclined her head to listen. "What did you say, sir?" she asked.

"I am loving you." Was it the wind speaking to her? Or, had she heard correctly?

Turning her toward the bridge, the second watch officer guided Mary Ann into the secure, narrow walkway, out of the open wind and spray, pushing forward among shadows in the encompassing darkness. Then he was gone. Alone once again beneath the star- spangled heavens, Mary Ann awaited the captain, as he had directed her to do before the burial service.

CHAPTER 41

Yet, Mary Ann realized she was not alone. She felt surrounded by love. Several seamen scrunched against her, jarring her thoughts momentarily, as they streamed forward in the narrow bridge horseshoe toward the deck hatch. Mary Ann felt new hope in a way she thought no one else might ever understand. Perhaps it was the brilliant beauty of that starry night sky, or the vast stretch of eternal ocean, or the poignant occasion of the burial at sea, but for the first time since coming aboard the U-boat, almost a week ago, she believed she would survive this journey. Yes, she would live to go home to Mama and Daddy, her wee Maggie, and Jack and Eddie, and finish her nursing classes, and see her friends again. And not only that, she would return home with new power, born of spiritual growth and confidence. How she felt this deep in her soul!

For Mary Ann envisioned, as she waited on the open windy bridge of the German U-boat, which was moving her swiftly southeast toward an unknown fate, that she would live to tell this fantastic tale of sailing with the enemy. She would share this story with her future children and grandchildren. Already she could hear them begging, "Tell us more, Grandma! Tell us more!"

A ghost of wartime destruction, the captain duly arrived at her right side, distracting her from her lofty dreaming. "Marianne dear," his hand rested heavily on her shoulder, "it is now the time to take you below."

"What! Already? But, why, sir? Can't I stay up here just a little longer? It's too beautiful to go down!" Mary Ann implored him. *Surely, this could not be the end of her vision of the sea and sky?* How she loathed returning into the boat's rank interior and her cramped prison bunk!

"My dear," the captain urged in his wispy sing-song voice, "I am afraid it has been much too dangerous to keep you here so long. An attack must come any time!" He propelled her toward the front end of the bridge, past the nebulous outline of the sailor on watch. Then suddenly, the captain stopped her short, gripped her shoulders and murmured close to her ear. "Besides, Marianne, if we remain here longer under those stars, I must be tempted to kiss you."

"Captain!" Mary Ann's cry of shock burst in the night air.

"Ssst!" The captain silenced her angrily and shoved her toward the gaping red hole in the deck. "Be careful where you walk, Marianne!" he scowled.

Like the first night she had been brought aboard this enemy vessel, Mary Ann gazed down the hatch that lay near the iron wall. An open manhole cover on a New York City street, the hatchway led to a dank subterranean world, to the sewer, to the bowels of Hell itself. An overwhelming miasma of noxious fuel oil fumes and men's body odors wafted up the hole, obliterating the fresh ocean air.

"Come now, Marianne!" the captain summoned her, as he slipped into the hatch to guide her descent.

With the help of several hands, Mary Ann stepped onto the top rung of the narrow steel ladder and began her slow, clumsy downward progress into the reeking, hammering Hell at sea. Down she went through the conning tower, past the apple-faced sailor at the helm, into the steel soup-can tunnel extension. When she emerged into the control room, she noted that the men on watch did not bother to observe her arrival. They were too busy operating this machine of war, which must proceed on its normal, unhindered, destructive course.

Already, her little "Billy Baker" Fritz Baier had been replaced as the boat's steward by another man, an older, dark-haired sailor, who struggled from the forward hatch into the control room - a lion through a circus hoop - balancing a large, enamel food container. As she watched, he crossed the control room among its array of valves and pipes, glanced at her, nodded shortly, and then tugged open a large metal hatch at the opposite end of the room. Immediately, the loud, clattering din of the U-boat's diesel engines roared into the room. "WHUMP!" the steel door slammed shut with pressurized suction.

The captain nudged Mary Ann, and she looked at him fast, stunned to see his raw, grizzled face so clearly in the control room lighting. He was not a very handsome man, but then, how must she appear to him, all haggard and mousy in these submarine conditions?

"You will undress at once!" The captain growled at her like she was one of his men. "Someone here will assist you." And off he strode through the control room toward the forward hatch, firing orders in German to all points of the compass, leaving Mary Ann alone and vulnerable before the slow, sly stares of his men on watch.

A tough-looking fellow, his scarred, angular face giving him the lean, hungry appearance of a street gang fighter, rushed for Mary Ann. Leering around at his mates to garner their attention, he turned his full gaze on Mary Ann, as she unbuttoned the big rubber coat. *Why, it was as if the cocky fellow expected her to be naked underneath!*

Mary Ann felt her blood boil. "Oh, yeah, what are you looking at?" She challenged the sailor, just like Jimmy Cagney taking on the "coppers" in his gangster movies. She wanted to smack that brawny sailor good and hard in the "kisser," the way he was acting just now, ogling her and making snide comments to his mates. Oh, she knew full well what he was saying by the reaction of the other men in the room. She thrust the heavy oilskin coat at him. "Here, take it!" But the sailor backed away as if she was poison, so Mary Ann merely let the coat drop to the deck at his feet. "I'm going to my bunk. Get out of my way, please."

The sailor jumped out of her way, all right, his hands up in mock supplication. "Oooo," he mooed, and let her pass.

Yeah, yeah, go ahead, laugh at me, you wise guys, Mary Ann seethed, as she dragged toward the forward hatch in her dumb rubber pants with its yellow suspenders. *What the heck, let those fellows laugh all they wanted. She was the loony buffoon around here.*

Angry, humiliated, disheartened, Mary Ann slid through the forward hatch on her hands and knees. After all the good will she'd shown these men by assisting their dying mate, after that beautiful occasion up on the bridge with the stars and the ocean in the background, after thinking all was well around this place, didn't this one goon in the control room have to go and ruin everything! *Why did some fellows have to act so dumb anyway?*

Yet, thank God, that rowdy fellow hadn't followed her. Mary Ann emerged from the hatch and tripped toward the familiar green curtain on the left side of the passage. *She certainly knew her way around this U-boat! Didn't have to be led by the hand anymore!*

As she entered her tiny refuge, Mary Ann sensed the eyes of the angel face radioman watching her across the corridor. She didn't bother greeting him. Just snapped the green curtain across the compartment door and flopped onto the empty bunk in her rubber pants. *No sheet or blanket yet? That figures.* Those men probably wouldn't even remember to get her a blanket. They'd just let her in here by herself to rot!

The impact of her situation hit Mary Ann like an icy snowball to the head. She couldn't take it any more! For all her trying to cooperate and be kind, Mary Ann was weary of fighting in ths man's world. Either those fellows loved her too much, or they taunted her and made her miserable. There was no happy medium. No plain, relaxed acceptance, but always this crazy grabbing, needling, push-ing, pulling, prodding, nasty laughter, as if she was some kind of dumb animal with no human feelings or mind of her own. *Well, just stay away from me! Leave me alone, for Pete's sake!* She brooded at that drawn dirty green curtain.

But what really wrenched her apart, at this point, believe it or not, was the loss of that beautiful night under the stars. How she longed to remain up there on the bridge forever! The marvelous sense of elation and hope she'd felt had been ruthlessly shattered after re-entering this Hell. Had her surety to survive been unreal, after all? Now she was back where she'd been, locked in loneliness, doubt, discouragement, and so angry that bitter bile singed her throat.

CHAPTER 42

Mary Ann discovered the problem later that afternoon on a routine, but ever-tortuous trip to the WC in the bow compartment. "Of all things, just what I need!" she despaired. Yet, she had no choice but to confide to the medic that she needed to speak to the captain, for only the captain could tell the medic in German, from English, what her problem was.

Hours later, or so it seemed to Mary Ann, the captain finally poked his head through the green curtain and glared at her. "Moeglich says you ask for me?" he grumbled.

A surge of panic shot through Mary Ann to see the captain's mottled face at the curtain. She had never summoned him before, but this was an emergency. Yet how could she explain her problem to him? He wouldn't understand anyway. A girl never told a man such private things!

With a swift move, the captain was in the compartment, closing the curtain securely behind him. The scowl on his face had magically vanished. "Did you remember what I say to you under the stars early today?" he asked softly.

"What?" Mary Ann couldn't imagine what he was talking about.

The captain waved his hand to brush away the comment. "I

see," he murmured, then glanced around the tiny compartment and rubbed the back of his neck. "Then it must be something else you want from me?"

It suddenly dawned on Mary Ann what the captain had been referring to. His desire to kiss her up on the bridge! *Why the nerve of the man to bring that up now!* Her wavering trust in him plunged further, and she regretted asking that he come.

Apparently sensing her discomfort, the captain stooped on his haunches with a soft sigh near the side of the bunk and toyed with the hem of the tattered blanket, which the medic had earlier exchanged for her discarded rubber pants. The captain gazed up at Mary Ann, eye to eye. "What is wrong, Marianne?" he coaxed gently. "You must tell it to me why you ask for me."

Mary Ann squirmed, her leg bouncing on the bunk in nervous agitation. "It's embarrassing, sir!" She bowed her face into her hands to escape his stare.

The captain's low voice encouraged. "You must not be afraid to tell me what it is you want, Marianne. I think so, now, we understand each other better, yes?"

Mary Ann whispered the shattering news: "My time is coming, sir."

"Your time is coming?" He echoed her words in his soft, singsong lilt. "What is this, your time is coming? You don't plan to die, do you, my dear?" He queried with contrived alarm.

Disgruntled, Mary Ann looked over at him, where he squatted beside the bunk. *Didn't he understand what she was trying to say?* "I have nothing to use, sir!" she wept at him. "Nothing for the - the problem, and it's only going to get worse!"

For some moments, the captain remained immobile at the side of the bunk, chewing on his lower lip and staring at the back of his hand, as if it could supply the answer he sought.

"I see, I see," he murmured at last, then looked up at her, "but you must not worry about this thing you have, Marianne, for we will help you, yes?"

She could barely meet the captain's gaze. He stooped so closely she could see every weathered crease around his eyes, every strand of stiff black beard jutting from his broad chin, the high, wide bone that formed the arch of his nose. "How can you help me?" she asked. "Men don't know about these things."

"Ah, but of course, my dear," he extended a daring finger and soothed her wrist. "I understand very much about women. You need much gentle care and reassurance. We have things here on this boat that can help you."

"Like what?" she wiped her bleary eyes with the cuff of her sleeve.

"Marianne, you experience a very normal womanly thing," the captain went on with gentle authority. "We must take good care of you all the time. You are our little sailor, after all."

I am? Mary Ann wondered at his term, "little sailor." *She was their "little sailor?"* She confessed: "Sir, I never had to tell a fellow something like this before. My mother always said it was something private we women should keep to ourselves and not discuss with anyone. Not even other women!" She hiccupped suddenly and glanced at the captain. "Pardon me!"

The captain playfully tipped back his cap, revealing an oily mat of dark, boyish curls. "Well, with all due respect to your mother, I am glad you say it to me. It will help you to know that my men understand very much about the functions of women. Many of my crew are married, Marianne. Some even are the fathers of little children."

Mary Ann's head spun. "They are?" She heartened considerably at this news. *Had she thought these Germans all monsters, incapable of marriage and having families?*

"However," the captain sighed, eyes downcast in feigned sadness, "I myself am not yet married. I have no luck yet in finding a good young woman to love me." His dark eyes came up to her.

Shocked at the captain's directness, Mary Ann struggled to sidestep the issue, which she sensed only too well, was aimed at her. "Oh, I'm sure you'll get married one day, sir." And she had to admit, "You are a very nice man."

"Thank you. You say this to me, I am very happy for it." He slowly arose, looking distant and distracted. "Now, Marianne, I arrange for you what you need. Moeglich will make the delivery shortly. Please worry no more about this thing you have." He flashed a tolerant smile at her and parted the curtain to exit.

Mary Ann looked after him, wishing he could stay just a little longer to talk to her.

The Requisitioning

"I need rags, men! Any spare rags!"

"What? Rags? We've got rags, all right! All the blasted rags you want!"

"Our good Moeglich wants lots of rags, and any extra bunting."

"What for? Someone get hurt, sir?"

"No, no, no one got hurt, Kuhnl. Come on, come on, let's have them!"

"What's Moeglich going to do with all these cussed rags? Sew up a new medical coat for himself?"

"Just get me some rags for me, will ya! Hurry it up!"

"I have the rags, *Herr Leitender Ingenier.*"

"No, not those crappy things, *Heitzer!* Don't you firemen have any nice big thick ones around here without any grease on them?"

"The *L.I.* has to be so particular about rags? What is this anyway? I mean, who cares?"

"I'll tell you what it is, Karlchen. It's the female. I bet two to one it's that thing women get each month."

"Oh, yeah? What's that, smart guy?"

"You dumbhead, don't you know? It's when they lay an egg and it comes out all oozy and bloody!"

- 2 0 2 -

"You crazy bonehead, Kuhnl, where'd you learn about women? From the goats on your father's farm?"

"Aah, shut up, I know all I need to know about women, and I learned it first hand from my neighbor, Frau Kinzler, back in school!"

"Oh, ho, ain't that interesting! You must tell me about your nice Frau Kinzler!"

CHAPTER 43

1156 hours, EST. U-115 approached the light at Frying Pan Buoy on her way south toward Charleston. The night sky was clear with a moderate breeze stirring the surrounding sea to a swift choppiness. A perfect night for hunting!

As if to confirm the mood of expectation, a ship hove into sight from the southeast, its darkened form visible against the lighter horizon.

"Target speed 11.5 knots!" Ketter called down the voice tube on the bridge. He observed the approaching ship and felt deeply the primal urge to destroy, demolish, kill. It was pure ecstasy to stalk his quarry. "Course 236 degrees true," he rumbled a litany of directives.

0014 hours. First Watch Officer Paul-Karl Ullmann, who directed the surface attack, fired one torpedo. Ketter's loins ached pleasantly with the thrust of the torpedo from the tube. "My Marianne, what sweet agony I endure over you," the searing thought skimmed his mind, as the torpedo sliced the black sea toward its unwitting target.

BOOM! The torpedo struck the port side of the ship and smashed open a fuel bunker before bursting internal bulkheads. The ship's engines stopped dead. In spite of erupting fires and apparent lethal damage, the ship, singled out by Dietrich Heubeck in the

Groener ship identification manual as SS Hurley, a 5,800 British gross registered ton freighter, refused to sink. It would take another torpedo to finish her off.

"Blasted stubborn barge!" Ketter scowled and swung to his first watch officer. "Launch number three, Pauli!"

"At once, *Herr Kaleu!*" Ullmann responded sharply.

The second eel left tube number three at 0030 hours. It plunged into the heart of the freighter, which continuously radioed a desperate plea, "SOS SSS" - submarine attack in progress! Yet, Ketter didn't respond to Schazi's report from below that a shore station had acknowledged the freighter's SOS. Rather, his turbulent thoughts ran a slightly different course, one that would prove dangerous in moments to come.

The call by Franz Wirth that another target approached on a reciprocal course made Ketter disdainful. "The fool! She comes right into the trap, though her master has to see the fire from the other ship!"

"You suppose the Americans don't yet know we declared war on them?" A seaman queried innocently at Ketter's side.

"Well, how about we drop you off on shore and you go inform them!" Another man fired back from the opposite side of the bridge.

The bridge guards laughed. Even the normally humorless Paul-Karl Ullmann joined in the merriment, "And while you are there, pick up several newspapers with Superman comics inside, and bring me back a barrel of southern fried chicken!"

Within minutes, Ketter had his boat in perfect position to launch another torpedo. *Too easy, too easy, this shooting gallery,* he mused to himself, as Ullmann sent out another eel at 0103 hours. The torpedo traveled a mere 800 meters before crashing into this latest victim. Ketter observed the sinking, while composing a rather philosophical mental note to himself to be jotted into the war log when he went below: "She was slipping away quietly. No fire. No explosions. No ear-piercing screech of metal. Ships die in their own personal ways. Like men."

"Alarrrmmm! Patrol craft on starboard beam!" Willi Feiler's cry jolted the watch.

Ketter whipped around, trained his glasses on a narrow shadow skipping toward them from the wall of darkness, a frothy white bone wake curling at her sharp bow. "Clear the bridge! Take her down! Dive! Dive! Dive!"

Frightened rabbits before a hawk's razor-sharp talons, the men leapt into the open bridge hatch. They slid down the steel ladder without touching their toes to the rungs and struck the control room deck - THUD! POW! CRASH! Then scrambling over each other like mad dogs before a stinging whip, they scampered to their battle stations and hunkered down for the expected bombardment. Off-duty crewmen dashed for the bow torpedo room to add weight to the dive, while the claxon clanged with spine tingling urgency in the background.

"*Herr Kaleu*, we only have forty meters depth beneath us! Not enough protection!" The chief engineer's face was gray.

"*Verdammt!*" Ketter squinted at the overhead. The ominous sound of the patrol craft's propellers loomed closer. The U-115 clawed for puny depth. This was the time to say quick prayers to the Man Upstairs.

Click - BOOM! The first depth-bomb exploded to starboard, pitching frail human bodies about the control room like rag dolls in a rolling barrel. Another blast - Click BOOM! The hydroplanes failed, and the U-boat went down by the stern - "on her knees" - in the soft sandy ocean bottom.

CHAPTER 44

Like pressurized air blasting from a ruptured pipe, Mary Ann's demented howls reverberated throughout the length of the blacked-out, sunken submarine. She lay crumpled on the linoleum deck, writhing in agony, deafened and in shock, having been hurled from her bunk by the force of the explosion. Within seconds a pair of strong arms caught her up and dragged her to a sitting position. Then a calloused hand slammed against her face, cutting off her screams, indeed, her very life's breath!

"Be stille!" A harsh whisper warned in her ear.

Mary Ann flailed against the unseen man, twisting her head this way and that, in the effort to catch her breath. The man was literally crushing her to death in his manic embrace! His hot mouth worked near her ear. "Silence! *Der Zerstroyer kommt!*"

More explosions battered the boat. Mary Ann felt her life ebbing away. The blood flow in her ears thumped thinner, slower. Blood vessels in her head seemed to pop from the pressure, her eyes bulged, ribs cracked. *Such a senseless way to die!*

Gradually, the man relaxed his strangle hold. *Oh, God, oh, God, oh, God!* Mary Ann gulped frantically for air and crumpled into the man's arms. She vaguely heard water dripping somewhere and a strange drumming sound far away in the distant darkness. Low whispers relayed messages back and forth, man to man, along the blacked-out passage.

The drumming was coming closer, closer. Click - BOOOM! BOOM! More hellish blasts jarred the boat with back-breaking force. Again, that rough hand clamped over her mouth. In a frenzy of madness, Mary Ann gnawed at that restraining hand, *tasted blood!*

"Nein!" The man snapped her head back angrily. The overhead lights flickered on, and Mary Ann stared into fierce blue eyes in the swirling haze. The man's face hovered only inches from her own. Second Watch Officer Dietrich Heubeck regarded her with a look that could kill.

"God, it's you!" Mary Ann latched onto his jacket. Wanted to turn, turn, turn to him forever, even if it meant dying in his arms!

Click - BOOM! Lights failed. Iron bulkheads twisted and moaned. Mary Ann's frantic screams joined a chorus of hoarse moans from desperate crewmen. Heubeck pressed her face to his chest to snuff out her cries. The patrol boat above was listening. How long would this nightmare persist? Another minute? Ten minutes? An hour? Two? It depended on the patrol boat above and what faint noises it could detect from its sunken quarry. The least sound from the U-boat - a wrench dropped in hasty repair, a sudden cry of fright, a careless footfall on an iron deck - the patrol boat would send down another deadly barrage in an attempt to split the boat's iron sides and send sea water roaring in to drown the enemy occupants - and one unknown innocent.

So, U-boat men must roll over and play dead. Mary Ann squirreled deeper into Heubeck's chest. She felt the cold presence of Death creeping, listening, probing for her. She hated that American patrol boat on the sea surface! The fact that the craft was one of her own, attempting to kill the Nazi German enemy no longer registered with her. *That patrol boat was out to destroy HER!* And if she had the chance, she would swim up and mangle that patrol craft to iron shavings with her bare hands, for the terror it was causing.

Silence reigned in the U-boat. Lights flickered on. *Had the attack ended? Did the crew of the American patrol boat assume they were crushed, mangled, drowned?* Mary Ann turned in Heubeck's arms and begged him with ogled eyes for assurance. *Were they safe?* Heubeck brought his unscathed hand to her cheek and began to caress her in slow, soothing, circling motions.

Paralyzed by this unexpected gentleness, Mary Ann searched Heubeck's pale, handsome face. "Is it over yet?" She whispered.

He barely uttered: "Shh, shh, *meine Liebste.*" Then touched his fingertip to her lips, and slowly came down to her, placing his cool, moist mouth over her mouth.

My God! For the first time in her life, Mary Ann tasted a man's kiss. Heubeck pressed his attack tenderly, testing her at first, then when she didn't offer resistance, he pursued the kiss with increasing urgency. Mary Ann found herself surrendering to the handsome officer with the crystal blue eyes. Exhausted, totally devoid of the ability to defend herself, badly in need of comfort and protection, she allowed the second watch officer greater liberty. In sudden rapture, she felt his hand drift down her neck and along her fatigues front to feel for her hidden breasts.

The sour taste of Heubeck's mouth heaved into her lungs, reminding her of the reality of the situation. Stinging, bitter, foul, the taste of his kiss was in keeping with the poor sanitation conditions on board, and her own disgusting body odors and filthy, unwashed hair under the wool hat, which she now wore continuously since her night on the bridge. Her oily face with red, unsightly pimples on her forehead and cheeks would surely discourage any man under ordinary circumstances. She couldn't imagine that Heubeck might find her attractive, and so chalked up these precious moments to complete male desperation on his part.

Gripping his jacket lapels, Mary Ann intended to curb the officer's eager pursuit, but it mindlessly signaled to him an awakening desire in her. At once the man was on top of her, his thick tongue plunging down her throat, choking her. *What, in God's Name, was he doing?* Mary Ann let out a gagged squeal of protest. "Stop it!"

The second watch officer leapt to his feet, as if burnt by Hell fire - and just in time. Two harried crewmen, one clutching a large wooden box of tools, bounded softly in cloth-soled slippers through the passage on their way to the control room and the diesel motor room beyond. Mary Ann dragged herself to the bulkhead and watched the men scoot into the round hatch and disappear, then glanced up at the second watch officer in confusion.

Heubeck whirled on her, his face a mask of anger. "To ze bunk now!" His scathing whisper singed her heart.

Mary Ann started to her feet. A low voice called quietly in the passage. The angel-face radioman with the merry laughter peered at Heubeck from the sound room doorway. *Good Lord, had he noticed the second watch officer mauling her?* Shamed and embarrassed that she had tolerated such behavior from the man, Mary Ann tip-toed to her bunk and crawled back in the corner beside the desk. She heard the Angel Face and Heubeck talking in hushed, earnest conversation. *Were they speaking of her? No, it didn't sound like it.* Besides, that wouldn't matter, at this point. The U-boat was down and damaged, possibly unable to resurface. *Dear God!* Mary Ann scanned the overhead - what if they could never get back up to the surface! How deep were they anyway? Oh, don't even think such things! And yet - what if? What if the American patrol boat took the German crew prisoner and rescued her in the process?

Now the patrol boat, if it was still up there on the surface, had become a possible source of salvation to Mary Ann. She felt her hopes rise and fall, like rolling ocean swells. What if the U-boat crew had to abandon ship because of irreparable damage? Certainly, she would put in a good word for these men, once they were rescued. Say how they treated her fairly, and even - she traced her lips with trembling fingers - loved her, in their own individual ways.

- 2 1 0 -

CHAPTER 45

Damage reports came in to the Old Man seated on the chart box in the control room:

"*Herr Kaleu*, depth gauge and rudder indicator came loose."

"Hmm."

"*Herr Kaleu*, this is Schwabl. Engine room telegraph is broken and the diesel air supply mast is leaking."

"We're taking in water through the hull valve of the WC. We have placed buckets, so that it is directed into the main bilge. Also, Mueller has a badly sprained wrist, possibly broken."

"There is a possible chlorine gas leak in one of the batteries aft! I'm trying to locate exact area!"

"Good God, get an immediate reading on the concentration! A spark anywhere could be enough to blow us to the next realm!"

"That's enough!"

"Take me to periscope depth, chief. I want to see where our 'little tormentor' has gotten to."

"Aye, *Herr Kaleu!*"

"First watch, stand by to surface."

"Aye, *Herr Kaleu!*"

"Up periscope! There she is! Blasted, she's seen the scope in the fire's reflection! Down scope! Dive! Dive! Brace for water bombs!"

"Screws coming on fast!"

????

"What, nothing? She has run out of fireworks?"

"No "Wabos," boys. No water bombs for us this time."

"Herr Kaleu, vessel turning for another pass!"

"Verdammt! That blasted little 'Ami' is a feisty devil!"

"She's having trouble finding us."

"Sound reports patrol craft moving away fast. Probably headed toward rescue of crew of first sinking ship."

"Good, Schatzi! Periscope depth, chief. Ah, yes, there she is, stopped by the side. Quite risky with us in the area. Now, chief, surface! Let's get the blazes out of here, while our luck holds!"

CHAPTER 46

<table>
<tr><td>20 Marz 1942 Freitag</td><td>Friday, March 20, 1942</td></tr>
<tr><td>1115 Uhr CET</td><td>Two ships sunk. Total 15,000 GRT. One ship damaged, seen last to be</td></tr>
<tr><td>. . . . KURS HEIMAT!</td><td>sinking. TORPEDOES EXPENDED. RETURN TO BASE!</td></tr>
</table>

CHAPTER 47

Signal from Admiral Karl Doenitz to U-115:
   "An Ketter. Gut gemacht. Befehlshaber." (To Ketter. Well done. Commander-in-Chief Submarines)

The Merry Chorus

"Look, the Old Man has won the award!"

"He has earned it well, men!"

"One hundred thousand tons of enemy shipping sunk so far!"

"For a long time, he's had that blamed "itchy neck." He wants too much too soon. You've seen how he gets, boys. I do not like this in him. He's not so cool and reserved like the first commander I served under."

"We work and work our butts for him!"

"But now we go home, Shaub! We look forward to this! We've done well, after all, and have a successful boat!"

"Yes, and again we will be made to read on the three-week's passage to port!"

"The Old Man is a school master, having us read books and report on them. Then he forces us to join these blasted discussion groups, besides everything else we have to do."

"He keeps us busy, all right. What with submarine qualifications work, cleaning the boat, and the constant crash dives to keep us on our toes. He's a merciless slave driver!"

"I'd like some spare time to relax and sleep and not think of anything at all—"

"But women and great sex!"

"Ah, look at this notice, boys. There is a celebration set for 1900 hours! I've heard it from the bosun that the Old Man plans something real special for us, for all our hard work. He is not so heartless, after all!"

CHAPTER 48

Radiomann Konrad stuck his head through the curtain, *"Fraeulein, bitte, erwacken Sie!"* He summoned Mary Ann in his deep bass voice.

Mary Ann rolled over on the bunk and blinked up at him groggily. For once, she had been in a good, deep sleep, instead of the usual misty half sleep of fear and longing, and felt annoyed at this disturbance.

Konrad apologized for "wacken you" in his battered English, then directed Mary Ann to "come, at once, to ze *Zentrale.*"

"What, again?" She grumbled, yet managed a cooperative smile. She readily understood Konrad's request and no longer heard a difference between English and German. It all blended together to make sense to her. She sat up slowly, the usual dull headache drumming in her forehead, and pulled back the sea blanket. Yes, she already had her shoes on this time, she showed Konrad, since she must visit the WC quite often with her "time of the month" hanging over her. *Another annoyance, Heaven forbid!*

Then, like a sailor going on duty, Mary Ann stood on the steady deck - the boat was dived, she surmised - and followed Radioman Konrad into the passage. Scooting behind him into the round control room hatch, she emerged on the other side into a wall of human bodies. There was barely any room to squeeze in! *What's going on?*

Mary Ann carefully straightened up behind Konrad's tall frame only to bump the baneful photograph of Adolf Hitler on the bulkhead behind her. She discreetly slunk aside to avoid contact with the dreaded Fuehrer and gazed over men's shoulders into the tightly-packed control room.

Gradually, familiar faces merged into focus, including her kind friend, the medic, who stood a body-length from her. He nodded when she smiled at him then looked off toward the middle of the room. Of course, the first watch officer was easy to spot. He rose head and shoulders above the others.

Someone pressed against her left side persistently. Mary Ann teetered off-balance into the bulkhead. Annoyed, she turned and confronted the Devil himself. The noisome navigator looked very pleased, indeed, to get her attention, and Mary Ann found herself trapped between him and the bulkhead. His hand slipped along the back of her thigh and squeezed. She calmly pushed his hand away. His hand came again. *Don't make a scene!* She tactfully blocked that roaming hand.

Then Mary Ann caught sight of the captain near a silver pole in the center of the control room. Immersed to the brim of his white hat in the sea of his men, the captain was watching her with a cautious expression, undoubtedly gauging her reaction to this unexpected gathering.

"Come, Marianne, you will join me here!" He gestured above the heads of his men.

"What, there?" Mary Ann pushed down on the navigator's hand, as it inched between her legs.

Yes, yes, come! The captain was waving vigorously. *But there's no room to move!* She pleaded with her eyes and swatted that persistent hand. Bodies hemmed her in from all sides. Men were staring at her, frowning, commenting.

Then a slight space opened up in front of her. Mary Ann darted in, relieved to escape that lecherous navigator. Several willing hands guided her through the press of bodies. Naturally, each man had to touch her, as she squeezed through the ranks toward the captain. It seemed she must be a good luck charm or the relic of a holy saint, the way they reached out and patted her back and shoulders. This treatment surprised Mary Ann, for she had expected to be man-handled.

As she approached the captain, Mary Ann noticed a large, metal cross dangling on a thick string at his open shirt collar. *Was the captain openly displaying his religious beliefs?*

The captain caught her staring at the cross and grinned. "This is the Knights Cross I am wearing," he said. "It is for my good work of sinking many enemy ships, Marianne! My men make it for me out of affection!" His dark eyes penetrated her with a light Mary Ann had never seen before. He was obviously very proud of his achievement and delighted by the adulation given by his men, but, too, he seemed most intent on making her realize the significance of what he had done - sinking many Allied ships!

"I ask you to share with all of us in our little victory celebration!" he announced. "I am sorry it is not one that you yourself will like, but the men, they enjoy the drink they have earned and have requested that you are present for this occasion."

Mary Ann glanced around the crowded control room. *Was this some kind of nasty joke? Were these Germans testing her? Driving their victory in on her?*

Several open smiles greeted her, including, naturally, the usual curious stares and frowns of uncertainty and unexpected hostility. She saw mirrored in those many eyes the myriad questions: *Would she accept the invitation? Let's see what the American girl will do now. Look, what do you think of her? She is not so much to look at, is she? So, this is the girl who sail with us?* Back and forth, back and forth. It was in the eyes.

The captain gripped Mary Ann's arm to get her attention. "Well? What do you say to this, Marianne? The men await your reply!"

"All right, sir." She replied quietly, for how could she say, "No, I don't want to be here"? She must go along, cooperate, for to do otherwise might be viewed as an insult, or worse, and could bring sudden hostility down on her head.

"Sie sagt, 'Ja,' Maenner!" The captain's shout deafened Mary Ann, and he swung a brown-colored glass bottle above his head to urge his men on in celebration.

Mary Ann recoiled at the sight of the captain. *With his ragged, black beard, blood-shot eyes and small white teeth glistening like pebbles in his open, red mouth, he was a crazed pirate! Just look at him!*

Loud cheers burst from the throng of men in the room. Startled to tears, Mary Ann realized the precariousness of her position. *If only the deck would open up and swallow her!* Yes, she might care about these German sailors and feel gratitude toward them for saving her life, but at what price? Where should she draw the line? Was she a coward not to decline their invitation to celebrate their victory and return to her bunk where she belonged? After all, it was her Allied ships and men that had gone down in the depths of the sea because of these German submariners!

In desperation, Mary Ann sought to concentrate on the captain, focus on his gaunt, bearded face in the haze of overhead lighting and mildewy air. She wanted very much to understand and accept this invitation as a positive gesture. It was obvious the men wanted her here with them. They might view her as their 'little sailor,' as the captain had said, but it was not right that she should be present for this celebration. *Captain, I must change my mind, say, no thank you. I'm sorry but—*

Suddenly, a long, brown bottle with a gold label reading "Beck's" joggled in her face. Mary Ann looked up at a flushed face with a white-blonde mustache and two black moles on the right cheek. The sailor indicated most vigorously that she take a swig from the bottle.

"Oh, no thank you," Mary Ann politely declined the proffered bottle. Of course, she'd never had a drop of alcohol in her life! "The drink of the devil," Mama called it. For she saw what drinking did to Daddy, how he'd come home from the tap room all riled up and make Mama miserable with his harsh words and belligerent behavior.

But the blonde sailor insisted Mary Ann take a drink. He waved around to his mates to encourage her. The men whooped and hollered, like wild Indians, their faces leering at her in a kaleidoscope of expressions.

Yet again, Mary Ann found herself in the loathsome position of having to cooperate with these men. *Just one small sip,* she convinced herself, and with trembling hands, brought the bottle opening to her lips. She smelled the burnt-grain beer odor. Hated it! It reeked of the bad times at home. Those few bad times in which she waited at the hall window to watch for Daddy to come up the street from the tavern. Was he walking straight and proud, or weaving from side to side?

Mary Ann took a quick swallow of the beer then lowered the bottle with a faint smile. "That's all, thanks." She wiped her mouth on her sleeve.

But the blonde sailor was not satisfied. He grabbed the bottle from Mary Ann and forced the opening to her mouth, as if feeding a fussy infant. *"Trinkst Du, Fraulein!"* he bellowed.

Enthusiastic "whoops" spouted from the crew. Mary Ann panicked, looked to the captain for help, but he was laughing and shouting right along with his men, enjoying this entire situation at her expense. *How she hated the man!* Hated them all for this humiliation they exposed her to!

The bottle was in her mouth. She feared the glass might chip her front teeth. The blonde sailor held her in the crook of his arm and smiled down at her endearingly, while Mary Ann coughed and sputtered, most of the bitter-tasting liquid coursing down her chin onto the front of her fatigues.

Enough? With a wink of his bright eye, the blonde sailor raised the bottle to his own mouth and bolted the remaining beer in one long draft. His protruding adam's apple jerked up and down, up and down, like a yo-yo, as Mary Ann watched with reluctant fascination. The other men were drinking as well, sharing several bottles of Beck's beer among themselves. For a moment, the crowded room rang with a loud salute, *"Prosit! Prosit! Prosit,"* then grew silent but for the chinks of bottle striking bottle in solemn celebration toasts.

From the protective ring of her blonde companion's encircling arms, Mary Ann looked on the scene of the German sailors drinking. She noted that many of the fellows looked unwell, thin, haggard, pale, like ghosts from the graveyard. Or was it the lighting in this room? She became aware of an array of bandages, bruises, cuts, and one bare arm in a sling. A fellow she'd not noticed before sported a white cotton patch over his left eye.

Yet again, Mary Ann felt sorry for these German sailors. Yet again, her heart was winning out in the battle against torn loyalties. A slow, warm sensation crept up her neck into her head. What little beer she'd drunk was taking affect. And it felt pretty good, if she had to say so herself. Now she began to understand why these men might need a drink and why she'd been invited to join their little party. After all they'd been through, they needed to relax and find a brief measure of peace from the chaos of near death and dying - and delivering death to other men.

One fellow across the way let loose with a loud belch, and a nearby mate swatted him on the head in mock disgust. Mary Ann giggled. *Wasn't it just like her silly brothers to do stuff like that?* When Mama wasn't around to hear, Jack and Ed held belching contests. Mary Ann, of course, had to be the judge.

Her blonde companion put his arm around her shoulders. Mary Ann glanced up at him. "Did you hear that guy before?"

The sailor nodded, as if he understood what she referred to, and gave her a reassuring squeeze. Another sailor, noting their pleasant exchange, sidled in closer to Mary Ann, slipping his arm around her waist. She raised her hand to his thick-muscled back and patted it gently.

Suddenly that wild-looking fellow with the eye patch was shouting at her. The merry-making in the room ceased, as the men stopped to listen. The man with the eye patch roared and gesticulated, wanting her to notice him. Mary Ann looked to the captain for an explanation. He grabbed her hand, at once, and pulled her from the arms of her amiable companions to his side.

"Marianne, *Bootsmanns Maat* Wirth wishes to tell it to you that he has several relations living in the United States," the captain explained.

Mary Ann whipped her head toward the eye-bandage man. "He does?" Her inhibition disintegrated. "Where, in America? Tell me!" *Oh, please let it be New York!* She wanted so much to run over and hug the man. All she knew was the man had a connection to her home, her family, her nation.

The man with the eye bandage was replying. The captain translated: "Wirth says, his aunt and uncle and cousins live near Chicago, Illinois, in a place called Jolliet. He wants to know, have you been there?"

Mary Ann wanted to cry. "No, I haven't. It's quite far away from New York, but I think I know where it is on a map." She smiled apologetically at the man, as if it was her fault for not personally knowing his relatives. Then she asked: "Do you hear from your relatives? Do they write to you? Have you met them?" She wanted to know everything!

Other crewmen had jumped into the conversation, jostling with each other to fire questions at Mary Ann and to plead with their captain to make her understand what they wanted to know. The captain promptly placed a thumb and finger between his lips and issued a piercing whistle. The men fell silent, though their eyes begged for the chance to ask.

Mary Ann smiled at them. "Don't worry," she said in the silence, "maybe sometime I can answer your questions, okay?" She saw the captain's disapproving look, then ducked her head in submission and grinned sheepishly.

"Marianne," the captain laid a firm hand on her shoulder, "I think my men will be too busy to talk with you soon, yes?"

"I know," she replied quietly. Images of men toiling beneath a whip came to mind. Everyone deserved some time to ask questions and learn. Everyone deserved to be cared for. Everyone deserved answers.

A strong voice hailed from a corner on the other side of the control room, *"Bitte, entschuldigen Sie, Herr Kaleu!"*

Bodies parted, elbows and shoulders twisted aside to make room for the bold comrade who thrust his way from the shadows through the crowd of men. Mary Ann glimpsed the dark-peaked hat and saw the solemn face of Second Watch Officer Dietrich Heubeck, as he stepped before her. With a deferential nod to his captain, Heubeck grasped Mary Ann's right hand and brought it to his lips.

Too shocked to react, Mary Ann could only watch as the second watch officer pressed his lips to the back of her hand, then brought it to his check. His blue eyes, heavy-lidded with devotion, came to her, and he began to sing. His deep, melodic voice heaved the German syllables passionately, the "r's" rolling from his tongue like a mountain stream splashing over round stones:

"Weit, so weit uber den Ozean zog ein Matrose—"

Mary Ann listened, spell-bound and painfully self-conscious by the attention the handsome officer lavished on her. Mesmerized, she watched his singing mouth - the mouth which had kissed her to new awareness - and concentrated on the translation the captain murmured in her ear:

"My naval officer sings to you of a sailor, who sails on a far voyage, Marianne. The girl who loves him weeps many tears because no message comes from him. The sailor lies on the ocean floor. No roses or edelweiss cover his grave. Only the tears from the girl who loves him and the wings of gulls, which fly over his burial place. In the evening hour, a cold wind brings him greetings from home." The captain sighed deeply.

"Und so, Marianne, I think, at the end, you need no more further explanation for this song, which my watch officer sings to you at this time."

No, she needed nothing more. It was all here before her. Mary Ann pressed her lips together to stifle threatening tears. She'd experienced all she needed to know of love, loss, and sorrow. And now, this handsome German officer, who moved her heart like the pounding surf, might one day be that sailor lying in an ocean grave. *Did he want for her tears to cover his grave? Oh, yes, yes, a thousand times, yes!* Her tears would fill the seven seas and surround the graves of every dead sailor of all nations and times!

Then the second watch officer brought his hands, one bandaged, Mary Ann noticed with a stab of regret for having bitten him, and framed the sides of her face. He gazed long at her, his face a mask of admiration, and proceeded to draw her head gently toward him. He kissed, first, her right cheek, then her left cheek, and finally pressed his warm mouth to her forehead under the wool hat, where he lingered for some moments. Enough to worry the captain, she sensed.

"Thank you, sir," Mary Ann choked, and watched the second watch officer turn away and blend into the whispering sea of men. Several pairs of eyes were watching her with longing, others quickly lowered away, when she looked at them. The room was beginning to empty out. A slow, steady flow of men stepped through the round hatch to go forward. Her blonde companion shoved his empty beer bottle at the little barrel-chested man, who stood looking after him with a contrived scowl on his elfish face.

Mary Ann watched the men go out, one by one. The need to do something, say something, drove her to call out after them, "Thank you, everyone! Thanks for—"

The captain gripped her arm tightly. "There is no need to thank them, Marianne."

"Oh, but there is, sir! They've been so sweet to me, and I want them to know—"

"They know this well, Marianne." The captain's hand slid along her back, as he guided her toward the hatch. "This is something they will not soon forget, my dear."

"Nor will I, sir," Mary Ann bowed through the hatch.

- 2 2 4 -

CHAPTER 49

Journal entry:

What a day! I'm at peace, and at the same time feeling all this was meant to be. I'm meant to be here, traveling on this U-boat. I feel it in my heart I was destined to make this journey. A crazy thing, but true. No one would ever believe me.

I know this boat is on its way back to Germany, but I am no longer afraid or upset. Must just go with it. I feel God is with me, taking care of me, so I can't be afraid. For this is His purpose for me, at this time.

I will live to go home, this I know, too, so I must patiently endure. For now, I live each moment in peace. Even the sea appears calm today, for the boat is barely rocking.

As I sit here wrapped in a blanket, writing at the captain's desk, I wonder why wars must happen. I know there are reasons, and these can be so deep and ancient, over the centuries defending one's self against aggression, or getting back at someone for old grievances. I've certainly witnessed enough of that in my own family, where pride and jealousy take over one's good judgment. Sadly, most of the trouble is over simple things that can get out of control, and it builds and builds til there's an explosion.

We people stubbornly stand our ground, right or wrong,

though we all like to think we're right and the other person is wrong, in what we do and say. Naturally, this leads to fighting and bickering. In the end, it seems no one wins. Everyone gets hurt, one way or another, and the hurts go on and on, from one person to the next, from one neighborhood to the next, from one generation to the next.

The fight can be over religion, who believes what, what practices they embrace - "I have the TRUE faith!" they argue. Mama says that sometimes. She believes our Catholic faith is the best, and inside, I wonder, What about the Protestants? What about the Jewish people, many of whom live in areas around our flat? Yes, I believe we Catholics have a beautiful faith, with our solemn Latin Masses and processions in honor of our great Saints. And, too, we have our wonderful Sacraments, our connections to God. But what do I say to my Jewish friend, Sarah? She loves her faith and heritage. And then, with politics, it's the same way. Who has the upper hand, the best lands. "That country used to be ours, we want it back!," or worse, "Those people who live there are less than human, let's get rid of them!" And so, armies are amassed olong borders. Clashes are inevitable. Pain and death continue.

Who is willing to stop this whole mess? Who is willing to lay down his or her armor, to forgive, let go, not hold that long simmering grudge? I often ask myself, can I do it? Is it humanly possible for me to do it in my own small life?

The real marvel of we people is that there is a higher call and purpose in each of us. The sad thing is, so many of us forget this, in dealing with each other on a day to day basis. We see only what we want to see. It is our personal challenge to rise above our everyday tendencies and strive to be close to God. God-like! Not act like an all-knowing king and expect everyone else to bow down and serve our demands, but to be God-like in the way of gentleness, kindness, forgiveness, knowledge, just every good thing.

This is the kind of God I believe we have. Not one that takes sides, or waits for us to trip and fall, so that He may throw us into eternal fire. No, I feel warm and hopeful inside, considering how beautiful and eternal God really is. I saw Him in the stars that night up on deck! I saw and felt Him like never before! What happens here on earth among His people will eventually find Truth and healing.

I can look at these German sailors, with whom I sail to an unknown port and think - I am no longer sailing with the enemy, but sailing with brothers, friends, family, neighbors. And if that is wrong to feel that way, then God must be wrong in His regard of His people on this world. That's how I'm seeing it from here.

Later:

I don't know where I am in time. Several changes of watches have gone through, so I assume a day has passed. Some clock I have, right?

But some nice things have happened today. First off, I have a friend to talk to, that is when he's not busy. He shares his life and listens to me as I talk about mine. Of course, we have some trouble understanding each other, which makes us laugh. Yet, it's the whole idea of bridging language and national gaps.

My friend is across the way in the radio room. When he came on duty before, he peeked in and asked if he could open the curtain. I was surprised and delighted, and so agreed. Since then, my little lonely world has opened up. I'm no longer shut away and left to myself, but able to see part of the passage and any fellows who pass by. It's so much better.

Konni, or Konrad, told me he is called "Konni" by his family and friends. I found out he is married and has a little one-year-old baby girl named Karen. His wife and baby live in a city called Danzig, which I think he said is in the former country of Poland. I can't figure out how Konni is in the German Navy, if he's Polish, or even what happened to Poland, if it's not Poland anymore? Shows how much I paid attention to the news back home, and I'm ashamed about that, believe me.

What made me happy was when Konni asked me about New York and my family. I tried to explain to him about Brooklyn being a borough of New York City, with the Bronx, Manhattan, etc., and that people of every background live there. He was most surprised and interested to learn that Irish and Italians and Polish and even German people live in neighborhoods near each other. There are problems sometimes, but mainly everyone seems to get along. Like Mama and Mrs. Rossi downstairs. And what really gets a lot of men together is baseball, the Brooklyn Dodgers, yes! I root for them, too. And when I sang, "Take Me Out to the Ballgame," Konni said he wanted to learn the words. Imagine that, a German sailor singing that song at his home in Danzig! What would folks think? But what a swell idea that is! Then we got to talking about my silly cat, Midnight, who walks on the piano keys in our parlor. Well, if that didn't get Konni laughing! He couldn't believe when I told him Midnight makes that walk every morning to say he wants his breakfast. I said to Konni, "Every day Midnight plays a little running tune," and then Konni asked if I could teach Midnight to play the baseball song. Now, there's an idea, if I ever heard one!

Right now, Konni's busy, so I won't bother him. The record player in the corner is spinning out a lively German song. Maybe, in time, I'll learn the words.

The captain and medic just went by out there. I haven't seen the captain since the party. He really looked bad. I wonder what's wrong?

Oh, oh, guess what, folks? I got work to do. Two sailors just

- 2 2 8 -

dropped off another big pot of potatoes on my bunk. Looks like I'm going to be peeling 'taters' for the next hour! The Cook has me do this every so often. Well, I don't mind. It keeps me busy. Yuck, most of these potatoes don't look or smell very good. I'll have to salvage what I can, but I won't dare eat them for our next meal, that's for sure!

Will write later, folks. Bye-bye!

CHAPTER 50

Oberleutnant Paul-Karl Ullmann pulled the thick wool scarf from his neck, as he entered the Wardroom after first bridge watch. "Where's the *Kommandant*, Gerhard?" He scowled at the medic, who was poring over a manual on the mess table.

"He's in the WC, sir, why?" Moeglich replied without looking up.

"Something's going on here," Ullmann snarled. "Ketter left the bridge like a drunken man. I demand that you tell me, *Herr Doktor.*" He pronounced the "Herr Doktor" with great sarcasm. "Is he ill? If so, I should have been informed of this immediately!"

As if to confirm Ullmann's suspicions, *Kapitaenleutnant* Ketter stumbled into the Wardroom and collapsed on his bunk beside the mess table, his face sweaty and pale with suffering. "Blasted stomach!" He growled.

"*Mein Gott!*" Moeglich scrambled to attend to the *Kommandant*, while Ullmann pressed into the tight space between the bunk and mess table and gripped the medic's shoulder with his long, bony fingers. "What is wrong with the *Kommandant*, Gerhard? You think you are so smart! You and he have been conspiring to keep the fact of his illness from me!"

Ketter groaned on the bunk, "Go ahead, tell him, Gerhard."

The medic looked brazenly into Ullmann's red-chapped face. *Do you really care, you dog face?* He wanted to blast the *EVO*, but answered in a cool, steady tone. "I will tell you, *Herr* Ullmann, our *Kommandant* has strong will-power. He will not give in, under any circumstances. I am certain it is his appendix, and I intend to operate to remove the appendix, as soon as possible. So, I will ask for your cooperation. We must get this boat dived to assure a steady operating theater, if you will see to this, please."

Ullmann straightened up fast, a slight smirk touching his lips. "Of course, *Herr Doktor*, I will see to this. But then, you are not a surgeon, Gerhard? What can you do in this situation? You're only a cussed pharmacists mate!"

Moeglich glared at Ullmann. "With all due respect, sir - and please consider the feelings of our good *Kommandant* who lies here in great discomfort - I have observed several appendectomies in the hospital courses I attended, and assisted in several, as well. Besides," Moeglich indicated the open book on the Wardroom table, "I have my medical manual right here with me to refer to through the entire procedure."

"Of course, of course," Ullmann mumbled, sounding much too pleased at the thought of a shipboard appendectomy. It wouldn't work. Couldn't work. The Old Man will die of shock, or he will develop an infection that will kill him, in the end anyway.

Awkward Franz Wachsmuth approached from forward with a large torpedo loading lamp dangling in his hands. "Is the Old Man going to die?" He inquired in a fearful, low voice.

Moeglich angrily waved Wachsmuth away. "For Heaven's sake, Franz, the *Kommandant* will not die! Not if I can help it," he mumbled to himself. "Now, get that lamp rigged. We've no time to waste to get this thing started!"

"Yes, Gerry, right away!" Wachsmuth dashed to the end of the mess table and began working diligently to attach the loading lamp to an iron rib in the overhead.

Ullmann eyed the medic. "So, then, *Herr Doktor,* I will have some words with our *Kommandant* before you proceed with what you must do here?"

Moeglich backed off to a respectable distance, but kept his eye on the viper. He knew what must come. Bits of Ullmann's conversation with the *Kommandant* reached his ears: "While you are indisposed, I am taking immediate command of this boat." Ullmann informed the miserable Old Man, whose only response was a grimace of pain.

Indeed, Moeglich had tried, with the Old Man's persistence, to delay the inevitable. Certainly, the second-in-command does replace the commander if he is ill, badly injured, or killed. That is proper military protocol, but what an irony that this must happen here, on this boat, with these two officers, whose long-smoldering feud had been felt by the crew. Gerhard Moeglich knew he and his mates were in for a rough ride with that blamed hard-nose in control, God help them! A more merciless man in the entire German Navy could not be found!

With a last look at the ailing commander, Ullmann lunged past Moeglich and Wachsmuth and strode determinedly toward the control room hatch. In seconds, the lively American tune, "Don't Sit under the Apple Tree with Anyone Else But Me" switched off. Bored, off-duty mates complained leisurely in their bunks, "Eh, come on! What is this?" little suspecting the storm bearing down upon them. Moeglich spat on the deck then glared up, scowling ferociously, at the speaker bolted on the steel rib.

"Achtung! Achtung! Attention, U-115 men! This is *Erste Wach Offizier* Paul Ullmann! At this present time, I am taking command of U-115, due to the poor health of our *Kommandant,* who has been diagnosed with an attack of appendicitis by our Pharmacist's Mate, Gerhard Moelich."

Silence blanketed the work spaces and passages in the boat. Even the diesel engines stalled in their eternal clattering. The lead mechanic on duty made a hasty round to check the pistons for any possible malfunction.

Ullmann's voice cracked: "There will be the necessary changes to bring this boat *up* to my personal standards." The ill *Kommandant* rose slightly on his bunk in the Wardroom, then flopped back exhausted, defeated, in agony, too far gone to care.

"I will not tolerate idiotic behavior. There will be no remarks of any kind, even in jest, against this command!" Ullmann droned. "Section officers will report any infractions of this rule to me with heavy consequences for the culprit."

A whole list of directives came from Paul-Karl Ullmann, some so picky and insane, that crew members shook their heads and laughed into their sleeves, albeit quietly. They'd known the *EVO* was a tough fellow, but this was ridiculous.

Ullmann was wrapping up. Finally! "This boat will be a model boat, men! One that our *Fuehrer* and the German people can be proud of! Carry on! *Heil,* Hitler!"

The close brotherhood of submarine men with the common task to make war on enemy ships and survive together in grim circumstances must now change loyalties to accommodate their new *Kommandant,* though the man be intensely disliked and mistrusted.

CHAPTER 51

"Psst, Konni? Konni?" Mary Ann called to Radioman Konrad in the radio room, when the lengthy announcement ended. "Could you please play some more English songs today?"

Konrad did not reply, or look over at her, but adjusted the headphones over his ears and bent to his work. Mary Ann knew not to bother him now. She was used to his sudden flourishes of activity in the radio room. A wireless message might come over the air any time, as he'd explained to her, and he must attend to it immediately. Then his long, thin fingers would - quick! quick! - tap the sender key. Or else, he might jot down certain messages on paper and give them to the second watch officer, who apparently checked them over before sending them on to the captain.

But the last time Konrad had been on duty over there, they'd had a swell time. "Today, I make a song to play for you in English!" He'd announced in his usual deep bass voice, those bright hawk's eyes sparkling at her beneath stormy, black brows.

"Oh, boy!" Mary Ann had clapped her hands with delight, eager to have some fun.

And then came a lively tune, "It's A Long Way To Tipperary." "An 'Englander' song!" Konni had yelled over to her above the chaos of crewmen's voices that quickly joined in singing, up and down the corridor, fore and aft. Mary Ann had laughed and belted out the words, like a true virtuoso, and swayed back and forth on the bunk, pleased to be part of the rollicky songfest.

Then an even greater surprise! Konrad had tuned in to a radio station from Charlotte, North Carolina. Mary Ann heard her all-time favorite hit song, "Chattanooga Choo Choo." There were the familiar advertising jingles for Gillette razor blades, Camel cigarettes, and Borax soap. *Home, home, home!* She couldn't believe it! And she wondered that the German sailors really liked the United States, with all its happy music and baseball games and wide-open land. Mary Ann had even considered running to the captain and begging him to turn his U-boat westward.

Presently, someone entered the corridor from the hatch and blocked Mary Ann's view of Konrad in the radio room. She glanced up. Looked again. First Watch Officer Paul-Karl Ullmann glared down at her from his lofty height. Mary Ann felt her chest contract with alarm. *What was he doing here?* "Sir? Um, hi," she managed a greeting.

The officer's cherry-red face, seared by cold winds from the open bridge above, expanded before her, as he stepped into her tiny compartment and drew the curtain shut.

"So, you are enjoying this boat ride very much?" he inquired in a pleasant voice.

Mary Ann was dismayed. *Since when had he become friendly?* This man was not noted for pleasantness, and yet, here he was, smiling down at her, like he was fond of her. A small warning bell went off in her head, but she ignored it, opened her mouth to answer, "Yes, sir, I do the best I can." She wanted to tell him she was grateful to him and the other men of the crew for their kind treatment of her. She wanted him to know that she intended to continue to cooperate and be a "good sailor," as she had promised the captain. .

She never got the chance to tell Ullmann.

His bony fist slammed her right cheek below her eye socket with such force it sent her reeling into the paneled bulkhead in a torrent of stinging pain and blinding star flecks. *Dear God, surely, her jaw was broken!* She felt for swelling, heard the officer raving above her: "Things are changing for you, American dog! From now on, I am in charge, so you do not have it so nice anymore!"

White terror knifed through Mary Ann, and she squirmed drunkenly to sit up. "Where's the captain?" she gasped. Knew, at once, this was the wrong question to ask.

With a snarl, the first watch officer caught her by the shoulders of her fatigues and dragged her up before his molten face. "The captain? You want the captain?" he murmured in a deathly calm voice. "I will show you the captain. I am now the captain!" He grinned maliciously. "And so, 'Ami' dog," he shook her like a wet shirt being hung out to dry on a clothesline, "you will know how I deal with an enemy prisoner on board of my boat!" And he flung her against the bulkhead.

In a daze of shock and pain, Mary Ann scrambled for the foot of the bunk to escape the first watch officer. "What happened to the captain? Where is he?" she howled at him. Sensed in her heart, the captain was dead. *This madman had killed him! Now he was going to kill her! Dear God, he was coming at her again!* "Help! Somebody help me!" she screamed.

No one came.

Who would come? Who could come? A military underling did not interfere with his superior, unless the fate of the ship and crew was in dire jeopardy. In a matter like this, it was the captain's discretion to deal with a prisoner as he saw fit.

So, the officer continued to punish his victim at will. He punched her in the stomach. "You want me to stop, American dog? You want for this?" He taunted Mary Ann, striking her wherever he could reach her, in the face, in the breast, on her arms and legs, until her whole body was a jarring welt. Mary Ann kept rolling toward the bulkhead to put her back to the man, but he continually threw her back to expose her most vulnerable areas.

"God help me. Mercy, oh, mercy, mercy," she gasped, and faded into welcoming haze. The brutal pounding seemed far away. Her body felt the assault, but her mind was traveling. She lay curled in half, shivering, her arms crossed tightly over her breast, her face turned into the leather mattress. "Enough, I beg you," she gagged on her vomit.

The rain of blows stopped suddenly, like the thumping feet of an army marching off the battlefield, leaving the scattered dead and wounded behind. "Have enough, dog? Have enough?" Mary Ann blinked up at the vague figure of the first watch officer hovering over her.

"Yes, please, no more," she whispered. Was he calculating the damage he had inflicted on her? He looked very satisfied, indeed, at what he had accomplished with this defiant, little enemy female.

"Stand up, now!" he growled.

Stand up? She heard the order from afar, but was unable to comprehend its meaning. She couldn't stand up. Not now. She only wanted to lay here and drift away into gathering fog.

"I said, stand up!" The command came like thunder, splitting her aching head.

Stand up? Yes, stand up, stand up. She must. Mary Ann willed her screaming limbs to the side of the bunk and pulled herself up on trembling arms. Then - she didn't know how - she stood unaided in her stocking feet on the swaying linoleum deck, helpless and stooped like an old woman. The first watch officer loomed at her side, a menacing reminder of her fragile fate.

"I take you now to your new bunk," he announced. "You no longer sleep in MINE bunk for this cruise!" And he swiped open the curtain, revealing her to Konrad in the radio room. Konrad glanced at her briefly with round, frightened eyes, then ducked out of sight behind the bulkhead. The message was tragically clear. Her "friend" would not save her.

Mary Ann receded into black despair. The deck yawed and spun beneath her feet, and she began to crumple down, down, but the cruel hand of her new master snatched her up by the collar and thrust her toward the Wardroom doorway. "Go!" he bawled.

A twig caught in raging flood waters, Mary Ann crashed into the cabinet containing the officers' china meal service with its ugly swastikas, then careened out into the Wardroom beneath a blinding white light. A pair of startled eyes looked up at her, following her wavering progress with remote pity. Another sailor scurried to get out of her way. Oppressive, embarrassed silence accompanied Mary Ann's pathetic transport. It seemed her pitiful presence here in this room infringed on a more serious routine in progress.

From her miserable, halting walk on the road to Calvary, Mary Ann glimpsed the sad-ox face of the medic, who sat on the other side of the drop-leaf mess table. He did not make a move to come to her aid, though her eyes begged for his assistance. Would there be no Simon of Sirene to help her carry this baleful cross?

Instead, the medic looked down at a figure lying immobile beneath a blanket on the lower left bunk. The man's eyes were sealed in dark hollows, his wavy, black hair rolling back from his high, sweating, grayish forehead. A thin, black, ragged beard crept across the broad, sagging jaw.

"Captain!" Mary Ann's agonized wail rang in the stagnant room, but the first watch officer rudely thrust her ahead. "Move!"

Mary Ann stumbled toward the galley hatchway. Far ahead in a white cloud of steam, the cook observed her approach beneath darkly-lowered brows. He was busy, so very busy slamming big cooking pots around with a deliberation that shook his bulging arm muscles. What would it take to slam the first watch officer on the head with a pan, or drive him through with a butcher's knife, as he goaded his brutalized prisoner along the passage?

Yet - nothing? Into the still, gray Petty Officers Room. Here, the first watch officer stopped Mary Ann with a blow to the ribs and pointed to an upper bunk on the left side of the narrow passage. "That is where you will remain from now on!" he rumbled.

Clinging weakly to the bunk support, Mary Ann looked up through churning mist to the top bunk. It appeared to be floating impossibly high above her head, and she knew, dreaded, that she would never be able to climb to that bunk.

"Go up!" The first watch officer spat at her back.

Mercy, mercy! "Yes, sir," she whispered. Prepared with all her last energy reserves to obey, placing her right foot on the edge of the lower bunk, where a man lay witnessing her wretched struggle. But she couldn't hold onto that upper bunk rail and pull up her body weight at the same time. Down, she clumped on her stocking feet, exhausted, shivering with pain and terror. She knew what must come. "I don't think I can make it, sir."

How must the helpless deer feel as it stands paralyzed before the headlight of an on-rushing locomotive? What must the lone man feel when he finds himself stuck in a dead-end city alley, while menacing gang members move in with knives and baseball bats?

Mary Ann sensed the violence building in the man behind her. She heard his scowl of impatience and bowed her head. *It must come. Now. Now. Now.* With an angry grunt, Ullmann seized her around her thighs and lifted her effortlessly over the rail of the upper bunk, scraping her ribs on the rail and striking her head against the low overhead. Mary Ann collapsed onto the upper bunk in a writhing ball of pain. Through her tears, she glimpsed the red-blotched face of the "new captain" peering over the bunk rail at her. His cold, lashless eyes, icy orbs of unadulterated hatred, stared in at her on a level, eye to eye. He grinned maliciously. In all his tainted glory and power, the man stood as the embodiment of the evil that threatened to annihilate all hope and goodness in the world. *Here was the true Nazi!*

Mary Ann closed her eyes and retched into the blue checkered sheet beneath her face.

CHAPTER 52

A short note:

Forty-four years later, at a reunion of U-115 survivors in Odenwald, West Germany, Alois Geissler, the boat's chief engineering officer from the 1942 patrol, shared with historian Steve Anderson, who also attended the reunion, about the day his commanding officer, *Kapitaenleutnant* Herbert Ketter, was operated on by Pharmacist Mate Gerhard Moeglich on the mess table in the Officers Wardroom. Together with the controversial account he later gleaned from Mary Ann Connor Carlino, Anderson assembled an amazing picture of brave people working under crude circumstances to save a man's life. Anderson was already familiar with, at least, two instances of emergency appendectomies performed by pharmacist mates on United States submarines in the Pacific, but he had yet to come across any information about the procedure being carried out on a German U-boat. The fact that it was U-115's commanding officer who happened to undergo the dangerous surgery made the story even more intriguing, certainly quite a coincidence, in light of the on-board situation.

"Clear the bridge!" Paul-Karl Ullmann took one last look at the twilight sea.

The third watch promptly disappeared through the open bridge hatch, with Ullmann the last to descend. He reached overhead to close the hatch lid and spun the wheel mechanism to seal out the rising sea. "Take her down to sixty meters!" He called, as he stepped down into the control room.

"Sixty meters, aye, sir!"

Two men sat rigidly at the diving planes and pressed down the hydroplane buttons under the observant eye of Chief Engineer Alois Geissler.

Ullmann stood near the chief, "Sixty meters should guarantee a steady platform for the surgery."

"It should, *Herr* Ullmann," Geissler tapped his right planesman on the shoulder. "Keep it on sixty, Willi. Eyes strictly on the gauge, gentlemen."

"Slow revolutions on E-motors. Course steady." Ullmann ordered the control room mates.

"Aye, sir!"

"I understand you will also assist at the surgery?" Ullmann confided to the chief.

"Yes, *Herr* Ullmann," he replied tersely. "It is the least I can do for our good *Kommandant!* My boys here know what to do." Geissler indicated his planesmen.

"Very well," Ullmann rumbled, "now let us go into the Wardroom. I want to see how the preparations are going."

The two officers filed into the control room hatch forward, Ullmann leading the way. They entered the Wardroom doorway and stopped short, noting the changed appearance of the cramped Wardroom. Half a dozen men, including the high-strung second watch officer, Dietrich Heubeck, were crowded at the mess table, being briefed by Gerhard Moeglich on "operating room" ethics. Indeed, the Wardroom resembled a hospital operating room theater, complete with the big flood lamp rigged beneath the sloping overhead and bunk sheets draped from the frames of folded upper bunks on both sides to form barriers.

Appearing lucid and having a rather chipper conversation with *Diesel Obermachinist* Holleder, the now-beardless, half-naked Old Man lay on his left side on the edge of the covered mess table. For a moment, Ullmann stood speechless at the efficiency he observed, while the chief pushed ahead into the Wardroom to take his place among the "surgical assistants." Everything was well organized, everyone seemed calm.

The medic caught sight of Ullmann in the doorway. "We should soon be ready to begin, *Herr Oberleutnant!*" Certainly, Moeglich was in control, in his element, as he directed Walter Jung to tighten the "surgical gown" - a clean, spare shirt from the supply locker worn backwards - which *Oberbootsmaat* Willy Scholz wore over his sweaty work clothes.

"Come, *Herr Oberleutnant,* see what we have, since you are interested!" Moeglich called, and Ullmann walked to the foot of the mess table. "Here," Moeglich pointed to various supplies on a baking tray from the galley, "you see ground sulfanilamide tablets to be the antiseptic agent. Over here, hemostats from the medicine chest. Also, a nice scalpel, which our man, Winkelhoffer, welded with a new, sturdy handle in the motor room. And an ether mask, an inverted tea strainer with a gauze covering. Pretty ingenious, yes!" Moeglich swung around and pointed. "Over here, metal tablespoons bent at the proper angle to serve as muscle retractors," he looked up at Ullmann and grinned. "And last, but most important, *Herr Oberleutnant,* you will see, *unser Smutje!* The cook is our main man!"

The brooding cook stood by the galley bulkhead, as Moeglich spoke on. "*Unser Smutje* will supply us with boiling water for sterilizing and anything else we need from the galley!"

Ullmann nodded. "So! Good, very good, *Herr Doktor.* It's too bad we have no more torpedoes. You could have milked the alcohol from them for a sterilizer as well, yes?"

"That is true, *Herr Oberleutnant,* but our Old Man used up all the eels to earn his Knight's Cross!" Moeglich smiled down at *Kapitaenleutnant* Ketter with open affection and patted his bare, white shoulder. "We have everything we need to perform a successful surgery, so don't you worry about anything, *Herr Kaleu!*"

"I'm in good hands with you, Gerry." Ketter smiled weakly and lay back.

Ullmann gazed down on his gravely ill commanding officer. "Good luck to you, *Herr Kapitaenleutnant.* You have a fine team here."

Ketter barely looked at Ullmann. "Thank you, Pauli."

Ullmann stepped back. "Good luck to all of you," he said, and then he pushed past the chief and exited the Wardroom, slamming the hatch shut behind him. The men in the Wardroom looked at each other. They were going to get away with their plan, after all!

CHAPTER 53

Quiet snatches of conversation floated in and out of Mary Ann's consciousness, like gentle waves washing up and retreating from the beach. Behind the closed curtain of her upper bunk in Petty Officers Quarters, Mary Ann sank deeper into currents of pain and despair. The captain was dead. This terrible realization slammed her body in a wrenching spasm and dragged her back to the surface of awareness. She would not survive without the captain. Tears of despair slid down her cheeks. She was truly alone. She would not live. Only the captain had been her one, steady source of life and protection in this dangerous submarine world. And more, he had loved her. Yes, yes, he had! And she regretted not having responded more kindly to him.

The distant calls of a wolf pack closed in. Men, coming off duty, entered the compartment, talking in fast German. Mary Ann froze in her upper bunk. *Dear God, what if they found her stashed up here behind the short, gray privacy curtain? What if this was someone's bunk she was lying in? Would the men drag her out? Attack her? Rape her? Finish her off for good?*

She rolled her head slightly to peer through a small slit in the curtain and cringed under the assault of a pounding headache. *Oh, no, the fearful navigator, with the devil's eyes, passed the narrow gap at close range.* Mary Ann pressed her mouth closed to stifle a cry of alarm. Lie still! Don't give yourself away in this narrow coffin, where even to raise one's hand to touch the top of the bunk space was not quite a bowed arm's length!

Exhausted, crushed, hopeless, in great pain, Mary Ann gradually settled into a restless dream, drifted in and out, in and out, a small, battered boat riding the ebb and flow of life. A heavy-hearted sea dirge tolled the end, and she sang aloud with all her soul, passion swelling her breast, like that of the second watch office in the control room: "Oh, Captain, my Captain, take me home with you. The gull cries on the ocean wave. I'm lost, and overdue. . . ."

Then Mama was waiting on the hallway landing outside their third floor Humbolt Street flat, a blue and white checked apron wrapped at her waist. Mary Ann climbed the great, bright stairway toward her mother, tears streaming down her face. "Oh, Mama, I love you! Please don't be angry that I've been gone so long at sea! I told the captain I must get home in time for supper tonight, and see, he brought me!"

Someone waited behind Mama. A child of eight? Mary Ann was startled to see her brother, Tommy, real and whole, his precious legs intact, as if no street car accident had ever happened. There he was, with auburn hair and freckles, ready to go play stickball in the vacant lot near Morton's Textile Shop.

"Sweetheart, it's you!" Mary Ann reached for Tommy, but he backed away shyly, as if he didn't he know her. His face changed, as she watched him. He seemed to grow older, a teenager. "Billy? Billy Baker! Weren't you on the submarine with me?" Mary Ann felt confused, sad, yet wonderfully relieved to know that her brother and the young steward from the boat were together in Heaven.

Tommy drifted toward the hallway window. Mary Ann crept near him, praying he would not draw away. She wanted so much to hug him, while she had him with her. She actually felt Tommy's little shoulder bone against her arm, then realized Daddy must be coming up the street from the tavern. Please let him be sober this time!

But when Mary Ann looked out the window, she viewed a calm ocean stretched against the distant horizon. To the west, the sun was setting in deep, orange glows, and in the east, the entire sky was ablaze with stars the size of baseballs. Along the zenith ran a definite line separating night and day, life and death. Mary Ann longed to go to those stars! She was actually standing on the line between night and day. She heard strange, beautiful voices singing far away in the stars, knew those were angels who sang to her. She gazed to her right, the stars shone under her. To the left toward the setting sun, Mama waited at the hallway window. Mary Ann calmly anticipated the Voice of God. It would boom out her direction, toward life or death, like the announcer at Grand Central Station in the city: "It is time to go down into the boat, Mary Ann! We cannot remain up here much longer."

"Yes, sir." And she gazed longingly at the stars. One last time.

Pain returned to her body in hammer blows. How long had she been away? Hours, it seemed, or maybe, it was only seconds? Someone had opened the gray curtain near her right shoulder. A blurry, white face loomed up beneath a black hat. Crystal blue eyes peered over the side rail. *Hello, dear angel! Had God sent His messenger?*

"Meine Liebste," a soft voice addressed her. A puffy hand ringed by a brown sleeve cuff slid over the bunk rail and soothed her wrist.

"Sir?" Mary Ann lifted her trembling hand toward Second Watch Officer Dietrich Heubeck. He began to lower the bunk rail, and Mary Ann watched him in a torment of agony and relief. "I was in Heaven, sir! I saw my brother and Fritz Baier. They were there!" She tried to explain to Heubeck, who mumbled, "Please, to come, sweet lady," as he encircled her back with his left arm and proceeded to roll her gently toward him on the bunk.

"But, sir, I don't want to get up! Please let me lay here, til I feel better!" She wanted back in that dream! But the second watch officer continued to urge her to the edge of the bunk. "Please, to come. It is necessary. It is necessary. Forgive! Forgive!" He apologized each time she moaned in pain, but he would not desist in prying her from the bunk.

As Mary Ann slowly emerged from her hidden niche, her gaze fell upon several crewmen huddled on two lower bunks across the central aisle. Among them perched the repulsive navigator, his devil's eyes unexpectedly blank, the hellfire snuffed out. The crewmen were staring at her, their mouths agape in silent horror, as if witnessing a ghoul rising from the grave, and Mary Ann knew by their frozen expressions of shock and outrage how badly bruised and battered she was.

Then, as if coming out of a trance, one man leapt to his feet and came flying around the small mess table to assist the second watch officer in easing his sweet burden to the deck. Other men, including the navigator, scrambled to seat Mary Ann on the lower bunk before the mess table. A bowl of water appeared beneath her gaze. Someone dipped a clean rag into the water, squeezed out the excess, and began wiping gently at her face. Mary Ann flinched, but did not discourage the care, while in the background, low men's voices soothed and crooned. Soon, the water in the washbowl grew darker with dried blood.

A cup slid below her chin. Mary Ann stared into a small, black pool of steaming coffee. She was coaxed to sip the coffee, and as she swallowed the first, oil-flavored gulps, she felt life and warmth seep back into her aching limbs. "It's good," she whispered.

Someone patted her back to reassure her. When Mary Ann looked up, a close ring of concerned faces surrounded her. Their eyes were watching her, as if waiting for her to reveal a great truth. Instead, she smiled weakly, in spite of the pain and swelling in her cheeks and jaw.

One would have thought she'd given those fellows a million bucks! Indeed, the rush of light-hearted laughter and relieved comments greatly heartened Mary Ann. She knew she was in good hands. These men would care for her and protect her. Gradually, the wavering, silver stars faded from her vision. Yes, she would go to those stars in due time, but for now, she would gladly stay here with these nice fellows.

Someone was grasping her gently under her armpit and began to coax her to her feet. Mary Ann looked up, perturbed. *What? She must be made to move again?*

With quiet words of direction, the second watch officer guided her by the hand beside the mess table, as another man led the way toward the galley hatch at the back of the room. The cook stood in the passage, his big, beefy, red arms folded across his t-shirt with the fearsome Nazi eagle, but he bowed his head, refused to see her sad condition, and stepped aside to make room for Mary Ann to pass, as she stumbled into the galley.

Immediately, Mary Ann noticed the familiar, large metal caldron boiling over in a white halo of steam on the small stove behind the galley ladder. Several gleaming objects roiled around in the pot. Something popped up. A sieve?

Then she entered the Officers Wardroom into blinding, white light. She kept turning her head down to avoid the glare, as she was ushered between a shifting group of crewmen toward the mess table. A white sheet draped the table, and every here and there, oddly-shaped mounds and valleys displaced the sheet. *Dear Lord, a man lay there!*

Mary Ann was frightened suddenly. *Why would a man be lying on the table like that?* She saw his bare chest, where the sheet ended. Beads of sweat dotted his pale skin, and a sparse growth of black hair trailed along the breastbone, then fanned out in wide circles around the flat, pink nipples.

Mary Ann blinked up in the harsh light. "What's going on here?" she gasped.

Masked faces surrounded her. She recognized the brilliant hawk's eyes of Radioman Konrad among them.

"What's going on! Somebody tell me!" She trembled with weakness and nagging pain.

The second watch officer cautioned her, "*Ssh, meine Liebste,* come, sweet lady, you will see," and he gently forced Mary Ann onto the lowered bunk at the right side of the naked man on the mess table.

"*Herr Kaleu? Sie ist hier,*" someone mumbled, and the man on the table slowly turned his head to look at Mary Ann. She saw the man's broad, grayish face crowned by limp, wet, black curls. His clean-shaven face was hideously smeared with a white, waxy jelly, and those dark, feverish eyes gazed at her, trying to determine who she was.

Then the man emitted a feeble cry. His thin, dry lips moved, as he pronounced her name: "Marianne!"

"Dear God, it's you, sir!" Mary Ann gaped into the suffering face of the captain. "Oh, dear God, you're here! I thought you were dead!" And she broke down and wept.

Someone placed a comforting hand on her shoulder. Mary Ann looked up through her tears at a masked face. "He's not dead! He's here!" She swung her gaze back to the captain. "You're not dead!"

The captain's narrow eyes, ringed by dark circles of suffering, regarded her with his usual amusement. "No, my dear," he murmured. He seemed ready to laugh, in spite of his misery. "I am not yet dead, only out of action for a short time."

"Thank God!" Mary Ann clawed at the table to get closer to him, touching impulsively at his bare shoulder. "But what's wrong, sir? What's happened to you?"

The captain sighed wearily, "Marianne, I have a bad appendix that must come out quickly."

"Dear Jesus in Heaven!" Mary Ann gasped.

The captain closed his eyes, a patient reaction to her rather volatile outcry. "Marianne, you must remain calm," he admonished gently. Even in his ill state of health, he could still remonstrate with her. She bowed her head contritely, "Yes, sir, I know. I'm sorry." Then she glanced at him. His eyes were regarding her intently.

"Who did this to you?" He lifted his hand toward her battered face. "I will kill him!"

Mary Ann shook her head, would not say, though she knew that he knew the culprit.

"Marianne, I tell the medic not to begin this surgery until I see you."

Mary Ann nodded. "Thank you, I'm so relieved, sir! Everything's going to be all right though. So please don't worry!"

The captain stared at her. "I want you by me for this surgery," he ordered quietly. "Soon, one day, you will be a fine nurse, yes?"

Mary Ann's heart jumped. *Be present for his surgery? My God!* Yet there could be no declining this supreme act of service to this man she cared for. "I'll be here for you, sir. You can count on me. I'll be praying, too."

A smile of contentment drifted over the captain's thin lips. "Good, Marianne, good." And he closed his eyes. He was ready.

CHAPTER 54

Silence descended on the Wardroom like a smothering blanket. The heat from the overhead lamp burned down with the intensity of a blistering summer sun on a Brooklyn street. The "anesthetist," a man with spiny brows above his make-shift mask, sat at the head of the "operating room" table, his back to the closed Wardroom hatch and the radio room, Captain's Quarters, and control room beyond. The medic huddled beneath a folded-back upper bunk draped with a checkered sheet. He must perform the appendectomy on his knees!

To the left of the medic, directly across from the newly "gowned and masked" Mary Ann, Dietrich Heubeck waited to assist, though the look of terror in his blue eyes did not bode well for future cooperation. Other members of the "surgical team" stood in their assigned positions at the foot of the mess table near the galley, while the medic talked continually in his even, quiet voice, appearing more to be calming himself than emboldening his assistants.

Mary Ann gazed on this surreal scene from her place at the captain's left side and wondered if she could endure the imminent drama. She'd never attended a surgery, as this wasn't her field in nursing. Bouts of pain and dizziness stymied her concentration. *Maybe she should just beg off, flag down the medic, and go and lay in her bunk for relief?* Yet, how could she dare desert her beloved captain at a moment like this? She must remain on guard, if for no other reason, than she owed him her life.

At the medic's prompting, the spiky-browed anesthetist began to drip tiny beads of liquid from a small vile onto the gauze-covered sieve, which lay tightly molded in the waxy gel on the captain's pale face. Immediately a sweet odor permeated the room, sending Mary Ann into a swoon. Ether! What if they all collapsed from the effects of that volatile liquid in this closed room? Yet, the captain was soon asleep, mercifully out of misery.

One last time, the anesthetist leaned forward and addressed the captain, but the captain no longer responded. It was time to get things started! An assistant gently pulled on the sheet covering the lower half of the captain's body. The sheet slipped toward his pelvis, revealing a smooth stomach with small, black, patchy moles on the left side. On an order from the medic, the second watch officer began draping several thin towels over the captain's naked chest and slightly freckled shoulders to preserve his dignity. Mary Ann timidly straightened one corner of one towel in an act of wanting to help.

Then in a solemn gesture of bestowing a priestly blessing, the medic raised his gloved left hand over the captain's flat stomach and lowered his little finger into the navel. Mary Ann sat forward, surprised, and observed this simple action with a soft ripple of embarrassment. She forced herself to remain objective, not to notice that the sheet stole closer to the captain's private male area and that several strands of black pubic hairs showed at the edge of the sheet. Certainly she had cared for male patients in her training at the hospital, mainly washing their extremities and administering back rubs. Sister Mary Vincent always sternly reminded the girls that they were caring for the sacred body of the crucified Jesus in any poor, sick men they nursed. In this instance, however, Mary Ann was not looking at the body of a strange man, but at one who evoked powerful emotions in her.

Then the medic stretched his thumb to touch the right pelvic bone and dropped his index finger onto a spot on the captain's clammy skin midway between the navel and pelvic bone. *So, this was the way to discover the location of the appendix?*

While the medic waited against the folded-back upper bunk, a garbed assistant, the boat's chief engineer - Mary Ann could tell it was he by the red plaid collar that stuck out at the neck of his "surgical gown" shirt - swabbed the surgical site with a dark-colored disinfectant. The medic's green eyes followed the swabbing intently. His total concentration reminded everyone in attendance of the gravity of the situation.

"Sind Sie fertig?" he mumbled, then nodded to Radioman Konrad, whose bright hawk's eyes stared at him in ready obedience.

Konrad picked up a small, gleaming knife from the tray, which the dour cook held forth in offering. With a somber move, Konrad offered the knife to the medic, who regarded Konrad for a long moment before taking the knife in his gloved hand. *Did he have doubts suddenly?*

The atmosphere in the Wardroom had become unbearable. Mary Ann felt her head spin. Nausea inched up her throat. Thumping pain tortured her trembling body. She blinked down at the captain's jelly-smeared face in a futile attempt to steady herself. *God help me! Don't let me pass out!* She clutched her cold hands tightly, viewed her captain lying in his helpless state about to undergo a surgical procedure in terrible circumstances by a group of men who had little, if any, medical knowledge. It was for this man that she was here! The others had brought her from her bed of suffering to answer her brave captain's call. She must focus on that, and nothing else. Not note how the knife blade had already sliced into his skin, weeping tears of blood.

She must remain here, steady and calm - a nurse's attitude! This good man whom she admired and respected must survive, for she, too, needed him for survival. And that dear man had summoned her to his side, he thought that much of her and her desire to be a nurse! Surely, it was an honor to be present for him. After all, he knew her quite well. Knew that she cared with all her heart. And he had responded to this care, respecting and caring for her in turn. Of all things, to be caring for and cared by a German enemy U-boat captain!

Tears welled up in her eyes, and Mary Ann willed the captain to live. Willed this with all the faith energy she could muster in her battered state. And she worried - a crazy worry - that the captain was not "under" enough? *Did that scruffy-looking "anesthetist" know what he was doing? How much ether to administer to keep the captain under?*

She looked to the medic. *Lord knows, she shouldn't have looked!* The surgical knife was penetrating deeper into the captain's stomach, and the chief engineer was applying sponges to absorb fast-running streams of blood. *Air! She needed air!* Hedged in by men's bodies and closed doors and steel bulkheads, Mary Ann was being crushed to death.

Look to the captain! Look at him! She struggled up on the bunk and forced herself to move closer to the captain's jelly-smeared face. *Now look at him! Look at the man you care for! You care for him? Then act like it! Be the nurse you're supposed to be! Look at this man who operates a vessel of war and carries the burden of combat and the fate of other men's lives on his shoulders! Think of the injuries and deaths of people the world over! Focus on that!*

Look at the captain. He resembles Mario DiAntonio, whose parents run the deli over near Ebbets Field. Imagine that? The captain looks like Mario! Why, that's who she'd been trying to think of, when she first saw the captain. *The captain looks like Mario!* Except for his mouth. What if the captain is part Italian and not totally German? He could be Italian with that dark, curly hair and brown eyes. *That she could only touch him. Soothe his brow. Secure that loose strand of hair—*

The medic's sharp voice snapped Mary Ann from her reverie. He was requesting assistance from Dietrich Heubeck, who gawked at the open wound in the captain's side, unable to move, or lift a finger to help.

"Sir?" Mary Ann peered up into Heubeck's masked face. "It's okay. You'll be okay," she used the expression, "okay." Knew he knew what that meant.

Still, the second watch officer couldn't move. His blue eyes begged for help, and it was obvious he felt shame for his behavior.

"Sir, please look at me," Mary Ann directed firmly. "That's it. Now pull yourself together. That's it, sit down. Sit. You'll be okay." Then she glanced at the disgusted medic and relayed the message with a quick head shake. *Let him go. Don't force him to do what he can't do.* And the medic turned to another man to resume his work.

By now, Mary Ann's nerves were shattered. *When would this thing be over?* Not just for her sake, but for all of them? *Look at these poor fellows!* Heubeck had collapsed back against the opposite bunk, his eyes cast down in defeat. He rocked side-to-side in a catatonic state, and Mary Ann reacted to this additional shock with gentle words of encouragement:

"Please don't feel bad, sir," she called softly to Heubeck across the captain's prone body. "You're a good person. Look what you've done for me, these past days. Why, if it wasn't for you. . . ." She smiled tenderly on the disheartened man with the crystal-blue eyes. "Ah, well, I know you don't understand what I'm saying, but please know I care, and understand."

No response. Mary Ann regarded the second watch officer with soft longing. Who would ever believe that she loved two men at the same time? Two Germans, no less! That one sitting dejected across from her, and this dear one lying near death on the Wardroom mess table. It seemed impossible, but this was the truth of how it was that formidable day many years ago - Mary Ann spilled this most urgent fact of the story, in the throes of her recall, to naval historian, Steve Anderson, forty-four years later.

Yet, let us return to that scene in the stifling Wardroom aboard U-115 in mid-March 1942, as Mary Ann remembered it:

The medic was busy directing another player in the crucial medical drama. In this case, the unruffled Radioman Konrad sought very
carefully to position a bent tablespoon into the open wound in the
captain's right side. Mary Ann wouldn't have believed it was happening had she not seen it with her own eyes - this crude, but most
adept way of exposing the muscle layers for the surgery to proceed.
In spite of her own torment from the beating she had received from
First Watch Officer Paul Ullmann, she observed the medic slowly
probing the surgical site for the inflamed appendix.

Again, Mary Ann looked to the captain, searching for any signs
of distress in the lines of his closed eyes. On cue, the "anesthetist"
leaned over and pried open the captain's right eye. Out cold, yes, the
brown iris well back in his head.

"So, far, so good," Mary Ann whispered to the "anesthetist," who
glanced at her stonily behind his mask. Then he settled onto the
wooden supply crate that served as his chair and seeped a few more
drops of ether onto the gauze-covered sieve over the captain's face.
Making sure?

Like that, the medic found the appendix! By the rush of excitement that swept the crowded Wardroom, Mary Ann knew at once,
and bent forward to observe the "surgical team" as the medic worked.
The medic was babbling on and on, describing what he saw and
what he was doing. He moved a probe and small scissors in the open
surgical site, then drew something out. A small, gray worm? Yes, the
appendix dangled on the scissors tip! It was whole, not ruptured,
which boded well for the captain's life. Several men clapped their
gloved hands.

With a quick twist, the medic placed the appendix on the tray
Chief Engineer Geissler held out, then returned to the care of the
open wound. But Mary Ann could not bear to watch this part of the
procedure. The sight of the thin sewing needle piercing a muscle
layer spurred another grievous stab of nausea in her stomach.

Yet, Mary Ann had to give herself credit. She knew she could never be a surgical nurse, not after this disturbing experience. But she would continue to do the one thing she knew she could do well: making those floor rounds in the hospital, bringing care, comfort, and attention to her patients. If nothing else, she gave love and support, when it was needed, and even when it wasn't. Always caring. This was her nature. This was, most assuredly, her call by God to serve His suffering people.

Now she looked on the sleeping captain. She felt for him, for all of them. The relieved medic - a hero in her eyes - was already placing a white bandage over the incision in the captain's side, carefully taping and trimming at the edges of the bandage as if he did this sort of procedure every day and thought nothing of it By the tone of his voice and the gestures he made, the medic appeared very pleased with his work. He had saved a man's life! Relief in the hot room was palpable.

Gauze masks, rubber gloves, and backwards-shirts-surgical-gowns came off and were being handed over for quick disposal. Smiles of satisfaction showed openly in haggard, whiskered faces. Conversation bantered back and forth like the calls of happy fans coming from a Brooklyn Dodger's baseball game. Only one man seemed out of place. The second watch officer pulled off his gauze mask with a rough tug, and before Mary Ann could offer any words of encouragement, hurled himself from the bunk, past the "anesthetist," and out the Wardroom hatch. No one noticed him going out.

Someone tapped Mary Ann on the shoulder. She looked up quickly to see the cook's large, hairy hand extended to her over the end of the mess table. A tough-guy grin cracked the cook's otherwise emotionless face.

"Hey, we did it, didn't we?" Mary Ann leaned forward to take his hand.

Other hands waved in her face. Mary Ann gladly accepted each man's proffered hand then reached for the medic's hand. "Congratulations, sir!"

The medic shook his large, shaggy head and gabbed and gabbed in excitable German, obviously explaining what he had done and how he had done it. Mary Ann smiled in reply.

Now her beloved captain lay on the table, oblivious to the riotous celebration around him. The "anesthetist" had removed the "ether mask" sieve from his face and was wiping at the white sealing jelly with a bit of rag. Mary Ann wanted to stay by the captain, as she had done for Fritz "Billy" Baier, so she waved her arm to catch the medic's attention. *Now, who in this room might be able to translate her request?* She glanced about the room. *Konrad! Yes, yes, Konni!*

CHAPTER 55

She never got the chance to care for the captain. The medic had escorted Mary Ann back to her tight upper bunk in the Petty Officers Quarters and drew the short privacy curtain to shield her from prying eyes. An hour later, when the boat surfaced into heavy seas, Mary Ann became too incapacitated to function anyway.

For long hours that strung into days, Mary Ann lay strapped on her bunk - a life saving act by the medic - as a strong North Atlantic gale raged beyond the steel submarine hull. The pounding waves and screaming winds deafened her. On occasion a crewman might show up, himself struggling in the writhing, heaving, bucking boat, to offer her a meager plate of cold food with thin, watery lemon slices on the side, or a half cup of distilled water or apple juice, but Mary Ann declined any food, could eat nothing, and threw up over the side rail what little she drank.

The most dreadful time arrived when the medic must lead her to the toilet compartment. Unstrapping her from the bunk, he helped her slip down to the leaping deck, which pitched her mercilessly about and dropped out suddenly under her tottering feet. A pale sliver of a ghost, her stomach caved in from the force of dry heaving, Mary Ann dragged along with the stumbling medic, whumping against bunks and bulkheads, and rolling over and over, side-to-side, banging her head, in the round, forward, cylindrical hatch that lead to her foul destination in the bow room. An insufferable trip, indeed! Why bother? How could one remain seated on the careening "head" in such violent conditions? Most of her urine ended in her filthy pants. Yet, the female captive had no choice when Nature called, unlike the men who employed tin cans or the bilge to empty their bladders.

And still the sea did not halt its relentless mauling of boat and crew and wasted female captive. Instead, it seemed the storm's fury increased to hurricane strength. The deck became the starboard bulkhead, and the overhead, the port bulkhead, as the U-boat battled for headway against house-sized waves. The hammering, crashing, thundering, roaring blended into a mammoth cacophony of madness. Hell itself now appeared a warm and welcoming abode, where one might go to escape this nautical torment!

The boat reeked of mildew and fuel and vomit and urine. The perpetual chill settled more deeply into aching bones. Meals for those die-hards with cast-iron stomachs consisted of greasy cold cuts on moldy bread, since it was impossible for the *Smutje* to eke out any meal from his galley stove.

The boat dived for two-hour stints every few hours, or when the first watch officer, acting as interim captain, deemed it necessary for crew morale. Tremendous relief enveloped the boat and crew at these blessed intervals. Still, the turbulence of the mighty storm on the sea's surface reached into the depths, gently rocking the tired boat like a baby's cradle. Then men off duty in their bunks and the deathly-ill female captive slept like the dead.

Indeed, Death stalked the bone-weary crew: a seaman of the third watch, the short-statured, boastful Otto Randtel with the "magic eyes," had been wrenched from his safety harness and swept overboard into the raging flood, as his helpless mates watched in distress. The navigator, Heinz Weber, as third watch officer, ordered the boat around to search for the unfortunate Otto, but the boat nearly took a fatal roll. And so, the rescue attempt was abandoned.

There was little time to mourn the loss of one shipmate; only to save the entire ship's company.

Further trouble mounted: the Old Man was not recovering so well from his appendectomy. He lay strapped on his bunk in his rightful Quarters with a high fever. The surgical wound had become infected, and the wretched medic treated his commander's condition as best he could with what flimsy medical supplies he had left in his kit.

In his delirium, *Kapitaenleutnant* Ketter called out the name, "Marianne," continually, so that men over-hearing grew more anxious for their Old Man. They glanced uneasily at one another and said: "It is so, he does have a feeling for the her, after all. We have seen this."

When the first watch officer, the replacement commander, came within range of Ketter's raving, his look grew blacker than the storm beyond the hull. He would have done with that foolish defeatist, if only he would get it over with and die.

By early Friday morning the storm began to diminish. The rain, sleet and hail moved off to the southeast. Ragged cloud curtains ripped apart to reveal hazy, silver stars and a lop-sided old moon swinging up the pre-dawn sky. Waves licked and leaped about the men's boots on second watch, and there had come a noticeable lightness to the men's spirits. Occasional jokes flickered among the watchmen, though their voices were lost in the vast seascape. Yet, it was heartily felt: the worst was over.

Below, in the boat, new life stirred. Strained limbs relaxed, legs and arms came loose from bunk supports, where men had hung suspended like gymnasts. Stomachs settled, heads were screwed on tight. Hot soup, the first warmth in nearly four days, revived flagging energy, and soon after, the acting captain ordered the boat shipshape, brooms and mops broken out, garbage collected, bagged, weighted, and hauled topside for disposal overboard. Loose objects, such as tools and books and boots and tin food cans and mess kits and chains and mattresses and dishware, unbroken, and cutlery and pots and pans were returned to their rightful places.

The cook in his galley was especially diligent in his reclamation of missing items. He lovingly caressed each pot, searching for dings and dents that might need extra attention, and he hung various cooking utensils on their hooks under the overhead or in the white metal cabinets where they belonged. For the cook had a system and no one better mess with it, or hold out on him when it came to a missing dipper or bowl or pan.

CHAPTER 56
Diary entry - Sunday, March 29, 1942

My dear, dear Diary, here I am! Never thought I'd live to write in you again. Never thought any of us would make it! I'm only too glad to forget the past awful days! Though my stomach still gets queasy at times, I'm feeling much better, and there's a reason for this. A blessed, blessed reason: the captain is back in command! When he came into the Petty Officers Quarters this morning, I couldn't believe what I was seeing. There he stood inside the open doorway, looking so thin and worn out, I almost didn't recognize him, but for his hat. He moved along the aisle to each man. Some fellows were still in their bunks, but they all jumped up fast and greeted their captain. And like a happy father arriving home, he grabbed for each man's hand, patting their backs affectionately, mingling and joking with the men - I could tell - everyone was laughing. The men cheered and "hurrahed," their smiles openly genuine and delighted, like this was the best thing that could happen to them. One could tell the captain felt very good about his reception by his men. Such tremendous relief among us all! We have gone from death to life!

   Then his eyes came to me. The captain walked over to me in my upper bunk and said, "I am back in the saddle again, Mary Ann." I remember smiling and saying, "He was a cowboy in the wild West." Then he brought me back here to his bunk in his own compartment, where, right away, I looked for you, dear Diary. There you were, under my mattress where I had left you! That first watch officer never found you! I asked the captain what day it was, and he told me it was early afternoon on Sunday, March 29th. What a shock! I've been sailing on this submarine since March 14th. Fifteen days!

Then I asked the captain when we will reach land. I nearly fell over when he told me we are in the middle of the Atlantic Ocean, halfway between Europe and America. I was pretty disappointed to find that out. I thought maybe we were closer to land than that, but, instead, we're far from anywhere! Sometimes I get the willies to think of the ocean depths beneath us. We must be like a tiny leaf floating on a big lake!

Yet, the captain reassured me that we would be reaching base in France in about two weeks. France! Two weeks! That long? "But why France and not Germany?" I asked the captain. That's how bold I am with him these days. I'm not afraid to ask certain things. But when he reminded me that Germany had conquered France almost two years ago, I let that conversation go by in a hurry. I was mad at myself for my stupidity in not even remembering France's fall to Nazi Germany. Then before he left, the captain promised to inform me each day how close we are coming to land. That helped me feel better.

Once in a while, I see the first watch officer go by in the passageway with his hard face. It spooks me to see him, but he doesn't look in here, or come after me. I don't exist to him, and that's just fine with me. I can forgive him for what he did, but I'll never understand why he beat me, except I am his enemy. Must he beat on a girl though? What did that prove?

Tuesday, March 31, 1942

The only thing I can do is realize each passing day brings us

HELL AT SEA

closer to land. There's been nothing to write about these last couple days. I sometimes close the curtain to rest or do some exercises to stretch my aching arms and legs, and to pray. Still feel a bit queasy now and then, but the ocean's been fairly calm. The usual routine going on. Even practice dives are something I've grown used to. My finger splint came off yesterday.

March 31 - later in the day

Konni and the one radioman named George, I think? "Schorsh," he calls himself, the cute fellow with the face of a cherub, keep me company. We can't talk too much, since they both get pretty busy. Konni tells me they must listen to every message they hear and write it down, even if the message is not meant for this boat. That surprised me to learn that! Sometimes the radiomen send out signals, perhaps saying where we are and what's going on. For sure they'd radio about any battles! Konni's hand goes like crazy on the sender button, and I can hear the beep-beeping of the code, like a little cricket chirruping on a late summer night. What I really enjoyed today was looking at a little red book Schorsh carries with him in a leather bag. Schorsh is an artist and makes drawings in his little book. I was so impressed to see the wonderful sketches he makes just with a pencil! Some of the sketches are of the men on duty. There was even one of the captain standing on the open deck under an iron-gray sky. It looked so real, I swear I could hear the wind and sea. That's how good Schorsh draws!

There are other good drawings in his little red sketchbook, too. Buildings and cathedrals and park scenes and people, especially girls, from where Schorsh lives. He says he is from Munchen, if I am spelling that correctly. The city is in Bavaria, in the south. But it's amazing to see the beautiful places in his city. The trees, the bright flower gardens, and the marvelous churches. Makes Greenpoint look drab! Still, I wonder how Schorsh would draw the skyline of New York, if he had the chance? Bet he'd do a swell job!

Good Friday, April 3, 1942

My Dear Lord Jesus goes on His cross today for all of us, everywhere, in every time. It is with a deep sense of wonder that I write here today, for I feel things in a way I never did before. Naturally, it is the result of this journey I make and passing close to Death's door.

I ponder the miracle that our God so loved His world of people that He sent a Part of Himself to live and die among us and for us. He did not remain apart and remote, like a king over his subjects, but actually entered His creation, His beautiful artwork, and made us glow with new life and hope. What an Artist that is! What a great God He is!

And who are we, as His people, traveling along on our own little pathways?

Look at this U-boat, for instance, so small compared to the sea and the war in which it sails. The captain brought this small boat all these days and weeks and thousands of miles to launch its own small fragment of war on the coast of my country, the United States. Such use of valuable human life and energy for destructive purposes!

And, sad to say, this is how we humans are toward each other. This is why our God had to come in person among us to say, "If only you love and tolerate and care for one another, without the need to hurt or get back at one another, you need never die, but will have eternal life in you."

Dear diary, I plan to use the three hours, from noon to 3 o'clock this afternoon, in total silence and prayers with the curtain closed, in memory of Christ's three hours on the cross and in loving concern for our poor world at war. All the people who are hurting and frightened and lashing out at one another. For sure, I've lived it here!

And now I can imagine how Christ must have felt looking down from His cross at the enemy Roman soldiers rolling dice, totally oblivious to Love Itself hanging right over their heads within easy reach! And so it goes with all of us. Do we look up at Christ, or roll dice in ignorance?

Later in day -

The captain held a small prayer service over the intercom a while ago. He led in both German and English, for my sake. How grateful I am!

Saturday April 4, 1942

A big surprise today! The cook invited me to come and help some of the men get ready for Easter tomorrow. We all had a hand in baking two big cakes in large oblong pans, along with preparing and icing the cakes after they cooled. What a mess it was in the Petty Officers Room, I was laughing so hard. Guys were smearing each others' faces with icing and getting the cook all worked up. Boy, he sure can yell! Other fellows were in and out of the room, all excited, adding to the chaos, I know, cause they knew I was there.

Plus, I got to know some of the men's names. There was Bernhard and Horst and Max and Eric and Claus, like Santa Claus! Hope I'm spelling their names right? And guess what, dear Diary? Guess who's going to be playing cards with the guys later on? Claus let it be known I should learn to play this card

NAOMI DESIDERIO

game they call "Skat." So, it looks like I'm going to be right in the thick of things. A big wheeler-dealer ha! It's a good thing I've played cards at home with Daddy and the boys. I may have a trick or two up my sleeve. Those fellows won't be expecting that!

Easter Sunday April 5, 1942

Woke up to find my room papered with colorful eggs and Easter crosses taped to the walls! Don't know who did it, but I have a pretty good idea who did the drawings. One beautiful egg, detailed with flowers and sun's rays, read "Klein Huenchen, Marianne." Everyone in festive mood, and I'm sure it has to do with our getting closer to land. Resurrection is in sight! We have less than a week to go!

Saw the first watch officer passing by in his usual surly mood. He glanced at the decorations and actually tore one off the wall and crumpled it in his hands, as he walked to the Wardroom. It seems all the world is his enemy. Not an ounce of joy in him. I have to feel sorry for him.

Monday April 6, 1942

Today was the big card game, dear Diary. Now I can play Skat as well as the rest of them! When Claus came and got me, I was really surprised. Didn't think he'd actually meant for me to come, when he said so the other day.

But there I was, in that long room in front of the boat, where the torpedo doors are, playing cards with a bunch of German sailors, as the others watched. What a mess in that room! It stunk to high Heaven, like 'dead socks and skivvies,' my brothers would say. But it was fun to be there. One fellow tried to explain

01321

that the room had gotten bigger, but I didn't know what he meant. It looked awfully crowded to me.

A cute fellow named Joseph sat next to me the whole time, and we got to kidding around with each other about the moves we made. At one point, I began to set down a card, but he poked me in the side to stop me. I knew he had peeked at my hand, so it got to be a contest between us as to who would sneak at peek at the other's cards.

When I finally caught on to the gist of the game, it was mealtime. I stayed right in the room and ate with the fellows. I wasn't too keen about sharing some sailor's mess kit, and only hoped it was clean enough. What a life, I tell you!

But we had a pretty decent meal - canned stew with rice, and apple juice, and the cake left from yesterday. I felt like I belonged, like I was one of them! It made me realize even more how special human beings are. There we were, pretty much in sad shape from the conditions in this boat, and yet we could find enjoyment in one another's company and make the most of what little we had.

I just sat there in wonder, much of the time. I kept thinking, isn't this something? What would folks back home think of what I was doing? Truthfully, I don't think of these fellows as Germans anymore. It seems like I've known them all my life, as if we all lived in the same neighborhood and went to school together. A lot of times I know what they're saying, simply by the shared human expressions and gestures. They get so excited when I try to talk German!

I'm not sure how long I was in that room with those sailors. Hours, I know. When I'd have to excuse myself to use the WC, as they call it, the fellows beside me got up and let me get by. Nobody thought anything of it. And when I came back, they left my spot at the table for me to sit. No one excluded me, or sealed off my place among them. The sailors fully expected me to return and join them, and it meant a great deal to me.

Then Max got out his accordion, and we all sang together. Though I didn't know the tunes, I hummed along. I will always remember the sailors' faces in the shadows, looking solemn and gentle and sad, as they harmonized. I had tears in my eyes to witness this calm scene of sailors at sea. It was as if I was hearing the voices of millions of sailors through the ages, sailing the world's oceans, from ancient explorers in unknown seas to those who sailed in times of war.

I realized I, too, am a sailor, as the captain told me that day, "You are our little sailor." Truly, in my heart, I am a sailor. A sailor at heart! We are all sailors, every one of us, on our separate, unknown courses in life, journeying toward the vastness of eternity. We sing of the sea, and of longing for home and family and peace. I felt great love in my heart for all my fellow sailors! Please, dear God, guide us all home to safe port in Heaven! Good night, dear diary.

CHAPTER 57

Dienstag 7 April 1942	Tuesday, April 7, 1942
1200 Uhr. Seegang 7.	Storm arising. From today on
Kurs: 87. Stellung:	we proceed by day under water.
45 11' Norden;	Approach western limits of
16 05' Western.	Biscay Bay. We have yet 28 cbm.
	fuel oil left.

Mary Ann sat up quickly on the bunk when she saw *Kapitaenleutnant* Ketter standing in the corridor outside the sound room compartment. "Captain?" she called softly. Never had she summoned him directly when he was nearby or involved with one of his men.

Ketter's head swung around. *Did he seem annoyed?* No, but he raised his hand to caution her to remain silent, while he talked to his man, Schorsh.

Then he wandered over to her in the tiny Captain's Quarters and stood by the open green curtain. "What is it that you want, Marianne?" he asked in a stern voice.

"Sir, I'm sorry to bother you, but what is that noise I keep hearing?" Mary Ann referred to several low, ominous rumbles far away in the sea depths. She had been hearing them, off and on, for the past couple hours, and they seemed to be coming nearer.

Ketter appeared distracted, as he scratched the back of his head below the hatband. Then his dark eyes, circled with weariness, met her's directly. "Those are bombs exploding, Marianne. We have entered the Biscay Bay, which is the transit for our German U-boats entering and leaving port." He cleared his throat and grinned, albeit lop-sidedly, up at the overhead. "Unfortunately, the British enemy employs a large number of airplanes and destroyers to search for our boats. Very often they drop their bombs at random to frighten us, but we use great caution to avoid any bombs."

A knot of fear formed in Mary Ann's stomach, but she only answered calmly, "I see," as if taking this news in stride.

Ketter sighed and continued his explanation: "You will hear the crashing and banging of bombs the entire day. It is the music which accompanies our run to port, yes?"

Mary Ann nodded. What could she say?

He offered additional information: "We run submerged by day and dash on the surface at night, so there is no chance the enemy will locate us. It becomes a game of hide-and-seek that we easily win, for the "Tommies" have trouble to find us this way."

Mary Ann lowered her head. "Gee, I never thought I'd meet the British this way," she mumbled.

"No," Ketter said, "you never thought you must meet the British." He looked so very exhausted, but remained unruffled by yet another series of explosions in the distance.

Mary Ann did not want the captain to leave. She needed him to stay and talk a little longer, and so she asked quietly, a nonsense question at a time like this: "How are you doing otherwise, captain?"

He looked down at her and frowned, taken off guard, "How am I doing?"

"Yes, please. How have you been feeling? You have no more pain or other problems since the surgery?"

"Ah, my kind nurse," he stepped into the small compartment, where she sat cross-legged on his rightful bunk. "But I am fine, thank you. I am happy that you ask this."

"Well, I do care, sir." She fumbled with the edge of her sea blanket. And she admitted, "I worry about you."

His dark eyes held hers, and Mary Ann felt compelled to say things she might not have said. Things she had kept in her heart on this momentous journey. Things she wanted him to know before further time went by. Before he went off to running the boat. Before the bombs found them. . . .

"Captain, I -" she struggled for the right words, the proper words to say to a man of his stature, "you've been very good to me. You saved my life! I am grateful to you and owe you a great deal!"

"Marianne dear, you have also been very good to me and a good member of my crew, yes?" A flash of small yellow-white teeth showed between Ketter's thin lips.

"It's just -" another rumble of bombs detonated in the distance, this time quite strong, as if an attack was taking place. She looked up at the captain. "I keep thinking, if things were different. You know." She struggled to express herself. "If things weren't like this, with the war, and us being in a situation like this, well—"

Ketter came closer. "What are you saying to me, Marianne?"

Mary Ann blushed hotly, avoiding the direct look in his eyes. "I would want to know you better, sir."

"Do you mean -" his low voice hesitated, then slowly went on in a quiet tone of disbelief. "You are suggesting that we must come together in a relationship?"

The crucial moment had arrived. This moment would echo forever in the depths of her heart. "Yes, I am sure I would like this very much, captain."

She'd said it! Heard herself actually speak her heart aloud to him, that, yes, she would willingly go out on a date with him. That she would want to be all dressed up in a pretty floral dress and white heels and walk with him in the open light of day, maybe to a park or along a tree-lined riverbank, such as Schorsh had sketched in his red sketchbook, or to sit in a nice restaurant somewhere, hold hands and talk. . . .

Kapitaenleutnant Ketter dropped to his haunches before her at the side of the bunk. Mary Ann was aware of him watching her beyond the fog of her confusion and trembling.

"Aah, Marianne, you cannot know how I feel now you say this to me."

She barely heard him, for he was speaking very quietly. She looked over at him. "Will I get to see you after we get to France?"

He stared at her for a long while without reply. She saw the tiny image of herself reflected in the dark brown depths of his eyes. Then Ketter lowered his head and sighed, "This I do not know, Marianne darling." He sounded dispirited.

Her heart collapsed. "Why?"

She knew, why. Yet, she thought there could be a chance! Couldn't there be a chance?

Ketter raised his head and regarded her. "I, too, want to see you in France, Marianne. You cannot know how much I would want for this." He wiped his hands across his face. Mary Ann thought she saw tears.

He went on: "Unfortunately, when this boat reaches port, there is very much to do. There are reports to make out and meetings to attend." Ketter became distracted, shook his head, then wiped again at his face and sniffled. "I must report to the U-boat Admiral, who is far away. Always a returning captain must report promptly on the facts of his war patrol."

"I'm sorry," she whispered, feeling depressed and disappointed, "I didn't mean to upset you by suggesting something that can't be possible." She fought back her tears. She mustn't break down in front of him! This man she admired and cared for must go to his duties. For his sake as well as her own in an enemy land. Especially, she must understand and let it go. Yet, a further, nagging question must be discussed, and she began carefully, fearfully:

"Captain, when we reach the harbor, will I be arrested and sent to a prisoner camp?"

Ketter looked up at her fast. "Arrested? Why, Marianne? You will not be arrested! You have done nothing to be arrested!" Did he seem to be assuring himself, or did he already know something?

She fumbled with the ragged hem of her fatigues shirt, rolling and unrolling it. "But, sir, you forget, I'm the enemy, and I'm not supposed to be here on your submarine. I'm sure the authorities will want to do something about all that!"

Ketter covered her trembling hand with his own strong one and squeezed gently. "My dear Marianne, you must not think such things anymore. Nothing bad will happen to you, I assure you!"

Mary Ann tried to read the expression on his lined, bearded face. She wanted to believe her captain. To hold to his words - and to him!

"I will tell you, darling," Ketter used the endearing term easily, as if she was already his own beloved, "when we arrive in port on the weekend, our boat will be met by the *Chef* of our flotilla. It is true that your presence on board my boat is already known to U-boat Headquarters, so someone from our Navy Administration will be there to meet you."

He gripped her hand. "This man may ask you several questions, Marianne. You answer them honestly, as you do to me. But your personal thoughts and feelings, you say nothing to him. Only the facts that brought you on board my boat. Do you understand these things I say to you?"

Mary Ann nodded her head, impressed by the gravity of his words and demeanor. "Yes, I understand."

"Remember, Marianne, you say nothing of what you and I discuss and feel for each other," he reminded her forcefully.

"I won't," she wondered that he doubted her? Certainly she wouldn't mention anything about their relationship!

He clasped her hand to his whiskered chin. Might he kiss it? "Marianne dear, I think you will see, you will be cared for in a nice way in port." And then he laughed quietly. "You think that a sweet, young girl who has endured a hard submarine patrol will be treated unkindly?"

"Well, I don't know. I guess I'm starting to get scared about how things will go when we get there." She could not mention to the captain that she felt terrified of entering the realm of and stepping onto the occupied ground of Adolf Hitler and the Nazis!

"You must try not to be afraid," Ketter assured her again, as he rose to his feet and gently released her hand. For a long while they watched each other.

"Captain?" she stammered.

"What is it now, my darling?" He seemed amused at her persistence.

"Is there a chance I'll be sent home to the United States after we get there?" Her eyes pleaded. This, she must know, most of all!

Ketter's eyes drifted to the side. "I cannot say this, Marianne. I will be very honest and say to you, I do not know this."

A prolonged rumbling rolled through the depths of the sea. Ketter scanned the overhead. His jaw tightened resolutely. "I must go, Marianne. I am sorry, if at this time, I cannot answer any further questions for you."

"That's alright, I understand, sir," Mary Ann settled in on herself, feeling alone and remote once more to face the unknown.

Kapitaenleutnant Ketter started into the corridor, then suddenly was back in front of her. His hand soothed her cheek, and her hand went up to him automatically. She wanted to bring his hand to her lips and kiss it, but dare not. It was time he moved on. Her captain had things to do. She must not delay him longer, when he had all their lives in his hands.

"Go ahead, I'm fine," she whispered.

Then he turned from her, a grim expression on his face, and headed for the control room hatch.

CHAPTER 58

<table>
<tr><td>Mittwoch 8 April 1942</td><td>Wednesday, April 8, 1942</td></tr>
<tr><td>2130 Uhr. Kurs 90.</td><td>Surface. Our advance is negligible.</td></tr>
<tr><td>Stuermisch.</td><td>Only about 14 sea miles over the</td></tr>
<tr><td></td><td>bottom while submerged, due to</td></tr>
<tr><td></td><td>strong underwater currents.</td></tr>
</table>

<table>
<tr><td>Donnerstag 9 April 1942</td><td>Heavy seas. Force 6 wind. Cloudy.</td></tr>
<tr><td>0630 Uhr. Kurs 88.</td><td>No sun or stars to be seen, so we do</td></tr>
<tr><td></td><td>not have exact position anymore.</td></tr>
<tr><td></td><td>We travel only by dead reckoning</td></tr>
<tr><td></td><td>on the chart. Dive for underwater</td></tr>
<tr><td></td><td>march.</td></tr>
</table>

The long hours floating submerged toward port passed slowly. The men off-duty in their various compartments whispered occasionally to one another:

"More WABOs! And now those damned water bombs are not so far from us!"

"The British dogs fly even in this nasty weather? Who has been worth these bombs that the "Tommies'" planes fly in such stormy conditions?"

"We cannot begin to anticipate our arrival at our 'front door,' Hans. We cannot relax our nerves for one moment in this stifling tomb."

"The run through *die Biscaya* will not allow us this luxury to relax, boys."

Not far away, alone and silent, seated on the edge of her bunk before the small captain's desk with the shaded lamp, Mary Ann ate the luke-warm gruel in canned milk, which the steward had served her. Thankfully, her weak bouts with nausea, as well as the continuous pounding of waves and the perpetual creaking and yawing of the boat had ended with the morning dive, and now she anticipated another day spent in writing, praying, and getting much-needed sleep in absolute silence - except for the thunder of bombs. No more opera music or jolly marches played on the phonograph machine. No more outbursts of laughter or loud conversation came from the men up front. If she heard anyone speak, it was in a voice hushed by caution. And when a man came through the corridor, he moved in soft-sole shoes, and might nod a greeting to her before going his way.

The underwater explosions seemed louder today than yesterday, but Mary Ann ate her meager breakfast without pause. She ate with icy hands, which could barely grip the bowl and spoon. She ate, in spite of having no appetite, for she'd heard from *Kapitaenleutnant* Ketter that food supplies aboard were dwindling.

In the sound room diagonally across from her, Schorsh turned the sound apparatus slowly and listened, listened, listened for the presence of British war vessels. Mary Ann barely saw the side of Schorsh's thigh from where she sat eating.

What could one do all day in the silent depths, with the hammering of Death probing for a victim? The "Sailor at Heart" could only do as she was told and accept conditions in the boat as they existed. She knew intuitively that the safety of the entire boat and crew was in her hands, as her own life was in the hands of every other sailor on board. It wasn't just for herself and her own survival that she remained silent and obedient to any orders. It was for all of them, her shipmates. The German sailors' endurance and camaraderie had rubbed off on her, during the patrol, and she had learned the lesson well.

Over her breakfast of gruel in the silent depths, Mary Ann philosophized on the concept of "shipmate," what it meant in everyday terms, and how it applied to her at this critical juncture. At once, she pulled out her diary from its concealed place beneath the bunk mattress.

"The world itself is a large ship floating in space, and all the world's inhabitants are shipmates." She scribbled. The idea sounded amazingly wonderful to her. Truly a statement of momentous proportion, in light of everything that was going on.

"Each nation is a separate compartment aboard ship, and every person in every compartment is a member of the 'Earth's' crew, each with a vital service to perform to keep our ship safely on course. Just like here in the submarine, there are the officers, who would be the leaders in government, business, religions, etc., in each of the Earth's compartments. Then there is the regular crew, like me, ha! But," she emphasized by underlining the word 'but' twice, "no shipmate is more or less important than another shipmate to the survival of the entire ship's company. Each member of the crew is equally special and important.

"I like to imagine how it would be if, say, instead of viewing a person and saying, 'Oh, he is German, or she is Japanese. Or, there is an African man, or an Arab woman. Or even, there is my Mother, my Dad, my brother, my sister. We would say instead, 'There is my shipmate!' What a feeling of harmony that would evoke in all of us to look upon one another that way. To say someone is my 'shipmate,' rather than a stranger or an enemy, or even a friend or relative. 'Shipmate' implies a stronger, more responsible bond. It means a personal obligation to the survival of all on board the Earth!"

Mary Ann lay back on the bunk, her right leg crossed over her up-raised left knee, and perused what she had just written. She recognized the power she possessed. That was how she felt it, at that moment. A new awakening! And what surprised her was to realize the power had always existed in her. Yet, she hadn't seen it so clearly, until now.

Mary Ann had another idea. She bounced up at once and set to work on the idea - a fiction account based on her experiences aboard the U-115. She'd never thought she would attempt such a task as writing a story about her life, and so wished she had started it sooner on this voyage, for it kept her occupied in the long hours in the silent depths with the rumbling of bombs beyond the hull. It got so that she no longer heard the menacing bombs, or felt the chill in the stale submarine air, or noticed the ceaseless growling of her stomach.

And if a member of the crew wandered by in the corridor and glanced in at her, he immediately saw a thoroughly busy young woman sprawled on the bunk, head bowed over her notebook, limp hair dangling from the back of her brown wool hat, the pen in her hand moving rapidly along the pages of her notebook. The captain happened by and looked in on her. So did First Watch Officer Paul-Karl Ullmann, who wanted to seize the notebook from her, but thought better of it, for the time being. Then there were the chief engineer, Alois Geissler; the short, stocky bos'n, Willy Scholz; *Diesel Obermaschinist,* Gerd Schwabl, and several others going on and off watches. At one point the blue-eyed second watch officer, Dietrich Heubeck, dawdled by the open curtain, hoping to catch her attention, for he had something he badly wanted to say to her, but when she failed to look up and see him, he walked off dejectedly to the nearby Officers Wardroom.

CHAPTER 59

Donnerstag 9 April 1942	Thursday, April 9, 1942
2135 Uhr. Kurs 90.	Surface! Same weather, poor visibility. Have ordered both diesel engines slow ahead to conserve fuel. When will this cursed overcast weather clear?

Freitag 10 April 1942	Friday, April 10, 1942
0035 Uhr. 46 03' Nord.	Broken cloud cover. Finally able to
08 54' Westen. Kurs 89.	obtain an exact position.

And what of the U-115 crew? As any surviving warriors would inevitably share with future historian, Steve Anderson, at their 1984 boat's reunion in the Odenwald:

In this continuous game of hide-and-seek with the British enemy and coming closer to home, the crew wanted nothing to go wrong. Between the raging storm and the British planes and destroyers scouring the sea's surface for any U-boats, the U-115 men had heightened their vigilance. Getting an exact fix on their boat's position was most vital, for who wanted to find himself running off course and wasting valuable fuel and time?

Once again, Hein Weber swung up the control room ladder, past Max Senghas crouching in the dim tower well wiping at a pair of large night binoculars with a scrap of cloth.

Senghas gloated at Weber as he climbed past him. "At last you have some stars to shoot, *Obersteuermann!*"

"Yes, yes, the Heavens have finally opened up to me, Max!" Weber shouted back. Then he was up in the roaring night on the bridge.

Leo Kuhlmey bent at the helm under an assault of cold seawater from the open hatch topside. "At last we will know how far we are from port!" he bellowed at Senghas.

"Such a hellish night," Senghas grumbled, then reached for the unwieldy sextant handed up by Franz Wirth in the control room below and passed it up to a waiting hand in the open bridge hatch. "This blasted storm will dog our heels all the way to port! This is, indeed, rotten weather!"

"Rotten weather, rotten moods," Kuhlmey scowled.

"Stop watch ready!" Weber's faint call came from the thundering night above.

Franz Wirth's ghost-white face peered expectantly up the ladder from the control room. "Stopwatch Ready!" he shouted back to Weber, and proceeded to count, "Ten ... five. ... two. ..."

"Zero!" Weber screamed in reply.

Wirth pressed the button on the stopwatch in his hand and began to read off the time span marked by the chronometer in the control room. Crouched in the tower, Max Senghas mindlessly wiped at another pair of night binoculars, his head tilted back to listen to the exchange between the bridge and control room. Kuhlmey ducked beneath another drenching. Yet neither man uttered a comment or curse, for this most important ritual of gaining the boat's correct position must be completed without interruption.

Several moments passed, then Hein Weber came scrambling down the ladder, a dark veil of rain and seawater coursing off his foul weather gear. His wizened, red face peered from his floppy sou'ester. "Just in time!" he grinned with his snaggle-teeth. "A bank of clouds is closing in fast!"

"Just get to the chart and tell us where we are, *Obersteuermann!*" Senghas growled.

"Don't worry, I'll get us in, Max, old boy!" Weber puffed. "A bee line straight into the garage, day after tomorrow, you'll see!"

| *Freitag 10 April 1942* | Friday, April 10, 1942 |
| *0600 Uhr.* | Dived for underwater march. |

| *Freitag 10 April 1942* | Friday April 10, 1942 |
| *2145 Uhr.* Surface. | Hurricane conditions. |

| *Samstag 11 April 1942* | Saturday April 11, 1942 |
| *0600 Uhr.* | Dived for underwater march. |

So close to port, and yet there can be no relief. Boat and crew are stretched to the limit of endurance. Breakdowns are inevitable, both in men and machines:

"Take her down to 80 meters, Chief."

"Aye, *Herr Kaleu.*"

"What's that noise?"

"She dives too fast!"

"We're taking on too much water, *Herr Kaleu!* Yet the pumps run like crazy!"

"Blow out tanks, Chief!"

"It does not help!"

"What in thunder is wrong? Has the storm caused us even greater concern?"

"See how the *LI* sweats blood to figure this latest curse!"

"Our Old Man will burst from the pressure!"

"And so, here in *die Biscaya*, our lousy boat is not in good shape! It's a dirty, mean trick!"

"Boat rises, *Herr Kaleu*, but our ballast tanks always run full again!"

"*Herr Kaleu*, I have already pumped out six tons of water!"

"Keep pumping!"

| *Samstag 11 April 1942*
2140 Uhr. | Saturday April 11, 1942
Surface. Weather has not improved. Fuel supply watched constantly. Pump situation repaired. |

Maybe, at last, there is hope?

Kapitaenleutnant Ketter sat at the table in the Wardroom and scribbled on a small sheet of paper. "*Leutnant* Heubeck," he rumbled, "have this message sent off at once!"

The second watch officer rose from the opposite bunk where he had been reading a book. "Of course, *Herr Kaleu*, right away." He duly reached for the small paper Ketter extended to him and glanced at the words. His blue eyes came up sparkling. "*Herr Kaleu*, this is very good news indeed! Then we are nearly there, yes!"

Ketter rubbed his hands together slowly and glanced around the room. "If all goes well, we will meet our escort in thirty-six hours. The Second *U-Flotille* in Lorient base will send someone to meet us at point 'Lucie two' on Monday morning." He looked at his eager second watch officer with a grim smile.

"We will be able to make those last kilometers, *Herr Kaleu!* You wait and see!" Heubeck pronounced with great feeling.

"This blasted storm," Ketter thumped the mess table with his fist, "it delayed us considerably. Nothing has been right."

"Don't you worry, *Herr Kaleu,*" Heubeck was searching in his jacket pocket and quickly produced the key to the cabinet containing the Enigma machine and coding books. "I will get this message off immediately, so that soon you will be stretched out in a nice, clean bed in a beautiful, sunlit room, yes?"

"We can't think of such a time just yet, Dietrich," Ketter scowled. "Let's just focus on getting this floating sewer pipe through the next critical hours."

Sonntag 12 April 1942	Sunday April 12, 1942
0548 Uhr.	Dive for underwater march following explosions of unknown origin. No enemy planes sighted. Pumps in working order.

Sonntag 12 April 1942	Sunday April 12, 1942
1930 Uhr.	Surface!

"Tower comes clear!" Chief Engineer Geissler called out.

Kapitaenleutnant Ketter urged his men waiting on the ladder in the tower below. "Hatch open, all clear! Watch topside!"

"Do you hear that, Hans? There is no sound of breakers crashing on the tower!"

"The storm has finally blown itself out, boys."

"Ah, scarcely a ripple on the sea, *Herr Kaleu.*"

"When have we last seen a night this calm?"

"Do you smell that, boys? What is that wonderful smell?!"

"It is the scent of land, *Herr Kaleu!*"

"We are now sitting on the 200 meter line. Our escort will come for us here in the morning!"

"This is surely a dream, *Leutnant!* After all those lousy days of bobbing like a cork and suffocating in our stink! Ah, the night before we make harbor. It is good!"

"If all goes well, at this time tomorrow, we will be seated at the homecoming feast, eating lobster and steak to our satisfaction!"

"Indeed, luck has been with us, *Herr Kaleu!* After those bomb detonations this morning, it has been peaceful all day."

"Don't relax yet, boys! Keep your eyes sharp!"

"Aye, *Herr Kaleu!*"

"You know that tonight will be the longest night for us, *Leutnant* Heubeck. I will keep looking at my watch and think, surely, an hour has passed, but then I will see that only five minutes have passed, yes?"

"Don't look at your blasted watch so often, Kutzop. You only torment yourself to see time move slowly."

CHAPTER 60
0530 hours

The faint light of dawn swirled through soft sea mist, but the splendor of the morning must be ignored for more pressing reasons. One last time *Kapitaenleutnant* Ketter ordered U-115 to the sea bottom. This close to port, to the goal, one did not dare relax his defenses. After all, British aircraft didn't take pity on pale, thin, half-starved German submariners who stood enthralled on deck by their first fresh, calm, land-scented morning in nine weeks. Then, too, an enemy submarine might lurk in ambush so close to the "finish line," waiting to pick off any careless, inward-bound German boat. Port, with its promise of new life, beckoned only a few kilometers to the East, but no man on U-115 must allow his mind to wander to the possibilities there just yet.

"A few more hours in the tomb," Ketter mumbled matter-of-factly to Chief Engineer Alois Geissler, as the boat dived away.

And so, the men waited on the seabed at forty-meters depth. The black hull of the submerged U-boat swung like a pendulum in a strong underwater current, then suddenly jolted forward on its keel, dragging along the rocky bottom. Men off-watch in their bunks caught themselves in the unexpected, jarring ride.

"What in thunder is that?"

"How are we supposed to get any sleep bumping around like this?"

But their angry words had no true edge. The men knew that very soon they would rise from this purgatory and enter through the harbor gateway to the promise of new life in Paradise!

0842 hours

Mary Ann glanced up from her writing, surprised by the entry of *Kapitaenleutnant* Ketter and the medic, Gerhard Moeglich, into her compartment. She dutifully tucked her notebook under the mattress and nodded to them, "Hello."

"It is time, Marianne," Ketter announced, his face set like flint. It was as if he didn't know her anymore.

"I'm ready, sir," Mary Ann replied.

The medic, a sturdy lifesaver and reliable companion to all on board - how often he'd assisted a green and retching Mary Ann - produced a thick roll of white gauze bandage from his pants pocket.

"Your head must be wrapped, so that your face and long hair are well covered," Ketter explained. "It will appear to any observers in port that a member of my crew has sustained a head wound. It is for security that we do this, Marianne."

"I understand," Mary Ann wriggled into position on the edge of the bunk and reluctantly removed the brown wool hat she had been wearing for three weeks. Her filthy hair fell to her shoulders like molasses oozing onto pancakes.

The medic spread his thick legs to either side of her legs and began to unwind the gauze bandage. "*Bitte.*" He directed her to tilt her head back, and Mary Ann gazed into his familiar, comfortingly homely face and smiled. "Hi," she said.

"Please be serious, Marianne," Ketter admonished her unexpectedly. "Let Gerhard do his work, for time is growing short."

"I know, I'm sorry, sir." *Why was she feeling so giddy? Relief that the end of the journey was coming? Or nervous about her reception in port?*

Crouching to her level, the medic lightly held the end of the gauze bandage against the right side of her face. Ripples of shock ran through Mary Ann, for she was sure any fellow would be repulsed to have to touch her pimpled face. Carefully, gently, the medic guided the stream of unrolling gauze up and over her head, round and round, over and over, one, two, three, four times. Gradually, the bandage pulled tighter on her jaw, when the medic turned aside fast and coughed into his fist. He came back to her, brow lowered, his green eyes concentrating on his delicate task.

Again, the boat jerked sideways with an awful grinding noise, sending Mary Ann tumbling into the medic, who swayed precariously, then crashed to the deck, taking her with him.

"Those rocks will tear our keel to shreds!" Ketter roared in English, as he dove for the control room hatch.

The medic and Mary Ann lay in a tangled heap of arms and legs against the bulkhead by the corridor. Loops of loose bandage draped their shoulders like party streamers. Mary Ann pulled up on her knees. "What's happening?" she gasped, for she could hear the captain bellowing out orders in the control room.

Someone gripped her elbow and brought her to her feet. Mary Ann looked up into the cool face of the first watch officer. Her stomach tightened. *Where had he come from?*

"Our boat is too light in weight, Miss Connor," he explained, as he guided her to sit on the bunk. "We need more water in the ballast tanks to hold us steady."

"I see," Mary Ann whispered. *Since when had the man become so well disposed toward her?* The medic was on his feet, like a bristling guard dog, while the first watch officer demonstrated the situation to Mary Ann with his long, white, bony hands, the hands that had brutally beaten her. She felt revolted to see those hands, that they could now be used to demonstrate a passing bit of information to her.

"Here, our boat is on the bottom," Paul-Karl Ullmann lay the heel of his right hand on the protruding knuckles of his left hand. "The sea bed in this area is composed of rock, and so the boat does not balance so well. If there is a strong underwater current, we slide like this." The heel of his right hand skidded across the knuckles of his left hand. "It is not good for the bottom of our boat that this happens." His hands went apart.

"I should say not, sir," Mary Ann replied quietly, her insides boiling with resentment. *Why be friendly now?* But then, it occurred to her, *what if he was trying to make up for his cruel treatment? Could he really be trying, in his own way, to admit he was sorry?* There were people in this life, who could never come right out and admit they were wrong, but had to show it in other ways. Of course, the first watch officer might be compelled to do so now that they were coming to port. In the end, Mary Ann managed a faint smile of gratitude to him for his explanation of the boat on the rocky bottom.

"And so," he concluded, "the *Kommandant* has ordered that more sea water comes into the ballast tanks to make our boat heavier, so that we cannot slide anymore."

"Good, thank you, sir," Mary Ann nodded. *Now go away!* She wanted to say.

Wonder of wonders! The captain had returned and stood looking at the two of them. Had he seen correctly? Then Ketter gestured for the medic to resume his bandaging work. Mary Ann rocked on her bottom on the edge of the bunk, like the boat on the rocky ocean floor, to get into a comfortable position. The medic seemed exasperated. *Can we get on with this thing?*

In the ensuing silence, he wound the trailing gauze around Mary Ann's head. She felt his fingers work along her chin and brush her cheeks, hair and forehead. Mary Ann found herself enjoying the process. *Cover it all up! My hair, my oily face, all my flaws! Hide them away!* Only her eyes, nose, and mouth remained uncovered. Scissors were produced, signaling the end of this part of the preparation for her reception in port. Then Mary Ann was directed to lie on the bunk, and the medic drew the sea blanket to her shoulders.

"You are to be our wounded mechanic, Marianne," Ketter gazed down at her. "You have sustained a head injury during an emergency dive. This is how we must enter it into the boat's log."

"Okay, sir. Sounds good to me." Her lips pushed out from the tightly-wound bandage.

"You must remain here until we put in at the pier," Ketter directed her to lay back on the bunk. "Remember, you are injured, so you must lie in a helpless manner when the medical personnel come on board to transport you to the base hospital."

"Yes, sir, I will." Mary Ann glimpsed the medic and first watch officer exiting the compartment, then gazed up at the captain, excited by this newest revelation of her fate in port. "I'm going to a hospital?" she burst out in a loud whisper. "I feel a lot better about going there, instead of someplace else!" Her overactive mind still envisioned a concentration camp.

Ketter leaned down to her. "Marianne, I will again warn you, you must not take this thing so lightly. Your situation depends on how you will answer and conduct yourself in port! Do I make this clear to you?"

"Yes, captain, I know!" She felt offended by his sudden doubt of her.

"You must know!" Ketter cracked.

"I do know!" She defended herself. "Look, captain, I can only take each moment at a time, like I did here on your boat. And look how I survived! Well, thanks to the kindness of you and your men, sir. But I'll be all right, I will! God is with me! I'll know what to say and do, when the time comes, believe me."

Ketter searched her bandaged face with tired, reddened eyes. "I believe this of you, Marianne darling," he mumbled. "I should know you by now, that your will and faith are very strong." And he smiled.

Mary Ann tried to smile back, but the bandages restricted her. Yet she smiled in her heart. "Captain?"

"What is it, Marianne."

"I love you, you know this!" The words tumbled from her mouth. She felt wetness seeping into the gauze wrap around her eyes. "I'll miss you, sir, I will!"

Ketter gripped her trembling hand beneath the sea blanket. "Ah, Marianne, I love you, too, with all my heart." His eyes locked with hers. Then he was coming down. His grizzled face hovered closely, and he placed a tender, lingering kiss on her puffy, chapped lips. His stale breath wafted in her nostrils, but she breathed it in. Savored it.

"Thank you for your love, my darling Marianne," his voice cracked with emotion. "I will survive to the end, because of it."

"I know. I feel this!" She shivered with wonder, as she watched his face rise against the ribbed overhead. She sought to imprint his face in her memory. Their hands were clutching. Then he was pulling away.

"I must leave you now, Marianne." She saw the sparkle of tears in her captain's brown eyes. "Soon, the time approaches. Remember all I have said to you."

"I will," she promised.

Kapitaenleutnant Ketter stumbled into the passage and closed the green curtain across his rightful Quarters, then entered the control room hatch. Mary Ann would glimpse his bearded face, one last time in passing, as she was transferred on a hospital gurney from U-115 to Keroman I bunker in Lorient port.

CHAPTER 61

Naturally, Mary Ann Connor Carlino did not relay the more intimate details of her sea journey with naval historian, Steve Anderson, during their interview in May 1986. Much of what is written in the previous chapters concerning her relationship with former German U-boat commander, Herbert Ketter, who died in September 2004 of pancreatic cancer, were gleaned from letters and memories she shared with her younger daughter, Mary Kate Carlino Nicholson, who lives in Roselle Park, New Jersey. I gradually put together the facts of Mary Ann's regard for *Kapitaenleutnant* Ketter in my own historical fiction novel, along with the actual accounts of her incredible sea experiences. It became for me, and hopefully for you, dear Reader, an inspiring story of courage, faith, and endurance in hostile conditions.

My kind friend of many years, Steve Anderson, who published his acclaimed nonfiction book, " The Paukenschlag Boats: The German Attack on The 'Sleeping Giant,'" in 1996, has been most instrumental in helping me complete my project. Thanks to him, I had the pleasure to meet with and interview surviving members of the U-115 crew, including the former commander, *Kapitaenleutnant* Herbert Ketter, who retired as *Konteradmiral* from the Federal West German Navy several years before the Berlin Wall came down in 1990.

Now, however, one last chapter remains to be presented for the sake of bringing U-115 and her young crew and their American female captive into port. Enjoy the ride in, dear Reader!

1000 hours

"Bring me to periscope depth, Chief." *Kapitaenleutnant* Ketter called down from his seat before the periscope eyepiece in the tower.

The easy hiss of compressed air escaping answered him. The boat began to float up to the surface. Alois Geissler watched the *Tiefen-wasser* and leaned gently on the shoulders of his two planesmen.

"Slowly," he directed. "Bow twenty degrees, stern, fifteen." His gaze went to the *Pappenburg* meter.

The periscope motor hummed in the tower, as Ketter prepared to take a look around on the surface.

"There she is! Our escort is waiting! Surface, Chief!" His order rang down the tower well.

Air bubbled and rumbled on the glassy sea surface as U-115's tower came clear. Ketter was up the ladder, undogging the hatch. These "blind" seconds could spell a submarine's doom! Drops of seawater splashed onto the eager faces of the watch, who clambered up the ladder beneath their Old Man. The hatch lid fell back with a crash, the tomb was opened, and fresh morning air filtered in.

Bright sunlight momentarily blinded Ketter, as he scrambled onto the bridge. His boots slipped on the wet deck, and he nearly went down on his knees, wrenching his still-tender surgical site. Ignoring the pain, he grasped for the iron lip at the forward end of the tower and shaded his eyes with his right hand. There, off port bow waited the minesweeper.

Immediately, *Obersteuermann* Hein Weber and two *Maroseno-bergefreiter*, Bernhard Uphoffner and Willy Feiler, took up their positions on the bridge. The signalman, Franz Wirth, flags in hand, wormed his way to Ketter's side.

"Tell our escort's captain we are ready to follow his lead," Ketter told Wirth.

"At once, *Herr Kaleu!*" The signalman scrambled onto the fair-water. His flags flapped like gulls' wings in the stiff, warm breeze and his arms performed the necessary contortions to alert the mine-sweeper to their proper identity and request for escort service.

Soon a reply came from the minesweeper's stern. *Yes, they acknowledged!* Wirth laughed, "So, there it is, *Herr Kaleu!* Now we can get our butts into port!" Wirth jumped down into the narrow horseshoe of the bridge and rammed his elbow on the periscope housing. "Oooowww!" he bellowed.

"Come right twenty degrees!" Ketter hollered to the helmsman in the tower.

"Right twenty degrees," Kulmey responded in the hollow.

"Proceed on electric motors," Ketter ordered down the voice tube to the motor room, then leaned on the tower wall and observed his boat quietly nose into the wake of the escort vessel. Ketter squinted at the mid-morning sun and its puffy cloud escorts with their iron gray bottoms in the azure sky. "A more perfect morning I have not seen in a very long time."

The west southwest wind toyed with the caps and jackets of the men on watch. Soft swishing sounds of the calm sea along the flanks of the submarine had a hypnotic effect on the men. Yet, all eyes continuously observed the bright heavens and scanned the barely rippling green water. Never let down your guard, not even when salvation seems certain and one can taste the sweet glory of home-coming!

1034 hours

Below in the boat, the ceremony of rebirth was in full swing. With faith in the eyes on the bridge, the men no longer suppressed their excitement at returning to port after their long, successful patrol.

Voices called back and forth, from one compartment to the next, up and down the central passage:

"How do I look, mates? The women will flock to me in droves!"

"Get out of my way, you dumb heads! I want to have a look in that mirror, too!"

"You know, I think I will keep my beard in port. I look pretty good with it!"

"What beard? Those few strands of hair on your chin, ha, ha! You look like the goats on our family farm!"

"Wolfgang, Hans, hurry! We can go up to the *Wintergarten* for the ride in! Man, I haven't seen the sun in nine weeks being in that cursed e-motor room the whole time!"

"We finished the tonnage flags, boys! Thanks to our Old Man who has won the Knights Cross, we can hoist these babies onto our periscope and look very impressive on our arrival at the dock, yes!"

Upon receiving the customary permission to go topside, several off-duty personnel climbed the tower ladder to the bridge. They came up with halting footsteps, staggering, blinking, tearing in the intense sunlight. Their faces resembled those of ghouls newly released from the grave, and they stumbled into the narrow horseshoe bridge, then fanned onto the cigarette deck at the rear of the conning tower. After nine weeks in Hell, it took a while for the men to get used to the fresh air, though their yellow-toothed, skeletal smiles revealed absolute pleasure to be up in the open air.

One of the diesel engine room mechanics swung up awkwardly onto the railing surrounding the anti-aircraft gun platform. Stretching out his arms in the wind, he let loose with a lusty wolf howl, "Ooowwoooo!"

The Old Man adjusted his crumpled dirty white cap on his head, more a deliberate gesture to hide the feelings of pride that swelled within him. His eyes were on the emerald-green land mass that rose from the sea, seemingly about to overwhelm the submarine.

On silent electric motors, U-115 passed through the narrows near Kerneval and Port Louis. The Old Man's gaze drifted to the white villa on Kerneval. It was as he expected, the U-boat Headquarters staff had been evacuated after the alarm at St. Nazaire. Now no well-heeled naval officers stood out on the lawn and patio to wave greetings to U-115 as she returned from sea. .

Yet, the haunting sense of doom soon dissipated, when Lorient appeared before the bulk of the minesweeper straight ahead. The U-boat's company on deck shouted and cheered at the sight of the port facilities and the buildings and houses of the city. And there was the supply ship, "Isere," tied up at the dock! Someone pointed vigorously from her stern. Already, the tiny figures of comrades hurried along the large ship's deck. A U-boat was returning from patrol! It was a dutiful pleasure to hail the in-coming, jubilant, battle-weary crew!

1115 hours

Unable to turn her head because of restricting bandages, Mary Ann stared at the familiar curved overhead and listened to lines of men hurrying by in the passage beyond the drawn curtain. Their laughter and shouts and singing were driving her crazy, at times, practically propelling her from the bunk to join them in their celebration. But she remained on the bunk as ordered, squirming around to reach a bothersome itch on her back right thigh inside her fatigues. *How much longer must she wait here like this? Where was the captain? Why didn't he come to check on her? Didn't anyone care? Had they forgotten her already? Fine! Too busy celebrating out there. But still!*

She felt strangely bereft and sad. The men were going away. She'd never see them again. Did she want for this sea journey never to end? Would she wish to stay aboard this boat, in these vile conditions, and sail forever? Yes, if it meant remaining with her beloved captain! *Now, wasn't that just dandy? Stay and endure it all over again? Such foolish thinking,* she chastised herself. She wanted to go home!

Then she heard something. *Wait. What was that?* Horns were tooting in the distance, and a drum banged away on the other side of the paneled bulkhead, "Boom, boom, boom," like the high school marching band at football games back home. They must be at the dock! *This is it, folks! We're here! This is the end of the journey! Oh, my stomach is killing me! Please, someone come, I have to use the toilet!*

1135 hours

Overhead, not far from the Captains Quarters midships, where Mary Ann lay in a torment of nerves, the crew of U-115 had "fallen in" on the foredeck. The happy, somewhat embarrassed men waved to the enthusiastic crowd of military, security, SS officials, and hospital personnel lining the quay. A pink chrysanthemum bumped *Heitzer* Karl Brauman on the nose and fluttered to the deck like a tiny parachute.

"See that, comrade?" Christoph Schaub poked Karl in the ribs. "Everyone aims for your big nose, ha!"

Crewmen craned their heads back to watch as the boat glided into the cool, shadowy cavern of Keroman I bunker. The shrilling of the Bos'n's pipe echoed in the vault, and the U-115 men snapped to rigid attention. In those young men's breasts, hearts beat high with pride and relief. The Old Man walked before his silent crew and eyed them with feigned toughness. His mouth moved, "*Maenner,* you look good! Well, done!"

A few smug smiles greeted his words.

Then with a sharp glance up at Paul-Karl Ullmann on the tower directing docking procedures, the Old Man turned to await the arrival of the flotilla chief. Already the gangway had been swung onto the U-boat's deck. *Korvettenkapitaen* Scheutze started across. The Old Man saluted smartly, then offered his hand.

E P I L O G U E
Roselle Park, New Jersey - May 13, 1986

"Ma, come in and sit down. Now that the kids are in bed, let's talk a little while longer."

"About what, Kate honey?"

"I think you know, Ma. There's more to your story than you've told me, isn't there? More than you told Mr. Anderson. Please, I want you to share it with me. I know it's been on your mind a long time."

Silence, then: "I've been wanting to tell you, Kate, but I don't know how you'll feel about me, once you hear what I have to say. And honey, you must never say anything to anyone about what I'm going to tell you! Not even your brother or sister, or one of your friends, and especially not your father. He'd never be able to handle it!"

"Ma, calm down! Don't get so upset! I understand how you feel, believe me."

"Kate, you have to remember, the events happened many years before I met your father. And please, say nothing to Mr. Anderson, should he ever approach you for more details of what happened to me when the boat reached port."

"Ma, you know I'm not going to say anything to anybody. I care about what you went through, so I feel it's very important that you talk about your memories. You have to stop worrying about what people think of you regarding that part of your life. You went through a terrifying experience. They should understand that, by now."

"But the memories are very much alive for me, Kate. Everything I felt at the time has come back to haunt me in ways I never expected. I've had to relive things I had buried, out of necessity, for all these years." Momentary silence. "It's strange though, Kate, until I met your father, I had hoped. . . ." A soft sigh. "Oh, never mind, just let me begin, and you can assume what you want as I go along. . . ."

She lay between clean, starched, white sheets and blinked at the late afternoon sunlight streaming onto the wall by her bed. Every time she closed her eyes, she felt the roll of the boat, back and forth, back and forth, as if she was still at sea. Yet, here she was, in her own private hospital room on a German naval base in Occupied France. Unbelievable!

Only a few short hours before, she'd been taken from the U-boat. After that, events had moved like lightning. Strapped to a narrow stretcher like an Indian papoose, she'd been hauled up the galley ladder by medical personnel from the hospital and taken out into a large, gloomy warehouse, where hammers and drills produced a deafening din and nearby arc welders threw up fiery sparks.

Now, as she lay in bed looking back on that hectic reception in port, she felt a surge of sadness. She hadn't had a chance to say, "Good-bye," to the men, let alone thank them for their many kindnesses and caring. For those four nightmare weeks, the boat and crew had become her world. Without them, she felt lost.

Then followed the trip by ambulance from the dock to the naval base hospital, where she'd endured interrogation by a bald, sharp-nosed German naval intelligence official, who scared her half to death with the way he wheedled answers out of her. Indeed, the captain had warned her to be careful how she answered, but she found herself caving in to such questions as: Did the captain give you sole access to his cabin? Did he, at any time, speak of his boat's operations to you? Did he or any of the other men become intimate with you? This last question had floored her, sent the blood rushing to her cheeks in open betrayal. "Nothing happened on the boat that was improper, sir!" she'd insisted. Knew the official didn't believe her, then wondered that someone might be trying to get the captain in trouble. And her mind ran, at once, to the first watch officer.

Yet the questioning was over fairly quickly and soon a medical doctor examined her and pronounced her fit, in spite of the rigors of her difficult sea journey. She'd lost weight and had developed an infection in her private area, due to poor sanitation, but nothing that couldn't be fixed with some medication. Her broken pinky finger had mended, and though the cut on her head looked a sight, in time, it would become a thin, white line under her long bangs.

But what happened next gave her great hope - a sure sign from God for her future survival! She was placed in the care of a French nun. A nursing Sister! Just like her beloved Sisters of Mercy at St. John's Hospital back home. Only this little Sister was dressed differently - a pale blue habit with a blue and white striped apron over top her front.

Sister Marie de Ste. Claire, the first woman she had seen in four weeks, immediately took her under her wing. At the sweet ring of Sister's soft, female voice with its lilting French accent, she felt sure she had died and gone to Heaven. Sister introduced herself as an Augustinian sister. Her convent was located in the countryside, "a beautiful place," she said. Then Sister wheeled her from the cold examining room, away from the accusative stare of that interrogating official, away from the memories of thundering seas and creaking metal bulkheads and hard men's violent curses, up an elevator to her quiet, serene hospital room.

And the first thing Sister did was to provide her with a good, hot bath to soak off the accumulated filth and odor of her submarine journey. How good it felt! She must have lain in the tub for an hour! Then once she was dressed in a clean hospital gown and terry robe, her first meal ashore arrived on a rolling cart. A most delicious meal, after surviving on gruel and rice for the last days, it consisted of roasted chicken, new potatoes, green beans with fresh butter, and applesauce, all served at the bright, open window overlooking the naval base grounds.

Oh, nothing could compare to this luxury! It was Heaven! To go from the foul, gray, claustrophobic Hell of the U-boat to viewing blue sky and white clouds and feeling warm sunlight on one's face. If she stood on wobbly sea legs and clung to the sill, she could look down on the courtyard below, where vivid green trees and bushes and lawn burst like fireworks before her eyes. Birds sang and flitted in harmony among tree branches and a gentle breeze from the far-gleaming sea rustled the nearby drapes.

Now burrowing deeper into the crisp sheets on her bed, she savored the cozy feeling that settled into her bone-weary frame. Everyone, so far, had been kind to her, well, everyone except that von Henzel fellow with the sharp nose. So the captain had been right. He had told her not to worry. That she would be well taken care of. And she was. So far. . . . She yawned til her jaw cracked and stretched her tired limbs. Her eyes closed. She was again at sea. . . .

Waves broke in great spumes of spray on the U-boat's iron bow, as it plowed the black sea. Overhead, a million stars hung like great misty globes in a hotel lobby ceiling. It was a beautiful night, one she could reach out and touch. In the distance along the faint horizon, ghostly ships crept in moonlit sheen. Allied ships, she knew. Tonight she stood lookout on the high tower and observed the convoy's silent passing. She felt responsible for those ships. They were her own! Surely, the captain understood her purpose on his boat. This night, she would stop him attacking those ships. It was her mission. That's why she was here.

He came to her, a laden spirit of destruction, his white cap glowing like a beacon in the darkness. She lay her hand on his leather arm and felt the soft give of his flesh. How she loved him! Her heart swelled with tenderness, as she said, "Please, sir, not tonight. Let them go."

The captain's weary face turned seaward. The ships had vanished. . . .

She woke with a start. Someone stood in the shadowy corner of her hospital room doorway. She struggled up fast, heart pounding, chills of alarm racing along her spine. The dark figure ducked into the hallway, as if trying to hide from her.

"Who's there? Is someone there?" she called out, shivering with uncertainty.

The uniformed man emerged into the direct daylight that cascaded through her high hospital window. The white hat flashed. "Forgive me, Marianne. I saw you were sleeping and did not want to disturb you."

She only needed to hear his voice. She bounded from the bed, dragging the bed sheet and blanket with her to the floor. It did not matter that she wore only a flimsy white hospital gown or that she had no slippers on her feet. She sprang across the cool linoleum floor and leapt into his arms, embracing him so desperately she thought she must squeeze him half to death.

"Captain, it's you!"

He was laughing in her ear. "What is this, Marianne? You are so happy to see me?" He sounded truly incredulous, his voice hoarse with astonishment.

She felt his arms encircle her waist. "Yes, yes, you have no idea!" She gritted her teeth against a threatening flow of tears. "Oh, Dear Lord in Heaven, don't let me lose my brains!" And she laughed out then struggled to calm herself, "Sorry, I'm sorry!"

Ketter backed away in order to take a closer look at her. He seemed in total, shocked delight that he could be the cause of all this fuss she was making, and she felt an overwhelming jolt of desire, that here she was, clad only in a thin hospital gown, with her reddish-brown hair, shampooed squeaky-clean and damp still, tumbling like a corkscrew whirlwind about her shoulders.

"Please, captain," she stammered, "let me take a look at you. Oh, wow, you look swell!" She glanced shyly at this fine-looking naval officer who stood before her. His dark eyes, beneath the brim of his peaked, snow-white hat, regarded her with that light of gentle humor and love she had come to depend on. However, his black beard stubble was gone, or otherwise she might not have recognized him in passing on the street. His mouth looked thinner, his jaw stronger, and he wore a spanking, double-breasted, navy suit jacket with two rows of gold buttons going down the front and gold rings on the sleeve cuffs. A tiny eagle emblem - she fervently ignored the swastika it held in its claws - was clipped below the right jacket lapel, while pieces of military ribbon looped through the buttonholes near his white shirt collar and navy tie.

"I can't believe you came to see me like this!" She gushed, then didn't know what else to say or do. But her captain surely did. He came closer, wrapped her strongly in his arms, and murmured in her hair, "I was afraid you would not want to see me again, my darling."

"Not want to see you?" She cried against his shoulder. "Oh, Heaven, don't even think such a thing!" She could not say the title, "captain." He was no longer "captain" to her, but had become some-one else. A new entity.

Ketter's hand slid up her back to the warm, bare skin at the nape of her neck. He rubbed gently along her smooth neck, then lifted his fingers into the thickness of her hair and pulled her head back to see him. His eyes watched her closely, gauging her reaction. She trembled with the reality of this man who held so tightly to her. Knew he felt her trembling. Knew he knew how much she wanted him.

"This is what I dreamed of," she felt herself breaking apart.

"I know this, darling," he whispered. Then his mouth came against hers, and she received his kiss with all fervor, her mind tumbling with the reality that this was a German U-boat captain who loved her. A man from another world. The enemy! This was the man she wanted to be with for the rest of her life! A good man! A decent man! A caring man!

"Dear God, what am I going to do?" she grasped at Ketter's shoulders, her breath coming in pants through their desperate kissing.

"My Marianne, shhh." Ketter touched a fingertip to her lips and traced their curved line. "Dearest one, listen. No, no, don't be anxious! You must listen to me very carefully."

"What? What are you going to do?" She begged in a voice torn with emotion.

Ketter guided her to the bed. "Please, Darling, sit by me."

She went with him, barely able to comprehend the gravity of the situation. Would he try to lay down with her on her hospital bed and love her? No, instead, her beloved sat on the edge of the bed, while the bedsprings squeaked in protest under his weight. She sat demurely at his side, and he turned on the bed to face her. His knee in its crisp Navy trousers pressed strongly against her thigh.

"Marianne," he began carefully, his tone serious. "I have arranged it with my flotilla chief that, if you will agree to it, we can be married quietly when I return from Paris in two days' coming."

The announcement struck her with all the violent beauty of an errant wave slamming the side of a ship. She reeled and bobbed and came about in the strong current.

Ketter went on: "I want you to be my wife, Marianne. This, I want more than anything I have wanted in my life! You are a good and beautiful woman with much caring in your heart."

She could not respond. Her mind whirled like a merry-go-round. Be his wife? *Be his wife!* How could this be possible? Yet, didn't she want for this, too? After all, she loved him!

Then her heart back-flipped with the reality of her captain's proposal. It would mean living in Germany. Becoming German! A Nazi? Oh, God, oh God! She would not be able to return to the United States to see Mama and Daddy and Eddie and Jackie and her wee Maggie, or Aunt Susie, or her nursing friends, or anyone else ever again! Dear God, could she do this thing? And how could he ask her something like this at such a critical time? She deliberately pushed the term "traitor" from her mind.

Now her captain sounded most desperate. He had obviously thought she would agree at once to marry him. "Marianne darling, I will come back from any future war patrols to find you waiting for me, that I can come immediately into your loving arms and find peace. But there is also the hope now, as well, that I can be given a shore posting very soon. Perhaps even here in Lorient, with my flotilla chief, Scheutze, and we can live here on the base. And you will be well cared for in my absences at sea. My flotilla chief will protect you."

He spoke of it so confidently. So, it was all planned? She pressed her hands to her face and rocked back and forth on the edge of the bed, "Oh, God, oh, God, oh, God." What could she say to this beautiful man she loved?

"Marianne, forgive me please. It is wrong of me to torment you in this way." She looked up to see slow resignation cloud his face.

"No, no," she shook her head and reached for Ketter's hand, brought it to her lips and kissed it. A fierce ache, born of strong womanly concern, fired by her recent experiences aboard his boat, took charge in her. "I love you, you know this!" she gazed at Ketter, tears falling.

He nodded, "I know this well."

"You can never lose me," she begged him. "You must know this! I love you too much to let this happen!"

How vulnerable her dear, brave captain looked, so lost and needing, like a little boy. What wouldn't it take for her to run away with
him to a place where no wars ever happened or enemies were made?
She would wrap him in a blanket of security and hide him away,
until the world was at peace again. Then! She would marry him.
Let the horrors and hatreds and death and dying go far, far away
and interfere no longer with the tender plans they dreamed to fulfill.
Let borders fall and armies dissolve and God's victory be forever
lasting.

"My love. . . ." Her voice faltered, as she reached out to soothe
Ketter's clean-shaven cheek. God in Heaven, what could she say to
comfort him, this good man she loved? "I will never go away from
you! Never!" Then her heart completed the words she desired to say
most of all: "I will sail with you forever!"

And she watched as his face softened with hope. She had made
her decision. There was no going back.

Her beloved Herbert - her captain had asked her to call him by his
given name, Herbert - had departed over two hours ago, on his way
to catch the evening train out of Lorient to meet with "the submarine Admiral, first thing in the morning, at his new office in Paris,"
he had said.

She lay on her hospital bed, staring out the tall, open window at
waning daylight. Her evening meal sat untouched on the end table
by the wall. At one point, a nurse had come in the room to check on
her and encourage her to eat, but she had ignored the woman.

She sensed Herbert out there in the dark, foreign world, going
away, away. She felt his departure like a premonition of death. What
if he didn't return? What if the Admiral sent him somewhere else
- to another base, or worse, back to sea? Her heart lurched with
a sickening thump. Dear God, what if she could've gone to Paris

with Herbert! Could that have been possible? Neither of them had thought of it, at least it hadn't occurred to her, in those last terrible moments before he departed for the railroad station.

She mourned that she hadn't had time to think clearly about their situation. So what if she didn't return to America! She could always write her family and assure them she was alive and well and happy. Surely, one day, she would see them again? Maybe even bring Herbert home to Greenpoint to live, when the war was over, for the war had to come to an end someday! It was possible to bring Herbert to America, wasn't it? After all, it happened all the time, with people from other nations immigrating to the United States! What mattered now was, she had found the one man, in all the world, that she loved. That he was German shouldn't, didn't matter! Nothing should have any bearing on the fact that they loved each other and belonged together.

Now she must wait - wait and pray. Yes, pray! Dear God, if it's meant to be. Yes, if it's meant to be, then it will be so. And it will be right and good and serve as an example to other people of what love and care and reaching across battle lines of hatred and prejudices should be. Wouldn't that be marvelous? And hadn't prayer always comforted her in times of greatest need? Look how prayer had helped her to survive her sea journey! Surely, God would help her in this situation. She had to rely on Him. He would show her the path to take. And so, she relaxed in her heart, assured that the answer would come.

At that a soft rapping noise caused her to pause. The gentle knock came again. Was someone wrapping at her door?

She rolled over quickly, straightening her hospital gown over her legs. Herbert! He was back already? Maybe he hadn't left, after all! She scurried over the floor to reach the door. Several people stood outside in the dim hallway. What was this? She strained to see their faces in the pale light from the window. She glimpsed a large bouquet of flowers clutched by someone out there and wondered that the bouquet might possibly be for her?

Then the tall figure carrying the bouquet moved toward her through the doorway. She scanned the hollows of the man's eyes, recognized the black, storm-line brow.

"Konni?" she cried, and backed up quickly, as a jostling group of men crowded into her room. She whipped the terry bathrobe from the foot of her bed and pulled it on quickly, securing the belt at her waist.

They surrounded her. Eight men from the U-boat, they meandered around her hospital room in clean-pressed Navy dress-blue uniforms, some with long, black ribbons streaming from the backs of their flat, round sailor hats, their smiles shy, and their low, excitable voices talking back and forth in German. How had they gotten in like this? She wondered, and felt a thrill of delight that they even wanted to come and visit her.

The cute angel face radioman, "Schorsh," or "Schatzi," as the fellows dubbed him, brushed past her with an apology, and headed for the open window to pull the heavy drapes closed, while the short, barrel-chested fellow who tossed the rain gear at her that day in the control room switched on the ceiling light. Another sailor, Erich - she recognized him from the bow room - was busy fiddling with the drawer in her night stand, pulling it in and out, bang! bang! just to have something to do in the awkwardness of being here.

The men were everywhere, it seemed. Oh, and there was her tricky "Skat" partner, Joseph! He flopped on her bed and stretched out, his arms tucked comfortably beneath his head right on her pillow. Well now! And he lay there grinning at her, winking every time he caught her looking at him.

She was beside herself with delight and nervous tension. Like silly, playful brothers, these sailors - her shipmates - had come to visit her. But what could she do with them? There was no room for all of them to sit down, though two of them had already perched on the window sill.

Right then, Konni shoved the bouquet of beautiful red roses into her arms. "For you, sweet Marianne, we bring these fresh blooms!" He bellowed at her, his hawk's eyes sharp and blue, as he followed her gaze.

"Thank you! Danke!" she blushed red as the roses and looked around the room. "I'm so happy all of you came! It's very nice of you!"

Then she wondered what these men would think to know she planned to marry their captain, when he returned from Paris? Dear God, she would be the wife of their captain! And, at once, she felt older, more mature, in the midst of the men. She would have to become a "mother" to these men, for wasn't that the way captains' wives treated their husbands' crews?

A harried nurse suddenly appeared in the doorway and looked thoroughly annoyed at the impromptu gathering of milling men in this young lady's room. Her mouth opened wide with an order that silenced the men. They looked at each other, surprised. What? They were just visiting their shipmate in the hospital! Wasn't that a good thing to do? Can't we stay a little while longer? Please, please, please? One did not need a translator to know what the men were saying to the intimidating nurse.

The men had to go. No arguing, no pleading. The nurse stood her ground, her fingers furiously tapping her folded arms. The men filed out of the room behind the nurse.

Konni was the last person to leave the room. "I think of you always, Marianne," he gazed down at his little shipmate. "I will never forget you in all my life." With that, he gathered her up, roses and all, and kissed her directly on the mouth. She backed away fast, shocked by his kiss, and tried to maintain her presence of mind.

Then Konni was out the door. She hurried after him and stood watching from her hospital room doorway, as the eight men paraded down the hall. Typical of young fellows, they pawed and punched at each other like playful kittens. And when the nurse turned to glare at them and remind them they were in a hospital, they acted like nothing had happened.

The men were filing, one by one, into the open lift carriage across from the nurse's station. Each man had to turn and look at the small figure in the doorway down the hall, perhaps trying to secure the image of her, clutching her red roses and waving, before she went out of sight forever. And she waved at them, certain she would see them again very soon.

Late that night, in a groggy haze of confusion, exhaustion, and mumbled protests, Mary Ann Connor awoke into the stern face of Sister Marie de Ste. Claire. Forced to change into a nun's heavy garments, Mary Ann was silently escorted from her third floor room at the former French naval base hospital in Lorient, German-Occupied France, down winding stone stairs and through a musty basement passage into the still, alien night. The two women arrived at the convent of the Augustinian Sisters in Sacre' Coeur shortly before dawn.

Mary Ann did not dare look back.